I0586349

CHARM, STRANGENESS, MASS AND SPIN

Stephen Dedman is the author of the novels *The Art of Arrow Cutting* (a Bram Stoker Award nominee), *Shadows Bite*, the Shadowrun novels *A Fistful of Data* and *For a Few Nuyen More*, the non-fiction book *May the Armed Forces Be With You: the relationship between science fiction and the United States military*, and more than 120 short stories published in an eclectic range of magazines and anthologies.

He has worked as a bookseller, book reviewer, editor, actor, museum exhibit and experimental subject, and taught creative writing at the University of Western Australia and the Forensic Science Centre.

His work has been nominated for the British Science Fiction Association Award, the Seiun Award, the Sidewise Award for Alternate History, the Spectrum Award and a sainthood.

CHARM
STRANGENESS
Mass
and
Spin

Stories by Stephen Dedman

NORSTRILIA PRESS

NORSTRILIA PRESS

norstriliapress.com

Norstrilia Press

11 Robe Street, St Kilda, Victoria 3182, Australia

Cover design by Martin Livings
Book design by David Grigg
Typeset in Adobe Garamond Pro, Aladin, Alegreya Sans, Concert One, and Alboroto

ISBN: 978-0-6453696-2-5 (print)
ISBN: 978-0-6453696-3-2 (ebook)

To Dave and Sally, Lee and Lyn, and Martin and Izz

Contents

AMENDMENT

"What's on now?"

"Lunch?"

Carol shrugged, leaned against the wall outside the hucksters' room to let a knot of people pass, and looked at her pocket program. "'The Future of Sf', 'Politics and Parallel Worlds', 'Jobs in Space', or *Moonraker*," she read. Lee grimaced. "Hey, it was filmed on location," Carol said, blandly.

"Yeah, with centrifugal force provided by Ian Fleming spinning in his grave," said Lee, who'd hated every Bond film since Connery had quit. "Who's doing the Parallel World panel? Heinlein?"

"No. H. Beam Piper, L. Neil Smith—"

"Give me Liberty, or give me Lunch!" intoned Lee; both men were fervent Libertarians. "Personally, I'll take lunch. McDonalds?"

Carol returned the program to her pocket. "Okay, as long as you promise not to run around yelling 'It's a cookbook!' this time."

Lee grinned. "Promise." They headed for the door, but were intercepted halfway across the lobby by a teenaged gopher in a *Battlestar Galactica* jacket and flared jeans. "Lee," he panted. "The Day Manager wants to see you, she says it's urgent."

The grin twisted into a frown. "Did she say what it was about?"

"Something about the signing session for Heinlein," said the gopher, not quite going into a defensive crouch. "She says there's someone here from L.A. who might cause trouble."

"What sort of trouble?"

"I don't know. All I know is what she told me. Come *on*."

1

Lee glanced at his watch, a cheap digital. "Yeah, okay. I guess there's no such thing as a free lunch-break." He turned to Carol. "Are you free for dinner?"

She batted her eyelashes. "No, but I'm inexpensive."

The grin re-appeared. "Great. Be seeing you."

PENNY, the day manager, was a solidly built woman with a *Property of Klingon Rollerball Team* button atop her huge right breast, opposite her name badge. "So this Preacher guy's a big fan of *Stranger in a Strange Land*," Lee repeated, to show he'd been listening. "So're a lot of people; I don't think it's a great book, but that doesn't mean he's crazy."

"It would if he liked *Number of the Beast*," muttered one of the *Illuminati* players behind him. Lee smiled; Penny glared.

"And he's bought a day membership because he wants to meet Heinlein," Lee continued. "So what? What's he done?"

"What *hasn't* he done?" said the day manager, heavily. "He's a doper and a thief and a pimp, and he's spent more time in jail than out, but I'm not worried about that, I'm worried about what he *might* do."

"What might he do?" asked Lee, patiently.

"Anything!" Penny drew a deep breath. "Look, Lee, you don't know this guy. He named one of his kids Valentine Michael. He was thrown out of a con in L.A. for supplying pot to minors, allegedly in exchange for sex. He used to be a Scientologist, and there are rumours he was a Satanist as well. He ran a nudist commune out in Death Valley, for Christ's sake!" Lee laughed, but turned it into a cough. "Three former members of his harem are in jail for murder!"

Lee raised an eyebrow at that. "Harem?"

She nodded, almost dislodging her glasses. "They stabbed and hacked three people to death and wrote lines from Beatles songs on the walls with their blood. The girls confessed; the D.A. tried to prove that Preacher was involved and they were protecting him, but there was no hard evidence and he couldn't make it stick, and Preacher just found himself some new women."

"When was this?"

"About ten years ago. '69 or '70. It was in all the papers—at least, it was in L.A.," she admitted. "But a lot of witnesses said he was heavily into knives and swords. Throwing them, too."

"Why do they call him Preacher?"

"It's what he calls himself. Sometimes. His women call him Charlie."

"Have you seen him here?"

"Not personally."

"Do you know if he's carrying a knife?"

"No, I don't *know*, but even if he's not, one of his women might be carrying it for him. I'm not expecting him to be violent, but he might... I don't know... ask Heinlein what human flesh tastes like, maybe offer to bring him some. Even if all he does is get his women to strip off in the signing session, or ask him to autograph their breasts, Heinlein's seventy-three, something like that could kill him." Lee, who'd lived in New Orleans for nearly half his life and had briefly worked as a janitor and bouncer in a local burlesque club, swallowed a smile. "They say Preacher once met one of the Beach Boys, kissed his shoes, and ended up taking him for a hundred thousand dollars and some gold LPs," Penny continued. "I'm not asking you to frisk him or anything, just... keep an eye out for him. Okay?"

Lee shrugged. "Look, this is Texas; it's perfectly legal to carry a knife. And there's a stall in the hucksters' room selling everything from shuriken to bastard swords. But if you want me to shadow this Preacher for the rest of the day, I'll do my best, though you'll need another redshirt for the art show... What does he look like, anyway?"

She laughed. "That's easy. Very short, not much over five foot. Long hair, beard, and he still dresses like a hippie though he must be pushing fifty. There are two ways to find him; one is to stand downwind of him, and the other is to look for all the women. You can't miss 'em."

"Why not?"

"They're a sad fanboy's wet dream," said another of the *Illuminati* players before Penny could answer. "None of them are exactly what you'd call good looking, but they'll fuck anyone he tells 'em to. Great if you can't afford to be fastidious."

"*And* your health insurance is paid up," said the first.

"Yeah, there is that. Come on, Orris, are you going to attack or not?"

"Okay," said the third player. "Survivalists, aided by the Society of Assassins, will attempt to control..." He looked at the cards before him— the C.I.A., Girlie Magazines, and the Secret Masters of Fandom—"the C.I.A." Play continued until Lee had walked out of the room, when the first player looked up and asked, "Was that necessary?"

Penny shrugged. "Kills two birds with one stone. I don't want him doing security at the art show; he can be too damn gung-ho, and he's got a temper. But he loves spy stuff, so this keeps him happy as well as busy."

"Unless this Preacher stabs him," Orris muttered.

"Better that than he stabs the Guest of Honour," she said. "Can one of you stop conquering the world for five minutes and put these room changes up?"

LEE found Preacher in the fan lounge, playing steel guitar and singing softly to the three shabbily-dressed (and scantily-clad for early December, even in Dallas) women clustered around his feet. He was heavily tanned, dressed in an ancient fringed buckskin jacket and much-patched jeans, and while his hair was long and wild and too dirty for Lee to do more than guess the colour, his beard was neatly trimmed into an iron-grey goatee.

Two fans were talking in one corner of the room, near the urn. Lee walked across the room, made himself a cup of coffee, and stood where he could watch Preacher while looking as though he were following the conversation; something about the coincidence that Aldous Huxley and C.S. Lewis had died on the same day. Preacher continued to softly wail about Devil's Canyon, but he looked straight at Lee and grinned as he sang. His dark eyes looked like something out of a Lovecraft story, and Lee reluctantly found himself turning away from his gaze. He forced himself to look back. Neither Preacher nor any of his women seemed to be armed, unless there were weapons in the guitar case. He watched as a young woman, a little older than his daughters and much prettier than any of the harem, walked around the cluster to get to the urn; Preacher stopped playing long enough to reach into a pocket and hand her a business card, which she glanced at, then dropped on the table next the sugar-bowl. Lee picked it up as she walked out with a cup of coffee, and pocketed it without reading it. He looked at Preacher, who grinned back.

"Crystal," Preacher said, without looking away from Lee, "go get me a banana smoothie." One of the women—Lee guessed her age at thirty—shot to her feet as though goosed and was out the door with a speed that Lee could only admire. "You a cop, man?"

"No," replied Lee, automatically. Preacher's grin widened a little more.

"Yeah, well, if you're after some dope, I'm not holding any, and if you're selling, I don't have any bread, either."

"You came all this way without any money?"

"Just enough for our memberships. The Lord will provide what we need," Preacher replied, and winked. "You from around here?"

Lee nodded. He suspected it would be safer to tell Preacher as little about himself as possible, and it wasn't exactly a lie; he'd lived in Dallas and Fort Worth for several years in the fifties and sixties, though he hadn't been back since his divorce. "You're supposed to wear your badges at all times," he said, feeling like an asshole. One of the women opened her mouth to speak, but Preacher reached into his pocket and removed four badges. Without reading them, he handed two to the women, and clipped a third to his jacket. "Anything to keep the peace, badge man."

Lee glanced at the badge he was wearing; it was yellow, indicating a one-day membership. The only name on it was 'Gypsy', while the women's badges—clipped to the waist-bands of their torn-off jeans, just above the crotches—read 'Preacher' and 'Crystal', but Lee knew that members were free to use any names they chose. "Long way to come for just one day," he said, mildly.

"Yeah, well, we just want to meet Mr Heinlein." One of the women giggled.

"So do a lot of people," said Lee, softly. "I'd like to meet him myself, but he doesn't have much time. He's not well enough to go to the room parties, or anything." He sat on a table near the group; he would have towered over Preacher even if he'd squatted on the floor, but from that height, it was like staring down into an abyss. "Did you bring a book to autograph, or anything?"

"I thought I might get one here," said Preacher.

"I thought you didn't have any money."

"No." He grinned. "Not right now, but sometimes good people give us money."

"You know he won't sign an autograph unless you can prove you've given blood in the past six months?" Preacher stared at him warily, trying to tell whether he was telling the truth. "He needed a lot of transfusions when he was sick, and he has a rare blood group; he thinks everybody should give blood as often as possible. It was in the progress reports," Lee added, trying not to smile, "and the program book. Look, it may not be too late to get down to the blood bank."

Preacher nodded. "Yeah, well, if Mr Heinlein wants blood, we got blood." He glanced at one of the women, who instantly sashayed out of the room. His smile said 'Your move'.

Lee managed not to swear. "Just thought you should know," he said, as blandly as he could manage. "Hate you to be disappointed after coming all this way."

Preacher grinned back at him. "Thank you. Anyway, badge man, it's nice talking to you and all, but I've got to go take a piss. You can stay and talk to Gypsy if you want." He stood, and Lee straightened up. The top of Preacher's head was level with his chin, but that didn't make him any less threatening; he was, Lee realised, taller than Attila the Hun, and about the same height as the Marquis de Sade. Preacher weaved past him and headed into the corridor, leaving Lee standing there flat-footed. He mumbled something to Gypsy, then ducked out of the room as she laughed. He watched as Preacher headed for the lift, then jogged down the stairs to the lobby, emerging in time to see the little man disappearing into the men's room. He walked past the door, and leaned against the wall on the far side, outside the hucksters' room where the signing sessions were being held. He reached into his pocket for his programme, and discovered Preacher's business card. 'Charles Manson,' it read. 'President, 3-Star-Enterprises, Nite Club, Radio and TV Productions.' No address or phone number. He shrugged, and pocketed it again.

According to the program, Heinlein wasn't going to be making any appearances before the signing at 1600, which was fine by Lee. His years in fandom had taught him that it was often a bad idea to meet people whose work you admired, and he'd liked a lot of the old man's earlier work, particularly the short stories. He stood there for a minute, watching the door, and noticed Carol walking out of the art show. "Hi, Lee. What did Penny Dreadful want?"

Lee waited until he was near enough to speak to without raising his voice, but was cut off by a shout of "Ozzie?" He turned around, and saw a balding, chunky man in cowboy boots, checked shirt and too-tight Levis waddling towards him brandishing a clipboard. Lee tried to smile, managing to show his teeth in a narrow grimace. "Hey, Shitbird!" the man called. "Long time no see! How're they hanging?"

"Hi, Dan." Lee had never made friends easily, especially during his days in the Marines, and didn't consider Dan as more than an acquaintance even after a dozen years of meeting at cons. Dan shoved the clipboard at him, peered at Carol's name badge—or stared at her breasts; Lee wasn't sure which—and introduced himself to her. "Anyway, Ozzie, I've got a petition here for you to sign."

Lee sighed inaudibly and took it. "What's it for?"

"Getting rid of some of the pain-in-the-butt red tape you have to go through just to buy or sell a gun, and a couple of other bullshit laws."

Lee laughed softly, and handed it back immediately. "You still flogging this horse?"

Dan flushed.

"Nah, I think the laws as they stand mostly make sense," Lee continued. "People living in cities don't need guns and most probably shouldn't have them. Look at me, for example."

"Yeah," spat Dan. "I did, and I thought that was a Marine Corps ring you're wearing. I must've been mistaken. Which side're you going to be on if the Russians invade, Oswaldskovich? You still reading Karl Marx?"

"Not lately," replied Lee, neutrally. "And the Russians aren't crazy enough to invade. *Nuke* us, yes, maybe, if Reagan doesn't clever up, but invade?" He shook his head. "Be seeing you, Dan."

Dan turned to Carol. "What about you? With the rising crime rate, women *need* guns, *especially* handguns, and *especially* in the cities."

She shrugged. "Maybe, but how would we stop men getting hold of them? No thanks."

Dan snorted. "Look, if you outlaw guns, only outlaws will carry guns. Prohibition's never worked for drugs, why would it work for weapons? Shit, there must be nearly half a million unregistered guns in the U.S., guns brought back from World War II or Korea, M-1s, M-2s, M-14s, Thompsons and God knows how many pistols..."

Carol shook her head, and watched him stomp off. Preacher walked out of the men's room an instant later, and Dan wheeled around and offered him the petition. "I take it you voted for King," said Carol, *sotto voce*.

Lee nodded. "Is that a problem?"

"No; so did I. I didn't expect him to win, but I thought it was time for a president who wasn't white. Why did that guy call you, uh..."

"Shitbird?" Lee smiled crookedly. "It was one of my nicknames when I was in the Marines, because I was such a god-awful shot. They also called me Oswaldskovich because I was reading *Das Kapital* and studying Russian. I wanted to get into Intelligence. Actually, I wanted to be Herb Philbrick."

"Who?"

"A spy, on a show called 'I Led Three Lives'. It was my favourite TV show when I was a kid, probably before your time; it must have been cancelled in '55 or '56. Richard Carlson, you know, the guy from *It Came From Outer Space*, played him. I discovered James Bond a few years later. I even bought myself a little pistol, but the only person I ever shot with that was myself—by accident, of course. It got me busted down to private and three months of K.P. I am possibly the *last* person on Earth who should be trusted with a gun." He glanced at Preacher, as he signed the petition and walked down the corridor chatting to Dan. "One of the last, anyway. I used to be a real hothead. Sure, I was young, which is a pretty good excuse for being an idiot, but not for being an asshole. I used to pick a lot of fights, I even hit my first wife a few times, until she left me. After she and I were divorced, I had a nervous breakdown and ended up in hospital; God knows what I might have done if I'd had a gun *then*. The thought scares the shit out of me." He drew a deep breath. "But as I said, that was years ago. I like to think I'm a better person now."

She wrapped an arm around his waist. At thirty-five, an assistant librarian at the University of Texas and twice divorced herself, she'd lowered her expectations when it came to meeting men her own age. Lee lived too far away to have much potential as a partner, his sense of humour was unpredictable and she didn't share his enthusiasm for *The Prisoner*, but he didn't drink, was in good shape for a man of forty-one, and had been a pretty good friend for several years without ever trying to pressure her into sex. Maybe, she thought, it was time for *her* to make a move. "We all do stupid things when we're young. Jesus, some of the things I did in my student days... You still want dinner?"

"Sure, after the signing. Where shall we go?"

She shrugged. "I don't feel like getting dressed up. Why don't we try room service?"

PREACHER and his women arrived at the hucksters' room a few minutes after four, by which time the slow-moving queue had already extended out the doors and down the corridor almost as far as the lobby. Preacher, Lee noticed, had a new-looking paperback of *Stranger in a Strange Land* in one hand, and the three women were giggling as at some secret joke. Lee stood behind them in the queue, trying to see what they had in their carry bags, and wishing that someone had given the committee an excuse to call the cops. The queue inched forward, and he realised that he was sweating. It took nearly twenty minutes for them to get inside the doors of the hucksters' room, and he was pleased to see another two redshirts flanking the table and that the sword merchant's stall was on the other side of the room from the queue. Without realising he was doing it, Lee began counting the people between Preacher and Heinlein, counting them off as the queue shortened. Twenty... nineteen... eighteen... Dan walked out past him, carrying copies of *Starship Troopers* and *Farnham's Freehold*. Fifteen...

Preacher was four or five yards from the table when Lee heard some-one clear their throat from the doorway. He turned around, to see Penny standing there, her face red. "If I could have your attention, please," she began. A few people turned around; most—including Preacher—didn't. Eight...

"There was just a news flash on the radio," said Penny. "I checked with the other stations, in case it was a hoax. It isn't. John Lennon..."

Preacher turned around, and everyone fell silent. Lee saw the older man's eyes gleam as Penny continued, nervously but loudly. "John Lennon has just been stabbed outside his apartment building in New York. He was dead on arrival at the hospital."

There was a stunned silence that seemed to last for minutes. Lee stared at Preacher, softly, who had turned stark white. "Come on," said Lee, softly, kindly. "You look like you need to sit down."

"No..." whispered Preacher. He stared at Penny, his eyes seeming to become deeper and darker, and then a Buck knife appeared in his empty hand as though by magic. With a scream of rage, he launched himself at Jenny. Lee stepped into his path to block him, and Preacher leapt up and slashed at his face. Lee recoiled, stumbling backwards, and Preacher weaved around him. Lee spun around to face him and make a grab for the knife, hoping his longer reach would give him an advantage, and felt another blade enter his back and grate against his bottom rib before be-ing withdrawn. Preacher laughed, and Lee stumbled forwards and aimed a kick at his knife hand. Preacher merely dropped the book and caught the knife with his other hand, then leapt back out of Lee's reach. A stu-dent tackled him from behind, knocking him down, then two more rushed in to grab his arms. Lee turned around to face the woman who'd stabbed him, and saw all three standing there, knives drawn, looking as though they were waiting for orders. Preacher screamed wordlessly, and the women rushed at Lee, two with their knives held high, one aiming for his belly. They stabbed him fifteen times before he blacked out.

He half-woke two days later, seeing only whiteness, feeling as though he was floating. Only the stink of disinfectant and the dry dead taste in his mouth convinced him that he wasn't in heaven. He tried to focus, then to sit up. "Take it easy," said a voice from incredibly far away. "Give me a second to call the nurse."

"Where am I?"

"Parkland Hospital." The whiteness became a flat plane, a ceiling. "Don't try to move," said the voice. "You lost a lot of blood; I've seen a few people knifed in my time, but no-one with as many holes as you. You're lucky to be alive."

"Are you a doctor?"

A short laugh. "No, but I used to be a cop. Name's Tippit; people call me J.D."

"I'm Lee Oswald. What're you in for?"

"Heart bypass," said Tippit. "I was sitting at home on the weekend, watching the game, and next thing I know they're rushing me into the trauma room."

Lee managed to move his eyes enough to see vases of flowers on the nightstand. "You've had a lot of visitors," said Tippit. "Your lady friend's been here most of the time since you came out of surgery. But they've kept the photographers and reporters out. Everyone's calling you a hero."

Lee shook his head. "All I did was nearly get myself killed."

Tippit laughed. "Well, take it from me, you may's well make the most of it while it lasts. People don't remember heroes very long."

"Yeah," Lee replied, then grinned broadly. "You know," he said, mostly to himself, "I always wanted to be a hero."

TRANSIT

I HAD JUST TURNED NINE WHEN Aisha walked into my classroom, stopping the conversation and stealing my heart in the same instant.

I think we all stared, and then, as Aisha looked back defiantly, we dropped our gazes back to our books as though we were suddenly interested in Stigrosc prime number theories. Pat, our teacher for the day, smiled a little thinly. "Class, this is Aisha, from al-Gohara."

A few of us looked up and muttered greetings, as Pat guided our new classmate to a seat near the doorway. A message from Morgan flowed across my book. *Pregnant*, e opined.

I glanced at Aisha's golden-pale profile out of the corner of my eye. *Don't think so*, I replied.

Must be. Look at the size of those boobs.

It was hard not to, despite Aisha's loose and very opaque sky-grey robe, but that would have been even more impolite than passing notes in class—and class was meant to teach us social skills: we would have learnt math much faster at home. *Can't be*, I protested. Aisha was taller even than Pat, at least two metres, but all the al-Goharans I'd seen were taller still, and Aisha probably wasn't much older than we were.

Morgan stared at er book for a moment, obviously gossiping to someone else. I stole a quick glance at Aisha's face, which was beautiful. Especially those eyes, rounder and darker and larger than any I'd seen outside of books. I love you, I thought, and was startled to see I'd written it on my book. I erased it hurriedly, relieved that I wasn't still passing my notes to Morgan, and went back to my math. A few of the kids were starting to talk again, but none of them spoke to—or about—Aisha.

Maybe they don't have contraplants on Al-Oasis, Morgan suggested, a moment later.

They must have, I replied.

Muslims aren't like us, Morgan countered, and then, *I bet they cut Aisha's thing off.*

What?

They do that. They used to, anyway. Ask my dad.

Why?

E couldn't answer that, and there was almost nothing about al-Gohara in my book or my ramplant, and I couldn't access the library during class without Pat noticing. All I could remember was that al-Goharans, being Muslims, liked to travel to Earth once in their lives, and their world was only one solstice jump from daVinci, with the worlds being in conjunction every six point something years (math isn't my forte, and I don't think anyone human *really* understands Stigrosc cosmography). From here, they went to Marlowe or Corby or Ammon, but that usually meant staying on daVinci for up to a year waiting for the next solstice. I was only three or four years old last time they'd visited, and the al-Goharans usually stayed near Startown, where they'd built a mosque, and didn't socialise much, but I'd never heard of them bringing their children here before. I wondered whether Aisha even spoke Amerish, and tried to imagine a voice that would match those eyes, that golden face, those breasts...

Aisha suddenly looked up, jacked out of er book, and then walked over to Pat's desk and whispered something. Pat looked startled for a moment, and then nodded. "Of course; I'm sorry, I didn't think of it. Will you be coming back today?"

Aisha smiled, whispered something else, and then walked out of the room. I remembered reading that Muslims had to pray so many times a day—though whether that was an Earth day, an al-Goharan day, or a daVincian day, I had no idea. Maybe I could ask Aisha.

AISHA was standing in the shade under the trees at the edge of the basketball court, leaning against one of the old cedars with a book in er lap, but it was obvious from the way er eyes tracked that e was watching the game, or the players, or maybe their clothes: smoke and mirrors were back in fashion again, and modesty wasn't. I found myself watching Morgan's legs, as usual—e liked to wear the briefest, tightest shorts possible, to show them off—but kept wondering what Aisha's must look like.

I'd accessed the library as soon as class was over, and discovered that the gravity on al-Gohara was .82, the climate generally warmer but less humid, and the day nearly thirty standard hours; the ship, the *Arakne*, (Stigrosc don't give names to their ships, but they allow the human passengers to christen them if they wish to) had only arrived three days before, so e was probably still adjusting. I summoned forth all the courage I thought I might have and had never needed before, and walked over. "Hi," I said. "I'm Alex. I'm in your class." Aisha nodded, and we watched the game for a moment. "Do they play basketball on al-Gohara?" Another nod. I wondered what I was doing wrong, and realised that I was asking yes-no questions. "How do you like it here?"

The only reply to that one was a quick glance, and an expression I couldn't read through er shades. The solstice isn't for nearly a year, I thought; you're going to have to talk to someone sometime...

I saw Teri weave past Shane and slam-dunk the ball amid scattered applause, and Aisha muttered something; the words were unrecognisable, probably Arabic, but the tone said, clearly, 'Not bad'.

"Do you want to practice your Amerish?" I suggested.

Another glance, and then, quietly, "Don't you have any friends?"

"Sure," I replied, slightly nettled. "I'm just lousy at basketball, is all. If I were as big—I mean, *tall* as you, I'd probably be great. *You'll* probably be great, when you get used to the gravity; everyone will want you." At least I managed not to bite my tongue.

"The gravity isn't a problem," e replied, and muttered something that sounded like 'initially'. "It's less than Earth's, and we've been training for that. It's—"

"What?"

"Nothing. You just do things so differently here. I wanted to come to your school—it's been so boring on the ship, with no-one else my own age—and I had to pester my father to let me, but it's..."

I waited.

"Don't girls go to school on daVinci?"

"What?"

"I suppose I should have learnt more about the place before I came here. I'm sorry I didn't, but there wasn't very much about it in our library: we don't travel much, except the men, and that's usually only on

Hajj... Do your girls decide not to come after they turn twenty-five, or is there some sort of law against it?"

I stared, calling up words from my ram and trying to understand what Aisha was saying, and hoping that I didn't look as stupid as I felt, if that were possible. "Or have they just sent me to a boy's school by mistake? I haven't even found a girls', uh, bathroom—"

A painful silence followed. "We don't have segregated schools," I began, "or segregated toilets, or segregated *anything*. We can't: we're all... we don't..." Oh, gods, I thought; this must be what Morgan meant when e said that Aisha's thing had been cut off. "I'm not a... I mean, I *am* a..." I took a deep breath. "Can I ask you a question?"

"I don't know. Can you?"

I tried to smile. "Do you know what 'monosex' means?"

It must have been Aisha's turn to stare to me. "What? No. What?"

"Or 'maf'—'hermaphrodite'?"

"You mean, like the Chuh'hom?"

"Yes. Monosex is the opposite; it means to be male or female, but not both..."

"But..." Aisha edged away from me slightly. "You mean *you're* a hermaphrodite?"

I nodded. "We all are."

"You mean, everyone in the school?"

"Everyone on the *planet*..." I replied, and then a thought hit me. "Well, except..."

Aisha slid slowly down the tree to sit with er arms wrapped around er legs, murmuring something in Arabic. I waited. "I've never met a hermaphrodite before," e said, weakly.

"I've never met a—girl," I replied, after a moment's thought.

A suspicious stare. "How come you know what the word means?"

I shrugged. "Old films and novels. Besides, we call our sports teams girls and boys—no-one wants to wear uniforms, so the ones with the shirts are girls. I don't know why; it's probably something that used to mean something once, like giving out gold and silver medals, or talking about 'going the whole nine yards'—" I glanced at the outline of Aisha's breasts, and suddenly guessed the origin of the custom. The feeling of knowing, discovering, *that* was more of a buzz, a jolt, than anything I could remember ever learning in class.

14

The game ended, and kids started drifting back into the classroom. I stood there silently, not wanting to leave Aisha.

When everyone else had disappeared, Aisha looked up, er golden face even more pale than usual. "This is too—" e looked around. "Do you think the toilets would be empty now?"

"Huh? I mean, yeah, sure."

"Great." I offered my hand, to help er up, but e ignored it and struggled to er feet without my help. We walked to the doorway, and Aisha stopped, until I offered to go inside and make sure there was no-one else there.

"Can you tell the teacher that I'll be back tomorrow, initially?" Aisha said, when e emerged.

"Sure," I said. "Will you be?"

Aisha hesitated, and then shrugged. "I don't know. I'll have to ask my father."

I nodded. It had never occurred to me before that monosexes had fathers, though it probably would have if I'd thought about it for a few seconds. "See you," I said, wondering if I'd ever see Aisha again, and knowing I had to.

I spent most of the afternoon accessing the library, to find out what I could about monosexes. There was a lot of stuff I'd never imagined, like needing separate pronouns for each gender—'he' and 'him' and 'his' for males, 'she' and 'her' and 'hers' for females. They seemed sort of redundant, but Amerish thrives on redundancy, and the female pronouns sounded exotic enough that I practiced using them whenever I thought of Aisha.

Monos were extremely rare away from Earth, except in some religious enclaves where no-one had maf chromosomes: otherwise, it required major surgery, which almost no-one bothered with. The first human mafs were born a few years post-contact, but the chromosomes were discovered by humans, not Stigrosc: Stigs don't believe in genetic engineering. Mafs remained a minority on Earth for more than a century, but many of them—us—travelled to habitable solstice worlds, where there was unrestricted birthright. Others became crew on the Stigrosc ships, or emigrated to the neutral worlds; Stigs can't tell one human from another, and the Nerifar say we all taste the same, but Chuh'hom and Tatsu find it much easier and safer to communicate with mafs. Meanwhile, on Earth, as gene surgery became easier and cheaper and more countries adopted 'one couple—one child' laws, mafs were seen by many govern-ments as a way of avoiding serious gender imbalances in the population, and various incentives were offered to prospective parents—cheap health insurance, exemptions from combat service, places in the schools or the civil service or diplomatic corps reserved for mafs, that sort of thing. Ac-cording to the library (which was at least seven years out of date), mafs made up sixty-eight percent of the population of Earth—and more than ninety-nine percent of the permanent populations of Marlowe and Avalon, where the al-Goharans would also have to stop en route.

There was nothing in the library—at least, nothing I could access—about how monosexes made love. I was wondering about that when school closed, and I guess I still looked pre-occupied when I went home: my mother, who is normally very careful not to invade our privacy, asked me what was on my mind.

"There was a new kid in class, today," I replied. "Off the *Arakne*. Her name's Aisha."

"Is that the one who's pregnant?" asked Rene, without jacking out of er eternal *Vaster than Empires* game. Sometimes I think that unrestricted birthrights are over-rated; I get on okay with Kris, but I think Mum and Dad should have stopped when they'd had one kid each. "She's not preg-nant," I snapped. "She's..."

"She?" asked Kris.

Okay, *sometimes* we get on okay. "It's old English," Mum explained. "I didn't think the al-Goharans brought their kids with them..."

"They never have before," Dad agreed, without looking away from the holo. "How long is the trip? Two or three years each way? Hell of a time for a kid that age to be travelling—how old is e?"

That was Dad all over, making a judgement before e had any of the facts. "I don't know; she's tall, and her Amerish isn't too good, and she dresses like... I think she's about twenty-five or twenty-six," Kris stared, and almost dropped er book. "In al-Goharan years, which is—" My ram converted that into thirteen to thirteen point five standard. "Nine, roughly, so she'll be about twelve when she gets to Mecca."

"Great," said Dad. "Three years of er life wasted going to see a crater."

"Mecca's not a crater any more," I informed er. "Well, it is, sort of, but the radiation's down to a safe level, and they've built a new mosque and stuff. There was a load of new data for the library on the *Arakne*—stuff about Earth and a lot of other worlds, and only a few years old."

"Anything about how to get rid of razorvine?" e asked, sourly.

"Not that I noticed." As far as the library was concerned, razorvine was unique to daVinci (lucky us). It was probably a mutant strain of our terraforming fauna; it grew at about the same rate (much faster than the cyberfarms could process it into anything useful), and in everything from deserts to rivers, but was much harder to kill. Anything buried beneath it might be lost forever: it blocked infra-red and radar, and thrived on spotlights and X-rays. And it wasn't even attractive—the same monotonous tarnish colour as the solamat we use for major roads, with inedible seeds that you couldn't pick without the risk of losing a few fingers. Dad's a builder, so e regards it as a personal enemy, but most kids play hide and seek among the thickets at least once—or as often as we can without our parents catching us—and there are the usual stories about secret tobacco farms hidden within razorvine jungles. "There *are* some new games and shows, from Musashi," I added, and Rene and Kris grinned, "and I don't know what else."

Dad grunted, and watched the holo for a few more minutes, then stretched. "Want to shoot a few hoops before dinner?"

"Sure, Mum," said Kris, heading outside. Mum glanced at me, then folded er book. I was the last one outside. As usual.

"A MUSLIM monosex," Dad muttered, as e collapsed onto the bed. My parents' room was well sound-proofed, of course, but easy to bug on the rare occasions that I wanted to listen in. "Okay, e's nearly an adult, e's got er implants, you'd expect er to have crushes and fool around a little, but there are *dozens* of kids er own age here, why—"

"E'll only be here a year," replied Mum. "Besides, it may be good for Alex to get to know some off-worlders. You know e's good at xenology; e might even be a diplomat."

"Not if it needs math," said Dad.

Mum sighed. "E's better at languages than we ever were, and e enjoys them. I wouldn't be surprised if e learnt Arabic before this friend of ers flies away."

"What good will that be?"

"How many mathematicians do we need on a world this size? Biologists, builders, designers, artists, yes, but mathematicians? And what if e wants to go off-world?"

"Why would e?" retorted Dad. "What the Hell can e get off-world that e can't have here?"

AISHA arrived in class a few minutes later than the rest of us, clad in the same loose grey hooded robe or another exactly like it. Her dark eyes were slightly clouded, and I guessed she was having trouble adjusting to the shorter days. I thought of pointing out that she'd get more praying done this way, but I wasn't sure how she'd take it, and I couldn't think of anything else to say.

Our teacher for the day was Jai, an old fossil with a murmuring voice and an inexplicable enthusiasm for economics, both of which e used to try to explain the half-million years of human history pre-Contact. Most of us were already confused long before e came to the impact of third wave tech, and when e admitted that the whole thing had collapsed soon after the Stigrosc arrived anyway, most of us became irritated as well.

"This is irrelevant, isn't it?" asked Teri, while a few of us chuckled.

Jai bit er lip. "I rather hope so. You see, history is a wonderful labor-saving device; it saves us re-inventing and re-discovering so much. True, all these economic theories were based on the idea that resources were scarce and humans needed to work to survive. By the first century pre-Contact, of course, the scarcities were usually manufactured for commercial or political reasons—so that the rich could stay rich, or nations could control their populace by denying them food—and the work ethic had become a cancer. Many people worked at jobs they hated because they'd been convinced that there was no other way to survive; by the time the Stigrosc came to Earth, it would have been cheaper to simply feed, house, educate and entertain most of these people—but that would have violated the work ethic and destroyed the illusion of scarce resources. In this regard, capitalism and communism were almost indistinguishable—and when the Stigrosc arrived, and *gave* us cyberfacs and habitable planets, asking only for those ideas and data which were free to every human, both systems became, as you say, irrelevant. Our new economic system is, to a large degree, another gift from the Stigrosc—but, unlike all previous human economic systems, it is founded on the idea that human demand will never outstrip resource availability. If this happy state of affairs should change, then we will need a new system—and those of you who've been paying attention will have some idea which ones *not* to try." E drew a deep breath, and then—apparently for the first time—noticed Aisha. E glanced at the book open on er desk, and asked, "I gather things are the same on al-Gohara?" She was silent. "The cyberfacs and robots provide what is needed, and no-one is compelled to do work that they hate?"

18

Aisha shook her head violently. "No, of course not," she lied.

"Of course, there *are* some people who cling to the old ways," Jai continued, "simply because they are human ways—or, more importantly to many of them, *not* Stigrosc ways. Most of them are still on Earth, because they regard Earth as a human world, or because they *own* parts of Earth in a way they can never own part of any other world. What good this ownership does them now, I leave to you to imagine; if any of you succeed, please explain it to me. Aisha, it's nearly noon; do you want to go and pray? Now, are there any other questions?"

"TELL me about your world."

We were sitting under the old cedars by the basketball court again. Aisha glanced at me, and shrugged. "Why?" she asked. "You don't want to go there, do you?"

If all the girls there are like you, I thought, I might, but I didn't say that. "I won't know until you tell me," I replied.

She smiled slightly, beautifully. "It's warm, and much drier than it is here, and the sun's not quite as bright—"

"I know all that. Tell me about the people."

"People are people." She looked warily at me, daring me to challenge her.

"How much difference does having two sexes make?" I asked.

She looked even more wary. "I'm not going to discuss sex with—well, you're a *boy*."

"I'm also just as much a girl as you are," I replied, mildly.

She looked thunderstruck at that, then shook her head violently. "There's more to it than having a—besides, you don't have..." She looked puzzled for a moment.

"If you want to know what I *do* have—" I began.

"I don't—"

"You can access the library."

Aisha blinked, and then laughed. I waited until she'd finished, and added, "That's how I know what you've got. Sort of. I mean, I... unless you..." I sat there, trying to find the words.

"Have I been circumcised?" she asked, at last. "No. That was a primitive custom, much older than Islam and fairly explicitly condemned in the Qur'an—you *have* heard of the Qur'an?—and while some Muslims on Earth did it, so did some Christians. By the time the Stigrosc arrived, it had been stamped out nearly everywhere, like foot-binding or breast implants. But there's more to being a woman than just the body."

"We can all get pregnant, if that's what you mean."

"No!", she said, shaking her head again. "More than that!"

"What, then?" I asked, but she stood and walked away. I tried following her, but she kept walking faster, and her legs were much longer than mine. I walked faster, and she began running. Finally, she ran out of the school and down the razorvine-edged road to Startown, and I didn't follow her.

THE next day was Saturday, and I'd resigned myself to not seeing Aisha. Kris had slipped out early to play basketball and get out of gardening, which we both hated. Mum always maintained that if we did it often enough, we'd come to enjoy it as e and Dad did, but e let me go after an hour of cauterising the razorvine that was beginning to encroach on the watermelons. I spent the rest of the morning with a portrait program, trying to see if I could produce a fair likeness of Aisha, and maybe slot both of us into an old movie, a pre-Contact one with monosex characters: *The Princess Bride*, maybe, or *War for the Oaks*. That way, I could just superimpose her face on a female body, rather than have to try to imagine hers. Unfortunately, nearly all of the female bodies in the art history catalogue were of women from Earth gravity, while the few from the Martian Republic were *too* tall and slender. I'd always known that ideals of beauty varied between eras and ethnic groups, but seeing the demonstration flash before my eyes was startling. I'd never imagined that there were so many ways to mutilate living bodies.

I managed to devote three or four hours to Aisha's face, and another two to her figure, before succumbing to the temptation to access some pictures of female genitals. They looked incomplete, even deformed, with just this little bump where the penis should be, but apart from that, they looked just like mine or Morgan's. Males, I discovered, had external testes where the vulva should be, in what looked like an uncomfortable, if not hideously hazardous, position.

After forming a recognisable template of Aisha, I scanned us into *Forbidden Planet*; the eyelines gave me a little trouble, but once I'd fixed that, it looked wonderful, and it even made sense.

On Sunday, I made the mistake of reading a love poem by Andrew Marvell, 'To His Coy Mistress'—*Had we but world enough, and time*—and became determined to see Aisha again, or at least to *try*. The library told me that Sunday wasn't a religious holiday for Muslims—their Sabbath started Friday and finished Saturday—and there was nothing to stop me walking up Tranquility Road to Startown; Aisha, a lightworlder, did it every day. Mum let me go with nothing more than the usual caution to be home before nightfall (razorvine is attracted by light, and can supposedly move fast enough to engulf anyone walking with a lantern), and I slipped out before Dad could object.

The streets of Startown were all but empty, but there was a soccer game in progress (if you can use soccer and progress in the same sentence) on Eagle Street two blocks from the mosque, and it had drawn quite a crowd—some of them in long-sleeved robes, some in jeans and shirts. I watched for a few minutes, scanning for Aisha, but though I noticed a few pale and beardless faces, I couldn't see any women present at all, or anyone under fifteen. I attracted some stares, not all of them friendly, but no-one questioned my right to be there.

A few minutes after the whistle blew for half-time, I heard the sound of a single, powerful voice booming from the direction of the mosque, and everyone turned and walked towards it. I followed until the last of them had disappeared inside the doors, and then headed back towards my home.

I'd reached the edge of Startown when, suddenly, it began raining. I heard doors open behind me, and laughter, and turned to see al-Goharans rushing out into the street, most of them staring at the sky and catching raindrops in their mouths as they laughed; a few even removed their skull-caps and let them fill with water before upending them over their heads. I turned about, but though I searched down every street, I couldn't see Aisha anywhere. Eventually, after the rain stopped, I returned home, hearing the waterfed razorvine growing around me as I walked.

That evening, I began learning Arabic: the library had teaching programs for most languages, even ones that had been dead since before contact. It was a little easier than Chuh'hom Oratory, and it might even be useful.

"WHY?" Aisha demanded.

"Why what?"

"Why are you learning Arabic? And why do you want me to help you?"

"Well, al-Goharans are going to be staying here after every solstice," I replied, reasonably enough. "We should have *someone* here who can speak to them without an interpreter."

"We all speak Amerish."

"Then why do you learn Arabic?"

"The Qur'an must be read in the original; all translations are invalid."

"What do you speak at home?"

"My mother used to call it Amerabic," she replied, and a beautiful smile suddenly appeared on her face. "Sometimes we'll start a sentence in one language and want to say something that's easier in the other language, so we switch. It's whatever language we think in—here, everyone speaks Amerish, so I think in Amerish."

I nodded. "I went to Startown yesterday, and everyone there was speaking Arabic."

"That's—you did *what*?"

"I went to Startown. I watched the soccer game for a while; then it started raining, and everyone seemed to get a big kick out of it."

"It doesn't rain very often on al-Gohara," she replied, looking at the cloudy sky with distinct approval. "I don't think I've ever seen it rain like *that* before."

"Then why weren't you out dancing in it like everyone else?"

"I—" She turned to stare at me; her beautiful face turned pale, and then pink. "That's none of your business. Anyway, I'm sure it'll rain again before I leave, initially."

I realised, suddenly, that all the times I thought she'd said 'initially', whether or not it made sense, she was really saying 'inshallah'—'if Allah wills it'. "Oh, sure," I replied. "Or maybe you can stop at New Seattle on your way back. Do you mind if I ask you a question?" She continued to stare, so I didn't wait for her to answer. "Are there any other girls—or women—in Startown?"

"No."

"Why not?"

"That's two questions..." She turned away from me, and watched the basketball game for a while. I was beginning to suspect that the reason she almost always headed for this clump of trees at lunchtime was that she *liked* talking to me, but wanted to make sure there were always plenty of witnesses, as though she was willing to regard me as a girl from the neck up. "Do you remember what Jai was saying last week about scarce resources and the Stigs?"

"The parts I stayed awake for."

"What she, he—what should I call him?"

"E," I replied, without hesitation. "We're all 'e', except you."

"Okay. What e said doesn't really apply on al-Gohara. There's one resource that's still scarce, and the Stigs control it: that's passage to Earth. The hajj, the pilgrimage to Mecca, is one of the five pillars of Islam, but there isn't enough room on the Stig ships for all adults to make the journey even once, so places are awarded randomly by a computer. At least, they are on al-Gohara; I don't know how it's done on other Muslim worlds."

I thought about this for a moment, and asked, "And women aren't allowed to go?"

"It's a little more complicated than that... women *are* allowed to go, but not without their husbands, so unless the husband has also won a place on the ship, the woman gives it to her husband. Or sometimes to her father, or an adult son, or she can trade it, inshallah. And there are some who think the computer may not be perfectly random—"

"Trade it? For what?"

Aisha shrugged. "Favours. Prestige. Luxuries that the facs don't make. A better marriage for her children, maybe, inshallah."

"Arranged marriages?"

She nodded. I refrained from whistling or swearing, but it was a near thing. "Some women complain about not going, but the men just blame the Stigs for not having bigger ships: some even say they're doing it to weaken our faith, because the Stigs won't even let us fill the ship, just in case someone wants to leave the worlds we visit en route, which no-one ever does. The imams and califas have tried petitioning the Stigs, but they don't seem to understand about religion, and almost no-one from," she hesitated for a moment, "other worlds, the non-Islamic worlds, ever wants to visit Earth. Anyway, if the Stigrosc cared enough to want to break our faith, they could leave all of us stranded on al-Gohara forever."

"Sounds like you're lucky to be here."

"Lucky?" She considered this, moving the tip of her tongue tantalisingly across her upper lip, as though tasting the air. "I'm lucky to be going on hajj, and glad I'll be an adult by the time I'm there, but I miss having other girls around. Men are boring."

I had to know. "How did you get a place when other women don't?"

"My father wouldn't leave me on al-Gohara alone."

"What about your mother?"

"She's dead," Aisha snapped. "Okay? Can *you* leave me alone, now?"

I walked to the other side of the playing field, so I could see her and pretend I was still watching the basketball game. The game ended a few minutes later, and I saw Morgan, wearing little more than a translucent helix of swirling silver light, glance at me meaningfully before walking off hand-in-hand with Teri.

DESPITE that setback, I finally *did* persuade Aisha to coach me in Arabic, after only four weeks of mispronouncing words and hideously mangling the grammar. In a moment of random curiosity, I learnt that she was named after Muhammad's third wife, and that her name was also Japanese for 'manipulating an overly sympathetic or soft-hearted person', a discovery that we both found hilarious.

Weeks passed, and though I became fairly good at reading and speaking Arabic, I couldn't write it or think in it. Aisha couldn't invite me to her home, nor come to mine, but occasionally she'd let me walk with her almost as far as Startown, on the condition that I stayed on the other side of the road. The only people who ever saw us were the razorvine clearing patrols, and they must have mentioned it to Dad, because one evening e said, with all the casualness of a sun going supernova, "Some al-Goharans volunteered for the clearing crews today, want MacLeod and me to teach them how to handle the lasers."

No-one spoke. I just stared at my dinner and kept chewing. MacLeod was Morgan's mother, and I wondered if e'd put them up to this.

"I don't know whether they were getting bored, or whether they just liked the idea of killing something," Dad continued, "but there was at least a dozen of them. There's nothing else happening at the moment, so we said yes."

"Maybe they want to thank us for our hospitality," replied Mum, mildly.

"Or maybe they don't want us coming any closer than we have to," said Dad. E seemed remarkably calm about the idea of armed al-Goharans: of course, the lasers have genescanners and safety switches built in, so you can't actually aim them at a human, and bouncing them off a mirror is much trickier than the thrillers make out. Dad wasn't setting me up to be murdered, but I wondered what e thought would happen to Aisha.

Kris looked from one to the other. "Why would they thank us for that? It's free. I mean, if we said no, the Stigs would stop coming here, right?"

Dad shrugged, and turned er attention back to er soup. Rene's eyes bugged. "No more Stigs? You mean no new games?"

"Relax," I told er. "It'll never happen. It's in the treaty the Stigs signed before they gave us Avalon and Terranova—that a ship would visit every human world every solstice, so we could always go back to Earth, or out to any new worlds..."

"Okay," said Dad. "What do you think would happen if, say, the al-Goharans landed and discovered that there was no mosque at Startown, or no food or water, or no cyberfac? Would the Stigs still keep coming?"

"The Stigs would," I replied, "but the al-Goharans might not..." My voice faded out, and we stared at each other in silence until Mum said, softly but pointedly, "None of us understand the Stigrosc well enough to know what they'd do. Or the al-Goharans, for that matter."

AISHA heard about the al-Goharan crews that same night, and the next day she asked me not to accompany her home again, in case her father heard about it and ordered her to stay away from the school altogether. On daVinci, that would be considered probable cause for a charge of child abuse, but I decided not to tell Aisha that: I was still wondering what I *should* say when she leapt up, and volunteered for the basketball game, on the sole condition that whatever team she was on would be the girls. I stayed on the sidelines and watched. Despite the gravity, she moved beautifully, like a gazelle with breasts.

To my irritation, this became a set routine for a few weeks: we'd be talking about something, when suddenly she'd stand up and join in one of the games. She wasn't quite as fast as Teri, and she had trouble allowing for the gravity when she had to throw the ball any distance, but she knew how to use her height and her reach, so she was always selected, while I usually had to sit back and watch. On days when it was too wet for basketball, she would sit in the classroom and watch the rain through the roof. "This is wonderful," she murmured. "Our buildings are made the same way as yours are—though the ceilings are higher—but they're designed to keep the sunlight out; I don't think this would ever have occurred to us. Even when it's not raining, I love watching your clouds, all the shapes, the way they move..."

I've never been that enthusiastic about rain myself, but I nodded. "You should see it in winter, when it thunders—but I guess you'll be gone before then..."

"Yes," she said, still beaming, and then, unexpectedly, "It's my birthday tomorrow."

"Happy birthday. How old will you be?"

"Twenty-seven: that's about, oh, nine and a half of your years."

I hesitated, then plunged in. "Of course, you could stay here."

She stared at me, and then shook her head sadly. "My father would never let me, Alex."

"So don't ask er." There was a shocked silence as I did the math. "In half a year, you'll legally be an adult—"

"Not on al-Gohara—"

"Right; you're *not* on al-Gohara. You're on daVinci, and subject to daVincian law—so you might as well enjoy its benefits. When're you considered an adult on al-Gohara, anyway?"

She looked away, as though she was fascinated by the way the rain trickled down the windows. "On my wedding night," she said, finally, very softly.

"*What?*"

"Of course, most women don't really treat you as an adult until you have a child of your own. Boys are legally considered men after puberty—do you know about puberty?"

I grimaced, and nodded, remembering my first and (so far) only period, before I had my contraplants inserted. "Sure," I croaked. "Is this part of your religion, or—"

"Some of it," she replied. "Some of it is tradition, I guess. Our ancestors weren't just Arabs; they came from every continent on Earth, and they brought a lot of different traditions with them." She shrugged. "My mother used to say it was intended to keep the birthrate up—we can't breed as fast as you can—but she may have been joking, I don't really know."

We sat there in silence for nearly a minute, before I asked, "Is this what you meant when you said that there was more to being a woman than... well, having female parts, being able to get pregnant..."

She nodded. "Well, it's also important *not* to have—male parts, or you'll never be trusted around the women. If you were to come to al-Gohara, the men wouldn't want to know you, and you'd be barred from places that were only for men *and* only for women, and you certainly wouldn't be able to marry. Men are permitted to marry non-Muslims, but women can't, so even if one wanted to... It'd be the worst of all possible worlds." She turned to look at me, and I noticed that she was on the verge of tears. "For you, that is. For us, it's—"

"Home?"

"More than that. It's... a world we created for ourselves." She looked down, and then scrambled to her feet and rushed out into the rain, looking at the sky, letting the rain run down her face. I just sat there and watched her, trying to think of the right thing to say, and finally I walked out behind her, stood within arms' reach but too scared to touch, saying nothing, nothing, nothing.

WEEKS passed, and we spent them saying nothing, until Cori was giving us a lesson in xenology. Aisha was as fascinated as I was, possibly more so; unlike the rest of us, she'd actually *met* Stigrosc and Chuh'hom and Nerifar. Cori was becoming slightly bogged down in the details of Nerifar triads, thanks largely to Teri's love for asking unanswerable questions, when Morgan interrupted to ask, "Nerifar don't have any religions, do they?"

"No," replied Cori, er relief apparent. "They have a complicated ethical code, which is almost entirely concerned with sex and food, but because they don't believe in owning any more than they can actually carry—which isn't much—it's short enough for most of them to memorise."

"Like a hafiz," I interjected. Cori looked blank. "Someone who's memorised the complete Qur'an," I explained.

Morgan glanced at me, er expression unreadable, and then smiled back at Cori. "But they don't claim that this ethical code was handed down to them by any sort of deity?"

"No. It was originally composed as a series of songs—peace treaties from various wars, marriage vows, divorce decrees, medical treatises, lessons for children, proverbs and parables, that sort of thing. But because it's never been written down, there's no standard version; it's sung differently in different clans, new verses are always being added, and a few were changed or edited out when they were discovered not to be true, like the one about kidneys..."

"In fact," said Morgan, er smile becoming wider and er voice impossibly sweet, "none of the other species we've encountered—or that the Stigrosc have encountered and told us about—have anything we would call a religion, or a deity."

Cori considered this. "The Nerifar... don't, the Chuh'hom... don't, the Tatsu don't... We don't really understand enough about Stigrosc or Garuda culture to be sure; they often seem to regard the universe as a sentient being on a time scale beyond our comprehension, which I suppose you could consider a deity..."

"But they don't believe that it handed down a set of laws they had to obey?"

"Only mathematical laws—which for a Stig or a Garuda, is pretty important. But not their ethical codes."

"And none of them believe in a single ancestor for their entire species?"

"No."

"What about the Garuda egg?" asked Jo.

Cori nodded. "Well, the first Garuda presumably *did* hatch from the first Garuda egg, but the 'Garuda egg' in their histories contained *everything*, so it's probably a metaphor—or a poor translation—of the Big Bang. The Nerifar don't have any similar stories—the only mentions of eggs in their coda are instructions on how to care for them and when not to eat them—but the Nerifar didn't know the rest of the universe existed until the Stigrosc landed on their homeworld."

Morgan nodded. "Do any of them worship their ancestors?"

Cori considered this. "No. Chuh'hom worship the community; they believe in a form of reincarnation, but they're still arguing about whether souls can travel between planets, and if so, how fast." Chuh'hom love to argue, and their committee meetings should be avoided at all costs. "The Nerifar eat *their* ancestors, and never speak the names of the dead. Male tatsu worship their mothers, and no-one knows what the females think. Stigrosc revere their descendants, and if Garuda worship anything, it's the sky."

Morgan grinned, and sprang er trap. "Would you agree that only humans had religion because it was invented by human monosex males and enforced with violence, to compensate for the fact that they couldn't bear children, that their role in creating children was ridiculously small and for all they knew, might have been non-existent, performed by someone else—the same inadequacy that produced lunatic ideas like penis envy, sentient sperm, and women as mere incubators? That its mainspring was the idea that the *father* was the creator, not the mother; the father was omnipotent and omniscient, the father knew best—but not better than *er* father, or er father before er, and so on until the golden age before women fucked everything up?"

There was a brief silence while Morgan paused for breath. I glanced at Aisha; her face, normally pale, was the colour of dried bone. Cori began saying, "Well, I think that's a—", but Morgan was unstoppable. "And that becoming complete, becoming mafs, so that *everyone* could create children, could know that feeling, did even more to kill off the old religions than the bombing of Mecca and Rome?"

Cori—who was only eighteen or twenty, and had never been a mother—gulped, and began again. "I think that's an oversimplification; I don't think there's ever a single cause for anything as complicated as—" but I didn't hear the rest, because Aisha had run from the room, and I followed her.

SHE was running down Tranquility Road, and I could *feel* her screaming, though she was saving her breath for the race. Her legs were much longer than mine, and she was nearly acclimatized to the gravity, and I didn't have a chance of catching her before she reached Startown unless she let me. She was at least halfway there before she began to collapse; fortunately, she slowed down enough that I could catch her before she hit the solamat. Holding on to her wasn't easy—standing up, my eyes were on the same level as her breasts—but I supported her as best I could while she cried onto the top of my head.

"It's okay," I murmured into her blouse. "E just doesn't understand, that's all."

She sniffed. "Do *you* understand?"

"No, but... I'm *trying* to understand. Besides, I..." I took a deep breath and said it very quickly, "I've been in love with you ever since I saw you and... well, Morgan and I used to..." I tried to remember an Arabic term for 'go steady', and couldn't think of one.

"What?"

"Well, I guess you could say we were... girlfriends, or something. Nothing serious, just kid stuff—kissing games, that sort of thing." She pulled away slightly and stared at me through her shades. "You don't play games like that on al-Gohara?" She shook her head violently. "Well, I guess it's different for you. We all have the same sort of, uh, equipment, and we get to see each other naked in the change rooms, at the beach, places like that, or look in a mirror... but I think Morgan's a bit jealous." I shrugged. "I guess that's one thing we haven't gotten rid of."

Aisha raised an eyebrow at that, and then began crying again. "Thanks for coming after me... I'm glad we can say goodbye."

"It's—what?"

"I can't go back to school. Not after *that*."

I stared at her, suddenly weighed down by a horrible feeling of heaviness, of sinking. "Goodbye, Alex." She grabbed my head, kissed me quickly and violently, and then let go and turned away. I tried to yell something, but my mouth seemed to be stunned. I watched her walking, and then ran after her.

"And do what?" I panted. "Stay at home all day every day until *Olivia* arrives?" She kept walking. "Okay, you don't want to go back to school, you don't have to, neither do I, we can still see each other."

"No we can't."

"There's an empty house, way out of town, all on its own; it's a great place, completely private, and I have a key." She stopped, and looked curiously at me. "It belonged to Mad Cousin Yuri. It's a long story. Anyway, it's at the end of Barrows Road, you know, the turn-off we just passed..."

Aisha shook her head, and started walking faster.

"Send me a note if you change your mind," I called. No answer. "Or send me a note anyway, any time you want to talk. Please?"

She stopped, and turned. "Inshallah," she murmured.

"Is this why you call him Mad Cousin Yuri?" Aisha asked, staring at the half-finished artworks that lined the walls.

I nodded, wondering how Aisha had convinced her father to let her out unchaperoned. "E was my father's cousin, not mine: e wanted to be an artist, and e was pretty good at it, but e hated working." Aisha laughed. "E convinced erself that the only way e was going to finish anything was by removing erself from society altogether, so e petitioned for a house out here, no one around but the friendly neighbourhood razorvines. A lot of people tried talking er out of it, but e had the right to a house of er own, and the builders couldn't claim to be too busy or anything, so it got done; they cleared the land, built a road and the house, and moved er stuff out here. E stayed out here for three weeks." Aisha laughed. "E came back occasionally, staying for a week or two at a time—and usually with a model or two, rarely on er own. Dad never really let er live it down—it was the first house e'd ever built, which is how I got a key—but Yuri was too easy-going to get upset. E managed to finish a few small things—some portraits, a lot of sketches, a statue or two—but e was just too fond of the cafes and the bath-houses."

"Isn't there a bath here?" asked Aisha, a little nervously.

"Sure—down the hall, second right. You want to take a bath?"

"I'll need to wash before I pray..."

Stupid of me. "Yes, there's a bathroom—down the hall, there."

"Then why did e have to go to bathhouses?"

"Ah," I said, sitting down on a chair that was twice my age. "Well. We go to the bathhouses for sex—I mean, *I* don't, you have to be at least eleven, that's about thirty-one of your years—but that's what they're for. I think that's where my parents met, or at least—" I noticed that Aisha was looking disturbed, even slightly revolted, and shut up. I'd had to wait five weeks before she contacted me, and another four before she'd agreed to meet me here, which left only eleven weeks and three days before *Olivia* arrived—Time's winged chariot hurrying near, as Andrew Marvell would have said.

"We may be more different than I thought," she said, softly, staring at the picture that Yuri had been working on er final visit here. It was a sketch of er favourite model, Kai, the one e used to joke about being buried with. E was very pregnant, and topless—or bottomless, rather; Yuri hadn't drawn er below the waist, just a halo of curly hair, a beautiful round face, and beautiful round breasts with large nipples the colour of Aisha's eyes. "I mean, I shouldn't be lying to my father, I shouldn't even be here with you, especially not *alone*..." I waited for her to say more, but she didn't. "Why not?" I asked. "I mean, we're not even *doing* anything—"

"But we *might* be!"

"- and what if we were? Whose business is that but ours?"

"You don't understand!"

"No! I don't!"

We glared at each other for a while, and then she shook her head. "What do you want?" she asked, softly.

"Where do I begin? I want to—I want us to be able to see each other whenever we want."

"I'm leaving in eighty days."

"You could stay here; you could be happy here—" She raised her eyebrows at that, and then blinked, as though the idea had never occurred to her before. "Anyway, we were talking about what *I* want. Next thing on my list is, I wish I knew what *you* wanted."

She continued to stare, and then shook her head. "So do I," she whispered. "Alex, you've been wonderful, you've been kinder to me than anyone since my mother..." She turned away, and I could tell she was about to cry; I reached up and out to touch her shoulders, comfort her, but stopped when my hands were only a few millimetres away. "My mother," she repeated, rather stiffly. "Was executed. For adultery. *Now* do you understand?"

I had the feeling that I was understanding less and less the longer I knew Aisha; I shook my head.

"My father brought me with him on this trip because he didn't trust my mother's family to watch me, he thought I might disgrace him—"

"That's—"

She turned and faced me, tears in her eyes and a crooked smile on her lips. "And how do you get on with *your* father?"

"That's not the point." I took a deep breath. "Okay, so maybe it is the point. But I know *my* father is wrong about you—and about a lot of other things. Is yours?"

"I'm here with you, aren't I?" She glared at me, then glanced briefly around at the windows, and then removed her scarf. As I stared, she shook her long hair free, pulled her jacket open, stepped out of her skirt, and then stood there wearing only a pair of pants and a strange harness-like garment covering her breasts. A moment later, that popped open, and then she removed her pants and sat down on a chair opposite me, legs slightly apart and one foot propped up on the seat. She was even more beautiful than I'd imagined.

"Now do you understand? On al-Gohara, I'll be my mother's daughter until I'm my husband's wife. Here, I'd be considered a freak, mutilated, incomplete—and that includes emotionally as well physically, sexually. We couldn't even have children naturally!"

I admit, I hadn't thought that far ahead—I couldn't legally switch off my contraplants until I was fourteen—and I was surprised that Aisha had. Of course, if 'naturally' meant 'without gene surgery', then she was right, but so what? Or was that against al-Goharan law, too? Suddenly, uncontrollably, I began laughing.

"What's up?"

I took a deep breath and leaned back in my chair. "I'm just glad I didn't fall in love with a Stigrosc; that would have made my life *really* complicated."

Aisha stared, her eyes bugging slightly—and then she, too, burst out laughing, which set me off again. I slid out of the chair and kneeled in front of her, close enough to almost taste her, close enough to hear her heartbeat. I reached out and stroked her hair, running my hand along the side of her face down to her lovely neck—and felt/heard the cry of the muezzin, transmitted through the bone from an complant, calling her to *zuhr*, noon prayer. She looked into my eyes sadly, then grabbed her clothes and ran to the bathroom, while I collapsed face-first onto her chair.

I heard the bathroom door slide shut, and then open, and she disappeared into Yuri's bedroom to pray (it's considered inappropriate to perform *salat* in a bathroom). When she re-appeared, fully clothed, I was sitting back in my own chair.

"When *Olivia* arrives..." I began, as she walked towards the front door. She stopped. "Just in case I don't see you before then," I said. "*Olivia* won't be able to wait for you; it'll only have an hour or two to rendezvous with the shuttles before going to the jump point. If you're not on the shuttle in time, your father will have to choose between you and waiting another six years for er hajj—six years *here*. Which do you think e'll pick?

"We can hide here," I continued, quickly. "Or, better still, we can hide in the razorvine; even if they can find us, they'll never be able to cut us out in time—"

"I can't stay here either," she said, "not in this house, not on this world..." and then she walked out. I stared at her back, waiting for her to turn around; then, when she disappeared behind the next hill, I grabbed one of the razorvines that was snaking around the house, feeling the thorns bite into my palm and my fingers, standing there silently, knowing that Aisha wasn't coming back, and understanding nothing.

THE clouds were the same grey as Aisha's robes, and the razorvine rustled and groaned alarmingly as I biked down the road towards the starport. I'd crept out of the house as soon as the sun had risen, after the longest night I'd ever stayed awake through. I hadn't heard from Aisha since Ramadan began, five weeks before, and that had been just another goodbye. She hadn't even answered my mail; maybe her father had taken her book away. If e had, e'd know I was here, waiting; if not, she would.

I watched the first bus arrive as the shuttle hangar unfolded like a flower, then heard another bike behind me. I turned, and saw Morgan, dressed in jeans and a fine mesh jacket against the morning cold, dismount and walk towards me. "Saying goodbye?" e asked.

I didn't answer; I just turned my attention back to the shuttle. I couldn't see Aisha, but maybe she'd boarded while I'd looked away.

"I've been reading about monosexes," e said, sitting next to me. "Boys, girls... they were almost never friends. They didn't understand each other well enough, they were taught to want different things... It was really a scary idea, not being friends with your lover. I was really glad we'd gotten past that." I said nothing. "E's not going to stay, you know."

I saw a figure in grey, slightly shorter than the others, walking towards the ramp, and reached for my nocs. It was Aisha, and she looked around before sliding up the ramp and into the ship. "I thought we were friends," said Morgan. "We were friends for a long time, since we were kids. I thought we might even be lovers, one day. You know, you hurt me pretty badly, dumping me like that."

"I'm sorry," I said, quietly.

"Especially dumping me for er," e said, with some real bitterness in er voice. "A monosex. Someone who's not even *complete*. How do you think that made *me* feel, knowing I couldn't compete with half a person?"

"She's not half a person," I replied, dully.

Morgan shrugged, as the first bus pulled away and another crowd of al-Goharans filed into the shuttle. "Well, e'll be happier with er own people."

I opened my book: no new messages. Morgan opened er jacket as the sun broke through the clouds. "So, what happens now?"

I looked at er for the first time that day. "We're friends," I said, gently. "You're one of the best friends I ever had, and I'm sorry I hurt you."

E smiled, and shrugged. I leaned over and kissed er. "And I'm going to miss you," I said, and ran towards the shuttle, yelling "Wait!" at the top of my lungs.

THE pilot was Jessi Vokes, Teri's mother, and e *knew* that I was still nearly twenty weeks short of turning ten—but e also knew that there wouldn't be another ship leaving for nearly four years. Faced with this dilemma and a strict schedule, e called my mother, who—to my astonishment—told er that I had er permission to leave, and woke Kris and Rene so we could say goodbye. Perhaps fortunately, fathers don't get a vote in these matters. We lifted off only a few seconds behind schedule, and docked with *Olivia* with time to spare.

The human crew here are doing their best to keep the mafs and the Muslims apart, so I haven't seen Aisha in a week—and, fortunately, her father hasn't seen me. But I have seen Nerifar, and Chuh'hom, and I hope to see some Stigrosc when they've finished shedding their skins. The ship's library is even better than the one on daVinci, and full of recent data about the planets we'll visit.

The atmosphere on Marlowe is rich in neon and the aurora look like waterfalls of blood, especially during the season they call Not-and-Live. Aisha and I will legally become adults there, long before *Isis* arrives. I think I could be happy staying on Marlowe, despite the weather, but if Aisha decides to continue on her hajj, I'll follow. They say Avalon is as beautiful as Earth was between the Ice Ages, but if Aisha doesn't want to stay there, either... well, I've always wanted to see Earth. And after Earth, we have time. And worlds enough.

Oh Have You Seen The Devil?

"I RECKON HE'S DEAD," said Kate, cheerfully.

The journalist managed not to wince, but he stared into his glass to hide his sour expression and wondered whether he should risk drawing attention to himself by contradicting her. Fortunately, Michael broke the silence by asking, "How would we know? Nobody knows who he is. Or was, if he *is* dead.."

"Well, the jacks aint caught him, that's one thing certain," said Bill. "They couldn't track a bleedin' elephant through a snowdrift, much less through all this bloody fog."

There was a murmuring of assent at this; September had been unusually foggy, even by the standards of the East End, and the police were not much loved by the clientele of the Ten Bells.

"Maybe *he's* a jack," suggested Esme.

"A Jack Tar, more like," said Jenny. "That's why he's been quiet. His ship's bin out to sea, but next time it's in port..." She drew a finger across her throat.

"I reckon he's a Jew, like that Lipski," said Maggie. "No Christian would –"

The door opened to admit another shabbily dressed woman and the sound of the church bells, and Michael shook his head as she weaved towards the bar. "Right-o," said the landlord. "Those of you's got homes to go to, go there. The rest of you, clear out anyway."

"One drink, Johnny?" the new arrival mumbled. Her Swedish accent, slightly marred by her missing teeth, was thick enough to tell Michael that if she wasn't quite drunk, she was well within spitting distance of it.

"You got any push?"

She looked around, then pointed at Michael. "He'll pay."

"Hell I will," said Michael, shooting her a look as poisonous as the cheap gin. "Sounds like you've had enough already, Liz—more'n enough. You comin' with me?"

"You can't send us out in that," Esme whined. "'E might be out there, waiting for one of us."

The landlord snorted, and the man they called Mr Memory shook his head. "He's never done it on a Monday night. Only Friday or Saturday. Nor when it was foggy, neither."

"Don't mean he won't," said Jenny, uncertainly. Mr Memory eked out a living as a sideshow freak at Tom Norman's penny gaff show with his ability to memorize and reel back long strings of numbers or other words—a popular joke at the Ten Bells was that he drank to forget—but his tendency to see patterns everywhere meant that he was less reliable as a prophet.

The crowd stared at him for a moment, until Michael asked, with mock politeness, "You know when he'll do it again, then?"

"A Friday or Saturday, or maybe Sunday; Friday, Saturday, Sunday, it's a pattern. And it'll probably be the end of the month, like it was when he killed Polly Nicholls. It'll be this weekend, if it's not foggy."

Everyone stared, a few of the women gasped, the journalist made a note on his cuff, and Bill nearly choked on his gin. As far as anyone could tell, Mr Memory utterly lacked a sense of humour and had never told a joke, drunk or sober. Michael was the first to ask the question on everyone's mind. "D'you know who he is, then?"

Mr Memory blinked. "No. Do you?"

This started most of the drinkers in the pub laughing. "I wish I did," said Michael. "I could do with a hundred quid." He glared at his common-law wife again, then emptied his glass and walked towards the door.

"Couldn't we all," said the landlord. "Righto, everybody, you heard the bloody bells, so clear out."

Sluggishly, the drinkers obeyed. "'We have heard the chimes at midnight, Master Shallow'," Mr Memory muttered as he disappeared into the fog. The journalist sighed, and headed home.

MICHAEL rolled over in his bed and glared at the snoring woman next to him. He'd known she'd been a whore when he'd let her move in, and had never held that against her, but far too often she'd disappeared with whatever money was in their rooms, and sometimes anything she could carry easily that she could pawn or sell, staying drunk until all the money was gone. Not that he was a saint in that regard, either—he'd done three days for being drunk and disorderly back in July—but sometimes she didn't leave him enough to pay the rent, or took something he'd managed to steal from the docks. She always came back—she seemed to like him better than any other man, at least while she was reasonably sober, though less than she liked gin or rum—but he was fairly sure she'd added injury to insult by giving him the pox after one of these jaunts, too.

He turned his back on her, and before falling asleep, made a mental note to lock her in and to take all his money with him when he left, as well as his best hat and coat, his new razor, and his clasp knife.

THE editor looked up as the journalist walked in, and grunted, "Mornin', Bulling. Any luck?"

Thomas Bulling, still more than slightly hungover, shook his head. "No new evidence at the inquest. Nothing from my friends at the Yard. I talked to Le Queux, and he said he hasn't heard a bloody thing either, nor have Springfield or Hands; they're even starting to run out of theories that're worth printing. And I went 'round the pubs in Whitechapel and Spitalfields, like you asked, and folks are saying Leather Apron's dead—either that, or he's skipped town, probably on some cattle boat, or been locked up in Colney Hatch. It's been two weeks, two weekends, and nobody's found a clue, much less a body."

"Not in Whitechapel, leastways. Some woman's been killed and ripped up, near Gateshead; they've sent Dr Phillips up there to look at the body, just in case. Maybe he *has* moved on."

"Want me to go up there?"

"No, go back to the inquest. Did they say anything about the doctor who was paying for quims or whatever?"

Bulling shrugged. "They don't think he's the killer, just the boy who buys the beef, but the killer might be working for him. But since nobody knows his name or where he lives, just that he's American, that's not a lot of good. But I've got an idea that might help…"

"If it involves killing some poor whore, I don't want to know about it."

"Nothing so crude. What if we published a letter from this Whitechapel Murderer?"

"How do you propose –" The editor blinked, then grinned. "Have you got it?"

"Not yet, but give me a minute… and some red ink…"

The editor handed him an old Waverley pen. "It'll help sell some papers, anyway. And who knows, maybe it'll inspire the *real* killer to write a letter that gives the bobbies a clue."

"Good point."

"And see if you can come up with a better name than 'Leather Apron' or 'Whitechapel Murderer' while you're at it."

"Already done," said Bulling. "What do you think of 'Jack the Ripper'?"

MICHAEL returned home from the docks to find Liz gone and the padlock he'd put on the door tossed onto the sagging straw-filled mattress. The cow must have had a key, he thought sourly, as he searched the squalid little room to see what she'd taken with her. While all of her clothes were gone, at least she hadn't stolen his other coat… not that a pawnshop would give her much for that. Even if she'd saved some money of her own from sewing or cleaning or from begging from her church, it probably wasn't enough to stay drunk on for more than a week—two at the outside, and she'd be back. She'd always come back before.

THE Chief Constable looked at the facsimile and snorted. "'I keep on hearing the police have caught me but they wont fix me just yet.' No wonder Bulling says he treated it as a joke. He's probably laughing fit to burst."

"Shall I file it with the other one, sir?" asked his clerk.

"No, send it to Abberline, just in case. All the newspapers will have it by now, and they'll probably print it, and if this lunatic *does* strike again, they'll ask why we ignored it." He looked at the accompanying note again. "Tell Abberline that it's bound to be a fake, not that he won't work that out himself."

"How do we know?"

"*If* the real murderer decided to write a letter, which I very much doubt, he might send it to us, or he might send it to a newspaper, but he wouldn't send it to the Central News Agency. Only a journalist would think to do that. Bulling most likely wrote it himself—no, *don't* write that down: we've no proof. Is Dr Phillips back from Gateshead yet?"

"MICHAEL! Michael Kidney!"

Michael spun around, not quite overbalancing. The fog had lifted, but it had started raining heavily and water was dripping from the brim of his hat, so it took him a moment to recognize the driver of the laden cart as Bill, another regular at the Ten Bells. He waved, and was about to continue on his way to the pub when Bill called, "You still looking for your missus?"

He hadn't been, but it occurred to him that it would be reassuring to know where she was. "Have you seen her?"

"I think so. It looked like her, anyroad. D'you know the Queen's Head, on Commercial Street?"

"Yeah." He knew most of the pubs in and around Whitechapel, but that one was memorable because Liz had been arrested there for drunk and disorderly a few months before.

"She was just leaving, with another woman. Heading north. I waved at 'em, but I had a load to deliver so I couldn't stop."

"When was this?"

"I dunno. Ten minutes ago, maybe. Likely she won't be far away."

"'ERE! Gummy Amy! That's Leather Apron gettin' 'round you!"

Liz stopped kissing the well-dressed man she'd met in the Bricklayer's Arms, just long enough to look around and notice two laborers standing on the footpath nearby, clearly intent on seeking refuge from the heavy rain inside the relative warmth of the alehouse. She stuck her tongue out at them, showing the gums that had earned her one of her nicknames, but pulled her escort out of the doorway far enough to let the two men squeeze past. The man she'd been kissing raised his sandy eyebrows at the accusation, but he looked more amused than outraged; he glanced across the street, and with a faintly murmured, "Shall we?", led her across the road towards Berner Street.

Forty minutes later, another workman saw her in the doorway to number 63, kissing a sailor in a black cutaway coat, and heard the sailor comment, "You would say anything but your prayers."

Shortly after half past twelve, she was seen outside the International Working Man's Educational Club with yet another man—first by Police Constable William Smith, and then by Michael Kidney, who ran towards her with an expression of such utter fury that Liz's prospective client quickly retreated along the street. Liz spun around to face her lover, who grabbed her by the shoulders and snapped, "You're coming home now."

"No," she replied. "Not tonight; some other time."

She tried to wriggle out of his grasp, and staggered backwards through the gateway into Dutfield Yard, screaming softly as she fell onto the slippery cobblestones. Michael glanced back into the street, and saw a Jewish-looking man watching him; he yelled, "Lipski!", and the man fled, not slowing until he'd reached the shelter of the nearby railway arch. Another man, emerging from the Bricklayer's Arms, also took fright and headed in the same direction. Michael smiled, and strode towards Liz, who scrambled back into the shadowy yard.

"You don't get to tell me what to do," she said. "I got more'n 'nough for the doss house, still, and I'll come back when I want, if I want. I met a man tonight, a real swell; he said my mouth was bang up to the elephant, best thing he'd ever stuck his pogo in. He gave me a whole shilling and bought me gin and a rose too and –"

"What d'you want fuckin' flowers for? Fuckin' flowers is for fuckin' funerals." He reached for her wet tangled hair with his left hand and tried to pull her to her feet. She struggled until she'd slipped out of his grasp, then turned away from him and tried to pick herself up off the cobblestones. He grabbed at her again in the near-darkness, grasping the check silk scarf tied around her neck and twisting it. Liz clawed at the makeshift garrote, gasping as it began to choke her, but Michael was too drunk and too angry to notice. She fumbled in her pocket, hoping for something she could use as a weapon, but found nothing more dangerous than a comb, a pencil stub, or a spoon. Her fist closed around a small bag of cachous as she blacked out for the last time.

Michael continued to tighten the noose for nearly a minute after she'd stopped moving, before the realization of just what he'd done slowly cut through the alcoholic fog in his skull. He let her fall, then turned the body over and stared at her. He slapped her face twice, hoping for a reaction, some sign of life, then tried to think.

Mr Memory had said that the Whitechapel murderer would strike again that weekend, end of the month, if it wasn't too foggy. Well, here it was Saturday night, maybe even Sunday morning, raining too heavily for fog, and Michael hadn't heard of any other attacks yet—and that was the sort of news that travelled fast. So, if he could make this look like Leather Apron's work, maybe the jacks would blame the murderer instead of him.

Michael blinked, remembering that he still had his clasp knife in his pocket, then drew a deep breath, knelt by Liz's head, and tried to remember what he'd heard about the murders of Polly Nicholls and Annie Chapman. He knew that their throats had been cut, and that Dark Annie had also been butchered, but he couldn't recall any of the details of her mutilations. He opened his knife and hacked at her throat, trying not to weep, then froze at the sound of a horse and cart approaching. He hastily backed into a corner away from the passageway into the yard, glad that his clothes were mostly black enough to blend in with the soot-caked walls in the near-darkness, black enough to conceal the blood-stains on his sleeves. He waited silently, and bit his lip as he heard the horse shy.

The carter probed the darkness with his buggy-whip, crying something in a foreign language as the tip of the shaft poked Liz's lifeless body. Michael held his breath as the man grunted something in a foreign language, then climbed down from the cart. Michael raised his knife in case the man came any closer, then nearly sighed aloud with relief when, after a moment peering into the darkness, the man turned on his heel and walked towards the door of the International Working Man's Educational Club. Michael dropped his knife into his pocket and hastily slipped out of the yard, heading south and turning the corner into Fairclough Street before slowing his pace to something approximating normal.

Inspector Abberline glared across the mortuary table at Dr Phillips, and repeated the question. "Do you really think we have *two* lunatics running around ripping up women in Whitechapel?"

George Bagster Phillips refrained from pointing out that Catherine Eddowes, the night's second victim, had actually been murdered in the City of London, not in Whitechapel: he knew that Abberline was well aware of that, and was fuming because this placed it in the jurisdiction of the City Police, not the Met. This had enabled the commissioner, Sir Charles Warren, to personally destroy what might have been a vital clue, some graffiti found near a public handbasin where the murderer had left part of Eddowes's apron. "It's possible, but that's not what I said," Phillips replied patiently. "There are similarities, but there are also differences. This woman, Elizabeth Stride, was also drunk and believed to be a prostitute, as were the other victims, and died either from strangulation or from having her throat cut, either of which would have silenced her. But she wasn't mutilated like Eddowes or Chapman –"

"The killer may have been interrupted," Abberline interjected. "The man who found her, Diemschutz, said her body was still warm. Nicholls wasn't mutilated, either, and neither was Tabram."

"It's certainly possible that he was interrupted. I don't know whether whoever stabbed Martha Tabram also slashed the others—the attacks do seem to be getting worse—but I don't think it likely."

"I disagree."

Phillips shrugged. "All I can say for sure is that Annie Chapman was killed and mutilated with a blade that was at least six inches long, narrow, and very sharp; Nicholls and Eddowes were killed with the same knife, or at least one very similar. Tabram was stabbed with something larger, possibly a sword-bayonet, as well as something as small as a penknife. And Stride's throat was cut with a blade that was rather blunt, probably less than six inches long but an inch wide, with a rounded or beveled tip. That could have been done by anyone, with or without any anatomical knowledge, in just a few seconds. So if it *was* the same killer, he acquired a much more suitable knife sometime in the forty-five minutes between the two attacks."

Abberline looked sour. "The papers are already calling it a double event, and calling Stride the fifth victim, counting Tabram and Emma Smith. And we received a postcard from 'Jack the Ripper' yesterday, taking credit for both; it'll be in the papers tomorrow, along with the letter we received the day *before* the murders."

"Do you think either is from the killer?"

"More likely they're both from a journalist who doesn't know any more about the killer than we do. Of course, everyone has a theory. Stride's common-law husband, Kidney, came into Leman Street yesterday, full up to the knocker, saying that he could catch the killer if he was in charge of the case, but when they questioned him, he couldn't actually tell them a damn thing." He stared at the body on the table. "Why does he do it? I could almost understand if he was an ordinary sadist, but all of the women were already dead when he mutilated them, weren't they?"

"Apart from the cut throats—maybe—yes, I'm sure they were."

"So why does someone cut up women's bodies that are already dead? Present company excepted, of course," he added hastily.

Dr Phillips was silent for a moment. "Maybe it's not about pain. He doesn't hide the bodies, he knows they'll be found; maybe it's about the way they're displayed. Maybe it's all about fear. Maybe he just wants people to be afraid."

THREE weeks later, Michael was back in the Ten Bells doing his best to drown his sorrows, when he thought he heard his name. He looked up, and saw that the landlord was reading from a newspaper. "What was that?" he asked, as clearly as he could.

"The Ripper sent Mr Lusk, the cove from the Vigilance Committee, a letter and half a kidney," the landlord repeated. "He said he'd taken it from his last victim, and ate the other half."

"Catherine Eddowes," said Thomas Bulling, reclaiming his paper. "The Ripper *did* take one of her kidneys." Mr Memory nodded his agreement.

"Bloody hell," said Esme. "What sort of nutter takes a bloody kidney as a keepsake?"

"Maybe he was signing his work," said Bill, who was sitting opposite Michael. "Maybe Kidney's his name."

Michael, white-faced, tried to lurch to his feet, then held onto the table to steady himself. "You saying I'm the Ripper?"

Bill held up his hands in a placatory gesture. "Nobody's saying that. You can't be the only bloody Kidney in London."

"They usually travel in pairs," said Bulling.

There were some subdued chuckles at this, but most of the pub's clients, atypically silent, waited to see whether a fight was about to erupt. Michael stared at the carter, then sat down again. "I spoke to the jacks. They know it wasn't me."

"I know," said Bill. "It was just a joke."

"Not very bloody funny."

"A bad joke," Bill conceded. "I know you're not the Ripper. I know."

Michael grunted, and looked Bill in the face, still wanting to erase that faint smile with one good punch… and then, in what was either a flash of drunken delusion or horrible sudden clarity, he realized *how* Bill knew.

I know it wasn't you, the smile seemed to be saying, but I also know that you killed Long Liz. That's why I took the other whore's kidney—I thought it would lead the jacks to you, but they're too bloody stupid to pick up a clue, even one as obvious as that. But whether they think you did the others or not, you can't prove I had anything to do with it and they can still hang you for Long Liz, so I wouldn't go talking to the jacks again or trying to claim any rewards if I was you.

Michael stared helplessly as Bill finished his beer and walked out of the pub. The Ripper stopped briefly to exchange a few words with the once-pretty redhead standing outside, then vanished into the thick October fog.

SHADES OF GREEN

THE DESCENDING JUMPSHIP WAS A MIRROR BUBBLE, so perfectly featureless that even estimating its size was difficult. A so'ar glided over it, using the updraft from its antigrav to boost it to a greater altitude, while smaller creatures fled from the noise. Mai looked up from her microscope as the ship eclipsed the small white disc of Lila's distant sun. She watched the so'ar for a moment, wondering whether this counted as learning behaviour; none of the clan had ever observed anything to suggest that the so'ar were even as intelligent as Terran birds, though as Neve had once pointed out with some heat, they *were* noticeably smarter than most plants.

The ship extended three landing legs, which sank slightly into Lila's soft soil as the antigrav field was powered down, revealing a small Danielite flag on the main airlock door. A ramp of reddish memory metal began extending from beneath it. Mai smiled slightly, and counted down from ten. Before she reached 'three', Tad was sprinting from the base to the flat area that served as the landing field, naked but for a filter mask which he adjusted as he ran. The airlock door opened and the pilot walked out just as Tad reached the bottom of the ramp; he collided with the pilot, who grabbed him and lifted him off his feet, an easy task in the low gravity. The two friends looked into each other's eyes through the visors of their masks, and Tad asked, "What's wrong?"

"There's trouble on Ararat," replied the pilot, setting Tad down on his feet at the base of the ramp. "Food shortages. The Inquisition are being unleashed, there are rumours of Zhir visiting secretly, people want to escape, and... I think I'd better speak to the whole clan. Are they here?"

"Only Mai and I; the others have gone north in the rover to gather more specimens. I can patch you through to them, but it's only audio."

The pilot, Chevalier, nodded, and they walked to the base in silence. Mai finished her notes, switched off the microscope, considered grabbing some clothes, and decided against it. "We'll need to contact the others," said Tad, as soon as he removed his mask. He and Chevalier kissed quickly, then the pilot sat down and unfastened the spider-silk tunic she wore over her shipsuit; it was as warm inside the pressure tent as it was outside, too warm for more than one layer of clothing. "How's your work here going?" she asked.

"Exhausting," said Mai, cheerfully, before Tad could answer. She liked and respected Chevalier, despite the pilot's propensity for infecting Tad with her own wanderlust. "It's a hell of a lot of planet for only five of us."

Chevalier nodded, looking around. "Not a hell of a lot of house, though." The tent, a semi-cylinder divided into compartments with thin screens, had been designed to look as roomy as possible despite its small size, but it was much too cluttered for this to work.

"We're rarely all here at any one time," replied Mai, "and privacy isn't a major problem for us. We may have to do something about the place before when the baby arrives, but that's five months away."

Chevalier's eyes flickered downwards to Mai's abdomen. "Congratulations," she said, softly.

Mai smiled. "Thanks," said Tad. "Now, what's happening on Ararat, and what can we do to help you?"

Chevalier sighed. "Where to begin? I wasn't there long enough to get all the details, but something's caused a serious food shortage; some people are blaming it on sabotage, others on divine intervention, though it was probably just someone's incompetence. Either way, there's been panic buying and hoarding, and stores are running low. The Inquisition's response has been to crack down on the usual scapegoats, herding them up and sending them to the camps. At present, they're slowly starving them, but I doubt it'll be long before someone's 'shot trying to escape'.

"Fortunately, I have some... contacts on Ararat who can help smuggle people out. I have eleven refugees in the tubes. The sooner I go back, the more I can save; I don't know how quickly the situation could turn into a full-blown purge, but I don't want to waste any time. That's why I want to leave these eleven here, return to Ararat, collect some more refugees, bring *them* here, and so on. You're barely two standard days from Ararat;

Daniel is ten. By the time I came back from there, everyone might be dead."

Tad looked stricken. "What about other flights?" asked Mai. "Larger ships?"

"There's one due in five days, from Covenant; it may be able to do something about the food shortage, but it won't take any refugees." Covenant was the first world the Zhir had given humans, and a stronghold of the Universal Faith; their Inquisition was even more feared than Ararat's.

Mai nodded. "Do they have filter masks?"

"You can't buy them on Ararat," Chevalier replied, apologetically. "The only people who use them are the police, so they're restricted equipment. Getting *any* survival gear on Ararat is almost impossible; there's no demand for it, so no supply. I have one spare, on the ship, which I can leave here if you like, but I thought the air here was safe, better than it was on most terraformed worlds."

"Not quite," said Mai. "It has more oxygen and a good ozone layer, and the pressure's adequate, but the CO_2 level's too high even during the day, and it can climb to ten percent at night. The methane level's a little high, too, but what do you expect from a planet that's nearly half covered with swamp? None of the tests have shown anything dangerous... but the protocols say that we sample the air for two years before we risk breathing it without filters, looking for seasonal contaminants—pollens and spores as well as microorganisms."

"You've been here for—"

"*Local* years," Mai pointed out.

"But that's... that's nearly thirty years! When were you ever sticklers for protocol, any of you?"

Mai glanced at Tad, who passed a hand across his chest in the clan gesture for 'ex-lover's privilege'. Mai sighed. "That's unfair. You're as much an out as any of us, but do you ever try using jumpdrive without getting into a suspension tube first?" Chevalier winced at the thought. "You're trying to get your refugees to safety. Without filter masks and other survival equipment, this place may not be any safer than Ararat. We've tried exposing some lab animals to unfiltered air at different times of the year, and many of them have shown allergic responses; there's even been a few fatalities. We've been able to treat the symptoms, and we've had good results from using immune suppressors, but exposing humans to this air isn't worth the risk. If you take your passengers to Daniel—"

"That's—"

"You should be able to get the necessary equipment there for *many* more refugees. You could then return to Ararat, pick up more refugees, bring them back here with the filter masks and so on, and shuttle between the two for as long as you can."

Chevalier frowned as she considered this. "What about food?" asked Tad.

The pilot's expression became even more sour. "Again, you can't buy any on Ararat, not even with my contacts. I have a few days worth on the ship, mostly concentrates, and you wouldn't *believe* what I was offered for those. I know your farm's just large enough to feed you and provide you with experimental animals, but you have plenty of biomass here, the whole planet seems to be green, can't your food converter deal with it?"

"The farm provides barely half of our food, and we only have two converters," replied Mai. "One here, one in the rover, and I'm not sure how quickly that can get back here. At maximum capacity, they could each provide a subsistence diet for ten people. Again, it's a problem of possible contaminants in the biomass; some of the fungi are poisonous, the algae indigestible, and—how much biochemistry do you know?"

Chevalier shrugged. "Paramedic level. No xeno stuff."

"The biology here is seriously xeno. *All* the large land animals we've studied so far have chloroplasts in their hide, so they can photosynthesize like plants. And all the species we've examined use copper for oxygen transport, so their blood is also green. That's not unknown on Earth—squid and octopi do it—but it's enough to make the converter nervous. It breaks everything down very thoroughly before deciding that it's safe to reconstitute as food, and that takes time; it also discards much of the stuff we put in as not worth the risk. Apart from the fact that you'd also need to add mineral supplements to the food..."

Chevalier held up her hands. "I get the picture, but I don't think you appreciate how bad it is on Ararat. If I wait twenty days before making another pick-up, there may be no-one left to save!"

"I've seen a purge," said Mai, softly. "On New Geneva. I was only twelve, so I was safe, but I remember how many died." She shrugged. "But you're right; there are too many unknowns on both side of the equation. Whether you decide to go to Daniel first or not, I'll respect your decision. We'll do what we can to feed them and provide them with filtered air." She glanced at Tad, who nodded. "That shouldn't be a major problem if they stay in the tents, though that's going to get very claustrophobic very quickly. I know we have one spare mask here; the other's probably in the rover. The water purifiers should be able to cope with a few dozen people; we'll worry about that if we get to that point. Shall I contact the others?"

WHEN the Zhir had first visited Earth, three centuries before, they had offered transportation to newly terraformed worlds to those humans they regarded as worthy. It had taken the Zhir several generations to re-alise that humans, unlike them, are not strictly monogamous by nature, and do not inherit most of their behaviour genetically.

The Universal Faith had been born on Covenant shortly after it was settled, and had quickly spread to other human worlds. It was a synthesis of common features between the Zhir moral code and many of Earth's major religions, but it could have been quickly reduced to a list of 'Thou Shalt Nots'. Genetic engineering, taboo to the Zhir, was as strictly for-bidden as murder, though cloning was routine. The only legal alternative to monogamous heterosexuality was celibacy. Though the Zhir rarely vis-ited human worlds, the Inquisition enforced their laws. Usually, they were content to sterilise the outlawed 'mutants' and perhaps segregate them into enclaves; killing an 'out' was rarely punished, but officially sanctioned purges were rare.

The situation had changed when the Zhir had invented the suspen-sion tube. Before this, no organism larger than a single cell could survive Zhir jumpdrive, and people travelled by having braintapes downloaded into android bodies or clones, while their originals stayed at home. The tube had made it possible for people to physically escape their home-worlds in search of a better. 'Outs' who could afford to do so fled, and eventually found—or founded—worlds where the Inquisition did not reign. These worlds were usually tolerated for the same reason the en-claves had been tolerated; many people enjoyed visiting them, enjoyed escaping occasionally to a more relaxed society with less rigid rules, then returning to their normal lives and forgetting that the outs existed until it was time for their next visit, or the next purge.

"WE'LL head back immediately," said Loren when the situation had been explained to him, "but even by the most direct course possible, travelling without a break, it's going to take nearly four days."

"That's local days," Tad translated, for Chevalier's benefit. "Call it six standard."

"Did you tell them what to expect?" asked Neve. "If there are twenty-two of them before we return, there'll barely be standing room at the base."

"I promised to get them to safety," said Chevalier, shortly. "I told them they might not get to Daniel immediately, and would have to make their own way from there. If anyone complains, they're free to come back to Ararat with me when I return."

Neve nodded, though she didn't look convinced. "Are any of them carrying anything that might be useful?" asked Indira. "Or dangerous?"

"I'll ask, but I doubt it," replied Chevalier. "They wouldn't have made it through the starport with any food, or weapons, or anything else restricted or particularly valuable—unless it was *very* well hidden. I scanned everyone and their luggage—not that any of them had much—and found nothing."

There was an uncomfortable silence. "Okay," said Tad. "If everyone's agreed, I guess we let them out of the tubes."

Kimi looked at the filter mask as Chevalier handed it to her. "Why do I need this?" she asked. The other refugees looked even more confused. The pilot explained as best she could, but with a minimum of delay. She had only five masks, including her own, and was waking the refugees four at a time and hastily escorting them to the tent. The first four went along with it with only muttered protests until they'd passed through the tent's airlock, where Kimi immediately turned to Chevalier and wailed, "What sort of place *is* this?"

Chevalier looked confused, and glanced around the room, then looked from Kimi to Mai. Kimi, who was a few weeks shy of fourteen standard, was dressed in Ararat's traditional costume for unmarried women travelling outside the home; a hooded robe with long sleeves and a full ankle-length skirt, colourful but shapeless. The other woman in the party, Grete, wore much the same, but began removing it as soon as she'd peeled off her mask. Mai and Tad glanced at each other; Tad, summing up the problem quickly, ran behind a screen and returned wearing a pair of shorts, holding out another to Mai. "Hi," said one of the men, removing his mask with obvious relief. "I'm Erik."

Chevalier looked imploringly at Tad. "I have to get the others," she said, her voice softened and slightly distorted by the mask.

"Of course," said Mai. Grete, Erik, and the other man handed over their masks eagerly; Kimi did so with obvious reluctance. Mai looked at the young woman carefully, trying to judge her age. Thirteen? Fourteen? Young to be an out; the Inquisition was usually lenient on adolescents, unless... Mai glanced at Kimi's abdomen, but the garment was baggy enough to hide the slight bulge of an early pregnancy. Chevalier hurried into the airlock, and Mai attempted a smile. "I'm sorry," she said, mainly to Kimi. "We've been living here for years, and we haven't had many visitors, except for Chevalier, so we weren't dressed for company."

"No problem," said Erik, who wore jeans and a soft grey sweatshirt under his long coat. "It's good to be warm, and after all, it's your home; we're sorry for intruding. You're scientists?"

"Biologists, yes. What do you do?"

"I'm—I *was*—a chef. Jose's a teacher: English and history." Mai glanced at Grete, who had stripped down to a sleeveless knee-length shift. "I'm an actor," she said, a little too quickly, and looked around for somewhere to put her heavy robe.

Mai and Tad looked at each other, wondering how to ask the next question. Jose saved them the effort. "Erik and I have been together for three years," he said. "*He's* too good at his job to be fired, but gays aren't allowed to teach in the schools."

Grete smiled. "Three years is a lot more than I ever managed."

Mai nodded, and turned to Kimi, who looked away. "The pilot said you were short on food, as well as room," said Erik, in an attempt to be helpful. "I'm afraid I didn't bring anything with me, but if there's anything I can do to make what you have more palatable..."

"I'll show you the farm," said Tad, sounding slightly relieved, and led the way to the airlock. Jose followed them out, leaving the women alone.

"I like the gravity here," said Grete, when it was obvious that Kimi still wasn't about to speak. "It makes me want to dance. How come the Zhir didn't take this place? They're light-worlders, aren't they?"

"They are," said Mai, "but the gravity here is point five six, which may still be uncomfortable for them. Or they may have other reasons; land fauna—animals—are extremely rare in known space, the forms here may be unique, and Neve thinks the Zhir want to see whether they have the potential to become sapient."

"Sapient?"

"Intelligent."

"Do they?"

"I doubt it. They don't need intelligence, and this planet wouldn't make it easy to develop any sort of technology; there's almost no useful metal near the surface. Mind you, if they ever *do* become sapient, their first religion's going to be sun worship."

Grete nodded, and looked around as the airlock's outer door opened and Chevalier ushered in another four refugees. "I have a feeling we're all going to know each other very well by the time this is over," she said, drily.

GRETE's prediction had already proved largely true by the time Chevalier returned with another eleven refugees, four standard days later. Mai doggedly continued to work as best she could, spending most of her waking hours at the microscope, but it was difficult to ignore the background conversations while Grete and Jose did their best to keep people amused and morale high. Only Kimi remained completely silent, which pleased Mai almost as much as it worried her. Kimi also refused to remove her concealing robe when there was any risk of anyone seeing her, despite the warmth inside. Mai wondered what she would have done if the tent's toilet had been as open as the shower; fortunately, it was the one place where seclusion was possible, and while the other refugees occasionally grumbled about the length of time Kimi spent in there, there had been no threats or violence.

Indira, Neve and Loren returned to base just as the sun was rising again, and hooked the other tent up to provide some much-needed room. When Chevalier landed two days later, bringing another eleven refugees, Tad tried again to persuade her to go to Daniel to collect some tents, food, and bedding. "There are thirty-eight of us here now," he said, as they walked back to the ship together. "Everyone's already on half-rations, and most of that's processed algae and fungi and recycled shit, plus an egg every eight days and a mouthful of fruit juice. We're having to walk further and further every day to gather enough plants to feed the converter. People are trying to sleep three to a bed, for less than six hours a day each, while everyone else talks or tries to work. We have enough water to drink, but not enough to wash in. It's hot in there even at nights, and during the day it's like a sauna, right down to the dress code. We can't possibly deal with forty-nine, much less sixty."

Chevalier shook her head. "I may be able to rescue another fifty-five people in the time it would take me to get to Daniel and back. In twenty days, they might all be dead. Is anyone asking to go back to Ararat?"

Tad sighed. "Not yet," he said, as the airlock door opened. "I think the girl who you brought here in the first flight may want to go, but she hasn't said anything, and I mean that literally."

"Kimi? I was worried about her," Chevalier admitted. "She doesn't seem like an out, does she? But she was on her way to the camps, like the others." She looked at Tad, her expression bleak. "Of the twenty-three I could have taken that day, I had to choose eleven. I chose her because she was so young. Of the other nine, seven are still in the camps, three are here, two are listed as 'missing'. I had less than three minutes in which to choose. Have you ever had to do something like that?"

"No."

"No. Of *course* I wonder if I made the best choices. But what else can I do?"

"What you're doing is wonderful, and I'm sure it's a lot more danger-ous than you're telling us; I feel as though *we're* letting the refugees down, not you. Look, can you try to get some tranquillizers? Something that calms people down, makes them eat less, sleep more, and give off less heat and less CO2? The best we have is anti-histamines; we have plenty of antibiotics and antivirals in the medkit, and we can synthesize more, but we never thought we'd need this many tranqs."

"I'll see what I can find."

"If they can sleep standing up, that'd be even better," muttered Tad, as the airlock door slid closed. "See you in four days."

"MAI? Have you seen Kimi?"

Mai looked up from the microscope and stared blearily at Jose. "Not unless she's suddenly become a Hell of a lot smaller," she said, more mildly than she felt. "Why?"

Jose looked around the room uneasily, and unconsciously hitched up his briefs, the only item of clothing he wore. Like many of the refugees, he'd lost enough weight that his clothes no longer fit. "Erik said she didn't collect her meal, so I tried looking for her. She's not in either of the tents."

"Maybe she went outside," Mai suggested. "Ask—who's in charge of the masks?"

"Hye," said Jose, who had a teacher's knack for remembering names and timetables. "Thanks."

Mai nodded, and tried to return her attention to her work. Jose re-turned ten minutes later, with Erik, Hye and Loren in tow. "She has a mask," said Loren. "I tried calling her, but she doesn't reply. She may just have gone to get some privacy or some sleep."

"Have you located her?"

"Just over half a klick away, almost due south."

"She went out four hours ago," said Hye. "I was asleep. Beth gave her a mask, gave me the list when she went to bed, and... well, that was two hours ago." They all looked at the window; even the summer nights on Lila were more than eighteen hours long, and the mornings very cold. The landscape was mostly flat, and the tents clearly visible from kilometres away, but they were surrounded by swamps and treacherous ground.

Mai sighed. "Are any other masks out?"

"Two," replied Hye. "Tyler and Andy went out to stretch their legs, run a few laps—" Erik snorted. "They won't have gone far," Hye conceded.

"Call them, tell them to come in. Keep trying the radio, but if there aren't any signs of movement in the next ten minutes, get the Morpho ready and send out a search party."

THE Morpho, named after a spectacular species of butterfly, was a two-seat ultralight aircraft, its paper-thin wings lined with bright blue solar panels. It could coast for as long as the sun was up, but its reserve battery was small, and only expert pilots took them out at night. Mai had reluctantly yielded the pilot's seat to Neve and the observer's position to Tad. Indira, Loren, Jose, Tyler and Hye took the remaining five masks and headed south while Mai remained in the tent, manning the radio.

"Why no lights?" asked Tyler, as he adjusted his visor. "Because of the animals?"

Loren nodded. "Most of the fauna here photosynthesize; waving a bright light around is like walking into a lion's den carrying a side of beef."

"Are any of them dangerous?" asked Jose.

"Not really. We haven't found any nocturnal species, and the only things you couldn't outrun are the fliers." He pointed over at a riverbank a few hundred metres away. "Mind you, some of the bugs can sting, and the cavernmouths are best avoided even at night."

Jose set the visor to magnify. "Why do they sleep with their mouths open?"

"Their jaws are flush with the ground, and heavy; they bite by bringing the upper jaw down, instead. They lie there waiting for something to wander by."

"Does it?"

"Sometimes. They seem to be omnivorous, eating plants as well as animals, but a lot of their energy comes from photosynthesis. We don't know how much, yet, because they make lousy test subjects; very lazy and uncooperative, no interest in science at all."

Tyler laughed, but cut it off when a call came through from Tad. "We should be right on top of the mask," he said, "but I can't see anything on the infra-red that looks like a girl, or any tracks. She must have ditched the mask a while ago. I'll keep going south, see if I can find anything; can you pick up the mask?"

"Will do," replied Indira.

They trudged along in the direction of the signal for a few kilometres. "She shouldn't be too hard to spot," said Tyler, trying to sound reassuring. "Not in that robe. She must be the only thing around that isn't green."

"She could have ditched it," said Loren.

"Not her. Besides, it's already getting cold. Never thought I'd feel so goddamn glad to be cold. The place is going to be like an oven if we try to squeeze any more people in there." He stretched luxuriously. "And cramped? I've had *sex* with people with less skin contact."

No-one responded. A few minutes later, Tad called to say that he'd found Kimi—unmoving, but still warm, probably just asleep. "We'll fly back and get the rover," he said. "Easier than trying to carry her back. Can you guys look after her?"

MAI sighed in relief as Tad carried Kimi back into the tent. "She seems okay," said Viviana, a pathologist who'd arrived in the third wave of refugees, and who was their most qualified medic. "She's been breathing the air outside for a couple of hours. I pumped her stomach, too."

"She'd eaten some of the fungi," growled Indira, as Tad lowered her gently onto a bench. "Probably just the same sort the mice ate safely, the ones that look like big yellow morels, but I'll want to check under the microscope—and it's time you had some sleep. I've made sure there are a couple of empty spots in one of the beds."

"I'm okay," murmured Mai.

Indira sighed. "I'll leave everything the way I found it. What're you working on?"

"It's not important," she said. "Doing chromosome counts and that sort of thing for some of the specimens you brought back. Just busywork, really." Indira nodded. She knew that continuing to work was important to Mai, a way of staying sane in insane circumstances, but she was also concerned that she might be overdoing it. "When did *you* last sleep?" she asked Tad.

"The same time she did," he replied, a little muzzily. Indira shook her head, wrapped her arms around both of them, and steered them towards the mattresses.

Five hours later, she woke them, her dark eyes gleaming despite her own fatigue. Mai stared at her. "What's wrong?"

"Nothing," said Neve, who was standing behind her. She sounded as excited as a five-year-old on Christmas Eve.

"Is Kimi—?"

"Still asleep," said Neve, impatiently. "Viviana's watching her. Look, the stuff you and Tad have been doing, the biochemistry and genetics... we've found something."

Tad opened his eyes, as did Grete, the third in their bed. "Wha- ?"

"The chloroplasts in the cavernmouths and so'ars," said Neve. "They don't match the rest of the animal—not genetically, and not biochemically. Indira recognised them; they come from one of the green algae that're common in the shallows, the sort that the water purifier filters out."

"Volvocines," said Indira. "Motile colonies with sixteen haploid cells, except in the zygote phase; a lot like some Earthian *Gonium* species."

Neve nodded. "How much do you know about sea slugs?"

"Not a lot," replied Tad, yawning.

"Sea slugs absorb the chloroplasts from some of the seaweeds they eat, so they can photosynthesize in seasons when food is hard to come by," said Neve. "It looks as though *all* the macrofauna here are doing the same with these algae."

Tad blinked. "Useful," he mused. "The animals get free energy and need less food, and the algae get to travel."

"It gets better," said Indira. "I think we may be able to do the same."

"*What?*"

"I want to feed the algae to some of the mice," said Neve, hurriedly. "If it doesn't harm them, I want to try it on Porky, then—"

"Photosynthesizing humans?" said Mai, obviously appalled.

There was an uncomfortable silence. "Well," said Indira, finally, "if you used immune suppressors to stop any allergic reaction, it'd solve some food problems..."

"Without genetic engineering," said Tad, impishly. "I say we try."

Mai looked around the group, and realised that she was outvoted. "*I'm* the biochemist," she said, flatly. "The mice, okay, but not Porky, not until I've run some tests."

KIMI revived a few hours later, and Viviana and Mai moved her to one of the beds, despite protests from the other refugees. "What were you trying to do?" the pathologist growled, as she took a temperature reading from Kimi's navel. "Commit suicide, or just kill your baby?"

Kimi blushed. "It's still alive," Viviana continued, her tone still rough, "in case you were curious. I just hope there isn't anything teratogenic in the air."

"Tera—"

"Anything that causes malformation in embryos," explained Mai, sadly. "You and I are the *last* two people on this planet who should try going outside without a mask."

Viviana looked at the two of them, then gathered up the samples she'd collected. "I'm going to run these through your lab," she said.

"I'll join you in a moment," said Mai, nodding, and sat on the mattress beside Kimi, waiting for her to speak. After a few minutes, the girl began crying. Mai continued to wait.

"I don't belong here," Kimi snuffled. "I can't stand it any longer."

"Would you rather go home?"

"I don't know!" she wailed. "Sometimes, yes."

"Chevalier should be back tonight," said Mai. "She can take you back, if you want..."

"I don't know," Kimi repeated, with less force. "What do you think'll happen if I do?"

"The Inquisition will send you to a camp; it won't be as crowded as this one, or as hot, but there probably won't be any more food. They may keep you alive until your baby is born, or until you lose it, or they may abort it; I don't know enough about the law on Ararat. You'd need to ask

Yannis, or someone like that. But I've seen a purge, when I was a little younger than you are. A few people were just sterilised and released, but not many, and I suspect they bought their way out. The rest... disappeared. No-one ever said what happened to them, and even young kids learned not to ask."

"They won't let the baby live, if I go back," said Kimi. "I know that much. They won't abort it, that's illegal, but they'll kill it if it's born. Its father's already dead—beaten to death by vigilantes, not the Inquisition."

Same people, different wardrobe, thought Mai, but said, "Do you want the baby?"

"No," she said, hollowly. "I don't really feel like it's mine. I was raped, and I'm glad the bastard's dead."

Mai nodded. The Zhir were physically incapable of non-consensual sex and tended to mete out equal punishment to rapist and victim, but the Inquisition would sometimes extend mercy to the victim if they were convinced of her non-compliance. "How long ago did it happen?"

"About eight weeks before I left Ararat," she snuffled. "Dad was scared that I'd be killed, too; that's why he smuggled me onto the ship."

So she was still in the first trimester. "We can abort it, if that's what you want," Mai said. "I don't know whether that would make it safe for you to go back to Ararat, but it's up to you."

Kimi was silent for nearly a minute. "How do you feel about your baby?"

"I planned her, I wanted her and still do, I love her," Mai replied. "But our circumstances are very different, and so are we. I can't make your decision for you."

"How does Tad feel?"

"The same, though maybe not as intensely. Same with all the clan; I wouldn't have done this without their approval. For one thing, I needed Loren's—"

"What?"

Mai looked at Kimi, and realised she might just have blundered. "His sperm," she said, softly.

"It's not Tad's child? But he's your *husband*."

Mai took a deep breath. "They're both my husbands. Neve and Indira are both my wives. I spend more time with Tad because we work together better in most ways, we're more compatible, and I would've loved to have had his child, but he has genetic defects that made it too risky; it was *his* choice too, not just mine. And Neve's, because she's Loren's primary partner the way I'm Tad's. And Indira's, too, because we all have to live in these tents. We'll all raise the baby, care for her, love her, *teach* her." Kimi stared at her, her face ashen. "That's why we call ourselves the clan. Oh, we came here as three couples—Tad and I, Loren and Neve, Indira and Amaka. We were all outs, we'd all had other lovers before, but we drew boundaries, and we managed to stick to them until Amaka died in a stupid accident. Indira turned to Neve, and they became lovers, and then I joined them, Neve and I had been lovers before, and... well, now we wonder why we ever bothered with any rules apart from making sure we weren't hurting each other."

"But that's..."

"What?"

"Unnatural..." Kimi said, her voice almost a whisper.

Mai shrugged. "Unnatural for whom? The Zhir claim that they're naturally monogamous, that it's somehow hardwired into their genes, and maybe that's true—they haven't let us study them to be sure—but even if it is, they're Zhir, not humans. You might as well say that the way the animals here breed, with the female laying eggs and the male squirting sperm into the water at the right cue, pheromones or sound or whatever, is natural. It's certainly natural for *them*, and for amphibians on Earth, and humans certainly *could* do something similar. There's at least one authenticated case of a virgin birth that I know of, after a girl bathed in bathwater into which her brother had ejaculated."

Kimi shuddered.

"Asexual reproduction is perfectly natural for many species, too," Mai continued. "Personally, I prefer the method most humans have used for the past few million years, though Indira might not agree with me. Most of the time, humans use 'natural' to mean 'comfortable' or 'aesthetically pleasing'; we even call farms 'natural', which is ridiculous. The same goes for 'moral', or 'decent', or even 'human'.

"There were—and maybe still are, on Earth—human cultures that believed it was moral, even natural, for a man to have as many wives as he could support. There were cultures that believed it moral, even natural, for some ninety percent of brides to be visibly pregnant. There were cultures that lacked any concept of paternity, and others which apportioned it out among a woman's lovers according to how often they'd had sex with her around the time she became pregnant. I'm not saying that what was right for them, or for us, is right for you; you're old enough to decide for yourself what you believe is 'natural' for humans." She stood. "I'll give you whatever help I can, but *you* have to make the choices."

THE first fight broke out later that day, after the egg ration was handed out and one man accused another on welshing on a bet. Yannis, the only lawyer there, stepped into the breach and sent the accuser outside to gather plants, then listened to witnesses and appointed a jury. When Chevalier arrived a few hours later, she was greeted with hostile silence. The new refugees she'd brought with her looked around the cramped quarters with obvious dismay.

"We can't take any more," said Mai, as she walked Chevalier back to her ship. "We've collected most of the edible plants for a kilometre, and the large land plants seem to be drying up and dying; Loren thinks that's a seasonal thing, not our fault, but even so, it means we're having to gather more seaweed to get enough biomass. That's hard work, which means people have to eat more, and there *isn't* any more to eat; people are already feeding their *clothes* into the converter. The CO_2 level inside the tent is nearly what it is outside, we had a fight this morning and a suicide attempt last night, and there's a dozen people we don't trust to give a mask to in case they decide not to come back. I'm worried that someone's going to get mad enough to wreck the place, or the food converters, and then we'll *all* die. Can't you go to Daniel *now*?"

"The Governor on Ararat has resigned," replied the pilot, heavily. "The Inquisitor-General is Acting Governor, and is flexing his muscles, trying to scare people out of voting against him. The election's in six standard days, and whoever wins, there's going to be bloodshed. Oceans of it. I probably won't be able to get anyone out after that—not for a week or two, anyway. If I can just make another two trips..." She looked at Mai's face. "I'll take the second lot straight to Daniel and come back with survival gear, unless you think I should bring them here and take some of those who've been here longest..."

Mai shook her head. "I think that'd cause more trouble than it's worth. We *need* Erik, and Jose won't go if he stays, and there's no safe and fair way to pick their replacements. Another eleven people?"

"That's all. I promise." The airlock door slid open. "Who was the suicide?"

"Kimi Kooiman. I've asked her to decide whether she wants to stay here or take her chances on Ararat. She's still deciding."

Chevalier winced. "Please, no..."

"What's wrong?"

"Tad was worried about her, so I did some asking around. My contact in the Inquisition, my most important contact? He's her uncle."

Mai stared at her, then at the turquoise sky as though expecting to be hit by a thunderbolt. "It gets worse," said Chevalier, grimly. "The Inquisition's a family tradition. Her father's a sergeant, both of her grandfathers are lieutenants, Kimi herself was an Inquisition cadet. Still is, technically; she's on sick leave. If I take her back, I'll be lucky to get offplanet alive, and I sure as shit won't be able to help anyone else."

Mai was able to swear in three languages, but she couldn't think of an obscenity strong enough to do justice to the way she felt. She stood there silently, her fists clenched, and Chevalier nodded agreement. "I'll be back in four days. Sorry I couldn't get any tranquillizers."

Mai shrugged. "It's okay. Neve and Indira may have found something better."

LOREN stood on a bench, drew himself up to his full height (at 191 centimetres, he was noticeably taller than Indira, and towered over the rest of the clan), cleared his throat, and waited for the hubbub to subside so that he wouldn't have to shout to be heard. "If I could have your attention for a moment, please... as the old joke goes, I have good news and bad news, though you may have to decide for yourselves which is which.

"There's going to be one more shipment of refugees in four days, and that will be the last. After that, Chevalier will be going to Daniel to pick up food and tents and survival gear, then bringing it back here so that those of you who'll have to wait to be evacuated can at least do so in more comfort, but she won't be back for three weeks, and some of you may be here for months unless she can bring a larger ship back."

There was some grumbling at this, but it was soft enough that Loren could talk over it. "Okay. In the meantime, it's going to be uncomfortable here. Quite apart from the crowding and food problems, the life support system can barely cope as it is; the carbon dioxide level in here is only a couple of percent lower than it is outside. So I'm going to ask for volunteers for an experiment. Though the protocols say we're not supposed to try breathing the air outside without filters for two local years, I don't think we have a choice anymore. We've tried letting some of our lab animals breathe it, and the only problem we've found is an allergic response which we can counteract with medication. I'm not saying it's risk-free; there may be long-term effects that we can't predict, and we're not considering any volunteers who're pregnant." He glanced at Kimi, then at Mai. "Dr Ochoa has spent the past few hours breathing unfiltered air from outside; do you have any observations?"

"It doesn't smell any worse than the farm," said Tad, drily, as everyone in the room turned to stare at him, "and I don't feel any more tired or short of breath than I do in here, but I'd suggest that at first everyone who goes out, goes with a masked partner, just in case. Are there any volunteers?"

Tyler was the first to raise his hand, but no-one could have said who was second.

ANDY was the first to reach the far end of the landing field, but Tyler tagged him as soon as he turned around to look at the rest of the racers. Yannis was still five metres behind them, with Tad and Beth hot on his heels. Everyone else, masked or unmasked, had slowed down to a jog. Tyler grinned, and kissed Andy's bald spot. "God, that felt good," he panted.

Viviana was the last to catch up. A relatively recent arrival, she was still carrying some extra weight, though she carried it well. "I'm a swimmer, not a runner," she puffed, as she checked Hye's pulse. "Is it safe to swim here?"

"I wouldn't recommend it," said Neve. "The cavernmouths are territorial about their patches of shore, the leeches grow as big as bananas, some of the jellyfish sting, and swallowing the water isn't a good idea."

"Pity," said the pathologist. "Well, *you* seem okay. Next."

"I thought most of your patients were dead," muttered Hye.

"True, but they never complain. Never threaten to sue, either," she said, grabbing Yannis's wrist. "Okay. I want you all back inside in an hour. Those of you who aren't masked, come straight to me for a checkup. Those of you who are, keep the masks on; you'll get your turn later."

"An *hour*?" said Tyler, plaintively, digging his toes into the soft moss.

Viviana looked at him, and at Andy, who was stroking his back. "Okay," she sighed. "Ninety minutes, but if you're any later than that, I'll send out a search party with nets and stunners." Beth and Hye also split off from the party, as did Grete and Mikhail. "Pity we can't do something about the food, too," said Viviana, as they walked slowly back to where they'd left the baskets.

"We're working on it," said Neve.

By the time Chevalier returned, the refugees were going out in groups of threes and fours, with only one masked watcher to a group. The pilot was astonished to find the tent less than half-full, and amazed at the warmth of the greeting she received from the refugees inside. "Where is everyone?" she whispered to Indira.

"Out getting food before it gets dark," the phycologist replied. "I called them as soon as I saw you landing, told them to bring their masks back." She explained the situation as quickly as she could, as they walked towards the ship. "It's done wonders to restore their sense of perspective. People are hoping that you've managed to rescue some of their friends, rather than worrying about squeezing another eleven people into the tents."

"How's the food situation?"

Indira grimaced. "Not much better. We can send more people out looking for converter fodder now that we're not using masks, but they're having to go further and further, and there's only the one rover; in three weeks..."

"The ground still looks green," said Chevalier.

"Moss and lichen, mostly. Gathering that and converting it takes even more energy than collecting seaweed, or even hunting."

"What about fishing? Ararati should know something about that."

"We've set up some traps, but the stuff we're catching still has to go through the converter. We'll eat cavernmouth if we have to, but I don't think the converter will deal with that any—" She froze as she saw Tad running towards them. "I... I'm sorry," she said, quickly. "I wanted to warn you, but..."

Chevalier stared as Tad hurtled towards her, completely naked. "Jesus!" she exclaimed, hugging him. His skin, formerly a pale gold, had a distinct greenish tint. "You look... what's happened to... Is that meant to be camouflage, or..."

Tad glanced at Indira. "I didn't have time to tell her," she said.

"It's okay," said the geneticist, soothingly. "I'm just using myself as an experimental subject."

"Without telling us first," growled Indira.

Tad shrugged. "What would you have done if I had? I made sure it was reversible first." He looked up at Chevalier. "Some of the local green algae form small colonies; if you break down the colonies and inject yourself with the individual cells, they reproduce inside you, but only the ones that reach your skin and can photosynthesize survive for very long. After a few days, it reduces your need for food and oxygen—not completely, but enough that the converters should be able to feed all of us. I'm not sure how long it will last without needing to top up with more algae, but we have antibiotics that will reverse it in a few days."

Chevalier blinked as she absorbed this. "Jesus," she muttered, looking at Tad's skin. "You'd better keep this a secret; can you imagine what the militias could do with this? Camouflage *and* logistics taken care of in one injection."

Tad shook his head. "I hadn't thought of that, but I don't think it's a problem." He slipped out of Chevalier's grasp and turned around, showing that his back had only a faint greenish tint, unlike his chest and face. "You have to keep one side of you facing the sun," he explained, "and stay out of shadows. More importantly, you have to be naked, or as near as possible; wear any more than a g-string, and you won't be able to absorb enough sunlight, so no armour, not even a helmet. I suppose it might have some limited usefulness for scouts and snipers, but that would be all."

Chevalier looked him up and down. "Will it work with darker skin?"

"I think so; you'd get a darker green, but no darker than some of the plants around here. Indira's volunteered to be the next subject."

"You're braver than I am," muttered Chevalier. "Both of you. I mean that."

Tad smiled, almost seeming to glow with the praise. "It seemed worth the risk," he said.

Mai looked up from her microscope as she heard the jumpship descending, and glanced at the com screen, a slight frown creasing her forehead. It had been barely twelve local days since Chevalier had left, and she hadn't expected her back until the next night. She heard Kimi come running up to look out of the window, and stared uneasily at the ship. Had something gone wrong?

The ship extended three landing legs as the antigrav field was powered down, and Mai reached for a pair of nox. The flag on the main airlock door, though barely visible through the rain, showed not the rampant lion of Daniel but a mountain peak topped by a wooden ark. She looked around the base; everyone except Kimi and herself was outside gathering food, photosynthesizing, or enjoying the first shower they'd had in weeks. The blood drained from Mai's face as the ramp extended and the door opened, and she saw the armoured figures emerging, two at a time, carrying large guns. They advanced slowly, and not just because the rain had turned the landing field to sticky mud. Urgently, Mai reached for the radio, wondering who was wearing the masks and listening—if, indeed, anyone but her still bothered to do so. "Unidentified ship on landing field," she said, broadcasting on all frequencies, "you are on a restricted planet, a biological reserve. Do you require assistance?"

To her relief, none of the clan or the refugees answered. "This is the *Dove*, from Ararat," came the reply, in a hard voice that she didn't recognise. "Please identify yourself."

"Dr Mai Long," she replied, then, drily, "How can I help you?" She glanced at Kimi, wondering what she was thinking.

"By staying where you are," the voice replied. "How many of you are there?"

"Just two," said Mai, without hesitation, "and we're not armed." She muted the radio, and turned to Kimi. "Do you recognise the uniforms?" she asked.

The girl shrugged. "Just militia in space armour. Why?"

"Do you know why they're here? From the look of those guns, I'd say it wasn't to tell you it's safe to go home."

Kimi glanced at her, her expression unreadable. "I don't know."

Mai stared at her, then looked around for the shift that Viviana had given her; she had no wish to meet an invading army while wearing nothing but a maternity bra. She considered opening the inner airlock door, to keep the soldiers out, but those guns looked more than capable of puncturing the pressure tents, and she suspected that they'd be carrying knives, too. The first pair of soldiers entered a moment later. "Into the centre of the room," one of them barked, looking around at the squalor.

"We're not armed," Mai repeated, obeying.

One soldier stared at her, while the other checked some type of sensor on his wrist. "Just the two of you?" he said.

"Unless you count unborns, yes," said Mai, drily.

"You're both pregnant?"

"Yes."

"Where are the men? Our records say there should be five people here, all scientists."

"They're out in the hoverover," said Mai, truthfully. "Collecting samples."

"What about the refugees?" The inner door slid open again, to admit another two soldiers. Mai glanced at one of them, noticing the insignia on his sleeves. He removed his helmet and visor, and stared at them appraisingly. "Just the two of them, sir," said the first soldier.

The officer—an Inquisitor, Mai realised—nodded sharply. "Check the rest of the place," he barked, while his aide removed a com from his pocket. "You're Dr Long?"

"Yes."

"And you?"

"Kimi Kooiman," said Kimi, after a moment's hesitation. "Sir."

The Inquisitor nodded, and glanced at his aide, who nodded. "You're from Ararat?" asked the Inquisitor.

"Yes."

"What're you doing here?"

Kimi hesitated, and looked nervously at the aide. "I was brought here, sir."

"By whom, and why?"

"Chevalier," she replied. "My parents wanted to get me offworld during the purge; they didn't think I'd be safe."

"Kooiman..." mused the Inquisitor. "Your name's familiar."

"I have family in the Inquisition, sir."

The Inquisitor raised an eyebrow, and turned to his aide, who nodded again. Mai, startled, realised that the com included some form of lie detector—then glanced at Kimi, and realised that she'd recognised it long before she had.

"And you're *here?*" asked the Inquisitor.

"Yes, sir," said Kimi, quietly. "I was raped. My parents were worried that I might not receive a fair trial during a purge."

The Inquisitor's mouth quirked slightly. "That doesn't make what they did legal," he said, mildly, "but we'll deal with that later. If they can lead us to the people-smugglers, we may be able to help them... Where are the other refugees?"

Neither woman answered, and the Inquisitor sighed. "I know you weren't the only one to leave the planet..."

"No," said Kimi, while Mai tried not to wince. "But the others aren't... They're not here. You can look if you want, but you won't find them."

Mai bowed her head slightly, hoping to hide her look of confusion. What was Kimi trying to do? Whose side was she on? "We're the only *human* beings left on this planet," said Kimi, flatly. The Inquisitor stared at her, then at his aide, who nodded.

"Check your records," Kimi continued. "This is the only base on the planet, and the air outside isn't safe to breathe without filter masks. How many refugees do you think escaped?"

The Inquisitor looked sour. "What about Chevalier? Where's she?"

"Long gone," said Kimi. "Weeks ago. She took the last load of refugees with her."

"Shit," muttered the aide. The Inquisitor turned to him, but he shrugged. "The gimmick says she's telling the truth, but that's—" He paused, listening to the voice in his headphones. "Duggan says his scans show no other humans with a kilometre; the heat and the rain and the CO_2 make it impossible to be sure of any readings past that range. He's located what looks like a small rover, but it's a long way away, near the horizon. Small and Lechler report that they've found a food converter, but not much food. Five chickens and a pig, though."

One of the soldiers laughed. "Shall we arrest *them*, sir? I could do with some fresh—" The Inquisitor glared at him, and the soldier fell silent.

Kimi cleared her throat. "I'm a cadet," she said, quietly, "and I know a little law. You can arrest me, or any other refugee, you can arrest Chevalier if you can find her, and take us back to Ararat for questioning... but unless you have proof that any of the scientists here have committed crimes *on Ararat*, they're outside your jurisdiction." She smiled thinly. "I think that goes for animals, too."

The Inquisitor turned pink, then bared his teeth in a snarl. "*Knowing* the law isn't the same as *being* the law." He took a deep breath. "If the others are gone, why're *you* still here?"

"I didn't want to go with them," she said. "I want to go home."

The aide nodded, but the Inquisitor ignored him. "Well, you're lucky we left one tube empty," he growled. "And you're not quite right about the law. If anyone here has committed any crime here *against* an Ararati..."

Kimi laughed. "Nobody here has harmed me, Lieutenant, or even tried," she said. "On the contrary; they've treated me very well. Or are you accusing her of corrupting me? I only turned fourteen a few days ago, but I assure you, I'm my own person, I make my own decisions, I know my own mind—and I'd like to get home and see my family. Or are you going to make me stay here, and keep the jumpship here, while you search the entire planet?"

One of the soldiers snickered, and the Inquisitor turned around, but their expressions were unreadable through their tinted visors. "Okay," he said, heavily. "I want this place searched, *thoroughly*; if you find *anything* that contradicts her story, tell me. Otherwise, we lift off in an hour."

It was still raining when Chevalier landed, but everyone was waiting at the edge of the field anyway. The pilot had radioed as soon as her ship had jumped into the system, saying that there was a larger ship following her—a Lanumoanan liner, with enough room for all the refugees. The eleven who were to go with Chevalier, a few hours ahead of the others, were chosen by a lottery; most of the refugees didn't even bother lining up for their numbers, though they did line up to say goodbye to the pilot. The cheer that greeted her when she walked down the ramp drowned out the calls of the cavernmouths.

"I guess I won't be back for a while," she said, half an hour later, as she prepared to leave. "Not with the Inquisition gunning for me. I'll make sure someone else drops in to see if you need anything, and lets you know if anyone suffers any after-effects from the injections."

"Thanks," said Tad. "The place is going to seem really empty, when everyone's gone."

"Make the most of the privacy," advised Chevalier. "Are you going to reverse the treatment, too?" she asked, watching Viviana and Beth dispensing antibiotics over by the tents.

"When we've got the farm back up to speed," replied Tad. "I feel pretty sluggish, but I don't know whether that's psychosomatic, a side-effect, or just hunger. Thanks for bringing food, by the way."

Chevalier nodded, and looked over at Mai, who was dancing in the mud with Erik. "How much longer are you going to stay here?" she asked.

"I don't know. It depends on what we decide is best for Kimi."

"Kimi?"

"The baby. We decided to call her Kimi." He sighed. "We'll teach her what we can here, but I'd hate her to have to stay in this swamp if she wants to go somewhere else. Of course, if she *decides* to stay, or to come back, that's her choice. Not everyone wants to spend half their life between planets, like you."

Chevalier smiled. "No, they don't. What about you?"

Tad stared at the green vista, and the half-green people that surrounded him. "I think it's about time I put down some roots," he said.

THE CHEERFUL BUSINESS

"DAMN-FOOL NOTION," muttered the dentist drunkenly, then coughed explosively without spilling a drop of his whiskey. "Knew something like this would happen if they gave the goddamn vote to women; Jesus, it was bad enough when they give it to niggers." He coughed again, and skulled the whiskey as soon as he'd stopped. His wife suppressed a sigh, and re-filled his glass. "Making it illegal—*illegal!*—for a man to get a simple goddamn drink!" The dentist stared at the bartender. "So, Jim, what're you going to do now? Get an honest job?"

The bartender laughed. "Oh, I'll find something pays better than *that*. What about you, Doc?"

"Stay drunk until New Year's, I reckon. After that, maybe move on." He shrugged. In five years, Dodge City had grown from a camp where buffalo hides could be traded for whiskey to the 'queen of cow towns', also known as 'the wickedest little city in America' and 'the beautiful, bibulous Babylon on the frontier'. The city had also given the world the expressions 'Boot Hill' and 'Red Light District'. He'd be sorry to go, though it'd be a novelty being able to leave a town voluntarily for once.

"Wyatt's been doing some thinking," said Jim. "About the future and all. Reckon you'll want to talk to him about it."

THE deputy marshal looked around the room, leaned back in his chair, placed his long-barreled Colt revolver on the table and poured the muddy dregs of his coffee into the spittoon. The men assembled—three of his brothers and three Mastersons, as well as Holliday: Wyatt was a great believer in family businesses—looked at him expectantly. "The way I see it," he said, "Prohibition isn't going to work, and it sure isn't going to last, but it isn't going to be all bad. We can see it as a problem, or we can see it as an opportunity. This is my town, and I am damn sick of seeing drunken—" He was about to say 'Southerners', but remembered in time that Holliday was from Georgia and amended it to "cowpunchers coming riding in and shooting up the place. So it'll be left up to the Law and Order Party to shut down the saloons, but Hell, there's only so many of us, and even in a cow town like this I bet there'll be a whole *load* of saloons need closing. Damn things will just keep springing up anywhere every time the cattle go through. Some of the owners may even try to pay us to look the other way and let them stay open."

He looked at the assembly—another three deputy marshals, a deputy sheriff, two bartenders, and the most murderous dentist in Kansas. Only their fellow Republicans called them the Law and Order Party; they were more commonly referred to as the Dodge City Gang or the Fighting Pimps. "The way I see it, there'll be big fines for selling liquor or public drunkenness; Hell, it could even be a hanging offence."

Holliday regarded him thoughtfully. "Where'll we get the liquor from?"

"We'll find somebody to sell it to us," replied Wyatt. "There'll always be moonshiners, and I bet some of the big breweries and distilleries will find a way to stay in business. If that fails, we can bring it in from Mexico. We won't be the only ones to see money in this: the thing will be to do what we have to make sure nobody tries to take it away from us. Nobody. Fortunately, the mayor is with us on this, so... are we all agreed?"

THE novelist walked out onto the balcony of the Great Western Hotel and looked up and down Front Street. To the north of the railroad, shops selling everything from birdcages to buckshot; to the south, the red light district, a large collection of businesses trading in a narrower range of highly prized commodities and services. He raised his Stetson to Squirrel Tooth Alice as she sauntered into a dance hall, then turned to his friend and said, "Fine place you have here, Wyatt. Real peaceable, good air, everything a man requires. Man can carry a gun, right out in the open, feel like a man, long as he's a friend of the law, and it's about as unlike New York as you could wish for. It's good to be back, even in such tragic circumstances." Ned Judson—better known by his *nom de plume* of Ned Buntline—had come to Dodge for the funeral of Ed Masterson, the city marshal, who'd been shot at point-blank range by a drunken cowboy.

Masterson had been popular in town—far more than his brothers or the Earps—and the funeral had been one of the biggest in Dodge's history.

"You figuring on staying here, Ned?" asked Wyatt, frowning slightly.

"Only wish I could, but I have business to do, deadlines to meet. Pity you can't come with me; I could make you even more a hero than you are already."

"Didn't exactly help Hickok."

"Hell, Bill'd still be with us if he'd stuck with the Wild West show instead of going back to Deadwood." He looked over his shoulder and smiled at the women who walked out of the Green Front Saloon: Judson was well known for enjoying female company and was, as was his custom, travelling without either of his wives or any of his mistresses. "And he forgot to sit with his back to the wall, he was too damn old, his eyesight was getting bad; you want to be an old hero, you do it somewhere safe. Is it true you wear an iron shirt?"

"Where'd you hear that?" asked Wyatt, softly.

"One of your whores said something about it."

"You aim to put that in one of your books?"

"No." Buntline was a seasoned politician, and his experience with the Know-Nothing Party had convinced him that Americans wanted legendary heroes and villains, not facts. When the facts contradicted the legend, he'd print the legend.

"Yeah, sometimes," Wyatt admitted. In fact, he wore the twelve-pound vest under his shirt whenever the weather was cool enough. "Won't help me if they shoot me in the back like Bill, though."

"I don't think Bill much cared whether he lived or died, anymore," Ned mused. "Never made any plans for the future. What about you? What're you going to do? You're making a nice piece of money here, but that can't last forever."

"I'll enjoy it while it lasts. After that..." He shrugged. "Funny thing is, I've been dreaming about a city, lately, but no city I've ever seen. Bigger, with bigger buildings. And..." He hesitated. "You know guns, Ned; you ever seen a repeater, a carbine, that fires fast as a Gatling gun?"

"No, and I would have if one existed. Hell, every soldier in the army would have one. Why?"

"I've been dreaming about *them*, too. Funny looking guns, two pistol grips and a big cylinder. One dream in particular; three men in fancy police uniforms and two in suits, armed with guns like that. They're in some building, all brick and stone, and they tell another seven guys to line up against a wall, and then they just gun them down. Been dreaming that one a lot.

"And there's other dreams, too. Beating two men to death with a wooden club, about this long; looked like a baseball bat, but heavier. And being in prison."

"You've been in prison before," Ned reminded him.

"Only once, and not a prison like this one. It was big, and nobody but the guards ever talked. If that's my future, I don't care for it much."

"Would you rather end up like Bill?"

Wyatt's Colt was out of its waxed pocket in an instant, but he didn't fire. It was the gun Ned had given him on his last visit, minus a third of its sixteen-inch barrel; Ned liked to proclaim that no man should be allowed to carry a gun with a barrel shorter than his penis, but drawing one of his over-long Buntline Specials took too long for Wyatt's taste. He'd only shot one man fatally in his time in Dodge, but he'd pistol-whipped dozens of cowboys before throwing them into the lockup, and eleven inches of barrel made an excellent club. The pimp stared at the Peacemaker for a moment, then pocketed it again. "I don't know, but I reckon I'll die with my boots on anyhow. How about you?"

"Me? I'll most likely be shot by a jealous husband." He watched two girls walking down the street, and grinned. "In about forty or fifty years, maybe, with one of those little Gatlings you've been dreaming about. I'm in no hurry."

THE barman looked at the small pile of coins on the table, and shrugged. "Sorry, Wyatt. Takings just ain't what they used to be."

"Town's getting too small for the lot of us," said Holliday. "Even if we cut Kelley out, it's never going to make us more'n we need."

"Kelley stays in," said Wyatt, firmly. While he liked money almost as much as he hated physical work, he always divided proceeds fairly, and not just with his brothers. "Less'n one of you wants to be Mayor?" Silence. "Okay, Doc, what do you suggest?"

"Maybe we could expand."

"You mean rob stage-coaches, or something?"

"Well, that's a possibility," replied the dentist, "but I was thinking more of a few of us staying here to run things, and a few of us trying our luck in other towns and the others maybe joining them later. Not just cow towns, either; there's mining towns, new ones, where there's lots of money and not enough whiskey."

"Virgin territory for whorehouses," said Wyatt. "Morg?"

Morgan Earp nodded. "I agree, the action here isn't what it was, and Short and the Mastersons have most of it sewn up." Holliday snickered; as well as the legal ten percent commission on the taxes he collected as county sheriff, and his income from the saloons, Bat Masterson was claiming $800 a month for the care and feeding of only seven prisoners. "And we may be better paid for our services elsewhere, but where?"

Wyatt sipped at his bitter coffee. The strange dreams had become more frequent, and now they were punctuated by images of reading newspaper headlines while in bed in an opulent hotel room. He was never able to remember any of the names from these papers when he woke, but there were frequent mentions of Prohibition, taxes, gangs, gun battles and—strangely—St Valentine's Day. "Wherever the money is, and the law ain't," he replied. "Texas, maybe. Montana. Arizona Territory. We scout around until we find somewhere there's enough for everybody."

TOMBSTONE *boasts... two dance houses, a dozen gambling places, over twenty saloons and more than five hundred gamblers... Still, there is hope, for I know of two bibles in town.*

A big camp this with a big future.

This is a terribly out of the way place. It is furthest from N.Y, by rail and telegraph than any other city in the U.S.

Several more shooting scrapes—but they are of such frequent occurrence that their novelty has ceased.

Every house is a saloon and every other house is a gambling hell.

"Virgil's been hearing good things about Tombstone," said Jim, handing the telegram to Wyatt. "He wants us to meet him there."

Wyatt pulled at his long moustache. He and Mysterious Dave Mather had been growing rich selling gold-plated lead bricks to cowboys in Mobeetie, but despite his fearsome reputation, word was starting to get out and suckers were becoming harder to find. "Okay. I'll send word to Morg and Doc that we're moving on again."

Jim glanced up as the doors swung open to admit McIntire, the deputy sheriff. "Evening, constable," he said, affably. "What can we do for you?"

WYATT looked around the ornately plush Oriental Saloon with deep satisfaction. It was a far cry from his first home in Tombstone; after being run out of Mobeetie, he'd had to share a one-room dirt-floored adobe shack with Jim and Virgil and their women. The women had been even less happy than they had, particularly as water had been scarce in Tombstone then and few of their clients had been willing to pay two dollars for a bath. Wyatt's innovation of the fifty cent bath, with just enough water to wash the nether regions, had not been appreciated. But their fortunes had grown with the town, as the brothers had made thousands by staking claims and selling them at a huge profit. Virgil had become deputy town marshal, then promoted himself after the former marshal was fatally shot under suspicious circumstances (to wit, while he and Wyatt were trying to disarm one Curly Bill Brocius) and appointed Wyatt *his* deputy. True, Virgil had been voted out a few months later in favour of Ben Sippy, but within six months Sippy had fled town and the job had reverted to Virgil. Wyatt had missed out on the office of sheriff after an election in which it was suspected that many cowboys and even some of their horses had voted twice, but he'd avenged himself on the new sheriff, Johnny Behan, by taking his woman. The Earps had muscled in on Tombstone's liquor and gambling trade, becoming part owners of both the Oriental and Alhambra saloons in return for protection, so the local wits said, from racketeering gunmen. The booze was smuggled up from Mexico by a local family, the Clantons, and their associates, including Curly Bill.

Of course, there had been problems. The silver near Tombstone was now being mined by the Gilded Age Mining Company, and the saloons' clients were mostly miners and cowboys on modest salaries, rather than prospectors who instantly gambled or drank or whored away what little money they made. Doc Holliday was out on bail for a stagecoach robbery which Behan and the Earps had been unable to solve. The brothers had torched the Arcade Saloon when its owner had balked at paying protection, and the resulting fire had spread and destroyed sixty-five other businesses, including the Oriental itself. Newman 'Old Man' Clanton had been ambushed in Guadalupe Canyon while rustling cattle, leaving his hot-headed son Ike and the smarter and more ambitious Curly Bill in control of the Earps' source of whiskey. Ike had even gone so far as to threaten Wyatt, Virgil and Holliday; Virgil had clubbed him senseless with his own rifle and arrested him for carrying a concealed weapon, and there was no way that would be the end of it.

Wyatt was suddenly troubled by the old dream again; the seven men shot on St Valentine's Day by killers in police uniform. Slowly and carefully, he put his coffee cup down and walked out of the saloon, heading towards the court-room two blocks away. He saw Tom McLaury, an ally of the Clantons, outside Spangenberg's Gun Shop with his hands in his pockets, and without preamble walked up to him and smashed his left fist into the cowboy's face. Discovering that McLaury was unarmed, he hit him about the head and left shoulder with the barrel of his pistol, then turned his back on him and walked into Hafford's Saloon to buy a cigar.

Virgil, Morgan and Doc Holliday met him there a few minutes after two. "There's a lot of sons of bitches in town looking for a fight," said Virgil. "I spoke to Johnny Behan, and he said he's going to go disarm them."

Wyatt nodded. "Curly Bill with 'em? Or Johnny Ringo?"

"No," Morgan replied. "Tom and Frank McLaury, Billy and Ike Clanton, and Billy Claiborne. They're heading for the O K Corral; if they've got horses, it could be a running fight."

"I'd kill them on sight," suggested Virgil. "Let them have it."

"All right," agreed Holliday.

Wyatt glanced at the double-barreled 10-gauge shotgun he was carrying. "You won't get close enough if they see you with that." Virgil looked down at the gun, then at Doc Holliday's knee-length duster, and handed the shotgun to the dentist, who was already brandishing a nickel-plated revolver. "Morg, you'd better deputize these two," Wyatt added, taking his own badge out of his pocket. "Make it look official."

The fighting pimps met the cowboys in the vacant lot between two boarding houses. "You sons of bitches," yelled Wyatt, "you have been looking for a fight and you can have it!"

"Throw up your hands!" yelled Virgil. Before the cowboys could react, Holliday shot Frank McLaury in the stomach with his pistol, then brought the shotgun out, pointed it at Tom, and fired both barrels. Almost in the same instant, Morgan shot Billy Clanton in the chest at point-blank range. Each of the Earps had fired at least twice before Billy, wounded in the right wrist as well as the chest, was able to draw his pistol and return fire, wounding both Morgan and Virgil before receiving another bullet in the chest and collapsing outside Fly's boarding house. His revolver empty, he called for more cartridges until he was disarmed and carried away to die. Tom McLaury, unarmed, died almost instantly, but Frank managed to draw a pistol and fire at Holliday, hitting the holster on his hip, before running into Fremont Street. Doc found him there a few seconds later, dead on the sidewalk. A passer-by, who'd picked up the cowboy's revolver, found himself staring into the muzzle of the dentist's nickel-plated pistol. Holliday stared malevolently at him as he dropped the gun and urinated in his pants, then laughed.

"Don't worry," he assured him, and everyone else who remained in earshot. "We only kill each other."

VIRGIL was to discover the truth of that two months later, when he was ambushed by Ike Clanton and Curly Bill Brocius. Within a week, the *Tombstone Nugget*'s headlines read 'EXEUNT EARPS'.

"Town's dying," said Holliday, and coughed explosively. Morgan nodded; the town was still bustling, but mostly with out-of-work miners and a sudden incursion of preachers. Wyatt had been forced to sell his faro concession at the Oriental, and all of the brothers had been stripped of their badges. "Allie says we should get out while the gettin's good."

Wyatt scowled. He and Allie, Virgil's common-law wife, had disliked each other since their first meeting. "I'm not stopping her," he said. "But I'm not running away from a fight, either. I telegrammed Crawley Dake a week ago and asked for his help in putting together a posse."

"How much did that cost?" asked Morgan. Dake, the territory's Federal Marshal, was a notorious skimmer of funds.

"Oh, he's keeping most of the money," Wyatt admitted, "and he'll probably deny everything if anyone ever asks. But he sent me what I asked for; it'll be arriving on the train today."

"The posse?"

"Well, them too." Wyatt stood and stretched. "I reckon Curly Bill and the others will be drinking up in Charleston; usually are, this time of year. And I reckon we ought to remind them who's the boss around here so they don't ever forget. Are you boys with me?"

There was guarded agreement, and they played poker until the train arrived. They were met at the station by more than a dozen gunmen, including the youngest Earp brother, Warren. Wyatt, with a theatrical flourish, opened a large trunk that had also made the journey, revealing a six-barrelled .45-70 Gatling gun, capable of firing a thousand rounds a minute.

"Boys," said Wyatt, "meet the Tombstone piano. There's going to be some dancing in Charleston tonight."

HOLLIDAY looked up from the newspaper, chuckling. "'Doc Holliday is another famous killer,'" he read. "'Among the desperate men of the West, he is looked upon with the respect born of awe, for he has killed in single combat no less than eight desperadoes. He was the chief character in the Earp war at Tombstone, where the celebrated brothers, aided by Holliday, broke up the terrible rustlers.' I like the sound of that; it has a better ring than 'MURDERED IN THE STREETS OF TOMBSTONE'. Want to hear what it says about you?"

Wyatt grunted, which the dentist took as assent. "'Wyatt Earp is equally famous in the cheerful business of depopulating the country. He has killed within our personal knowledge six men, and is popularly accredited with relegating to the dust no less than ten of his fellow men.' The cheerful business." He chuckled again. "No wonder they all gave in."

Wyatt grunted again. Despite the terrible power of the Gatling gun, their attempts to hold onto Tombstone had failed. After Morgan had been gunned down there, the family had divided despite Wyatt's objections. Wyatt had followed Holliday back to Dodge City, rejoining Bat Masterson and Luke Short and other members of the 'Dodge City Peace Commission' in a successful attempt to retain control of the city's saloons and brothels. The opposition had capitulated, leaving the commission slightly wealthier but with little else to do. "So where do we go now, Doc?"

Holliday took a sip of his whiskey and stared at the mirror over the bar. "Well, I've had this dream for many years now..."

Wyatt, startled, nearly dropped his coffee cup.

"Dreamt about opening my own hotel and gambling establishment— a really big, high-tone place," the dentist continued. "Anyway, I know this small town on the way to Californy, no law at all, and it's just crying out for a good keno game..."

"Sounds good. What's it called?"

"Las Vegas."

AL Capone was sipping his breakfast coffee when he noticed the obituary in the *Tribune*. Wyatt Earp, the famed gunfighter turned movie producer, had died peacefully in his suite at the Hollywood Hotel on January 13. The rest of the obituary was less reliable: Capone knew that the eighty-year-old Earp had devoted most of his later years to preventing any unflattering features of his life story getting into print or film, and financed his own westerns with profits from his Vegas casinos and shake-downs from both the studio bosses and the screen extras union. Still, he felt a certain regret for the death of a kindred spirit. He remembered, with a certain surprise, childhood dreams of walking to the OK Corral with murderous intent, protected by a steel vest and accompanied by his brothers Frank and Ralph; of shooting a cowboy in the back in a railway depot; of conferring with a large group of fellow thugs and killers; of firing a 'Tombstone piano' into a crowd... He even wondered, occasionally, how much larger his own illegal empire might have become had Prohibition still been in force in the 1920s.

He looked up warily as Frank 'the Enforcer' Nitti walked in. "Al, we have got to do something about Moran. Everybody knows he killed Lolordo, and it's making us look bad."

"I'll do something," said Capone, mildly. "I'll kill him real good, and as many of his men as I can, and I'll do it so nobody ever forgets who the boss is around here." He put the paper aside, and smiled. "I'm going to have him hit on Valentine's Day; it'll be like the O.K Corral all over again. Can you get me some cop uniforms?"

THIS PLEASING HOPE, THIS FOND DESIRE

PAPAIOANNOU'S OFFICE HAD A VIEW OF THE CITY—a real view, not just a hologram—and his desk was wood from a tree that had actually grown in a forest. He wore new thousand-dollar suits tailored to hide his wearable computers, and his cloned auburn hair was coiffed by a hairdresser whose annual income rivalled his own—but whenever Best walked into his office, the bio-ethicist always felt distinctly outclassed, as though he was wearing a patched sweater, odd socks, and an Einsteinian nebula of silver hair. He took what consolation he could from the fact that the MBA had walked downstairs to see him, rather than calling him up to his own office.

"What's this about you pulling the plug on the James project?" Best asked, as soon as the soundproofed door had slid shut behind him.

"It's just a recommendation," said Papaioannou, then flinched inwardly at his apologetic tone. Best was merely one of Proteus Biotech's project managers, and Papaioannou wasn't accountable to him; technically, he outranked him in the company's labyrinthine hierarchy. Part of the problem was that Best was some twenty years his junior, and more handsome than Papaioannou had ever been, or could ever be without major bodysculpting. Another part was that though Best's salary and benefits were slightly smaller than the scientist's, he played the stock market well enough to pay for a far more extravagant lifestyle, and always dressed accordingly. He'd also ensured his future with the company by marrying the granddaughter of one of the directors, while Papaioannou always felt that he was hanging on to his own job, which was informally described as "the company's conscience", by his fingernails. Proteus had often made it plain that it regarded consciences as a hindrance, which the

81

bio-ethicist suspected was partly responsible for Best's success: if the exec had a conscience, which he doubted, it certainly didn't seem to be keeping him awake at nights.

"And I didn't actually suggest pulling the plug," Papaioannou said, trying to sound more forceful. "Just putting any announcements or human tests on hold until we've done some more research. Giving the results to a journal for peer review, not to the press office. There are too many unanswered questions in James's reports."

Best kicked a chair aside to loom over Papaioannou's desk. "This phage she's developed is one of the most important discoveries made since penicillin," he said, forcefully. "Not to mention being potentially more profitable than Viagra: the venture capitalists will be queuing up from here to Wall Street. Okay, and a few monkeys have died, but letting that stand in the way of goddamn *immortality*..."

"Increased longevity," said Papaioannou, mildly but firmly. "And faster healing. We don't know that it's immortality."

"Some of those mice she has are what, eight years old? That's at least twice as long as they could have lived normally. And none of them show any signs of aging."

"Body parts can still wear out—especially brains," the older man replied. "And there may be side effects other than the ones James has acknowledged."

"So it's also a contraceptive. So what?"

"The spermicidal effects seem to be lasting, maybe even irreversible. And I'm not ready to generalise from intelligence tests performed on mice, to humans," said Papaioannou. "I want to wait to see how the primates fare."

"That'll take years!" Best protested, then lowered his voice. "Do you want to be the one who has to explain that to the families of everyone who's going to die between now and then?"

Papaioannou leaned back in his chair, his expression unhappy. "No, but I'm worried about the side effects. Do *you* want to be the one who has to handle the litigation?"

Best looked sour, and after a moment's hesitation, he sat down and looked uneasily at the antique bookshelves that lined the office walls, then over Papaioannou's shoulder at the view of the poorer side of the city. Best's corner office, Papaioannou knew, overlooked the river and King's Park: he must really have thought he was slumming it, being here.

Both men knew that most of Proteus's multi-billion-dollar annual profit now came from phages. As antibiotics became less and less effective in the twenty-first century, pharmaceutical firms had turned to nanotechnology to produce new ways of combating disease and come up with phages that located and devoured cancer cells. Then retroviruses. Now people were taking phage-filled capsules to cut down cholesterol, or kill acne bacteria—but there was, as yet, no cure for old age.

"Some of our directors are in their nineties," the MBA said quietly, as though imparting a great secret. "They may not be able to wait very much longer. Even if James's treatment doesn't stave off senility, there's no evidence that it brings it on any earlier. And so what if it makes them infertile? Infertility and immortality seem like a pretty good combination to me, and most of them can't stand the kids they already have anyway. If they want more, they can go somewhere where cloning isn't illegal, can't they?"

"And what if other companies are this close to finding the same secret, and get the jump on us? Would that be fair to our shareholders?"

"It's not just the sterility," said Papaioannou. "You *do* know that the process has a less than fifty percent success rate, don't you?"

"Damn close to fifty percent," said Best sullenly. "Even higher in some of James's original groups. And even the unsuccessful fifty percent lived close to their normal lifespan—well, apart from the ones she dissected."

"And this was when she was a student? Before she had assistants?"

"Yeah. So what? We funded her research even then, gave her a scholarship that paid her fees for her last year, put her through her post-grad studies, gave her a holiday job..."

"And stopped her publishing her results."

"Commercial confidentiality. We paid her more than enough to compensate her. She signed the contract, and she's never complained."

Papaioannou shrugged. "Perhaps. Have you read the reports on her experimental subjects that died? The rats and monkeys?"

"Yes, but I'm not a veterinarian."

"Many of them show indications of memory loss, sleep disturbance—nightmares, if you like—greatly reduced pain threshold, and no sex drive."

"Still seems a small price to pay for living forever," said Best, leaning back in his chair and putting his hands behind his head. "Especially if you're already facing Alzheimer's and menopause and all the other problems of old age anyway. Besides, weren't *you* the one who didn't want to generalise the effects on lower animals?"

The bio-ethicist stared at him for a moment, his expression unreadable. "Has this treatment *already* been tested on humans?"

"Not to my knowledge," said Best, blandly.

"But you think James might have done it?"

"How would I know? She hasn't asked my permission."

The scientist nodded and looked at him closely. "How easy would it be for her to administer the treatment to someone?"

"Well, it doesn't take surgery... just an injection, or a series of injections if you want it to take effect more quickly. You *have* read the reports, haven't you?"

"Yes. Have you?"

"Yeah."

"What about her psych file? Have you read that, too?"

Best shifted in his chair, his smugness slightly diminished. "Yes, but it's full of crap."

Papaioannou raised an eyebrow inquisitively.

"Okay, maybe she was abused as a child as she says, but Jesus, we can't refuse to employ people just because of that, can we? So she hates her father and his... what was it, his boss? But they're already dead, so who gives a damn?

"And she failed her compulsory bio-ethics unit at university. Big deal—so did some of our best scientists. That's why we keep you around, isn't it, doc?" He smiled; Papaioannou didn't smile back. "And the drugs, the extreme risk-taking behaviour, the self-harm stuff... well, that was all a long time ago. She's still alive, isn't she?"

The bio-ethicist didn't reply.

"Okay," the exec conceded. "So she has some issues, some problems, but I don't believe this stuff about paranoid tendencies: she's no more paranoid than most people who work here. She's brilliant, she can cope with her problems. And as for that crap about her being a lesbian..." The smile became a smirk. "Sure, maybe she had some girl-girl sex when she was at university; how many girls don't, at least once? But she's not gay *now*."

Papaioannou looked away from him for a moment and turned his chair and pretended to examine the books on the shelves, hoping to hide his disgust. He'd heard rumours that the executive had been exercising his *droit de seigneur* on many of the young woman who'd applied to Proteus for scholarships, but he'd always dismissed the gossip as motivated by jealousy. When he could trust himself to speak, he said, "You've had sex with her?"

"Sure."

"You initiated it?"

"Of course. The first couple of times, anyway. The last time, she came to me."

Papaioannou spun his chair around suddenly and stared. He opened his mouth to speak, closed it again, then, with a faintly strangled tone, said, "Have you ever actually been down to her lab, personally?"

"Of course."

"Ever looked at the animals?"

"The successful test subjects, yeah. Like I said, I'm not a vet, but they seemed fine to me. The failures... well, she'd already autopsied them, dissected 'em, cremated 'em... whatever it is you do with failures."

Papaioannou looked at the executive's manicured hands, his rings, and his platinum Rolex watch. "Do you have any pets, Mr Best?"

"What? No."

"Ever kept mice or rats?"

The exec snorted. "Hardly. I had a few robodogs when I was a kid, but that was a long time ago."

"Do you think you could... for example... tell a female mouse from a male?"

"What?" Best laughed, then realised that the bio-ethicist was serious. "No, I guess not. Not quickly, anyway."

"I've been down to James's lab too," said Papaioannou. "I've examined the animals who've had their lifespans extended. They're all female. Every single one of them."

Best stared at him, for once at a loss for words.

"That doesn't prove that all the failures were male," Papaioannou continued. "The gender of her experimental animals isn't noted on her files anywhere, and no-one in the company ever asked before, and now those bodies have been dissected and cremated. But the chimps and monkeys who're unable to sleep for more than a few minutes at a time... *they're* all male."

Best's handsome face turned grey as he considered the implications of this. "You mean it only works on females?"

"The phage sterilises males—it's spermicidal—but the increased longevity... yes, it certainly looks that way."

Best grimaced. Immortality for sale... but only for women. He tried to imagine his own wife outliving him by centuries, remaining vital while he aged, maybe taking a string of progressively younger husbands. Women treating men as short-lived pets, or ephemeral playthings. He imagined trying to put this idea across to the board of directors—nearly all of whom were male—and shuddered.

"Yeah," he said, eventually. "I can see that would cut the market share down. It'd hardly be worth selling the stuff. 'fact, it'd probably be safer not to."

Papaioannou was silent.

"Okay, doc. Your point's well made. When it comes up at the next meeting, I'll tell them I agree with you: delay the announcement, and any human testing, until we can run some tests on primates and do something about licking that particular problem. I mean, there has to be a solution, doesn't there?"

Papaioannou hesitated, then shrugged.

"Doesn't there?"

"I don't know," the bio-ethicist admitted. "The problem might be linked to testosterone levels, or the phage may see Y chromosomes as being damaged and destroy them... James's reports are too vague. It'll take a lot more research—*independent* research. And how long that will take..." He shrugged.

Best shuddered slightly as he stood, and walked towards the door. Papaioannou watched him leave, then said, "Mr Best?"

The exec, who was about to press the button to open the door, stopped suddenly. "Yes?"

"Knowing Jenny James as well as you do... how likely would you say it was that she'd used *herself* as an experimental animal?"

Best looked around, and was silent for a moment. "I'd say the odds were better than fifty percent," he admitted. "Maybe closer to ninety percent."

"I agree," said Papaioannou. "She's a habitual risk-taker. By the way— and I realise it's a personal question—when you had sex with her, did you use a condom?"

"What? Why?"

"Because—well, I can't be absolutely sure of this without more tests, but in theory, at least… the phage could be sexually transmitted."

Best stood there, seeming older every minute. Jenny James had always used a femidom when they'd had sex– except for the last time, when she'd initiated the sex herself, and smilingly told him she was using something better. His fingers shaking slightly, he jabbed at the button. The door slid open, and he stepped outside.

"And—forgive me for asking—but have you made love to your wife since then?"

The exec's eyes turned wide, and he grabbed at the wall to prevent himself falling.

"Having any problems sleeping?" asked Papaioannou, softly.

If Best replied, it was cut off by the door sliding shut.

THE PRETENDER

THE KNIGHT STOOD BEFORE THE KING AND QUEEN, still in his armour. His face was flushed, except where it was scarred, and his close-cropped black hair glistened with sweat in the lamplight. Despite his youth, the scars were plentiful—it had been the custom of the court in less peaceful times that no knight without a face wound was permitted to sit at the King's table—and his face would not have been beautiful even without them. But his body was muscular and powerful, and even in armour he moved with the grace of some mythical beast, part cat, part dragon. He had been the Queen's lover for four years, and was also dearly loved by the King. He drew a deep breath, feeling as out of place in their chamber as a dead rat on a banquet table.

"We were on our way to Mass, and we saw an old priest praying at a great tomb outside the chapel," he said. "He greeted us, calling us the two most unfortunate knights who ever lived. We were unarmoured and afoot, with only our swords and daggers, and I thought he meant we'd walked into a trap."

"Did he know who you were?" asked the Queen.

The knight nodded. "Mordred asked him why we were so unfortunate, and the priest told him that," he hesitated, "that he was the son of the greatest king England would ever know, and that he would destroy him."

"How did Mordred take this?" asked the king, softly.

"He laughed; he told the priest his father was the late King Lot and that he'd had no hand in his destruction, and the priest laughed back. He said Mordred was no more Lot's son than water was dry; he named *you* as Mordred's father." He resisted the urge to stare down at the fresh rushes on the floor, and looked the King squarely in the face. "He then said that you'd had all the baby boys born that May-day cast out to sea in a boat that sank, drowning all but him."

There was a long silence in the small chamber, and then the Queen asked, "And what did the priest say to you, Lance?"

"Nothing," replied the knight. "Mordred was standing nearer the old man than I was, and he drew his sword and slew him before I could prevent it. I wish now that I'd killed him there and—"

"No," said the King, his face grey. He tried to smile, but only succeeded in grimacing. "Nothing else the old man said was true; why should the prediction that Mordred would destroy me be different?" He stared at the horn window, watching it grow dark, then reached for the Queen's hand.

"Mordred does not favour Lot." said Guenever quietly. "It has often been remarked on—"

"Neither do Agravaine or Gareth," replied the King, wearily. "I wouldn't swear that any of them are Lot's sons, except perhaps Gawaine; Margawse has long had a passion for young knights. Apart from their other obvious attractions, it kept them loyal to her rather than to Lot." He shook his head. "I don't know who Mordred's father may have been, but it wasn't I. I've never lain with a woman in my life, Gwen; you must believe that."

"And the story about the boat?" asked Lancelot.

"That may be true; I've heard it before," replied the King. "But it was none of my doing; even had I wanted to, my arm wasn't so long as to reach to Lothian and Orkney, not with Lot and Margawse still alive. Lot might have done it, or it might simply be a slander."

"What would you have me do, sire?"

"Nothing."

"But if Mordred believes these tales—"

Arthur shrugged his mighty shoulders. "Mordred is an intelligent young man, and I have no other heir..."

Guenever stared. "Arthur!"

"You may go, Lance," said the King, his voice betraying his weariness. "If you would, watch Mordred for me, and tell me who else he tells about this, and see that he comes to no harm."

Lancelot bowed his scarred head. "Yes, my liege." They watched him walk out and close the door, then Guenever said softly, "Mordred was born on May-day?"

"Or the night before. It's difficult, now, to find anyone who was there and might remember. Why?"

Guenever's lips moved slightly as she calculated. "So he was begotten the summer before. Was that during her time as ambassador from Lot's court?"

"Yes," replied Arthur. "Lot must have known that the child wasn't his, but that doesn't make him mine. Margawse had her own knights there to protect her, and there were many others at court who she could have seduced easily enough. Oh, she wiggled her eyelids and chest at me while she was here, but only succeeded in making herself look foolish. Neither of us knew then that she was my sister; Merlin did not tell us who my father was until much later." He sighed. "I wish he were still here."

"Your father?"

"No, Merlin. He warned me about Mordred before he was born—he even said it would be better if he died as young as possible, though he never suggested a massacre of boy-babies. If I'd done *that* so soon after being crowned, it would surely have destroyed me; no knight would have sworn allegiance to a murderer of children." He closed his eyes. Merlin had also advised him not to marry Guenever, warning him that she would fall in love with Lancelot, but he'd ignored his counsel. Though he was fond of Guenever, their marriage had been politically motivated. Guenever's father Leodegrance had been a staunch ally of Uther Pendragon's and Arthur had badly wanted his support. Unfortunately, Leodegrance had also shared the Pendragon's hatred of sodomites—and he was offering a dowry of a hundred knights and the great round table, the wheel of a giant's chariot that Uther had given him.

The Queen had remained virgin until her thirtieth year, when Lancelot had come to Camelot. Like Arthur, she had soon fallen in love with the young man, and the King had appointed him her champion and bodyguard as a gift to both of them. Occasionally, Lancelot's conscience would trouble him, and he would leave Camelot on quests, but always returned to Guenever. His King he loved without desire, just as Arthur had come to love Gwen, and none of the ill that Merlin had predicted had come to pass.

"Mordred is your sister's son; you *can't* acknowledge him as your own."

"No," replied Arthur. "But I need an heir, Gwen, or all we've achieved will melt away like snow as soon as I'm dead. You don't remember what Britain was like between my father's dying and my becoming King, with no-one to unite the baronies and lesser kingdoms, and Cerdic and Claudas and... If you were to marry Lance after I die, then it might gain us a few more years, but even he would need a successor eventually."

"And what about Mordred?"

"If he should ask any of us, we can tell him the truth; what more can we do?"

Sir Dinadan lay across Arthur's bed and mused. "Finding the father of a child of Margawse's would be like going on a quest for all the splinters of the true cross."

Arthur snorted and removed his crown—a thin circlet of gold, designed to be worn inside a helmet, but which somehow felt heavier than his jousting armour. Dinadan, better known as a satirist than a fighter, had been his friend for many years and his lover since Camelot had been built. "Don't say that in front of her sons, for Jesu's sake."

Dinadan looked up innocently. "So she had a passion for young men, and indulged it when she could; where's the harm in that? And what did they think that fool Lamorak was doing in her chamber every night? Who do *you* think Mordred's father was?"

"I don't know. I think she actually wanted a child who would give her power; she tried hard enough to seduce me," Dinadan laughed aloud, and the King grudgingly smiled. "I could ill afford to be amused at the time, I'm afraid; Leodegrance was still alive and very influential, and I was terrified of being unmasked—we all believe Lot had sent her down here as a spy. But Margawse never used that against me," he said, as though it had just occurred to him.

"Probably too upset that anyone could resist her."

"Perhaps, but it gave her a weapon, one that neither she nor Lot ever used..." He shrugged, collapsed onto the bed next to Dinadan, then turned on his side and kissed him. "Who was the second most powerful man in court twenty-three years ago?"

"Merlin. Not exactly a youngster, but he always liked pretty women. So has Kay; pity few of them return the liking. I think it's his tongue, myself; too sharp, and he likes using it too much, it could do someone a lot of damage..." Dinadan looked Arthur up and down. "Kay was young then, too, and as seneschal and your brother, he might have enough influence to interest Margawse. But Mordred doesn't exactly look like any of you."

"No." Mordred was tall and handsome, and his hair was golden, as Arthur's had been in his youth—but there the resemblance ended. He didn't resemble Margawse, either; she'd been tall, wide-hipped and full-breasted, with green eyes, a powerful laugh and long hair the colour of fresh blood. Sir Kay was brown-eyed and running to fat, and his thinning hair was brown; Mordred, though well-muscled, gave an impression of slightness, of hunger. Partly it was his narrow face, and his dark eyes—deep and intense, like those of his grandfather Gorlois, or his Aunt Morgan.

"Perhaps he doesn't believe it... and even if he does, why should he love you less for thinking you're his father?"

THERE were seats for a hundred and forty-one knights at the Round Table, several of them never used except by the palace cats. Margawse's sons watched silently as the name of Tristram magically appeared in gold letters on the seat that had previously belonged to Sir Marhaus.

"They say that Lancelot was barely able to defeat him," murmured Mordred to Gawaine a few hours later, when the feast had ended and the brothers had retired to Mordred's chambers. It had been two years since his encounter with the priest near Peningues, though he had never mentioned the incident. "Do you remember that Merlin predicted that the two greatest knights and best lovers would fight beside Colombe's tomb?" Gawaine merely grunted from behind his cup of wine. "Strange, when we consider how many ladies you and Gaheris have loved... Everyone knows that Tristram is loved by Mark's wife, La Beale Isoud, but who do you suppose Lancelot's lady might be?"

"I neither know nor care," replied Gawaine, quietly.

"Fitting, though, that he has taken the seat of a man he killed." He glanced at Agravaine and Gaheris, then into his cup before saying, "I wonder whose seats ours were, before we came to sit in them. Do you remember, Gawaine?" No answer. "Weren't you once the second greatest of Arthur's knights, or was that Lamorak?"

"Hold your tongue," replied Gawaine, as the aging Agravaine's once-beautiful face turned pale. "The King already has a fool, he doesn't need another."

"And the fool he has, he loves dearly," said Mordred. "Gods, but we are a sad and sorry lot."

"If ye're talking about our father, now—" said Gaheris, unsteadily getting to his feet and reaching for his belt knife.

"*Your* father," snapped Mordred. Gaheris froze, then fell back down on his stool, almost upsetting it. The others stared in silence, and then Gawaine said, "So that's it."

"Yes." Mordred turned to Gareth. "Get out of here, keep your pretty hands clean." Gareth turned to Gawaine, who nodded, then walked unsteadily out of the room.

"You knew?" asked Mordred.

His eldest brother shrugged. "I was old enough when ye were born to count the months, even if *they* weren't. Gareth was the only one still at home; I don't know what he may have heard. Who told ye?"

"A priest, near Peningues. He's dead now."

"Did he say who your father was?"

"Arthur."

Gawaine snorted. "That's ridiculous."

"Why? Because he's a sodomite? Our mother could have seduced a coil of rope."

"*You dare!*" snapped Gaheris. Gawaine, moving with surprising speed and precision for a man so obviously drunk, grabbed Gaheris's right wrist and twisted it, forcing him to drop his knife. "Hear him out."

"You know it's true." Mordred sneered at Gaheris. "You murdered her, not for lying with your father's killer, but out of jealousy because she wouldn't lie with you. You would have murdered Lamorak, too, but even naked and unarmed and half-asleep he was too quick for you, so you let us think *he'd* murdered her."

Gawaine let go Gaheris's arm as though it were something indescribably foul. "*Is this true?*" Gaheris glared at him, but said nothing, and Gawaine slapped him across the face with all his strength.

"Oh, excellent," said Agravaine, the colour slowly seeping back into his face. "How's he going to talk with a broken neck?"

Mordred laughed bitterly. "Well, that's Lothian justice for you, isn't it?"

"I didn't mean to kill her," said Gaheris, sullenly. "It was Lamorak I wanted dead, not her; anyway, it was Agravaine's idea, but *he* didn't have the courage. *You've* killed women who were trying to save their men, Gawaine, you must understand..."

"Then you have what you wanted," said Mordred. "Strange how everyone wants something. Pretty Gareth wants to be Lancelot in battle, pretty Agravaine wants to be Lancelot in bed... it seems almost everyone wants to be Lancelot, except Arthur, who'd rather be pretty Guenever. I wonder what it is that Lancelot wants? To be King, perhaps?"

"And that's what ye want, isn't it?" growled Gawaine.

"I'm the King's son; who better?"

"You're no son of Arthur's, boyo," said Gawaine, advancing on his youngest brother like a great tree slowly falling. "I don't know who or what your father was, but it—"

"I *am* his son," said Mordred, thumping his chest and staring into Gawaine's blazing blue eyes. "I feel it. I know it, in here."

Gawaine spat precisely into his wine cup. "Ye'll feel the point of my spear in there, come morning. I may not be the greatest knight in court any more, but I can still—"

"Kill your own brother?"

"Half-brother." He glowered down at Mordred, then shook his head. "Arthur would pardon me."

"Arthur pardons everyone," replied Mordred. "He's pardoned more murders than you could count; he'd pardon Lancelot and Guenever for adultery if anyone ever had the guts to accuse them—but there's one person the King can't pardon."

"And who's that?"

"Himself. If the people and the priests knew about his lust for the great Lancelot—"

"What a man *wants* isn't a sin," snapped Gawaine. "Anyway, ye have no proof."

"How he and Dinadan amuse each other, then."

"And what good would that do ye? Ye don't remember what the land was like before Arthur's day: I do. He's been the best King we've ever had."

"I agree," said Mordred, calmly. "I have no wish to usurp Arthur, merely to succeed him. Swear that you will not hinder me, Gawaine, and I'll accuse no-one of anything."

Gawaine considered this, then drew his dagger from his belt. "You will swear to this, too?" he asked.

"Of course," replied Mordred.

That was remembered as the year that Arthur defeated Claudas; that Brumant l'Orgilleus was consumed by flames while sitting in the Siege Perilous; and that Lancelot first saw his bastard son Galahad, and went mad.

GALAHAD was sixteen when his name appeared on the Siege Perilous, the seat reserved for the greatest knight in the world; he was also the most beautiful young man anyone had seen since the arrival of Gareth Beaumains more than twenty years before. He was loved, and hated, as his father had been, and by the same people.

He had a gracelessness about him, the result of a cloistered upbringing, and soon acquired a reputation for churlish manners. He declined all offers of love, courtly and otherwise—even those of Guenever—as politely as he knew how. Dinadan may have been the first to recognise that the young knight was in love with his King—or it may have been Mordred, but Mordred spoke to few people in court, and never to Galahad.

That was the year of the quest for the Grail, and so it was that the young knight and the grey-bearded satirist were riding together through the South March. "The King and Queen love my father well, don't they?"

"In their own ways, yes," replied Dinadan. "And your father loves them as he can. He loves the King but does not desire him; he both loves and desires Guenever. The Queen loves your father, but she needs to possess what she loves; she believes he betrayed her by lying with your mother all those years ago and may never forgive him. Almost everyone loves the King and your father—except for Sir Agravaine, who desires Guenever but loves only himself. Sir Kay loves no-one but Arthur and Guenever, not even himself—and I love gossip, and have already filled your ears with too much of it. Who do you love, young sir?"

Galahad blushed. "The King is a great man."

"That he is—but he is also the King, and his kingdom is more to him than his own happiness, which is why he may not always do as he pleases, no matter how much he may love you. He fears that if you were to become his heir after being his lover, you might find it difficult to keep the allegiance of many of his knights."

Galahad considered this. "Me, his heir? Is this one of your famous jokes?"

Dinadan smiled; it was well known that Galahad lacked a sense of humour. "Arthur may seem eternal, but he's as mortal as any man, and has already seen some sixty summers. When he dies, he expects your father to marry Queen Guenever and become King—and you, being your father's only son, will be next in line for the throne."

The two knights rode along in silence until sunset, when they set up their pavilions. Mordred and Agravaine found them there an hour before dawn, and slew them both in their sleep.

LANCELOT returned to Camelot a year and a day after setting out on his quest for the Grail, and found the King alone, staring north-west over the battlements. It seemed to Lancelot that Arthur had aged a decade or more since Galahad had come to court; there was now more silver in his hair and beard than gold, and he moved without his old vigour. "I'm glad you're back," he said, softly, without turning around. "It seems the best of my knights have gone, and many may never return. There's been no word of Galahad in three months. Your cousin Bors said he dreamed that Galahad found the Grail and has been taken bodily to heaven, but I suppose I'm the only one who's dreamed of Dinadan. Old fool should have stayed here. How did you fare?"

"I was found unworthy," replied Lancelot, as quietly. "Where is Bors?"

"He went searching for Galahad and Percivale. I wish him every success."

Lancelot nodded. "How is the Queen?"

"Not happy. She spends most of her days beating Kay at chess. I'm glad you're back," he repeated. "We all are. This is as much of my realm as I've seen in more than a year, and there are people who need to see me, but I haven't dared leave Gwen with no-one to defend her. Even Gawaine is gone, doing penance for killing Yvonet in a friendly joust." He shrugged. "I've made Gareth king of Lothian and Orkney; Gawaine was pleased to let him have it, and his other brothers made no protest, but it means I'm losing yet another good knight."

"When are you going?"

"In a few days. London, then Oxford, Caerleon, Cardiff, and back again before it begins to snow. Go and see Gwen; she's missed you as sorely as I have."

LANCELOT was asleep in Guenever's bed when Mordred and thirteen knights, armed and armoured as for battle, came to the door. "Traitor knight, Sir Lancelot of the Lake!" called Agravaine, loudly enough for his voice to be heard throughout the castle. "Come out of the queen's chamber, for know you well, you shall not escape."

"Who is it?" whispered Guenever.

"It sounds like Agravaine," Lancelot replied softly, "but smells more like Mordred." He looked around the dark room. "Is there anything in here I might use as a weapon or shield?"

Guenever shook her head. "How many of them do you think there are?"

"Ten, at least." He glanced at the furniture, finding nothing that would make a dent in armour or hold against a sword for more than a few buffets, then reached for his robe and began winding it around his right arm and hand.

"Traitor knight, come out and fight!" yelled Agravaine.

"They're going to kill us, aren't they?"

"Me, yes. They may want you alive."

"Why?"

"Because you're the Queen, and you have a better claim to the kingdom than—" He stopped.

"Arthur's dead, isn't he?"

"I don't know. If he is, Mordred can't very well accuse us of adultery... but Mordred will have to convince people of his death before he can claim the throne. He'd have a far better claim if you were to marry him than he would as Arthur's bastard, and I suspect that's the choice he'll offer you." He bit his lip. "If I'm killed, pray for my soul, and my kin will come to save you." Before she could speak, he padded over to the door. "Fair lords, leave your noise, and I shall open this door and admit you."

There was a moment's silence, and then Agravaine replied, "A wise choice. You could never defeat us all."

"First, I will have your word that the queen is not to be harmed."

"You have it."

"I must hear it from Sir Mordred." Silence. "Or is he such a coward that he has sent you to do what he dares not?"

"The Queen shall not be harmed," replied Mordred, his voice barely audible through the solid door.

"I can't hear you!"

"The Queen shall not be harmed, and you shall both be brought alive before the King."

"Before *Arthur*."

"Before Arthur. I swear it."

Lancelot smiled slightly, then opened the door, just wide enough for one man to enter. Sir Colgrevance charged in, and Lancelot slammed the door shut behind him and barred it, plunging the room back into darkness, and hit the knight across the face so hard that his helm was knocked askew. He caught the blade of Colgrevance's sword in his right hand, wrenched the weapon from his grasp, and thrust it through his visor. As quickly as possible, he and Guenever stripped him of his armour, which Lancelot then donned. There came a sound of splintering wood from the corridor outside.

"Someone's thought to fetch an axe, at last," muttered Lancelot, picking up Colgrevance's shield.

"Can't you take me with you?"

Lancelot shook his head. "I would need more knights to protect you, and a horse for you to ride. Bar the door when I'm gone; stay in here as long as you can." He kissed her, then donned his helmet and strode towards the door.

"Traitor knight, come out and—" Agravaine fell silent as the door opened and he saw a knight in full armour before him; before he could speak again, Lancelot brought his sword down between his neck and his shoulder, cleaving through his chest.

He heard the door slam shut and the bar slide home behind him, and held his ground, so that his foes had to climb over their fallen allies to reach him. The corridor was narrow, so that only two knights could meet him at a time, and he quickly mowed his way through them: Sir Gingalin and Sir Astamore, Sir Mador de la Porte and Sir Gromer Somir Joure, Sir Petiphase of Winchelsea and Sir Galleron of Galway, Sir Florence and Sir Lovel, Sir Meliot and Sir Melion.

When only Sir Curselaine and a barricade of dead knights remained between himself and Lancelot, Sir Mordred turned and fled. Curselaine fell a moment later, his helmet and skull in two pieces, and Lancelot clambered over the pile of armoured corpses to give chase. He saw Mordred banging on the door of a chamber, and dash in as soon as it was opened. Lancelot hesitated outside for a moment, then ran to the stables.

"Is Arthur dead, then?"

Mordred stared sullenly through the rain at the empty road, until Gaheris repeated the question. "I don't know. Aunt Morgan sent me a message to say she saw a vision of him killed on Salisbury Plain, but that may be to come, or she may be lying."

Gaheris nodded. "What will you do if he returns?"

Mordred scowled at him, but there was a knock on the chamber door before he could speak. "Yes?"

"Sir, the Queen would speak with Sir Kay."

"Then she will speak with me," replied Mordred. "Tell her I shall attend her presently."

"Do you want me along?"

"No. Keep an eye on the road, and be sure that if Gawaine or Gareth return that they speak only to us. Tell them Lancelot has slain Agravaine, Lovel and Florence, no more." He stood.

"Not that you hid in a lady's chamber while Lancelot was killing him?"

"Not unless you want Gareth to know who murdered our mother," replied Mordred, "and who let Lancelot ride out unchallenged."

"He was wearing Colgrevance's armour, and Colgrevance—"

"Lies dead in Guenever's chamber. I'll call you if I need help bringing him out."

"Where is Sir Kay?" asked Guenever. She had dressed in her best robe; several others were strewn over the dead knight near the doorway. Four of her ladies, including Mordred's lover Landoine, attended her.

"In his chamber," replied Mordred, smoothly, "awaiting punishment for the foul crime of sodomy. What would you with him?"

"He is seneschal of this castle; he, not you, rules in Arthur's absence." She did not refute the charge; the portly Kay loved beautiful men as well as women (he'd been one of the many men lured into Margawse's bed during her visits to Camelot), and it was well known that his sarcastic tongue-lashing of young knights was often the spite of a scorned or abandoned lover. She wondered who they'd used to entrap him.

"Do you expect my knights would follow such a man—such a sinner?"

It was an obvious trap, one that Guenever avoided easily. "And your claim to the throne, Mordred? Arthur has other nephews."

"But no other sons."

"He has no sons," Guenever responded. "I don't know who your father was, Mordred. Have you asked your aunt Morgan? I'm sure *she* knows."

Mordred bristled. He *had* asked Morgan le Fay, and he was sure she'd used her magic to look back to his conception—though he was also aware of the rumours that Queen Margawse had often enjoyed three or four lovers in a night. "I do not need Dame Morgan to tell me what I already know."

"Then perhaps you will believe the Lady of the Lake. Arthur told me he would visit her, and ask her, when he came to Caerleon."

If this rocked Mordred, he contrived not to show it. "And if he does not return, Lady?"

"Do you believe he will not?"

Mordred opened his mouth to answer, then glanced at the Queen's attendants. "Lady, I would speak with you alone."

Guenever hesitated, then nodded. "Don't shut the door," she warned Landoine. "I would not wish to be accused of entertaining knights in my chamber."

"If Arthur *is* dead, my Lady, would it not be better for the kingdom if we were to marry?"

"For the kingdom?"

"The land must have a King; marrying you would strengthen my claim greatly."

"I am already married," said Guenever, softly. "To marry another while the King lives would be treason."

"I could have you burnt for treason tomorrow," Mordred snarled.

"If the King were dead," continued Guenever, "Lancelot's presence here would *not* be treason. But I am prepared to wait for Arthur to return."

"How long will you wait?"

Guenever smiled sweetly. "Have you heard the bards sing of Odysseus and Penelope, Mordred? I've always admired Penelope."

Suddenly, there was a shout from the corridor outside. He turned around to see a page, breathless, holding onto the door frame. "My lord, Sir Gaheris sent me to tell you your brother Sir Gareth has returned."

Mordred glared at him, then turned back to Guenever without his expression changing. "You have fifteen days," he whispered. "On the morning of that fifteenth day, if Arthur has not returned, you will be burnt or married." And he hurried out of her room.

THE stake was set up in the square outside St Stephen's Church, and Guenever was led towards it clad only in her smock, while Mordred watched from the safety of a balcony. "Lancelot will rescue her," murmured Gareth, behind him.

Mordred flushed. Sir Kay had escaped the night before he was to be burnt, and he suspected that Gareth—though never a friend of Kay's—had been involved. He could ill afford another embarrassment; too many knights had already ridden out of Camelot, supposedly to search for Lancelot or Arthur or Gawaine, leaving him barely enough to maintain a guard. He had yet to appoint a seneschal to replace Kay, and the castle stank. The only good news was that no-one had—as yet—risen to challenge him. "He may try," he growled. "I want you and Gaheris waiting by the gate."

"I won't fight him," replied Gareth.

"Then go unarmed, and hope he doesn't fight you, but stop him!" He turned to Gaheris. "You may arm yourself, or not, as it please you, but go with him." His half-brothers stared at him coldly, but obeyed. Mordred watched as Guenever was tied to the stake, and then a horn sounded from the castle's tallest tower; four blasts, signifying four riders.

The rescue was swift, but bloody; twenty knights were slain by Lancelot and his three kinsmen, and many more fled from them, before Lancelot slashed through the ropes holding Guenever to the stake. He handed the Queen a gown and kirtle before lifting her onto his horse, then rode at full speed towards the gate. Gareth stepped aside to let him pass; Gaheris did not, but was knocked senseless with a buffet from Lancelot's shield. Mordred, watching in rage from the balcony, drew his sword and ran towards the gate.

An unknown defender of the Queen's had ensured that the bundles of wood at the base of the stake were green and damp, producing little flame but much smoke. In the confusion, no-one saw Mordred murder Gareth and Gaheris—and their deaths, like the others, were blamed on Lancelot.

ARTHUR walked across the battlefield at Camlaun, his horse having been slain beneath him hours before. Gawaine's ghost had appeared to him the night before, warning him to delay the fighting until Lancelot had arrived, but an argument between two of his young knights and two of Mordred's Saxon allies—supposedly someone had drawn a sword to slay an adder spotted in the grass—had escalated into a battle which killed thousands.

Gawaine had gone to France to avenge his brothers and had died there from wounds received in a duel with Lancelot; his last action had been to write a letter begging Lancelot to return to Britain to fight at the King's side. Arthur scanned the field looking for movement and saw a man standing near the body of Sir Kay's unmistakable blood-red horse. As fast as his armour and his wounds would allow, Arthur ran across the plain towards him.

"Kay!"

The man turned, revealing a black shield with a silver bend. Mordred's shield. Arthur continued to charge towards him, drawing Excalibur as he ran.

"Father!" yelled Mordred, mockingly. He walked delicately between the bodies, his own sword drawn. "Why have you forsaken me?"

Arthur stopped a scant ten paces from him. "Do you want to know who your father was, Mordred? I asked the Lady of the Lake, and she told me. I warn you, you may not be pleased by the answer."

Mordred took a step towards him. "Tell me, then. Who do you blame for my begetting, and your downfall?"

"Agravaine," said Arthur. "Your pretty brother. Your mother may have the excuse of having been drunk, but he wasn't. I didn't believe it, either, until the Lady showed me their images in her crystal."

Mordred staggered slightly, and the blood drained away from his face. "You lie. I *know* I'm your son; the first time I saw you, I knew it, I felt it *here*." He thumped his breastplate with the pommel of his sword. "I could not have loved you as I did *had* you not been my father—"

"If you loved me, it wasn't because you wanted me as a father," replied Arthur, grimly. "But you couldn't admit that, even to yourself; you've never had that sort of courage."

Mordred advanced slowly, his face contorted by hatred. "You lie," he repeated. "I've had women, nearly as many as Agravaine or Gaheris, I have sons, I don't love you and I am *nothing* like you!" He rushed at Arthur, and swung his sword with all his strength. The king parried with Excalibur, and the inferior blade shattered, one fragment piercing Arthur's helm and skull. Arthur thrust once, piercing Mordred's shield, left arm, breastplate and chest, and both men collapsed onto the bloody plain.

SOME say that Arthur died and was buried, with Guenever, in the Isle of Avalon. Others say that he sleeps with his favourite knights in a hidden cave, waiting for a champion to awaken him. No-one knows what befell the bodies of his enemies, nor praises the wisdom or courage of the pretender.

A SORT OF WALKING MIRACLE

THE ROOM WAS DARK, apart from the sick blue glow from the clock on the VCR, the reflection in the half-open eyes of the family Siamese, and a diffuse hint of light from underneath a closed door somewhere upstairs. The messenger stood for a moment, letting his eyes adjust, then reached into the pocket of his leather jacket for a penlight. A quick sweep of the room revealed thick carpet, an enormous television, a complicated stereo, shelves of books and tapes and trophies, a space heater, a leather-ish-looking sofa and chairs, a vase full of roses... It all smelled clean and rich and respectable, and new. He calculated quickly, then noticed a newspaper folded on the seat of the largest chair, and grinned. He picked it up, careful not to rustle it, and a picture of the New York skyline and the word BOMB caught his eye simultaneously. He flinched, and then read the rest of the headline and the first paragraph. Just a car-bomb in the World Trade Centre. He sat down on the arm of the chair, drew a deep breath, and looked at the paper again. The San Francisco Chronicle, Friday, March 5th, 1993.

1993. Jesus, he thought, I'm in the future. And San Francisco. Haven't been here since—

The cat glanced at him, then went back to sleep. He pointed the penlight at the floor, and listened. He had excellent hearing, and had always been good at listening, which isn't quite the same thing. Outside, still suburban streets. Inside, only one other person in the house, upstairs, awake. He switched the penlight off, pocketed it, and walked carefully towards the stairs, making no more noise than a cat.

There was a thin line of light showing under only one of the doors; he padded along the corridor, and knocked lightly. He heard someone inside jump, and then a girl's voice called, "Who's there?"

"A friend."

There was a disbelieving gasp from the other side of the door, and then the voice, trying to sound older, snapped, "I've got a gun..."

He opened the door slowly, and looked inside. The girl was sitting on the bed, cross-legged, wide-eyed, dressed in designer jeans and a silk blouse with a small roll of puppyfat showing between them. There was a thin paperback face-down near her feet, with a sheet of notepaper tucked inside it. He guessed her age at fifteen, maybe younger. She saw his scuffed leather jacket, his dusty Levis and boots, his shaggy hair and beard, and recoiled. He hoped he didn't smell too bad; he could barely remember the last time he'd been able to take a hot shower. "If you've got a gun," he said, softly, "why d'you need the pills?"

"What?" She glanced at the open jar in her hand, as though noticing it for the first time, and then dropped it on the bed, spilling the pills. "I—who the Hell are you?"

"My name's Colin Patterson, if that helps. It probably doesn't, but I'm not a burglar, or a rapist. Can I come in?"

"How did you *get* in?"

"That's a long story. Can I sit down?" He shrugged his khaki pack off of his back, and slid it along the floor towards her. "There's a gun in *there*, if it makes you feel better. Survival rifle: it should only take you a minute or two to assemble it... And a knife."

She stared at the pack, then at Patterson. "Get out! Get the *fuck* out and leave me alone!"

He didn't move.

"Did you hear me? I said, get out!"

"I heard you," he replied. "You were going to take all of those pills, weren't you?"

She stood, her face white. "What the Hell business is that of yours?"

"There's been an accident. Your parents are going to be late."

"*What?*"

"That's all I know. I mean, they weren't *in* it, they're not *hurt*, they're just stuck in traffic. They'll be home an hour or so later than you expect them. That's all she told me."

"She?" She stared, seeing the grey at his temples and in his beard, the creases in his forehead, then sat down again, her face crimson. "You're a friend of my mother's," she said, despairingly.

He shook his head. "I've never met your mother. *She* is... can I sit down? Thanks. She... look, what do you want me to call you? I know your name's Genevieve, but—"

"Jenny."

"Fine." He noticed the can of Diet Pepsi on the bedside table, and asked, "Can I have some of that? It feels like years since I had anything to drink."

She handed it over. "If you're not a friend of Mum's, then how did you get in?"

"Well, that's—"

"A long story. Right. Do you do this often?"

"Oh, yes," replied. "Yes, all the time." He took a long swig of the Pepsi, and grimaced; Jenny actually laughed, and then recoiled when she realised what she'd done. Patterson shook his head, and closed his eyes. "That's better," he said, and passed the can back. "Don't worry; I've left you enough."

"Huh?"

"To wash the pills down. If you still want to. But if you do, you'll die. I mean, *die*. Is that what you really want?"

She sat down, then curled up on the bed, kicking the jar and the paperback to the floor, and stared at the wallpaper that her mother had chosen years before. "Why else would I take a whole bottle of sleeping pills?"

"I don't know. Me, I've never wanted to die. That's sort of why I'm here—part of it, anyway."

"I've got reasons."

"Maybe you have. Want to talk about them?"

"Reasons you wouldn't understand."

"That's possible."

"And I don't have to explain myself to you!"

"I know."

Suddenly, she burst into tears. "Why *are* you here?"

"To help you," he said, softly. "If you really want to die, okay, I'll go; I think we all have the right to choose when we want to die. In my case, it was *never*, which was probably a mistake."

"And if you're trying to make a statement, if you think that the only way you can get people to care, to listen to you, to help you, whatever, is to try to kill yourself, or look like you tried... maybe you're right. You're probably not, but I don't really know. All I was told before I came here was that your parents were going to be—"

"In an accident," she repeated, dully. "Who told you that?"

"A girl. No-one you know... well, actually, she might be, I don't know. You see, there are these three women... or maybe it's only *one* woman, I... Did you ever see that movie of *Macbeth*?"

"What? The Polanski film? Yes; why?"

"Do you remember the three witches? One ancient, one middle-aged, one a teenager? That's what these three remind me of... but they're also a lot like each other, uncannily so. Maybe they're just grandmother, mother and daughter, but I really think they're the same woman, you know, like I was seeing them at thirty year intervals." He paused. "I know, that sounds bizarre, but they could do it. They send me through time, why the Hell not themselves?"

"They send you through time?"

"Well, yes and no... I really don't know, but... Have you ever heard of alternate worlds?"

"Like, what if the Nazis had won World War II? Or Kennedy hadn't been shot? That sort of thing?"

He nodded. "Most of them aren't *that* different—not the ones I've been to, anyway. Not that I've noticed, anyway; I haven't had time to study most of them. The way the woman—or women—explained it to me, the only things that change the worlds are deaths. Not all deaths—Hell, everyone's got to die *sometime*—but some deaths are..." He looked up at the light. "Jesus. I have to explain this nearly every time, you'd think I'd be good at it by now. Chloe warned me that I needed to practise... Anyway, most deaths are... maybe not inevitable, but... *fated*, I guess. Like in *Lawrence of Arabia*, you know, 'It is written that he should die'. Or at least *probable*. But some deaths can be prevented. Like yours."

She laughed sourly. "You mean I'm going to live forever? Shit."

Patterson shrugged. "I don't know how long you're going to live, or how you're going to die. I don't know what sort of difference you're going to make to the world. But the women sent me back here to talk to you, so they must think there's a chance." He grimaced. "Sometimes it doesn't work. If you really *want* to die, I can't stop you, and I won't. But most 'suicides' don't, and I don't think you do—"

"I—"

Patterson continued, ignoring the interruption. "Or maybe you're like Tom Sawyer, you want to 'die temporarily'. But there's no such thing. I don't think you know what dying means. Like most teenagers."

"And you do?" she said, sarcastically.

"I've seen people die," he replied, slowly. "Mostly when I was in Vietnam. I was drafted: I could—I *should*—have run away to Canada or somewhere, but I didn't. I guess going to war was a form of teenage suicide, too: fortunately, it's no longer fashionable.

"I saw suicides, there, too, including one Buddhist monk who set himself alight. I wouldn't have tried to stop him then, I wouldn't now, he chose the time and place of his death and that was his right, he may have been doing it as a gesture, a political statement, but I believe he *knew* what he was doing. He knew it was real. And when I saw that, *I* knew it was real. Never knew it before. Most teenagers don't. They think they're too young to die, just like they're too young to get pregnant, and they're *never* going to be like their parents, right?

"You can take those pills, if you want to. Like I said, I don't know what's worrying you. If you want to tell me, I'll listen; if I can help, I will. But I can't help you, *no-one* can help you, if you're dead... and I don't think you really want to be dead."

She sat up, and looked at him. "Haven't *you* ever wanted to die? I don't think I know anyone who hasn't—and a lot of my friends have tried."

"Not that I can remember. Maybe I did, when I was your age, but it was always too damn scary, even scarier than growing old. I just wanted to get away from home, have a life of my own. After that... well, the first time I saw Chloe, she—"

"Chloe?"

"The girl who sent me here. She calls herself Chloe Weaver, though I never believed that was her name. We were both staying in a backpacker's hostel, in Seattle, in 1985; some guy was doing tarot readings, and I asked if he could tell me where I was going to die. He asked why, and I said, so I could make sure I never went there.

"Chloe came up to me later—we were staying in the same dorm—and asked if I was serious about that. I said, sure I was serious. She said she could tell me where." He shrugged. "I liked her—don't get me wrong, she was too young for me, for one thing—so I called her bluff and said, okay, tell me.

"Right here, she said. Here in Seattle. This is where you're destined to die.

"I didn't laugh. She just looked at me, and asked if I believed her. I asked her *when*, and she said, tomorrow morning, a few minutes before noon.

"Okay, I said. What can I do to avoid it—apart from not being here?

"'Only that', she said—pretty coolly, I thought—and then, 'Were you planning to stay in town long?'

"'Not if I can get a lift somewhere. There doesn't seem to be anything going here.'

"'Are you looking for work?'

"'Well, it doesn't seem to be looking for me,' I told her. She smiled at that, and said, 'You might be wrong. I have a job for you. It doesn't pay well—but it'll get you out of town.'

"'Driving deadheads?'

"'What?'"

"'Courier work?'

"'In a way,' she said. 'You like to travel, don't you?'

"I don't remember what I said to that—probably yes—but the next thing I knew, we were standing in a forest: no buildings, not even a road or a telegraph line in sight, I could see all the way out to Mount Rainier and no signs of human life at all except the two of us and I wasn't too sure about her... I don't know how she does it. I've never seen any sort of time machine or anything, but maybe it's back in the future somewhere, or another dimension, or maybe it's really small. And if you were going to travel through time, would you carry a big machine around with you and show it to everyone?

"Anyway, next thing I knew, we were back in our dorm in the hostel. She told me that she needed someone to take messages through time, occasionally—messages to people like you, suicides who didn't really want to commit suicide, who were just trying to make some sort of statement and things got out of hand... She said she was getting too old for the work; I thought, at the time, she was trying to make a joke."

Patterson shrugged. "I got to admit, I liked the idea. I'd never been a lot of use to anyone before, and I thought maybe I'd get to save people like Tchaikovsky, you know... I mean, I'd heard Tchaikovsky deliberately drank contaminated water to give himself cholera, because he was being blackmailed for being gay, and I always thought, how fucking horrible and what a fucking *waste*... or Alan Turing... I guess you could say I had a call. And, like she said, it was a chance to see the world, and if I was good at it and didn't quit, I could save a lot of lives, maybe even talk down a war...

"So I said sure, and went and spent the last of my cash on some gear I thought would be inconspicuous and useful—which is why there's a survival rifle in there, and a survival knife: there was a big war scare on at the time, *Rambo* was breaking box office records, and survivalist gear was everywhere...

"And the next day, I got up and got dressed, and suddenly I was in England, in a small apartment that reeked of gas. There was a woman there, who'd tried to seal the kitchen and turned the gas on, but she obviously didn't want to *die*; she knew there was a girl coming around at nine, and she'd left a note on the table with her doctor's name and number. Unfortunately, the gas had seeped into the room downstairs, so when the girl arrived and tried to get help, the man who lived there didn't wake up... if I hadn't unlocked the front door, I'm sure she would have died." He shook his head. "A moment later, I was back in Seattle. Chloe—at least, she said she was Chloe, she looked *ancient*—told me I'd just saved Sylvia Plath. I didn't even recognise the name.

"She was the first; there have been dozens since. A lot of teenagers and students, like you. Most of them listen. I don't know how many try again."

They sat there in silence, then Jenny asked, "These women... Chloe... do you know who they are?"

"No. They know the future, so I guess that's where they're from. I think they're the same woman at different ages, a time traveller—probably someone I've been sent to talk down at some time."

"Maybe," said Jenny. "But—do you know that Pretenders song, *Hymn to Her*?"

"No."

"How about Greek mythology?"

"A little. Never read much, as a kid; my parents weren't into books. Still don't."

"There's these three women in Greek myth, the Fates: Clotho, the young one, the maiden, spins the thread of each life; Lachesis, the mother, measures it out; and Atropos, the old crone, cuts it off. The three of them decide when it's someone's time to die, and they can't be defied, they're more powerful than all the Gods and..."

Jenny looked up, and saw that the room was empty. She sat there in silence for a moment, then knelt on the floor and began picking up the pills. When the jar was half-full, she muttered, "Oh, the Hell with it," and set it on the bedside table, where she knew her mother would find it in the morning, and began getting ready for bed.

THE sun had just begun to rise when Patterson re-appeared in his scratched-out cave on the side of Mount Rainier; enough of its light broke through the perpetual cloud to turn the glassy, rain-filled crater that had been Seattle from a sickly glowing blue pool into a dull red eye. As always, it reminded Patterson of the cauldron from *Macbeth*, full of dead things, which is what he would have been if he'd been there when the missiles hit... No matter how far he walked between trips, Chloe always brought him back here. All the other cities were the same, anyway.

Sighing, he reached into his backpack for his radio, his binoculars, his Geiger counter, and the AR-7 survival rifle. No sign of movement, nothing but static on the radio, radiation low enough for him to walk down to the ashen landscape that had once been a forest.

His own words echoed in his ears. *If you really want to die, okay, I think we all have the right to choose when we want to die. But if you're doing it as a gesture, a political statement, and you don't realise that it's real until it gets out of hand... you'll die. Is that what you really want?*

No, he thought. I guess it wasn't what any of us wanted. He assembled the rifle, and walked warily, stubbornly, down towards the ruins, in search of food and some hint of life.

DEAD OF WINTER

WHEN YOUR LIFE IS FLASHING BEFORE YOUR EYES, and you're only twenty-seven, the least you could ask is that most of it wouldn't be boring. Unfortunately, mine was, at least until I met Leah. She was the one riding the bike and trying to avoid the truck that was bearing down on us along a tree-lined and potholed road only slightly wider than a razor-blade; I was merely sitting behind her and holding her in what I hoped wouldn't be a death grip, while pointing a digital video camera back over my shoulder. The ghost that was chasing us was...

Maybe I should start at the beginning. The beginning of the interesting bit of my life, anyway.

I MET Leah a few weeks after I'd received my doctorate. She'd conned a huge advance out of Carnelian Media to compile *The Encyclopedia of the Undead* (print and online versions) and was looking for a research assistant who could translate old manuscripts. I was looking for a job, and there wasn't much demand for historians. I knew almost nothing about the undead when we started—my thesis was on the history of the Adamites, whose only brush with the supernatural occurred when one of their number became spiritual advisor to the 'possessed' Louviers nuns. I'm still not sure why Leah chose me over dozens of other eager and well-qualified applicants. Maybe one day I'll work up the courage to ask.

We spent the next several months traveling around England, spending progressively less time in libraries and more sitting in supposedly haunted ruins. The day before she returned to America, we were sitting in the dark in what little remained of Whalley Abbey, waiting for a procession of chanting phantom monks. She asked if I'd like to go with her to the US, which was probably the most astonishing offer I'd ever had, at least from a woman. I sat there in silence for a moment, hoping some ghostly monks would wander by and rescue me, but they didn't. A few seconds later, I said yes.

I'm never going to trust a monk again.

I HAD been staring at microfilms of the old newspapers for hours when Leah leaned over my shoulder and murmured, "How's it going?". Her voice was soft (at least she knows how to behave in libraries) and I think I felt the stud in her tongue flick against my earlobe, but maybe that was my imagination. I removed my glasses, wiped them, and sighed quietly as she glanced at my notes, trying to decipher them. I decided to save her the trouble.

"It isn't the oldest case of the vanishing hitchhiker on record—that dates back to the New Testament—but it's the one of the best documented that I've found. There are several accounts which seem to refer to the same apparition, and they're remarkably consistent on many details, except the date. There's no dubious prophecies or any of the other stuff you find in other variants. Of course, it could just be the same story updated with each retelling—"

"What details?"

"Three of them, including the first, start in a dance hall. Someone offers to drive her home and she gives them directions, but disappears as they drive past the cemetery. None of the accounts I've found mention the address, but two of them, one in 1939 and one in 1957, actually name the dance hall. I've checked the papers, and the places did exist at the appropriate times. Different names, but—this is the interesting part—the same address."

"You're kidding." She stared at my scrawl, her eyes wide, then copied the address into her palmtop.

"No. Both accounts also agree on her appearance, and one mentions her name, which is consistent from another report from..." I flipped through the pages until I found the date. "1946."

"What was the name?"

"Annie. Fairly common name in this area, especially in the earlier part of the century."

"Description?"

"About five feet and a hundred pounds, light brown hair, white dress, blue scarf... the report from '39 doesn't give us much more than that, but the account from '57 describes her dress as 'old-fashioned' and mentions that hair was wavy and cut short. No pictures, though."

"Do they name the men who picked her up?"

"No."

She made a moue of disappointment. "Any other stories about the same woman?"

"One, so far. In 1966, a student claimed to have seen her on the street and given her a lift. It doesn't say which street, or any other details, but the description matches, and so does the end of the story..." I glanced at my notes. "And so does the time of year. December. Of course, that just could be because it's a slow news month, and the similarities might actually be a bad point. It may just be the same story being recycled wholesale by campus folklore or the local paper."

She glanced at her watch. "Okay, good work. Keep looking."

"What about the phantom biker?"

"Later. Can I borrow those print-outs?"

Half an hour later, she returned, a beatific smile on her face: for all her goth affectations of dress and make-up, Leah rarely tried to hide happiness or excitement. "What're you doing tonight?"

"I don't have any plans," I said, cautiously.

"Want to come clubbing?"

"I gather you're not talking about baby seals?"

She smiled, and stuck out her tongue. "You're no fun anymore." Actually, I never was—at least, no-one else ever thought so. "Have you ever heard of a place called Justine's?"

"I don't think so."

"The manager's invited us along. I told him I thought the place might be haunted, and he seems to like the idea."

I managed not to sigh. "A publicity stunt?"

"Maybe," she conceded. "He says Thursday's their Goth/Fetish night. But I haven't been dancing for a month, so even if nothing happens it won't be a complete waste, and I'd love you to come along."

I accepted with a little trepidation. I'd once thought Leah's driving had been erratic in England because she wasn't used to our road rules. I learned, unfortunately, that that had merely made her more cautious. I tried not to look at the road as we hurtled through the streets, and prayed that it wouldn't start snowing. She slowed down so we could look for a parking spot, and that was when I noticed the street signs. "This is where the dance hall…"

"Right."

The bouncer outside the club resembled Klaus Kinski in *Nosferatu* minus a few teeth, but he became quite affable when Leah told him who we were. The manager, who introduced himself as 'Cain', met us at a corner of the bar where it was possible to speak at a normal volume and be heard. It was easy to understand why no-one would have noticed a ghost there; the place was too badly lit, and too noisy. "So," said Leah, dispensing with the formalities in less than a minute, "how long has the club been here?"

Cain stared at the stage, where a young goth was wailing loudly in a fruitless attempt to be heard over the drummer and two electric guitars. "A year, maybe a bit longer. Why?"

"So you were open last December, but not the one before that?"

"Yeah, that's right."

She looked around the dance floor at the costumes people were wearing. Apart from the goths and vampire-wannabes, I could see enough black leather for a herd of water buffalo and enough chains to hobble them. Maybe that explained the way they were dancing. I also noticed a lot of mock uniforms, from military and police to a latex nurse's uniform so short it showed the tops of her stockings: not what I'd expected for the Bible Belt. Leah had bought me a new outfit in an attempt to help me blend in, but it obviously wasn't working; I suspect I looked more like an undercover priest. She, however, was in her element, all black lace and silk, goth to the max but still oddly beautiful. "Have you ever seen anyone in here dressed like this?" she asked, handing over a sketch.

Cain studied it, then handed it back. "Don't think so," he said. "She might come in on Wednesdays, the hair looks right—that's our women only night, so I'm not here. Friday and Saturday we have live music, and the place can get pretty crowded. What's this about?"

Leah told him the story we'd gotten from the papers. Cain smiled wryly. "And you think this ghost might come in here asking for a ride home?"

She shrugged. "Ghosts tend not to vary their routines."

"People change, though. I'm not saying a young woman who walked in here asking for a ride home wouldn't get one—it'd depend on the night—but if she disappeared from the car before she got there, how many people are going to come back and tell the story? Most of the 'singles' we get in here are married, so they're not going to tell anybody. Same with the college boys; their frat brothers'd never let 'em live it down." He shook his head. "I'd really like to help you, and not just because it'd make this place more interesting, but I don't know what I can do."

Leah didn't answer, and Cain shrugged. "I've got to go; the show's about to start. I'll be in the lighting box if you want me—and I'll keep an eye on the security monitors in case I see your friend."

We watched him leave. "What do you think?" asked Leah, sipping at her lemon lime and bitters.

"I believe he really hasn't seen anything." The moue reappeared, and I hastily added, "It's still one of the best documented cases we have."

"I know, but I'd like more. A photo, maybe. And I've never heard of a haunted night-club before." She sighed softly. "I think we should stick around for a while."

"You actually want to see the stage show?" I asked, a little alarmed.

She looked at me, one eyebrow raised. "I thought the English were into that sort of thing?"

"Not *this* Englishman."

"Well, you're a historian; haven't you ever wanted to see anyone put on the rack? Or try it yourself?"

"Not particularly," I said dryly. "Listening to this music is more than enough torture for one night."

She shook her head. "It's not for listening to; it's for dancing to... but I suppose you don't dance, either?"

"Not often," I admitted, "and not well."

"Pity. I've been waiting for you to ask me for a dance." Her tone was light enough that I suspected she was serious, and I drew a deep breath. As soon as I opened my mouth to speak she said, "I'd love to," and led me out onto the floor.

Dancing, she looked even more stunning than she normally did; despite her pale make-up and her black outfit, despite the horror-movie lighting and the funereal thudding of the music, despite the fact that (like everyone else on the dance floor) she was barely moving, she seemed so *alive* it made me feel like a waxwork. I drove her home, and was oddly relieved when she didn't disappear before we reached the motel.

The next day, I hit the newspaper morgue again, until I was fairly sure I'd found all the accounts of Annie the Vanishing Hitchhiker. Leah re-emerged a little after noon, and asked me to check the obituaries for women killed in road accidents in December before 1939, while she went out to try to find people who'd worked at the video library.

"Annie Gray," I said, as soon as she returned. "Born 1911, died Saturday, thirteenth of December, 1930. And here's a picture, taken when she was still at school; the hair doesn't match, except for the colour, and the paper doesn't mention her dress." I handed her the printout from the microfilm; Annie might have been pretty, but the photo was too bad for me to tell. "You realise this still isn't proof of anything."

She scanned the obituary. "It doesn't say how she died. Car crash?"

"No. Suicide, on a Sunday. It was her boyfriend who died in the car on Saturday night. They had an argument at the dance, and he stormed out. She ran after him, but he'd already gone. He didn't return—for obvious reasons—and she had to ask someone for a lift home. It's all in the coroner's report, and most of that was in the paper. It was probably the biggest story of the year: their answer to Romeo and Juliet."

"Did he suicide?"

I shrugged. "Not according to the coroner: he ruled it an accidental death. He was angry, and apparently it had snowed that night for the first time in years. It doesn't say whether he'd been drinking, but Prohibition was still in force, so if he had, he'd been doing it illegally. But *she* took rat poison, so the coroner didn't have much leeway there."

"Where are they buried?"

"There's only one cemetery in town. I don't think they would've buried her at the crossroads with a stake in her heart, not even here."

"Fine. Let's go there."

The microfilm room didn't have a window, but I could hear rain on the roof. "Why?"

"What?"

"What do you expect to see?"

She was silent for a moment. "A photo of the grave, and the photo of her, would be better than nothing. Are there any photos of the dance hall from the '30s?"

"Not that I've found."

"The book needs pictures. And not just pictures of ruined abbeys and stately homes; it's not *The Encyclopedia of English Architecture*."

"Is that all?"

"I'm a sucker for romance, okay? I love *Romeo and Juliet*."

I tried to raise an eyebrow, Spock-style, but I didn't have her talent for it. "And?"

"And we may be able to get some real evidence." When I didn't comment, she said, "You're an historian; wouldn't you like to be able to speak to people who'd actually seen the past?"

"Of course, but that…" I took a deep breath. "Why are you *really* doing this?"

"You're interested in the past. I'm more interested in the future. I want to know what happens next."

I looked at my notes. "If appearing once a year at Justine's and asking for a lift home is the best we can hope for, I'd rather *not* know. None of these ghosts seem to be having a good time."

She was silent for nearly a minute, then shrugged. "We'll go back to Justine's tomorrow night, and see if we can see her. Either way, we'll get to the phantom biker on Monday. Okay?"

THE music at Justine's on Saturday night was louder than the music had been on Thursday, but at least the people—mostly students from the college—looked more normal. I tried to retreat to the lighting box so I could see more of the dance floor through the security cameras, but Leah soon noticed that I was missing and tracked me down. She'd obviously been dancing, and she suggested that we alternate in the box, at least until eleven o'clock.

"Why eleven?"

"That's the earliest the ghost's been reported. Of course, it was also snowing every time, as well, and it's not snowing yet, but it may before midnight."

"You really think she'll turn up?"

"Old ghosts don't often haunt new buildings," said Leah. "Maybe that's why Annie keeps coming back, when so many other ghosts disappear. Anyway, go get your ass down on the dance floor. If she *does* turn up, I want you there."

I did as she asked, but always stayed in sight of the door. One young woman approached me and asked if I were waiting for someone, and I said yes, and she left. I didn't initiate any conversations, because I didn't want to have to explain what I was doing there, or why I had a hands-free cell phone plugged into my ear, or to suddenly break off in mid-sentence so I could chase a ghost.

It started snowing at approximately quarter past ten, and that's when Leah barred me from returning to the lighting box. "You haven't been dancing at all, have you?"

"I thought we were here to work."

"Is that all there is to your life?"

I tried to think of a short answer that I could bellow into her ear over the background music, and the best I could come up with was, "Shall we dance?"

She smiled, and dragged me onto the dance floor, where I did my best to imitate her movements while at least one of us kept an eye on the entrance. I'm not sure how long the woman in the pale blouse and the scarf (the lighting made it almost impossible to recognise colours) had been there before we noticed her. She was talking to a young man in a checked shirt, and I grabbed Leah's shoulder and spun her around. She pirouetted back to face me, then noticed my expression and turned around. I weaved my way between the dancers as quickly as I could, and reached the doorway just as they were about to leave. "Annie!" I yelled.

The woman looked over her shoulder at me, and blinked. "Do I know you?" she asked.

I tried to remember what we'd found of her biography. It occurred to me to say that I was a friend of her boyfriend's, but I couldn't remember his name, and I must have been silent too long, because she turned back to the man in the checked shirt. I couldn't hear what she said, but he smirked slightly as they walked out. Leah caught up with me as they stepped onto the pavement and headed for the parking lot.

"Someone's going to have to teach you how to pick up women," she said, shaking her head. "Your technique sucks. Come on, at least we can follow them."

We did, as discreetly as possible. He had a fairly new pick-up truck, but I guess they haven't changed very much in the past seventy years, at least from the back. The snow provided us with a little cover, but it also made it difficult to see inside his car, much less videotape it. As we'd expected, he headed towards the cemetery, and stopped and switched the interior light just after he passed the gate. Leah kept driving, then stopped half a dozen car-lengths on and reversed towards him. I kept my head down and kept the camera pointed back through our rear window.

Leah opened her door and stepped out. "Need a hand?"

He wound his window down, stuck his head out, and stared at her. "What the hell is this? A Dracula movie?"

"What happened?"

The stare became a glare. "What makes you think something happened?"

"It seems a strange place to stop."

"What the hell business is it of yours?"

"I thought you might need some help."

"I'm fine," he said, stiffly, then, ungraciously. "Thanks for the offer."

Leah returned to the car. "Did you really expect him to talk to you?" I asked as she drove away.

"Not really, but it didn't hurt to try. Besides, I wanted a better look at him."

"Why?" I asked, trying not to feel jealous.

"Because the ghost picked him out. True, he was standing near the door, but there may have been more to it than that. Maybe he looked enough like her boyfriend for her to trust him."

She glanced at me, and I realised what she was saying. "You want me to dress like him? Dye my hair? Is that it?"

"Maybe. Dyeing your hair isn't fatal, you know: I've done it dozens of times. Turn me upside down and I'm a strawberry blonde."

I tried to keep that image out of my mind for long enough to answer. "You want to try this again?"

"Next Saturday. We'll deal with the phantom biker until then, and go somewhere warmer when we've finished here. Okay?"

THE phantom biker was even better documented than Annie Gray, and though he was usually seen on the anniversary of his death in September, there were reported sightings at other times of the year as well. Better still, he was almost unique: there were many reports of phantom cars and trucks, and another phantom biker in Ohio whose legend dated back to just after World War I, but he only appeared as a speeding headlight, a fast-moving will-o'-the-wisp. Our subject looked and sounded real enough for several bikers to have identified his bike as a green Harley-Davidson with a forty-five cubic inch engine. According to the legend, the bike was war surplus, and may have been one of the reasons bikers still think of green Harleys as unlucky.

It was only other bikers who'd seen him, always heading east on a treacherous stretch of country road about a mile long and barely one lane wide, lined with handmade memorials but no lights. Most of the riders had seen his light behind them when they were speeding, and had slowed down to let him pass: they'd heard him, and sometimes seen him for an instant, as he passed them and disappeared. Others had only seen the headlight receding behind them as they'd sped away. A few of these had barely survived crashes a moment later, usually with trucks, which had led to a legend that the biker was a harbinger of death, like a banshee or whisht hound.

"The problem with death omens," I said, as we sat on a huge Kawasaki and waited for sunset, "is that you have to wonder how anyone else ever finds out about them."

She smiled slightly, but I was mostly talking to cheer myself up. She'd ridden this far cautiously enough, with me hanging on for grim life, but I didn't know what she'd do if she saw the phantom biker. The motorbike seemed to have twice as much engine as any car I'd ever driven, and only half as many wheels, and that didn't strike me as a good combination. "You know the legend says the biker's supposed to be the ghost of a returned soldier from World War II? Do you think he'll notice that our bike's Japanese?"

She shrugged. "All the best bikes are made by the sides that lost the war. Maybe it's what they do when they can't make fighter planes. Besides, we *want* him to chase us, remember?"

"Yes, but… why are you doing this? And don't say it's just for the book. Why did you decide to write the book?"

"I've already told you, I want to know—"

"What happens next. So do we all, but we don't go around the world chasing ghosts. Why are you so possessed with death? You're twenty-three: you shouldn't have to worry about the afterlife for another sixty, seventy years… Hell, the way things are going, we might be immortal." She didn't answer, and I had a sudden sinking feeling in the pit of my stomach, as though she might have some terminal disease and I might have said something incredibly stupid. "Am I right?"

She was silent for what seemed like a year, then said, "I don't know. I've been interested in ghosts for as long as I can remember, even though I don't think I ever saw one before last night. I used to wonder what it would be like to be a ghost before anyone I knew died, maybe even before I realised that you had to be dead to become one. I used to love *The Addams Family*, of course, and *Casper*. I thought it was so cool that ghosts could just walk through walls like that, who couldn't be trapped anywhere; it wasn't until later that I heard about haunting. And I can remember dressing in black for my grandmother's funeral—I think I was four—and how many flowers there were, and only later wondering where she'd gone. I've never managed to believe in heaven or hell, but it's hard to believe that something as real and alive as some of the people I've known can just *stop*... Have any of your friends or lovers ever died?"

"No."

"A friend of mine was shot when we were in high school. I wasn't there; my mother moved us around every year or two, following work. Another friend shot himself. A friend and one of my exes died in a road accident. Another OD'ed, which might have been an accident." She shrugged. "Maybe I just have a knack for choosing friends and lovers who're going to die."

I couldn't think of anything to say to that.

"Do *you* believe in ghosts?"

"I do now. Before last night, I wasn't sure. I still don't know what they are—but I don't want to be one. I don't think they're... autonomous, or even fully conscious; all the ghosts we've studied just seem to repeat the same actions. Either it's something they were doing just before they died, like Annie Gray, or it's something that was so much a part of their routine that even death didn't interrupt it, like many of the phantom monks and priests. The most likely explanation I've read is that events or emotions can be recorded somehow and recalled by some individuals."

"*The Stone Tape*."

I nodded. "Or maybe something less solid; what Hindus call the Akasha, and Price called 'psychic ether'. Either that, or we see ghosts in their haunts because we expect to. Maybe someone who knew about a death in that location saw or heard something, maybe because the place triggered a trace memory, and our imaginations do the rest. Maybe like other urban legends, they grow and become distorted in the telling." It was already becoming dark, but I could see that Leah looked disappointed. "I prefer to think the Akashic record is the most probable. That way, at least the ghosts can at least teach us something about their own time. But I don't *know*—and if we find evidence that there is a real after-life, that ghosts are autonomous and intelligent, I'll accept it."

She nodded, then lowered the visor on her helmet, for all the world like a knight summoned to tourney. "Ready?"

As I'll ever be, I thought. "Yes."

"Good. Hang on."

I did, and not just because she quickly accelerated up to 60 mph before I decided to stop looking at the speedometer. I wrapped my left arm around her waist, and rotated the viewfinder on the digital camera so that it showed the road behind me as it peered over my right shoulder. I'd attached it to my wrist with a lanyard, though I would rather have stuck it to the bike or my helmet and held onto Leah with both hands.

We made the run a dozen times without even a glimmer of a phantom headlight, though we did pass an obviously real Ford Explorer on the thirteenth. I didn't bother counting after that, but we continued making the same circuit every few minutes for another two hours—north at sixty miles or more, then decelerating and turning around, back to the beginning at a more leisurely speed, then north again. I was beginning to feel like one of the phantom monks who've been retracing their footsteps for seven centuries, and wondering whether my ghost might end up repeating this journey like a scratched track on a vinyl record, when I heard the roar of another engine behind ours, and looked in the viewfinder to see a bright round light maybe five metres behind us.

"Leah!" I shouted, then regretted it as she glanced back over my left shoulder for an instant. "Watch the road!"

To my relief, she did. She even decelerated slightly, allowing the light to approach us. I could hear the engine more clearly now: compared to the steady whine of the Kawasaki, the old Harley sounded like a tubercular tractor. I still couldn't see anything more than the headlight until we passed through a treeless stretch and the biker was illuminated by the moon. The bike was clearly a pale green, and the rider wore a brownish bomber jacket and an old-fashioned helmet with goggles. Leah looked in the rear-view mirror, and slowed until he was almost close enough for me to touch. I could see his face clearly enough for me to count his teeth, and to see headlights reflected in his goggles. I glanced up for an instant and saw a huge truck, almost wider than the road, bearing down on us. Our combined speeds must have topped a hundred miles an hour, and I knew we'd never be able to stop in time. I had the bizarre feeling that everything was in slow motion, and I could step off the bike and run for safety, if only I could get my body to cooperate.

Leah looked around, spotted a space between two trees on the far side of the road, and headed for the gap. The truck passed within inches of the rear wheel as we hurtled off the asphalt, and then we were skidding across leaf litter and mud. Everything went black for a moment, possibly because I had my visor buried in Leah's leather jacket and my eyes closed besides. I had just enough time for the exciting moments in my life to flash before my eyes, and to regret the things I hadn't done and the opportunities I might have missed, and then we were lying in the mud a few feet from the bike, sore but alive.

Leah turned to face me and raised her visor. "Are you okay?"

"I don't know." I checked the camera to make sure that it wasn't damaged, then did the same for myself. None of my bones seemed to be broken, and my leather jacket was scuffed but intact. The left leg of my jeans was badly tattered, but I established that it was soaked and stained with nothing worse than mud. "I think so. Are you?"

She stood, careful to put most of her weight onto her right leg, then removed her helmet and looked around. "Fucking truck driver didn't even stop."

"Maybe he thought you were the phantom biker," I said. "You nearly were." I hauled myself to my feet, brushed myself down, and discovered that I had an erection. Embarrassed, I turned away from Leah to look along the road. "No sign of *him* either."

Leah picked the bike up, and we cautiously made our way back to the motel. I showered, and was examining my bruises when Leah knocked on the door. She was wearing clean jeans and an old T-shirt, both still damp from her shower. "I'm too keyed up to sleep," she explained. "Can I have the camera? I want to see if we got anything useable."

"Sure. Mind if I join you?"

"I was hoping you would."

I looked down at my towel, and turned away again. "Give me a minute to get dressed?"

"If you insist," she said impishly.

For an instant, I thought about calling her bluff, then I grabbed a pair of chinos and a pair of boxers and disappeared into the bathroom.

WE watched the video over and over, adjusting the brightness and contrast and speed to try to get clearer images of the phantom biker. After an hour, we had a useable few seconds of the rider and his Harley before the lights of the truck washed the image out, as well as nearly two minutes of the headlight and engine noise. There was something odd about the whole thing that I couldn't quite define, and as we examined the final seconds frame-by-frame in search of stills good enough for the book, I kept wondering what it was.

Finally, when we were both so tired we could barely keep our eyes open, we chose three of the least blurry vidcaps to e-mail to Carnelian. "It loses a lot without the sound," said Leah, regretfully. "Still, the footage will look good on the website or the CD-Rom, or however they decide to use it. That should keep them happy."

I sat up, suddenly alert. "That's it!"

"What?"

"He's happy! It's not just a skull. He's smiling!"

Leah looked at me as though I were crazy.

"Think of all the other sightings we've investigated. Think of the ghosts. They're all either despairing or miserable, like the vanishing hitchhikers or la llorona, or angry, or lost or looking for something, or just repeating part of their regular routine like the phantom monks. Can you think of *one* who's been described as happy or smiling?"

Leah considered this. "There are stories of a few theatre ghosts who only come to shows they like—usually musicals—but those are the only ones I can think of at the moment." She glanced at her watch. "Jesus, it's nearly sunrise."

"Maybe I should go," I said, still staring at the screen, and wondering what it would have been like to have become a ghost on that road, on the bike, holding on to her forever.

"If that's what you want."

I was back in my own room by the time I thought of the right answer to that, and by then, it was too late.

It was after one when I woke, and to my disappointment, Leah was already out of bed, fully dressed, and answering her e-mails. "I didn't realise you were *that* tired," she said.

"It was an eventful night. What're we doing today?"

"Taking the bike back to make sure it's okay. I want to go back and see if we can get some better shots of the biker tonight. Maybe even something good enough for the cover."

I stared at her. "What? Why?" When she didn't reply, I said, "I thought we were going somewhere warmer."

"Not yet. I want to go back to Justine's on Saturday night. We can leave on Sunday whether we see Annie or not, but I want to try." When I didn't answer, she said, "We did something incredible last night. We have evidence that ghosts *do* exist. Okay, the video quality is a little Blair

Witchy, but it's still better than anything else I've seen. But if we can't do it again, the best we can hope for is an Ig Nobel. We can't stop *now*."

I winced. I'd heard of the Ig Nobel, of course: they award them for results that can't, or shouldn't, be repeated. "What if he only appears when you're about to be hit by a truck, or some other near-death experience?"

"Then that's one thing we have to establish," she said, calmly.

"I signed on for a research project, not a mutual suicide pact!"

Leah stared at me, and her face turned even more pale than usual. "Suicide? You think I'm suicidal?"

I hesitated. "Can we settle for 'obsessive'?"

Some colour slowly returned to her face. "Okay, I'll accept that. But Jesus, Alan, I don't think I've ever felt more alive than I do now! How about you?"

"Of course I do! That's why I don't want to throw it away—and I don't want to see you throw it away, either!"

"I can't do this by myself," she said. "If you don't come with me, I'll try to find someone else from the college—do they teach film there? Or journalism?"

"I don't think so." I tried to imagine Leah with someone else, or myself without her, and shrugged. "Okay, count me in. What exactly did you have in mind?"

I SPENT the day in the university library or on the web, finding out what I could about old Harley-Davidsons and looking for clues to the identity of our phantom biker. Leah had theorised that like the vanishing hitchhiker, he was trying to get home but was unable to reach there. I could only find one death on record that matched his description, a man named Edward Corby who died on that stretch of road in 1946, and unfortunately, it looked as though he was riding cross-country *away* from his home in California.

"How did he die?" Leah asked, as we finished our dinner. "Hit by a truck?"

"No. Ran off the road and hit a low branch. The tyre tracks suggest he swerved to avoid something, probably an animal, but no-one really knows."

"Any more details?"

I handed her a grainy black-and-white photo of a bomber crew. "Third from the right: he was a gunner on a B-17. One Purple Heart. Twenty-eight when he died, never married; closest living relatives are nieces on the west coast."

"You're amazing."

I suspect I blushed. "It's what I do best. I'll probably end up haunting a library somewhere, and no-one will know the difference."

"Is that your idea of heaven?"

"It used to be. It's still a long way from Hell."

We spent most of the next five nights riding along the same stretch of road at different times and different speeds. Most of the trips were fruitless, and we soon established that the biker would only appear once per night, and not only when there was oncoming traffic or some other threat: it just seemed to suit him to race us at some times, and not at others. We also learned that if we stuck close to the maximum speed of his Harley, we could get him to race us for several miles past the point where he died, though he disappeared if we stopped, or turned west, or put too much distance between us, or came too close to a house or a town.

I'd expected Leah to return the bike to the hire firm on Saturday, but she didn't. "I want you to go to Justine's tonight," she said, as we searched the Goodwill store for a new old outfit for me. "Make one last try to pick up Annie. I'm not sure she'll go with you if I'm there: everyone else who's picked her up has been alone, and male. Send me an SMS message if you have any luck."

"Where will you be?"

"I want one more ride with the biker. By myself."

"Why? We have video, audio, some good stills, we know he can vary his routine and leave the stretch of road that he's been haunting... I think that counts as proof that he's autonomous at some level, not just a death omen or a re-run of an old accident. What more do you think we can do?"

"Probably nothing, but maybe he'll talk to me if you're not there."

"We tried stopping. He just vanished."

"I just want to try. Okay? And tomorrow we'll head down to New Orleans, get away from this weather."

"You're saying goodbye?"

"Something like that."

I felt a sudden stab of jealousy, and wished that she found me as fascinating as she found him.

"Oh, cheer up," she said. "You look just like my mother used to look whenever I went out on a date. I'll be careful, okay?"

ANNIE turned up at Justine's at four minutes past eleven, and I was ready for her. Trying not to look too predatory, I intercepted a jock who was heading towards her, and said softly, "Hi."

She turned to face me, and looked me up and down, with no sign of recognition. "Hello."

"Are you meeting someone?"

"My boyfriend was supposed to drive me home," she said, "but he left, and I can't see him anywhere." She was silent for a moment, then said, "My mother's going to kill me if I'm not back by midnight."

"I have a car," I said. "Where do you live?"

She looked at me neutrally. "I don't think I've seen you before. Where are you from?"

"Oxford. England. My name's Alan."

"What are you doing *here*?"

"I'm an historian," I said, then remembered that they hadn't started building the university until after Annie had died, so I could hardly claim to be looking for work there. "I'm writing a history of the 10th Cavalry."

She seemed satisfied by that, if completely disinterested in the subject, which was just as well. "Could you take me home? I don't see anyone here that I know well enough to ask."

"Where do you live?"

"Charles Road. Out past the cemetery. I can tell you which way to go."

I looked at my watch, then remembered that it was a digital and hoped she wouldn't notice. "Okay."

Leah had been unable to find a 1920s car for hire and had rented a Chrysler that resembled something out of *The Untouchables*, at least externally. I reached into my overcoat pocket for my cell phone and pressed the 'Send' button, turned the recording equipment on, then drove carefully and slowly out of town. A few minutes later, Annie looked around and said, "You're going the wrong way!"

I was: Leah had told me to avoid the cemetery. "I'm running low on pet—uh, on gas," I said, hoping she wouldn't look at the dashboard. "I'll need to fill up before I go that far out of town."

She seemed mollified by that, at least temporarily, and I continued to drive south, following the route Leah had mapped out and wondering what the hell she had in mind. A few minutes later, we reached the limits of where the town had been in Annie's day, and she looked around again, her face pale and her eyes wide.

"There's no gas station out here!" she said. "There's nothing out here but farms! Where are you taking me?"

"I told you," I said, as calmly as I could. "I need petrol—and some antifreeze would be a good idea, too. I'm staying with the Robertsons; they'll have some."

She wasn't buying it. "Let me out!"

"We'll be there in a couple of minutes."

She drew a deep breath. "If you're kidnapping me, you've got the wrong girl. My parents haven't got any money. Just let me go, and I won't tell anyone."

I wondered whether all the recording gear was working, and whether it was possible to be convicted of abducting a ghost. "I'm not kidnapping you, but I'm not letting you out this far from town, either, not on a night like this. You'll freeze to—to death."

She stared at the door, and I wondered what would happen if she tried to open it. I hadn't tried to touch her, so I didn't know how solid she was, and this didn't seem like a good time to try. She wasn't wearing her seatbelt—did they have them in 1930?—and like a gentleman and an idiot, I'd opened her door for her when she'd gotten in, as well as closing it behind her. Was there something in the glovebox that I could ask her to pass me?

I saw a pair of headlights approaching along the narrow road, and prepared to steer onto the shoulder: the other driver was moving much faster than I was. A moment later, I realised that they were the headlights of two motorcycles speeding along the snowy road, neck a neck in some insane race. I pulled over and stopped the car, hoping they'd see me in time for one of them to fall back. My cellphone began vibrating, and I grabbed it and looked at the SMS message on the glowing screen:

I CAN SEE YOU. STOP NOW.

I did, but I was so busy trying not to skid that I didn't notice Annie disappearing from the seat beside me. I don't know whether she opened the door before she went through it, but before I could speak, she was running across the road ahead of me. One of the bikes pulled ahead of the other before they both came screeching to a halt, the faded green Harley barely two metres from Annie, Leah's Kawasaki maybe three metres behind that.

The biker raised his goggles and stared at Annie. "Are you crazy?" he yelled. "You could've been killed!"

"I need to go home," she pleaded. "If I don't get there by midnight, my mother will kill me…"

He seemed to hesitate, then nodded. "Get on, and hold on tight. Where do you live?"

A moment too late, I reached for my camera, and all I captured was a blurred image of the bike disappearing into the darkness with Annie on the back.

The passenger side door opened a moment later, and Leah slid into the seat, her helmet in her hand. "Are you okay?"

I stared at the empty road. "What did you just do?"

"An experiment." She smiled. "I wonder if anyone will ever see them again."

"If they don't," I said, "you've just destroyed one of our best pieces of evidence. And I wish you'd told me in advance."

She shrugged. "Sorry, but I didn't know if it would work. Besides, I think it was worth it. We've established that ghosts can be aware of each other, and interact. I think that's proof that they're autonomous, not just recordings. And I told you I was a sucker for romance."

I didn't reply.

"Come on. I'll race you to the motel."

"I'm not racing in *this* thing—not in snow and on the wrong side of the road!"

"Then I'll wait up for you."

I stared at her. Even in leathers and with her black hair a mess, she looked especially beautiful when she smiled. I remembered wishing I'd had the courage to touch Annie, then undid my seatbelt and leaned across and kissed her. She kissed back without the slightest hesitation.

"I thought you'd never ask," she said, a long time later.

I kissed her again while I tried to think of an answer. "If ghosts can change their routines," I said, at last, "then I guess I can, too."

AGE AND HUNGER

"SHE WAS DEAD WHEN WE ARRIVED," I repeated. "The next morning, I mean. She was alive when we left."

The cop leaned over the table in the interrogation room, his face so close to mine that I could smell his breath—which was probably banned by the Geneva Convention, or should have been. "Where were you between seven and ten p.m.?"

"Seattle Public Library."

"Can anyone confirm that?"

"Nearly thirty people. We have a list."

"What were you doing?"

I was fairly sure that if I told him were holding a *Hyakumonogatari Kaidankai*, he'd just look at me blankly. "Telling ghost stories."

Maybe I should start at the beginning…

WE were down to the last candle, and the blue paper shade around the lantern made many of the people in the lecture room look disturbingly corpse-like. What it did to the sushi was even worse.

Hyakumonogatari Kaidankai is an old Japanese ritual that supposedly summons an *aoandon*—a demon woman with long black hair, horns and teeth, and a white kimono. It was once used as a test of courage for samurai, and eventually became a popular game for townspeople, much as ouija boards did in the west. There was no sign that an aoandon had shown up this time, though someone had taken advantage of the darkness to eat the last of the sushi and dim sum from the table: I suspected the anorexic-looking long-haired girl who said she wanted to be a model and had been pointedly sitting with her back to the food. Leah was obviously disappointed, but she thanked everyone who'd stayed the distance, and said she'd let them know if and when we were going to try again.

Leah had become fascinated by *bakemono*, Japanese ghosts and monsters, particularly *gaki*, ghosts hungry for something they'd desperately wanted in life, be it food or money or booze or sex... but neither our publisher nor the university would pay to send us to Japan, so I'd been reading huge tomes of *kaidan*, Japanese 'weird tales', and while we were in Seattle to look at an alleged miracle, Leah had the idea of bribing students to get together for a Hyakumonogatari meeting. In exchange for free food, they had to tell at least one scary supernatural story, and sit there while the other ninety-nine were told or read out and the andon lanterns extinguished. It had attracted a mixed group of Japanese language students, anthropology majors, horror fans and writers, as well as an old Asian guy who'd dropped in, eaten a lot of sushi and drunk a huge quantity of tea while telling us an unnerving story of *tsukumogami*, century-old inanimate objects that take revenge if not treated with the proper respect—in this case, a *waniguchi*, a bronze temple gong that became a crocodilian monster.

Leah still looked disappointed when we returned to our hotel room. "Maybe the stories weren't scary enough," I said. "Or maybe they have to be told in Japanese: maybe the aoandon doesn't understand English." The one thing I didn't dare say was that maybe there was no such thing as an aoandon.

She nodded, and began undressing. When she was down to her underwear, she suddenly sat down on the queen-sized bed and asked, "Why do you stay, Alan?"

I would have thought the answer to that would have been obvious even when she was fully dressed, but she didn't give me time to reply. "You could be a professor by now if you weren't following me around chasing shadows like this."

I sat down next to her and kissed her. I could have told her how important it was to apply the rigorous standards of academia to the study of ghost stories (my doctoral thesis, which almost no-one had read, had been on the Adamites and the "possessed" Louvier nuns), but instead I said, "Research is more fun than teaching, and this way I don't spend *all* my time in libraries. Besides, our success rate's not that bad when you compare it to some other forms of research. How do you think the SETI people feel, or ripperologists, or..." I kissed her again. She kissed me back, but it was obvious that she didn't want sex, so I grabbed a book from the stack beside the bed and began researching tsukumogami.

BOB Sims was in his eighties, and bald and big-bellied as the small Buddha figurine on the top of the dusty display shelf in his rather shabby den. "I'm sorry you came all this way," he said, as he produced a ceramic bottle, handling it carefully. "I never said it was a miracle or anything like that, but when I told my daughter about it, she made a big fuss. I'm just lucky they kept my address out of the papers." He coughed so hard that the shelves seemed to rattle. "Not that I couldn't use a miracle or two."

I looked at the bottle, which was so dusty that it almost felt as though parts of it were covered in fur and sloshed as though it were mostly full. A pattern of darker cracks had appeared in the amber glaze, and this pattern certainly looked like a face—though much more like the old man from the Hyakumonogatari Kaidankai than the Virgin Mary or Jesus. "This is a sake jar," I said. "A, what's the word... *tokkuri.*"

He nodded. "It belonged to my first wife. Her family gave it to us as an engagement present: they didn't have much to give, and she said it was an heirloom, so... even when she died, I couldn't bring myself to throw it out." He smiled crookedly. "Even though it's been more than fifty years. Stupid, huh?"

"No," said Leah, firmly.

"I didn't realize the thing was still full," said Sims, and shrugged. "I thought I'd poured it out years ago. I didn't like the stuff myself, only drank it to be polite, or when there wasn't anything else. It's probably poisonous now. Aiko liked it, though. Maybe it reminded her of home— she didn't drink much of anything else, except beer, which is what I liked. And sometimes Scotch, when we could afford the good stuff."

"How long has this face been there?"

"Damned if I know," he admitted. "It wasn't there when we got it, I can swear to that. And I don't do much dusting." He burst out coughing again. "Not big on housework, and I can't afford to pay anyone else. My daughter gives me hell about it. But it was up there for years, without anybody touching it as far as I know. Then last year, I took my medals down to show my sister's grandkids, picked that thing up while I was rummaging on the shelf, and the face was staring at me. Gave me such a start I nearly dropped the damn thing. Betty—my sister—wondered what'n'hell was wrong, and she saw the face, and she started saying it was a miracle. I asked her not to tell anyone else, but she musta, or the kids did. I really don't think it's anything, any more than that face on Mars or whatever… but I'm not much of a churchgoer." Another bout of coughing. "'cept for funerals," he wheezed. "'scuse me. Lungs're bad today."

I put the bottle down and looked at the other items on the shelves. Apart from the small Buddha and an assortment of half-empty bottles of wine, there was a collection of framed photographs, a sheath knife, several ashtrays, a Zippo lighter, and a few dusty boxes that looked as though they might contain medals. The photos showed younger versions of Bob Sims, plus a few other men in U.S. army uniforms, a very pretty Japanese woman, three blondes, and assorted children. "Is Betty one of these?"

He nodded, and pointed at one of the women in the photos. "That's her. The short one's Dorothy. Married her in '59, had nearly forty years. That's Julie, our daughter. And that's Aiko. She and I didn't have any kids… funny thing is, it's her I keep thinking is still around, late at night, not Dorothy. Her voice, her perfume… guess that's why I couldn't throw her stuff out."

Or the other way around, I thought. He looked sadly at the other bottles on the shelf, then returned his gaze to the tokkuri. "Julie thinks I should sell it on whatchamacallit, eBay. Says a toasted cheese sandwich that looked like a face sold for thousands, that way. What do you think?"

I shrugged. "I don't know how much you'd get for it. How much is it worth to you?"

"I don't know. I mean, I don't need the money, and if it's just cracks in the clay rather than any sort of miracle, I'd hate to rip anyone off." He was silent for a moment. "I guess I'll just leave the decision up to Julie. It'll be hers—" He coughed again, and didn't stop for more than a minute.

Not sure where else to look, I picked up the knife from the shelf, careful to handle it respectfully, and waited for him to be able to speak again. "Did your wife give you this, too?"

"No; I took that off a Japanese officer on Guam. Why?"

"If it's as old as I think it is, it might be much more valuable than the tokkuri," I said cautiously, drawing the blade half out of the sheath and looking at the metal. "It looks like a *kozuka*, a samurai dagger." It felt old, too, and dangerous, but that was probably just my imagination. I sheathed it again and returned it to the shelf. "But if you don't need the money…"

"I don't." I was about to say he was lucky, but he shook his head. "Doubt I'd live long enough to spend it. Julie wants me to sell this place, says it's too big for me and it'd be worth a packet if I had it fixed up a bit, but I've been here fifty years and I hate moving." He looked at the photos wistfully, then at the tokkuri. "Sorry you came all this way for nothing."

"We were in town anyway," said Leah. "Call us if the face changes, or if… well, if anything else happens. It was good to meet you."

"WHAT was that about the knife?" Leah asked, as we headed back downtown. It was a beautiful clear October day, and she was looking out the windows at the trees, the innumerable shades of red and yellow like a frozen sunset. I was doing most of the driving, by now: I'd gotten used to the way Americans drove on the wrong side of the road, and at least the roads here were broad enough for that to mean something. Back home in London, when we have to drive, we drive wherever there's a space at least as wide as the car. In Italy, they're not even that fussy, but that's by the by.

"If it's real, it's a few centuries old," I said. "Samurai used to carry kozuka, daggers, around with their katana. They collected the heads of their enemies, and if they picked them up with a kozuka rather than their hands, they wouldn't have to touch the dead bodies."

"Why did they –"

"Trophies. Proof that they'd done it."

"Souvenirs."

I nodded. "What did you think of the tokkuri?"

"He's probably right; it's just a case of our tendency to see faces in random patterns. What do they call that?"

"Pareidolia."

"It felt *old*, a little strange, but not… you know, ghostly, no more than the rest of the house did. It certainly didn't feel dangerous, the way the knife did… it felt more… I don't know, like an old toy that someone had loved. But that was probably just my imagination, both times."

I love Leah's imagination, because she wouldn't be who she was without it… but while a feeling isn't something they let you cite as a reference, I had to agree there was something unsettling about the tokkuri as well as the kozuka. "I keep thinking I've seen something like it before, or that there's something I'm forgetting…" I shrugged. "Maybe the face reminds me of someone. Or maybe we've just been in too many Japanese restaurants."

Leah smiled, which made her even more beautiful. "Have you ever tried sake?"

"No. You?"

"Yes. I guess it must be an acquired taste."

I WOKE earlier in the morning than Leah, as usual, and booted the laptop while I waited for the kettle to boil. By the time Leah opened her eyes, I was on my second mug of tea and had managed to put together a sketchy bio of former Sergeant Bob Sims and his family, getting most of the information from a website put together by one of his nephews and double-checking it with public records and online news archives. "His story checks out," I told Leah, as she emerged from the shower. "He fought in the South Pacific, came out with a Purple Heart and a Bronze Star, then was stationed in Japan and Okinawa during the occupation as an M.P. Stayed there until the Korean War. After that, he returned to the U.S., brought his Japanese wife with him—"

"Didn't you trust him?"

"Yes, but I was curious. It gets even more interesting after that. They both became active in trying to get compensation for Japanese who were interned during the war. Then Aiko died in 1954, hit by a car while crossing the road, just around the corner from where he still lives. The driver was acquitted because of her blood-alcohol level. After that, it looks like Bob hit the bottle pretty hard for a couple of years, was discharged from the Army… then he seems to have dried out, and remarried in 1959. He was an ambulance driver then, with a spotless record, and she was a nurse… their daughter Julie was born in '64. No grandchildren. That's about all I can find." I looked at the family tree and photo album on the screen. "Nothing to suggest that he's trying to run a scam with the face on the tokkuri; he seems far too honest, and not greedy enough."

"I agree. He reminds me of my own father, in a strange way."

"I thought you hated your father."

"I did. Bob's almost exactly his opposite. What're we doing today?"

"Two schools: more phantom footsteps and other weird noises. I'll get the recording gear."

WE left Seattle a week later, and didn't return until the following July, after hearing about some reported sightings of uniformed ghosts at the military cemetery. It was raining heavily when we arrived and we didn't manage to photograph anything, and when we held another Hyaku-monogatari Kaidankai the next night, no ghosts or demons were kind enough to make an appearance, though the skinny woman and the old Japanese guy turned up almost as soon as we put the food on the table. The man told a story about a gaki, a hungry ghost, who consumed ink. Leah was sufficiently alarmed by this to check her tattoos as soon as we returned to our hotel, then had me check the ones she couldn't see in the bathroom mirror, so the night wasn't completely wasted.

After a late breakfast at Pike's Place Markets, we went out the next afternoon to investigate a supposedly haunted hotel, and were passing through Beacon Hill on the way back when Leah noticed that we were only a couple of blocks from Bob Sims's place; she stopped singing 'It can't rain all the time', and suggested we call in and ask to see the tokkuri again.

The house had been painted since our last visit, and the garden looked neater than it had the year before, but the name 'Sims' was still on the letter box. The rain had stopped, and there was an old woman trimming the hedge in the house on the left. She looked up when she heard us shut the van's doors, and called out, "You here about the job?"

"Excuse me?" I turned to look at her.

She lowered her voice, so that we had to step closer to the fence to hear her. "If you're after the cleaner's job, get her to pay you in advance. Nobody lasts more than a week before she fires them." She emphasized this with a powerful SNIP of the garden shears. "Accuses them all of drinking her precious booze."

"Mrs Sims?"

"And don't call her that, either." Another SNIP. "It's *Ms*."

"We were looking for *Bob* Sims," said Leah.

"You're a little late," said the neighbour. "Bob died two months ago." She looked at us more closely; we were dressed for fieldwork, which in Leah's case meant leather jacket, silk shirt, tight jeans and combat boots, all in immaculate black, and in mine a pair of cargo pants, an Oxford sweatshirt, and running shoes. "You look sort of young to be friends of his."

Before we could answer, the front door of the house opened, and a skinny sharp-featured woman trying to look younger than her forty-something years emerged. "Yes?" she demanded.

"Ms Sims? I'm Leah Corby; this is Dr Graves. We knew your father."

"Doctor?" she said, suspiciously.

"Not a medical doctor," I replied. "I'm an historian. Your father had an item that he asked us to look at when we were here last, and we thought we'd drop in." I'd learned it wasn't always a smart move to tell people we were researchers for the *Encyclopedia of the Undead and Paranormal.*

She peered at us for a moment, then looked up at the cloudy sky. "I guess you'd better come inside," she said grudgingly. "Wipe your feet."

The interior of the house had been changed almost beyond recognition: all new furniture, carpet, lighting, and a colour scheme so stark and unsettling it could only have been chosen by a professional designer who wouldn't have to live there. There was no sign of the tokkuri or any photos or Bob Sims's other mementos. "What item are you talking about?" she asked.

"The sake jar. The one with the face."

"That ugly old thing?" She sat down on a chair that looked as modern and uncomfortable as something out of *Alien.* She didn't invite us to sit, so we didn't. "I threw it out."

"Excuse me?"

"It wasn't worth anything, was it?" She suddenly looked alarmed. "I sent photos of his stuff to an appraiser, but they said that without proof of its provenance it was all just junk, so I just threw it all in the dumpster when I was cleaning the place out. If they lied, I'm going to sue them for —"

"You threw it out?" Leah repeated.

"They said I might get something for it on e-bay, but it didn't seem worth the hassle. I gave some of his army stuff to my nephews, but their parents didn't want them to have the knife or the lighter, and nobody wanted the bottle. The appraiser said it was only a hundred years old or so, and it wasn't rare, and it sure as Hell wasn't beautiful or anything." She looked around the room with obvious pride. "Why're you so interested?"

"Did the jar still look like a face?"

"An ugly one, sure. Sort of Japanese. Not that I'm racist," she added, hurriedly. "Some of my best clients are Japanese. Was that all you wanted?"

I wondered whether it was worth asking if she thought the place might be haunted, but I doubted I'd get a useful answer. We thanked her for her time and walked out. The neighbour was still chopping away at the hedge, and Leah stopped and asked her, "Excuse me, I know this is going to sound like a strange question, but… Alan and I collect ghost stories. Do you know if anyone around here says they've seen ghosts?"

The old woman stared at her, her clippers held up as though she were warding off an attack… then she shrugged. "You know what kids are like. One has a nightmare and thinks it's real, and tells other kids about it. And older kids always try to scare younger ones late at night, and then the younger ones tell the same stories when they're older. And they say it happened near here because that makes it scarier. When I was a kid it was escaped lunatics; now it's UFOs and aliens."

"UFOs?"

"Some of them say they've seen a bright light come around the corner late at night and up the street and go into the house next door. They say someone was killed by a car near there, though that was before my time." Another shrug, another SNIP. "I thought *she'd* be scary enough without that."

Leah smiled. "Thank you," she said, and we climbed into the van and returned to the hotel.

WE'D scheduled another Hyakumonogatari Kaidankai for that night, so went to the library at the University of Washington and spent a couple of hours looking through collections of Japanese ghost stories, assuming Leah was doing the same. So I was more than slightly surprised when she walked up to my desk and murmured, "Julie Sims collects rare wines and old Scotch—not to drink, as an *investment*. Apparently really expensive bottles of Scotch have become a traditional way to sweeten deals with Japanese clients. Some of the bottles are worth thousands, so I'm not surprised she's paranoid about… what's wrong?"

I looked up from my much-thumbed copy of *Japanese Ghosts and Demons* and the library's *Japanese Grotesqueries*. "I've just been reading more about tsukumogami—objects that come to life after a century. I knew there was something about that tokkuri that was ringing a bell very faintly… apparently, one of the harmless sorts of tsukumogami is a sake jar that, after years of not being used, becomes a *kameosa*. It still looks the same, except that cracks in its surface start to resemble a face. The other interesting thing about kameosa is that if you poured the sake out, the jar would magically re-fill itself."

Leah blinked. "A perpetual supply of sake?"

"Yes. If we still had the thing, we could test it, it'd be the best proof of—what's so funny?"

Leah stopped giggling, and took a deep breath. "And she threw it out, thinking it wasn't worth anything! Do you think I should call her and tell her?"

"And have her sue the appraiser?"

"Good point. I gather you're not feeling sorry for her, either?"

"No, I'm too busy feeling sorry for *us*. Somewhere out there, there may be a genuine magical item that could stand up to laboratory testing and peer review." I sighed. "Have you found anything else?"

"I've been reading about gaki. Do you know what they looked like?"

"Small clouds of black smoke, if I remember. Or skinny humans with swollen bellies and tiny mouths, unrecognizable as their former selves."

"Or small balls of light, like corpse candles. Or UFOs. Like the ones the kids saw go into Sims's house."

"Those could be *anything*. Or nothing. Every culture has their own explanation for will o'the wisps—ghosts, elementals, pookas, faeu boulanger, kitsune foxfire. Or swamp gas or ball lightning. What makes you think it's a gaki? If it is, what's it hungry for?"

Leah thought for a moment, then brightened. "Sake?" she suggested.

"A sake gaki?"

"Why not? Bob Sims told us that his first wife drank the stuff, that it reminded her of Japan. And she died on the street near the house. And he said he often felt as though she was still there. If the sake jar was a special sort of tsukumogami, a—what did you call it?"

"A kameosa."

"If it was always full with sake, no matter how much she drank, why wouldn't she keep coming back? And now that Julie Sims has thrown it out, what's the gaki going to do? I think she'd drink her wine and Scotch." She started giggling again, and soon, despite myself, I joined in, much to the irritation of the students in the otherwise eerily silent library.

When we were outside and could speak at a normal volume, I said, "I just wish we could find that tokkuri. Even if it's just an ordinary ceramic jar with interesting cracks in the glaze, at least we'd *know*. Now, all we can do is wonder is whether there might be a genuine magic item buried in a landfill somewhere in Washington state."

Leah shrugged, and looked down at the grass. "I don't know. I rather like that idea. Buried treasure. Didn't Oscar Wilde once say that we have so few mysteries left that we can't afford to solve any more of them?"

"Oscar Wilde also said he *didn't* want to be an Oxford Don," I reminded her.

"And you do." Her smile faded slightly. "Sims isn't in any danger from the gaki, is she? I've not heard of them taking revenge…"

"I don't think so. Most gaki are supposed to be annoying but harmless, except for the blood-drinkers. It could hurt her investment portfolio, but I won't lose any sleep over that."

"Me neither. Do you have enough stories for tonight?"

BETWEEN sips of tea and mouthfuls of food, the old Japanese man told us a story of the *futakuchi-onna*, the ghost of a woman who became so hungry that another mouth appeared in the back of her head, while her long hair grabbed food and fed it to this second mouth. When he'd finished and blown out the candle, he bummed a cigarette from a student and stood up as though to leave. "Have you ever heard of the *nurahiyon*?" I asked.

He stopped, and looked at me warily, but didn't reply. "The legends say he takes the form of an old man who enters houses at dinner time, drinks the tea and smokes the tobacco, and is so confident that no-one questions him," I continued. "They assume he's the master of the house. He's actually the master of the bakemono."

The old man smiled broadly. "I've heard of him, of course, but those kaidan are really just fables, little stories with a moral. The suppon-no-yūrei tells us not to eat too much turtle meat. Gaki tell us that it's harmful to crave things we can't have. Futakuchi-onna tells misers to feed their wives. Tsukumogami tell us to value the work of craftsmen who can create things that last, and not to be wasteful by needlessly replacing old things with new. And the nurahiyon reminds us to respect our elders and treat guests with courtesy." He bowed slightly. "Sayonara, Doctor—and thank you for the food."

He walked outside, cigarette between his fingers. A moment later, we returned to telling stories and blowing out the candles, but the aoandon didn't honour us with an appearance. We were about to go back to the hotel when Leah froze. "The knife!"

"What? What knife?"

"Sims' dagger. It's over a hundred years old too, right?"

"The kozuka? Probably much older."

"What if it's a tsukumogami? What if it wants revenge for being thrown in a dumpster?"

I stared at her, then glanced at my watch. "It's after midnight. Do you want to call Ms Sims and tell her that an antique knife is coming to kill her?"

"Well…"

"Me neither." We went back to our generic hotel room and slept until just before noon, when the homicide detectives knocked on the door.

"A WITNESS gave us a good description of you two," the cop said, "and an even better one of your car. No other visitors."

"She was alive when we left," I repeated, "sometime between two and two thirty. Have you established time of death?"

"Sometime between two and three."

I paled. "In the afternoon?"

"No, the next morning," he admitted. "You didn't go back?"

"No!"

The other cop reached under the table and produced a stack of photographs and a plastic bag. "I'm showing the suspect Exhibits A through to H," she said. "Photographs of the victim, and the weapon recovered from the scene."

I stared at the photographs of Julie Sims, feeling strangely thankful that I hadn't had breakfast. Her right hand grasped the hilt of the kozuka, which protruded from her throat; the blood splatter and the pallor suggested that it had pinpointed the carotid artery. She'd probably been asleep when she was stabbed, but her expression suggested that she'd woken up and had probably tried to remove the knife before going into shock from the pain and the loss of blood.

"Do you recognize this knife?"

I looked at the dagger closely. "It looks familiar," I admitted. "I think it's a kozuka, a samurai weapon. Bob Sims had one that was similar, but his daughter said she threw it in a dumpster when she inherited the house."

"Do you have any idea how it might have ended up in her throat while she was in bed?" asked the male cop, with feigned politeness.

"No." I answered the rest of their questions honestly while I waited for our publisher's lawyer to arrive. We were never charged: I found out later that the doors and windows were deadbolted from the inside, and the newly-installed alarm system was switched on. There were no signs of sexual assault, nor of a robbery, unless you counted some sealed but in-explicably empty bottles of expensive wine and scotch.

The kozuka was identified by other members of Bob Sims's family as a souvenir of his time in Guam, but the only prints on it were hers, and I didn't hear anyone suggest that it was a tsukumogami. Leah and I were probably the only ones who even thought it.

WE left Seattle as soon as the cops said we could, but came back a few months later and persuaded a Buddhist monk to perform an exorcism, a segaki rite, on the Sims house. It seemed like the honorable thing to do, particularly as the money from the sale was going to Bob Sims's family. The place had gone on the market already, but the buyers had moved out after a couple of weeks, and not because of the way beer kept disappear-ing from their fridge.

They said someone or something was stealing their money while they slept.

THE LADY MACBETH
BLUES

BIANCA WAS WATCHING CRYSTAL DISSECTING A RAT, carefully wielding the scalpel so as not to nick the intestines; the reek of preserved dead animal was nauseating enough that four girls and two boys had already bailed out. It was the second week of semester, and not too late for the squeamish to transfer to another class. Bianca had decided to tough it out, despite having little love or talent for science. Biotech was one of the few growth industries this side of the Mississippi, and with social security non-existent in fourteen states, the companies could afford to pick and choose. She stared as Crystal pinned the hide down to the ancient wax tray; when *she* dissected something, it actually looked the way it did in the textbook, as though it were nouvelle cuisine rather than a splatter-movie shot. Crystal looked up as though she'd heard her thinking, flashed a quick grin, and then froze. Bianca turned her head to see Mrs Hickey, her economics teacher, standing in the doorway. She looked so stricken that Bianca wondered who had died. Mrs Fish also turned to face the door.

"The Levin Bill has passed through the Senate," said Mrs Hickey, quietly. "It's just come over the net. Unless the President vetoes it, it'll become law by next January."

Bianca turned to Crystal, who had paled to a sickly yellow-grey. Mrs Fish nodded, then turned to the class. "I'll be back in a few minutes," she said, then walked—a little unsteadily—out of the room. Even after the two teachers had disappeared from sight, the room remained uncannily quiet until someone cheered. Crystal flinched.

"Come on, let's party!" said the boy who'd cheered. "Hunt's not going to veto it, and you know what that means? More jobs for all of us!"

"It means," said Crystal, coldly, "that we're going to lose some of our best teachers just because they're female and married." She knew there wasn't much chance that the President *would* act; the Levin Bill was too popular with the Promise Keepers and other traditional values groups, employers tired of paying for maternity leave and childcare, and many blue-collar unions. Hunt hadn't even protested when South Carolina passed laws preventing couples with children under sixteen (including first-trimester unborns) becoming divorced. Tough times, he'd muttered, required tough measures.

The boy hesitated, then shook his head. "Nah. The bill only prohibits government departments *hiring* married women, not—"

"That includes *re*-hiring," said Crystal. "And most teachers are on one- or two-year contracts, as are a lot of other workers. And it's not just government departments; it includes any company with more than ten full-time employees, or any employer who has or wants a government contract."

"Yeah, well," the boy blustered, his face reddening to match his hair, "that's good, too. Spreads the work around more. I'm not going to miss Hickey, or the Fish, and it's not *my* fault your father cut and run. You have to look at the big picture."

Bianca reached out and grabbed her friend's wrist, scared that she was going to throw the scalpel. "He's a stupid, ignorant pig," she said, softly.

"Sure," said the girl sitting behind her, "but now he's an *employable* stupid ignorant pig."

Crystal shrugged and smiled—a smile that was as technically perfect as the dissected rat on the tray, and just as dead. "What about your mother?" Bianca asked.

"Casual," Crystal replied, quietly. "They can fire her at any time, they always could, but there was always the prospect of her getting another job. I guess we'll have to move to some state that still has welfare."

"It's only an emergency measure," said Bianca. "If unemployment drops back below fifteen percent—"

"Which it never will," said Crystal. "How many jobs are there left that can't be done more cheaply and more efficiently by machines—or by one person and a few machines instead of five, ten, a dozen human workers? Not many, and next year, there'll be even fewer, at lower wages, and people will fight even harder to get them. Before you know it, men'll be shooting each other for the right to clean the sewers, and the government will say it's what we need to do to compete with the Asian economies, when what we really need to do is change the way we *think*."

No-one else in the room spoke, and Crystal realised that she'd raised her voice until it was audible throughout the room, and probably the corridor outside.

"You'll be okay," Bianca reassured her. "You won't have any trouble getting into college, and the supernationals will always need scientists..."

"Sure," said Crystal, sourly. "What the fuck, I never expected to get married anyway."

GETTING out of her antique wedding dress wasn't as difficult as getting in, but it was still a job for at least two people, and Bianca was glad that Crystal was still around; she wasn't ready to face Simon yet and had asked him to wait in another room while she changed. "I think I've just discovered how medieval knights must have felt. Thank Christ they don't expect me to wear it on the plane."

Crystal, who was none too comfortable in her bridesmaid's dress, laughed. "At least you'll never have to wear it again."

"No, but I'm already feeling sorry for my daughters. Ahhh!" She took a deep breath as Crystal unlaced her corset. "What's the point of making a dress that only gets worn once, anyway? Do you think we could give it to a museum?"

"Not while your in-laws are alive. What else did they give you, apart from the honeymoon?"

"Barrington House."

Crystal's face fell. "Oh, Gods. Do they expect you to *live* in it?"

"You've seen it?"

"Simon took me there, once. The place is a museum, and they won't let you change any of it. Sleeping in a slave-owner's bed is one thing— but they won't even let you have a cat, for fear it might scratch the furniture, and honey, trying to cook in an antebellum kitchen... You can't persuade Simon to ask for a transfer?"

Bianca shook her head as she struggled to remove her panty-girdle. Simon had studied and schemed too long to be given his position in R&D and wasn't about to give it up. "It'd be like begging to be disinherited. Besides, he couldn't take you."

"Yeah, well..."

"And I'd miss you, too." She looked at the clothes draped over the bed. "You know, it's hard to believe anyone except Jack the Ripper ever hated women enough to design shit like that. It wouldn't do any good, Crys. The family, the company—they own all of us."

"They don't own me."

"They own your work, and what're they doing with it?"

Crystal looked at the crossed Civil War (War Between the States, she corrected herself automatically) cavalry sabres on the bedroom wall, and grimaced. "Touche. Did they give you anything else?" she asked, hoping to change the subject.

"A GeneSafe. It's being put in tomorrow."

A second hit; Crystal bit her lip. The GeneSafe was Sanderson MedTech's profitable spin-off from the money-losing nanotech-based AIDS cure she'd helped develop. It was rapidly becoming a traditional wedding gift or sixteenth birthday present among the few wealthy enough to afford it; it was programmed with the genetic codes of the person in whom it was implanted, and usually one other—in most cases, the recipient's husband. Nanomachines would then constantly scan the body (except for the digestive tract) for foreign genetic material, which would trigger a very visible immune response. Reprogramming was possible, but required minor surgery. It served as a smart contraceptive and was as effective against sexually transmitted diseases as condoms but without the inconvenience to the male.

Crystal remembered the lecture she received after she'd designed her prototype machine. Society, her supervisor had told her, wanted a HIV vaccine, not an AIDS cure; transmission by blood transfusion and organ donation had been stopped so long ago that all those unfortunates were dead, and all new AIDS cases were regarded as self-inflicted. If they were to be cured, the diseased should at least be made to pay for the privilege. Crystal had looked into his face and resisted the urge to spit in it. "By 'society'," she said, sweetly, "I presume you mean that elite group that you and I will never be permitted to join?"

Her super, Adams, had flushed visibly despite his dark skin. "That 'elite' has paid for your work, babe, and has yet to get any visible return for that. You're lucky Old Man Sanderson believes in basic research, even if his spawn don't."

"That's because he's the only one who's lived long enough to see how it pays off," Crystal retorted. "How much has the company made out of the new lie detectors? That wouldn't have happened if they hadn't sponsored Elzanowski's pheremone research, and—"

"I know, I know," Adams had replied, wearily. It was an old argument for him, and he was usually defending the other side. "Your work will pay off eventually, and not just financially. Old Man Sanderson wants something that'll eat cancers, clean his lungs and livers and arteries, let him live the way he wants but for twice as long. That's what nanotech is going to give him, what *you're* going to give him... but that doesn't mean you're indispensable. There's a genius born every day somewhere, babe, but people with the money to pay for this sort of research—they're *real* rare."

Crystal snapped out of her reverie. "Anything else?" she asked Bianca, weakly.

"Not from Simon's parents. The rest of the family gave us—what did they call it in *The Lord of the Rings*? Something like mammoths?"

"Mathoms," replied Crystal, with a faint smile. "You'll probably get mammoths for your anniversary." Sanderson MedTech had managed to clone mammoths from frozen remains, but the embryos were still in the freezer pending a decision on who owned the copyright. The Siberian government needed the money and was expected to settle out of court eventually, but it seemed to enjoy making Americans wait.

"Albino ones, most likely," Bianca grumped. "Big hungry white elephants with perfect pedigrees. Jesus, Crys, almost everything they gave us is a registered antique, as though they expected me to try to sell some of them and run. The only new and remotely practical thing was a set of kitchen knives from Simon's grandparents. Good ones, sharp as scalpels, but isn't it supposed to be bad luck to give knives as a wedding present?"

"I don't know."

"Uh-huh." Bianca sniffed at her armpits. "Ugh. The house isn't air-conditioned either, is it?"

"Climate controlled," Crystal assured her. "It was the only way to preserve the fabrics. If anything, it's *too* cold."

Bianca nodded, and headed for the en-suite bathroom. "How often did you go there?"

"Once was enough. He's not a bad man, honey."

"No, I guess not." She sighed. "I just wish he'd stand up to his parents occasionally."

"He will."

"Then why didn't he marry *you?*" Bianca turned the shower on full blast, drowning out any possible reply Crystal might have made. Three minutes later, she stepped out of the tub, her eyebrows raised. Crystal shook her head. "They own him," said Bianca. "They own you. They own most of the fucking state, and they went to school with the people who own the other fucking states and a few other fucking countries. And now they own me. Did you see the pre-nup I had to sign?" She dried her face, and sighed. "Oh, fuck it, they say slavery's better than starving."

"They won't live forever."

"Won't they? I thought that's what you were working on?"

Crystal winced again. "If it works, it'll extend their life expectancy, but it won't do more than double it. The brain can't last any longer than that—160, 180, 200 years tops."

"Their brains are already 200 years old," said Bianca, sourly. "They think it's still 1850-something, and Abraham Lincoln's just an impertinent nobody with no future." She wiped the mist off the mirror and stared at her face. "God, I look like shit."

"You look gorgeous."

"Thanks. You're beautiful. Crys..." She wrapped the towel around herself and drew a deep breath. "You're right; Simon's not a bad man, I wouldn't have married him if he were, and you wouldn't have... uh... but I don't want to see his parents turn him into one. Will you help me?"

"Any way I can."

"Thanks." She finished drying herself, dressed for the flight, and freshened up her make-up. "Okay, let's go."

Simon and his best man were sitting in the den watching one of the news channels. A PR flack was defending the use of Sanderson MedTech's new lie detectors in screening job applicants. "These machines are ninety-nine percent reliable," he blustered, while a split screen shot showed the detector's needle unquavering. "They use nanotech to detect minute quantities of certain pheremones which are only emitted when somebody lies. We have to check our workers out thoroughly; even minor acts of negligence or sabotage can cost the—" Simon reached for the remote and muted the 3V as he heard the women walked in. "Ready?" Bianca, unable to speak, merely nodded.

Simon stood, and looked at both of them. "You're beautiful," he said, smiling broadly. "Rick, can you take Crystal home?"

BIANCA zipped her dress closed and tried to smile. "I'm sorry," said Rick.

"Hey," she said, trying a little harder, "if condoms never failed, I probably wouldn't exist."

His mouth quirked slightly. "You have an implant, don't you?"

Bianca nodded. "A GeneSafe."

"You sound worried. Is there a problem?"

"I hope not," she said, sitting back on the bed. "It's just that... if it's been triggered, it's fairly obvious."

"How obvious?"

She sighed softly as she searched for her shoes. Rick, one of Sanderson MedTech's battalion of lawyers, seemed to take care to learn only what he needed to know at the time. "Iridescent blue patches inside the eyelids, in the lymph nodes, and any places my skin's thin enough for veins to be visible. If there was enough of your semen to activate the nanos, it'll start showing in an hour or two."

Rick sat up slowly. "How long does it last?"

"Two or three days."

"And when's Simon due back?"

"Tuesday, but Simon isn't the problem. I told him about us months ago." Rick blinked. "It's his parents."

"You *told* him?"

"Of course."

"Why?"

"Why not? I don't like lying. I was fairly sure he wouldn't mind, and he doesn't. He married me mostly to get his parents off his back, and maybe keep the Sanderson empire running for another generation, though he hasn't shown much sign of that. I thought you knew that?"

Rick rubbed his face, and climbed out of the bed. "No. I don't get to talk to him as much as I used to. Does he have someone else?"

"Yes," she said, neutrally.

"Who?"

"If he hasn't told you, I'd rather not," she replied. She finished dressing and leaned over to kiss him. "Look, it'll be okay. If anything does happen, I'll let the computer screen my calls."

"I don't know," said Rick. "The Old Man has a lot of spies... Does he know about Simon and..."

"I'm sure he does—it's been going on for years—but they don't know about us."

"What do you think they'll do if they find out?"

She looked at Rick sadly. Nothing to you, she thought. Nothing to Simon, either. Something to me, maybe something to Crystal... but probably not, she's too useful to them. "They won't find out," she said, kissed him goodbye, and hurried home.

BIANCA stared at the blue spot on her wrist, then plunged her hands back into the soapy water to hide it. She stood there for nearly a minute before looking at her wrist again, in the faint hope that it was something she'd imagined.

It wasn't. It was still small and pale, and she might not have noticed it if she hadn't been looking for it, but she was sure that the spot would fluoresce faintly if she examined it under black light. It wasn't as though she hadn't been expecting it. She swore softly, and plunged her hands back into the dishwater, wishing again her in-laws had given her something practical—or at least less malicious—as a wedding present. An autochef, maybe, or even a dishwasher... but the ancient kitchen would have earned an approving nod from an Amish woman. Most of the dishes she was washing were genuine breakable antiques, and while some of the knives had monatomic edges, they were otherwise ordinary knives.

She left the dishes in the sink, wiped her hands on her apron, and walked into the bathroom to stare at her face in the mirror. Nothing yet. The silence of the dark, empty house was beginning to get on her nerves, so she reached for the 3V remote. The Chief Justice was defending the Supreme Court's decision that unmarried women could not claim damages for sexual harassment unless the alleged harasser was married. "We can't criminalise courtship behaviour," he sound-bit. A newsreader, aided by gory computer graphics, told the story of a man who'd turned up for a job interview armed with an Uzi and fired at those ahead of him in the queue. Eleven had died, three of them because they'd hesitated too long before running. Bianca shook her head and channel-hopped. Baseball, cartoons, basketball, soaps, low-g gymnastics from Mars, het softcore, het hardcore... she watched with dull amusement as the couple on the screen lit up cigarettes. Tobacco advertising had been banned everywhere but the adults only channels; she was surprised that the cigarette companies still bothered with the domestic market. More basketball, music videos, gaymale softcore, the *Star Trek* channel, more soaps. She switched back to the news channel, and walked back to the kitchen, rubbing at the spot on her wrist. Jesus, she thought, it's not as though that pre-nup gives them the right to both my kidneys or anything. I can leave if I want...

And go where? she asked herself. Unemployment was still rising, Levin Act or no Levin Act, and the price of a divorce had been increased to more than most people made in a year. Even if she'd been single, her chances of finding a job at twenty-seven were minimal. Social Security had been scrapped in every state except Alaska, Canada was deporting illegal immigrants by the truckload, her parents were living in a retirement home thanks to her income, and that only left the re-training camps. Shivering, she plunged her hands back into the water, half-wishing that Simon had gotten her pregnant. It might have mollified his parents; his mother was constantly buying gifts for the prospective grandchild, and she might even have done something to make her life less miserable if she became the mother of the Sanderson heir, though she doubted that they'd leave her in charge of her child for very long. But Simon was content to wait for his parents to die, as long as he had Crystal, and she knew she couldn't rely on Rick... and Crystal was apparently still determined to make his parents as near-immortal as possible. Bianca clenched her fists in the water, cutting her fingers on the monatomic edge of a kitchen knife. She withdrew her right hand, watching with little more than mild intellectual curiosity as blood dripped from the incredibly fine cut into the water. She stood there for several seconds, then wrapped a tea-towel around her wounded hand and walked to the bathroom.

The phone rang. She ignored it, letting the computer answer. "Bianca, dear," said her mother-in-law's sour syrupy voice, as Bianca fumbled in the cabinet for the first aid kit. "I need to come around some time before Saturday. The insurance company needs to check on the paintings, to make sure they're being maintained according to their dreary little agreement. I don't know precisely when, but I'll try to call you beforehand. Goodbye."

Bianca stood in the bathroom, staring into the mirror and trying to stop herself shaking. Simon's family found an excuse to visit and examine some part of the antique collection nearly every time Simon was out of town for more than a few days—as though they suspected her of stealing items or replacing them with forgeries. She attempted to bandage her fingers with her left hand, but after less than a minute, she dropped the kit in anger and stalked back into the kitchen and grabbed one of the knives. I'll show you bad luck, she thought, as she walked back into the sitting room and looked around at the paintings, wondering which one to start on.

She looked down at her bleeding hand. The mark on her wrist was now bright blue. She glanced at her left wrist; the mark there was smaller, but just as distinct—maybe even a little brighter. With a shriek, she stabbed at it with the knife, slicing across the vein and into the tendon. The mark remained. She drew a deep breath, and began systematically cutting along the vein. The monatomic edge sliced through the flesh easily, with almost no pain. She looked at the incision with faint approval, and then grabbed the bloody knife with her left hand and attempted to make an identical incision on her right wrist. A few seconds later, she dropped the knife at her feet, and staggered towards the phone.

"Crystal? It's Bianca. Look, I've... I need your help."

THE doctor looked down at the woman on the stretcher. "What happened?" she asked.

Crystal and the paramedic looked at each other. "We're not sure," said Crystal, cautiously. "She was unconscious when I arrived. The cut to the fingers might have been accidental—she was washing dishes by hand, including some sharp knives—but the injuries to the wrists look self-inflicted."

"You found her first?"

"Yes. She called me; her husband's in New York. I stitched her up and bandaged her as best I could with a first aid kit."

"You're a medic?"

"Geneticist, but I've had medical training."

The doctor nodded, and reached for Bianca's throat, taking her pulse, then pulled down her eyelids to look at her eyes. "This blue..."

"She has a GeneSafe," said Crystal.

"I thought so. Do you know what's triggered it?"

"It must have been the transfusion," replied Crystal. "She'd lost a lot of blood by the time I arrived; I had the paramedics give her a transfusion as soon as possible. Sometimes the GeneSafe reacts to the leucocytes, but the reaction is harmless." The doctor blinked. "I work for Sanderson MedTech. I wasn't on the team that designed this device, and I don't have one myself, but I know the principle."

The doctor nodded. "Well, if it makes you feel any better, I think you've saved this woman's life. Lucky you knew what to do."

"Yes," said Crystal softly. "Yes, it was."

BIANCA lay in the bed with her eyes closed, feigning unconsciousness. The silence, the smells of flowers and antiseptics, and the ache of the drip into her arm, was enough to tell her she was in a soundproofed private hospital room; she didn't need to see it. "Interfering nigger dyke bitch," muttered her mother-in-law. "We ought to send her to Malaysia, that'd teach her how easy she's got it here."

"We can't," replied her husband, whispering the way most people do around a sleeper or a corpse. "Adams has convinced the Old Man that she's going to make him immortal."

"Good a reason as any; the sooner he's dead, the sooner we inherit. Christ, Bobby, you could at least stand up to him behind his back, if you can't do it to his face."

"The longer he lives, the *more* we inherit," Bobby Sanderson said. "He has a real gift for making money; I know, part of it is reputation, but not all of it. When he dies—*if* he dies, come to that—Sanderson MedTech's stock is going to take a dive. We'll lose millions, maybe *billions*. Besides, if Adams is right, what do you think immortality is worth?" His wife stared at him blankly. "We can charge whatever we like for it—the government can't stop us—but it's worth a lot more than money. This is the fucking power of life and death! And while we hold the patent, *we* decide who lives and dies! Imagine what that'll mean to those assholes in Washington—or overseas. What do you think al-Sauds and the Kuwaiti sheikhs would give us for it? Or any other emperor, king, or President-for-Life? *Now* what do you think of the nigger dyke bitch?"

Bianca could almost hear her mother-in-law smiling. "I think we can put up with her for a little longer, in that case," she muttered. "But what happens if she decides to leave the company, and take her secrets with her?"

"Why should she? Adams swears she works harder than anybody else in the lab, on the same salary she started on; your hairdresser makes more than she does. And she hardly even goes home, except to feed her cats; she has a bed set up in her lab instead."

"What if *she* wants to live forever, too? Are you going to give her that?"

"It's not my decision, but if she's still useful to us, the Old Man might... and why not?"

"What if another company offers her a better deal?"

"Why would they? How would they know what she's done; *we're* not telling anybody. Look, we'll find a way to keep her here—why are you so worried, anyway?"

"Simon spends too much time in that lab."

Sanderson laughed. "What's wrong with that? The more he knows about R&D, the better."

"What if he's sleeping with her?"

"*Droit de seigneur*," replied Sanderson, drily. "Or is it *de rigeur*? Anyway, it's as old as—well, I'm not a historian, but Jesus, all work and no play... or are you scared she's going to bring a pup along to one of your D.A.R. meetings? They *both* have more sense than that." He always tried to be out of town whenever his wife and her Daughters of the American Revolution cronies gathered; marrying an aristocrat hadn't been *his* idea. The Old Man had arranged the wedding to win favour with her father, then the state's junior senator and heir to a dwindling but still prestigious tobacco empire. Bobby Sanderson sometimes wondered why she'd cooperated; it was obvious that neither of them had married for love.

"What about you?" she asked.

"Huh?"

"How much have you been exercising *your* droit de seigneur?"

"Jesus, you've got a suspicious mind lately! None since we were married," he lied. "Before that, I didn't keep count." He glanced at his Rolex rather than meet her eyes. "Where the fuck is Simon? He should've been here half an hour ago. I'm going out for a smoke; call me when he comes in, or when she wakes up, whichever comes first."

ADAMS looked nervously around the boardroom, suddenly conscious that his best suit probably cost less than most of the neckties he could see, and cleared his throat. "I'm not sure what rumours you've heard, but we do *not* have the secret of immortality, nor have we discovered the fountain of youth. What we have is a nanotechnology-based device similar to the GeneSafe, but far more sophisticated. It prevents and reverses the growth of cancers, removes blockages from arteries, fat from around the heart, tar and other crap from the lungs, and so on. It may even be able to prevent or at least delay the onset of Alzheimer's disease, though we haven't done enough testing on human subjects to be sure." He decided not to mention that most of their test subjects had been chimps, pigs and hamsters; few of the directors knew enough biology to understand the ways in which these animals were similar to humans. "It won't repair all types of existing damage, users won't look any younger though they should *feel* healthier, and some of us may already have over-stressed our bodies beyond it's power to heal, but barring accidents it should increase normal life expectancy by about a century." Silence suddenly fell over the room. Adams glanced at the Old Man, who was sitting at his left. "We haven't told marketing about this, of course, but in the meantime, we're calling it the Centurion."

"Thank you, Dr Adams," said the Old Man, as Adams sat down. "Of course, gentlemen, we can't just release a device like this onto the market *ad hoc*. The country is already paying too much in benefits to unproductive retirees; they just have too many votes." There were a few loyal chuckles from around the great oaken table. "What would happen to the economy if all of these people were to live for another hundred years? We're paying too much damn tax already! No, this has to be kept secret. It will, of course, be available to all of you gentlemen, and your families, for the bargain basement cost of a quarter million per, plus a check-up every five years at half the going rate. Note that this price will *not* be offered to anybody else; Dr Adams and I have worked out a scale based on five percent of the buyer's net worth, with a minimum price of half a million, and a top of twenty million. Obviously there are many potential clients who could pay much more, but there are more important considerations than short term profit. Despite Dr Adams's understandable caution, this *might* be immortality; who knows how medtech might improve over the next century? There are many people who could afford a Centurion, at any price we might set, that we may not want around for that long, overpaid entertainers and similar parasites, as well as some heads of state." He smiled frostily. "It's imperative that we use it carefully, selectively. I suggest we start with a maximum of one thousand, to be implanted over the next four years, and then reduce production to fewer than a hundred a year. It would, for example, be of no advantage to us to sell one to the President when he has only three years left to serve. But senators, congressmen, judges, other politicians and administrators who can continue to serve well into the next century..." he showed his transplanted teeth in a grin, "whose interests and concerns are parallel to ours, and whose gratitude can be depended upon, thanks at least in part to the need for regular check-ups..." He paused again, watching smiles break out across the room as the directors began thinking. "Thanks to Dr Adams's team, we need no longer be tied to short-term goals, we can make plans for the next century in the hope of seeing them come to fruition. We can be sure of *stable* government, not the current chaos. We can choose the next century's leaders *now*."

He took a deep breath. "For too long, cheap medical care has enabled less productive members of our society to survive into their second century, while the world's elite, the decision-makers, have been overworking and overstressing ourselves into early graves, wasting all that experience and learning. History has been rewritten by those too young to remember it, dishonouring great men and fine traditions..." He coughed; his face was turning red, and Adams watched him with genuine alarm, wondering if he was going to have a heart attack before they'd had a chance to implant his Centurion. The Old Man grabbed a glass of water, sipped it slowly, and continued more quietly. "Of course, there's another, more immediate advantage. You'll now be working for yourselves, getting what you deserve, instead of it going to your widows or your ungrateful heirs. Now—" He tried to laugh, but it became another coughing fit. "Sorry. Now, Dr Adams and I have prepared a list of potential clients, which I'll now hand around for everybody's approval—but for God's sake, remember that we have to keep this as quiet as possible! I know the rumours are already circulating; lie, if you have to. We can implant up to two of these a day without breaching security. The sooner I have your cheque, the sooner you get onto Dr Adams's list. Any questions?"

BIANCA spent two weeks in the hospital before she was discharged, and had been home for five days when Crystal visited. "Sorry I couldn't get here sooner," said her friend. "We've been completely snowed under at the lab..."

"I know," Bianca replied levelly, as Crystal collapsed into a rocking chair that had once belonged to Jefferson Davis. "Simon told me. Do you want a drink?"

"Coffee?"

"Fine." She walked into the antiquated kitchen. "Simon's told me about the... what are they calling it? The Centurion? Was that your project?"

"*Mea culpa, mea culpa, mea maxima culpa.*"

"What?"

"Most of it, yes. Why?"

"He told me they add about a hundred years to your life expectancy. Is that true?"

"In some cases. They haven't given you one, have they?"

"No," replied Bianca, dully. "Simon's father said I'm too young to need one, and his mother told him they wouldn't waste it on someone who'd already tried to kill herself. Maybe after a few years." She poured boiling water over the coffee bags and waited for them to brew. "What about you?"

"Too young, like you, and I can't afford one. Anyone under fifty either pays ten million plus or waits in line. You wouldn't believe the people who've visited the lab this week." She chuckled.

"No, probably not," said Bianca. She placed the coffee mugs on a silver tray, removed a small revolver from a drawer and slipped it into her apron pocket, then headed back towards the sitting room.

"Thanks," said Crystal, as she took her mug. "So, how're you feeling?"

Bianca sat opposite her, put the tray down on a small table, and drew the pistol. Crystal stared at it, her eyes wide. "You know," said Bianca, sourly, "before I went to hospital, none of the guns in this place were loaded? I made sure. I knew they hadn't been plugged or anything, the Old Man wouldn't let anyone do that to a firearm, but when I come back, surprise! Loaded firearms everywhere. They didn't bother with the old black powder weapons, but there's still enough for a modest massacre. I guess someone's trying to send me some sort of message." She looked at the pistol sadly, then pointed it at Crystal's face. "*You stupid fuck, do you know what you've done?*"

"Put the gun down."

"*The fuck* I will! *You sold out! You sold out to them!* Thanks to you, those monsters are going to live for centuries like fat fireproof leeches, until they own or control everything and no-one else can remember a world without them!"

Crystal shook her head, and wondered if she could tip the chair backwards far enough to get out of the line of fire. Probably not. "I thought you knew me better than that. Jesus, Senator Levin's getting his Centurion next week; do you think I want *him* to live for another hundred years? Put the gun down, and I'll explain." Bianca didn't move. "Okay. To answer your question, yes, I know *exactly* what I've done—much better than anyone else does. Oh, the Centurions do what Adams has been telling people they do—but more. You know those new lie detectors the company is making?"

Bianca blinked, then grimaced. "Yes. They're using them to screen job applicants and anyone who needs legal aid."

"Yeah, I know. Do you know how they work?"

"They detect some pheromone that people only emit when they're lying, right?"

"Right. So does the Centurion; it's an extra feature I didn't bother telling anyone about. When the nanos detect this pheremone, they head for the brain. Enough nanos in the brain, and they cause aneurysms. You also get the same blue patches inside the eyelids and in the lymph nodes that you have when a GeneSafe is activated. If you ignore this warning and keep lying, the aneurysms will rupture, causing massive hemorrhagic strokes, which should be fatal in seventy to ninety percent of cases." Bianca stared at her, horrified. "Of course, you have to lie a *lot* to cause this degree of build-up; consistently, and over quite a long period. I'm not expecting the first deaths for more than a year, and most of the Old Man's pet politicians should survive until the primaries. Longer, maybe, if they notice the warning signs, assume they're sick, and pull out of the race. It should increase life expectancy at least slightly for *some* users, though not too many, and if there's anyone on the list who's rich *and* honest, anyone who wouldn't secretly sell poison baby food if there was a buck in it, they might even live for the full two hundred years."

The pistol wavered slightly. "Fortunately," Crystal continued, "most of the people buying Centurions are already old enough that it'll take a long time for anyone to guess that the device may be causing the strokes, even if they can cross-reference the deaths with a list of clients—Adams is bright enough, but we can trust him not to stick his neck out or jump to any conclusions, and the Old Man probably won't live long enough to detect a pattern himself. Even if someone becomes suspicious, there's no known way—yet—to remove enough of the nanos to prevent this happening, so the only other safety measure possible is not to lie. Besides, the company will publicly deny that any such device exists... can't you just imagine the Board of Directors sitting in some Congressional hearing, swearing that their product is perfectly safe until they literally turn blue in the face? I wonder if any of them will have the grace to drop dead with their hands still on the Bible? Gives a new meaning to laying them in the aisles."

Bianca stared at her, her face dead white—then she carefully placed the pistol on the table so that it pointed away from both of them. "Is this true?"

"Get a lie detector and I'll say exactly the same thing," Crystal replied, more calmly than she felt. She waited for several seconds—it felt like hours—until Bianca nodded. "Okay. I'm sorry I doubted you, Crys."

"Forget it. I knew I'd fooled nearly everyone, but I didn't expect to fool *you*. Jesus, you had me scared." She began laughing, nervously at first, and then more heartily as Bianca joined in. Suddenly, Bianca stopped laughing, and her face turned pale again. "What about Simon?" she asked.

"Simon?"

"He's on the list for a Centurion—a fair way down the list, but he's a Sanderson, and he turns forty next year. Are we going to tell him?"

"Oh Jesus," Crystal said. "Do you think he'd tell his parents if we did?"

"I think he would," whispered Bianca. "He lies to them about you, but this... I think he'd tell everyone." Crystal nodded, her expression bleak. "What do we do? Do we let him get a Centurion? Do we ask him to keep this a secret, too, even if it means lying? Do we wait until he puts us on the list for Centurions, too? What the *fuck* do we do?"

"I don't know, honey," said Crystal. She looked around the dingy antique-littered room, and then shook her head. "I just don't know."

EMPATHY

"AND THIS IS THE DEATH CELL," said the guide. They'd split us up into two groups when we started the tour, and the other group had gotten the cute Asian girl while we'd gotten the droning old fossil who looked like he'd either been a guard here or an inmate. His broad Australian accent didn't make his narration any more interesting, either, just more difficult to follow. I'd learned to tone down my own accent; some Australians still seem to want revenge on the English for sending their ancestors here, even though they maintain it's the best place on Earth. "Anybody condemned to death was brought here before an execution and constantly watched while the hangman prepared the gallows. This used to be a couple of hours—they were woken up at half past five, and hanged at eight, usually on a Monday morning. I'm sure some of you face Monday mornings with the same sort of enthusiasm." No-one laughed, and the guide cleared his throat. "In the fifties, it was decided that to avoid the risk of executing someone who was legally insane, a team of three psychiatrists would sit here and watch the condemned man for the three days before he was hanged. If, at the end of that time, it was decided that he was insane, he'd be granted a stay of execution. At least, that was the theory. I don't think it ever happened."

"Having three psychs watch me for three days would be enough to send *me* insane," muttered Callum quietly.

The guide either ignored him or was too deaf to hear him, but a middle-aged woman shot him a dirty look. "You thaid 'condemned man'", lisped the girl with the pierced tongue and lip, who'd checked into the hostel just before we had and was standing in front of the group. "Weren't there women hanged here, too?"

"Only one," said the guide, "and that was in 1909, before psychiatry became fashionable." He sounded disapproving; I was about to ask if he'd been there as a witness, but Michelle saw my mouth open and trod on my foot as a warning. The guide cleared his throat. "Now, when the hangman had finished setting up the gallows, making sure that the trap-door worked properly and adjusting the length of the rope to suit the weight of the man—or woman—" he added, looking at Miss Metal, "then the condemned was walked from this cell to the gallows, which is what we'll do now, if you'll follow me. It's only a short walk—most of the condemned were out of here, shackled, hooded, and hanged in less than a minute. And that's despite the fact that most of them had a glass of whiskey beforehand. Shall we see if we can beat that?"

We tagged along as he led the way to the gallows, where the guide showed us the heavy rope with the rubber flange, which he informed us was easier to adjust precisely than the traditional noose. "If you get the length of the drop wrong," he explained, "it can either tear someone's head off—not that that ever happened here—or slowly strangle them. Now, if you look at the wall there, you can see where their feet kicked the wall as they died."

Michelle had been looking more than a little queasy before this, and on hearing this she gripped Cal's arm and closed her eyes, probably expecting him to guide her around. Tongue-stud noticed this and smirked. I'm not as sensitive or squeamish as Michelle, but I wasn't feeling great either; I knew I couldn't be smelling anything dead, or the shit and piss and other stuff that would have dripped onto the floor from all those corpses, but I couldn't help imagining that that's exactly what I *could* smell. I was enormously relieved when we were led from there to the old church, and Michelle seemed to recover somewhat. The guide stood next to the altar, pointing out how the sixth commandment on the wall had been amended to "Thou Shalt Do No Murder" because it was thought that "Thou Shalt Not Kill" was inappropriate under the circumstances. He continued to talk as though delivering a sermon, then directed us to look through the window. I did, but I couldn't see anything particularly interesting.

We were walking across one of the yards when Michelle turned around and looked back at the chapel. "What's up?" I asked.

"I thought I felt someone watching me," she said, staring at the window. The guide stopped, looked in the same direction, and smiled slightly.

"See anything?" he asked.

"A face, in the window," she said. "A woman's face. It's not—"

"Anybody else see it?" he asked.

"I can," I said. Slightly more than half of the people in our tour group, including Metalmouth, nodded or muttered or grunted assent; Cal said, "No," and a few people—most of them old or, like him, wearing sunglasses—indicated that they didn't.

"That's the same window you were looking through earlier," said the guide. "You can't see it from inside, but there's some sort of flaw in the glass that reflects the light so that it looks like a face. There's supposed to be some part of our brain that sees faces when they're not there—the man in the moon, the face on Mars, things like that."

"Pareidolia," I said, automatically.

"What?"

"The condition. Thinking things look like human faces. It's called pareidolia."

The guide looked strangely at me, then droned on, "Others, of course, say it's a ghost. Funny thing is, it's supposed to have appeared the day after a woman was hanged here."

Cal snorted; Steel Life shuddered slightly and giggled.

"Her name was Martha Rendell," the guide continued. "She was the only woman ever hanged in the prison. She murdered her stepson, and possibly her two stepdaughters, though she was never charged with that. Like most murderesses, her case became what they call a cause célèbre," I winced at his pronunciation, "because a lot of people thought she was innocent." He shrugged.

"Was she?" asked one of the old women.

"There's no reason to think so. I won't deny some people here were wrongly convicted, like the two blokes who did time for murders that were really done by Eric Edgar Cooke, but he was hanged too—the last man executed here, in fact—while they weren't. Anyway, if you'll come this way, our next stop is the flogging post…"

STAYING in a backpacker hostel that had once been a prison had been Cal's idea, of course, but we'd gone along with it, having previously stayed in a tall ship and a converted brewery in Stockholm, a lighthouse in North Wales, a castle on the Rhein, and railway carriages in Sydney. Fremantle Prison, an early Victorian limestone bastard product of military engineering and convict labour with later additions, hadn't looked too bad from the outside—not very different from my old prep school, in fact. The structure was ancient by Australian standards and heritage-listed, so they couldn't tear it down, and it was too big and too central to just be used as another museum in a small city that already had at least four. Some of the buildings had been turned into artists' studios and a children's literature centre, but the central location made it a logical choice for tourist accommodation. I probably wouldn't have been reluctant to stay there if I hadn't made the mistake of taking the somewhat grisly guided tour on our first day.

It didn't help that Cal and Michelle weren't getting on. It's bad enough sharing a house with a happy couple when you're single; traveling with a couple on the verge of disintegrating is much, much worse. Their relationship had been shaky even before we left home, and it had done nothing but worsen since then. While all three of us had interests in common, Michelle preferred shops, art galleries and theatre to sport, pubs and concerts, which sometimes resulted in compromises that didn't make any of us happy. She also seemed to be allergic to almost everything in Australia, with the pollen or mites or something aggravating her asthma: she had coughing fits if there was too much tobacco smoke in the air, she was eating almost nothing but salads and drinking only bottled water, and she tired easily if we had to walk any distance, much less do anything more physically demanding. Cal had complained that she was also snoring thunderously, and I suspected that unless she was into erotic asphyxia (which I doubted), she'd also lost any enthusiasm for sex. Cal had been eyeing up other women more and more obviously as we'd headed west from Sydney, and he certainly seemed riveted by Miss Bodymod. I found her two-tone hair (the left side unconvincing blonde, brassier than Michelle's; the right as dark as Cal's own) and the rings and studs in her face off-putting, but presumably he didn't, or maybe he hadn't yet looked up that far: she was nearly as tall as him, much bustier than Michelle and obviously braless, and Cal was unabashedly a breast man.

Michelle left the tour of the prison museum before it finished at the rifle range, and I was tempted to join her, but Cal had already made some snide comments about the amount of time I was spending with her rather than him, so I joined him in firing a gun at human silhouettes. He wasn't as good a shot as he would have liked: I matched his score, but was careful not to beat it. Miss Metal fared much better, saying as she handed the rifle back to the guide that she'd grown up on a farm and was used to killing things. She introduced herself as Letha, or maybe it was Lisa—the lisp made it difficult to be sure.

It being a Friday evening, we went to the markets and then on a pub crawl around town, with Letha tagging along. At breakfast the next morning, Cal looked fatigued as well as grouchy, and not quite as immaculately groomed as usual. "First snoring, and now nightmares," he muttered, jerking his head at Michelle. "Woke up screaming, and not in a good way."

Michelle stared bleary-eyed into her yoghurt as she stirred it, then said quietly, "I dreamed I was murdering someone. Children."

Letha, who'd joined us at our table for breakfast uninvited, looked intrigued, her dark green eyes almost gleaming. "How?"

"Poison," she said. "I was smearing something on the backs of their throats. I think it was some sort of acid."

"Probably caused by your sore throat," I suggested; there was a rasp to her voice, and a distinct wheeze as she breathed. She shrugged, and Letha nodded: Cal merely looked unimpressed. "What's the plan for today?" I asked, happy to change the subject.

"The thipwreck mutheum?" suggested Letha. "They have what's thuppothed to be a great exhibit on the *Batavia* mathacre, including the thkeleton of one of the victimth: you can see the woundth in his thkull. Or there'th another mutheum, uthed to be an athylum; there's thtill a padded cell there, and it's thuppothed to be haunted." She'd changed her 'You've Been a Bad Boy: Go to My Room' T-shirt from the previous day before for a black low-cut vest and a skull-and-crossbones pendant.

"I want to check my e-mail," said Michelle, when no-one else expressed any particular enthusiasm for Letha's plan.

"Yeah, me too," said Cal. "After that, isn't there a football game on in town?"

Letha nodded. "Tharkth verthuth Tigerth. You like Authie Ruleth?"

"Never seen it, except on telly—we couldn't get into a game in Melbourne—but I'm interested. You?"

"Maybe," she said, twirling a lock of her blonde hair around a black fingernail. "But the internet café firtht?"

"Yeah. Sure."

By the time we returned from lunch (Letha ordered fried squid tentacles, then let them dangle from her mouth and claimed she was Cthulhu), there was a huge queue outside the oval gates and Michelle begged off, saying she'd had to stand in line too long at the fish and chip shop and was already tired. The prison/hostel was only a short walk away up a fairly gentle slope, but I offered to go with her: I didn't feel any strong desire to see the game, having heard that the word 'rules' in 'Australia Rules' was used in the same sort of way that Aussies call a tall man 'tiny' or a redhead 'blue'.

Cal sneered, but didn't argue, and we left them there. We were nearly at the gates when Michelle asked, "Do you remember what the guide said yesterday about the woman who was hanged here? Martha Rendell?"

"Some of it."

"I did some research on the web while we were in the café. The guide was right about the case being controversial: it was the local equivalent of the Lizzie Borden trial, or the case of that woman who said her baby was taken by a dingo. She said she was innocent, and a lot of people believed her; they said she didn't get a fair trial, that an all-male court system found her guilty because she was living with a man who'd left his wife. The man was also charged, but acquitted. Even the people who thought she *did* do it were never able to suggest a motive."

"Do you think she did it?"

"I don't know. I don't know enough about the case. But maybe there's something in our culture that insists on sacrificing an innocent woman, every now and then."

"Lizzie Borden was acquitted," I pointed out, "and the dingo baby woman, Chamberlain, had her conviction overturned." I wouldn't have remembered the name if dingo jokes hadn't been all the rage in England at the time of her trial, even though most of us wouldn't have known what a dingo was a year earlier. "Besides, they haven't executed anyone here since that serial killer, Cooke, more than forty years ago—and they abolished the death penalty twenty years after that. You're being needlessly morbid."

"Am I?" she asked. "When I woke from my nightmare, Cal tried to hold me, but that felt worse, it felt like there was a monster on top of me, I screamed even louder until he got off me…"

I couldn't think of a safe answer to that, so I said nothing. Cal's been a friend of mine since junior school; he's charming when he wants to be, very good at getting his own way, but he can also be manipulative, jealous, vindictive, self-centred, and amoral. His girlfriend before Michelle used to say that his name was a misprint and he should've been called 'Callous'. I didn't know how much of this Michelle knew—they'd been living together for just under two years—so I just held the door open for her, then followed her into the hostel lobby. "Are you feeling okay now?"

"Yes. I don't know whether it's my asthma or the weather down here or what the problem is…" It was ridiculously hot for what was meant to be the end of winter—hotter than it was back in London, where it was summer! "… but I really feel like shit. I think I'll just lie down for a while, maybe take a nap. You go have a good time."

MICHELLE looked even more distraught the next morning at breakfast, and Cal even more sleep-deprived and sour. Letha had sat down at our table again, catty-corner from me, and when Michelle and Cal joined us, they could neither sit opposite each other or side-by-side. They sat there silently, stirring their tea—she clockwise, he widdershins—for nearly a minute, then she stood and walked over to the reception desk. Cal, sitting across from Letha, took a sip of his tea before saying, "You'll have to excuse Shelley. We didn't get much sleep last night."

Letha raised a plucked eyebrow: I wondered if he'd forgotten how much Michelle hated being called Shelley.

"Another bloody nightmare," Cal explained. "She woke me, and neither of us… well, we're going to ask for separate rooms for tonight, and until she gets over this. I've got to go and book. Back in a minute."

Neither of us spoke until he was well out of earshot, then Letha leaned across the table and murmured, "Thith could be your chanth."

I suspect I sneered. "You obviously think it's yours."

She shrugged, and that massive bosom shuddered. "I'm thtaying in Perth—even if I can't find a job, I'm not going back home. I've had enough of farmboyth. And I'm not looking for anything lathting, any more than he ith. I don't think the two of you would latht, either—rebound relathionthipth almotht never do—but at leatht you'd both get laid."

I opened my mouth, made several false starts at a response, and finally came out with, "Is that your answer to everything?"

"No, but it might make you both feel better for a while. Or it might not, but you won't know if you don't try, and I don't think you get many offerth. Ten or twenty yearth from now, women your own age might think you're a good catch, dependable and rethpectable and thafe, but now… nah. Girlth my age want thomebody more like him, thomebody thort of mad, bad and dangerouth to know."

She laughed at my expression. I hadn't expected her to know that quote, or any other: she seemed more the sort who'd think that Lady Caroline Lamb was someone's pet sheep or a puppet from a kid's show.

"You think that's what Michelle wants?"

"Maybe not quite *that* dangerouth," she admitted. "I think the'th re-alithing that the'th out of her depth, and might need rethcuing, and she's embarrathed about it. But be careful—the might drag you down with her, inthtead."

THERE was no question of Michelle and Cal spending the day together; Cal announced his intention of going paintballing with some others from the hostel, while Michelle and I headed for the quiet of the art gallery. From there, we headed to King's Park, a huge plot of mostly un-spoiled bushland close to Perth, the river and the university. The view from the elevated walkway was spectacular, though the city skyline was marred by the ugliest skyscraper I've ever seen—a glass and aluminium folly like an anorexic Gothic cathedral complete with flying buttresses, a bastard child of Lang's *Metropolis* and Giger's *Alien*. Many of the older buildings had been gutted and their heritage-listed facades stuck to the fronts of office towers, giving the impression of a town of masks. We stared at this false-face city in horrified disbelief for as long as we could bear, then turned our attention to the river. "I did some more research this morning," Michelle rasped. "About Martha Rendell. They say she killed her stepchildren—three of them—by painting the backs of their throats with hydrochloric acid. She protested until the end that she was treating them for diphtheria."

I didn't know what to say to that, so I said nothing.

"This morning, I dreamed I was on trial for murder," she continued. "They were saying the same things about me that they said about Martha Rendell—the prosecutor called her a sadist and a pervert; the judge described her as a 'moral deformity'. I told them I was innocent, but no-one would believe me, and then I woke up with Cal shaking me..." She was silent for a moment, then added, "It didn't end there. I mean, my nightmare did, but hers didn't. Even executing her wasn't enough for them. You remember Cooke, the serial killer, the last man they hanged here?"

"I've heard of him."

"They're in the same grave in Fremantle cemetery. They buried him, a serial killer, the last man they found evil enough to hang, on top of her."

I DIDN'T sleep well that night. It was obvious that the three of us couldn't continue to travel together, nor to share a house. Cal was pretty good at looking after himself, while I wasn't so sure about Michelle. The problem that kept me awake was, how to stay with her without looking as though I were stalking her.

It was nearly twenty to nine when I finally made it down to the café for breakfast; Cal and Letha were sitting together, talking and occasionally eating, but there was no sign of Michelle. I sat down and asked, "We still off today?"

"Yeah. Taking the ferry out to, what's it called, Rottenest? Staying there for a couple of days before flying up to Broome. You coming along?"

"I don't know," I admitted. "Is Michelle?"

"Dunno. Ask her."

"She's not here."

"Probably still asleep, then."

I glanced at my watch, then walked to Michelle's room. Maybe if I'd hurried...

CONVINCING the manager to open Michelle's room took several minutes, but less time than it took to cut her down from the ceiling and remove the pillowcase from over her head so that we could be sure it *was* Michelle.

The doctor estimated the time of death as shortly after eight o'clock, Monday morning. No-one ever explained the smell of whiskey.

WE had the funeral in Perth, which I suppose is as good a place as any for one, though I persuaded her parents that she'd prefer Karrakatta cemetery (which we'd spotted from the train) to Fremantle. The coroner eventually ruled it a suicide, to Cal's obvious relief. I'd moved out of the hostel by this time and into another a few blocks away, and Letha had relocated to Perth in search of fresh prey, but Cal had stayed in his cell-like room until they said we were free to leave the state. I only saw him at the funeral and the inquest, and they were more than enough, but I went back to the old prison the day before we flew back to London, to take one last look at the place where Michelle had died.

When Cal called out, to say the shuttle had arrived, I was standing in the courtyard and staring at the church window, sure that I could now see *two* faces. I turned away from the glass and took a long look at Cal. I thought I saw a vague flicker of regret, maybe even shame, but maybe I was wrong.

Maybe it was only pareidolia.

VALLEY OF THE SHADOWS

THE HERMIT WAS DOZING, but he woke as soon as he heard hoofbeats on the path through the ravine. Two riders, by the sound of them, and he had no doubt they were coming his way; the ravine didn't lead to anywhere else that anyone would want to go. He looked around his cave and grabbed his crossbow and his battered Bible. He nocked the bow and hid it under a thin blanket beside him, then let the Bible fall open to the psalms. It was too dark to read in the cave, but the hermit understood the value of appearances.

The cave was located high on a cliff face, and the only path that reached it was too narrow for horses, or even for faint-hearted goats. Any sound made in the valley echoed from the cliff opposite into the cave's small entrance; the hermit listened to the men's voices, only slightly distorted, and to their breathing. They sounded weary, and not angry, except maybe with the terrain. The hermit waited until a shadow fell across the entrance of the cave before calling out, in Latin, "Who's there?"

It was the younger man who replied, also in Latin. "I am Forese, squire to Sir Charles. We seek the hermit Anselmo. Are you he?"

"I am," the hermit replied, blandly. "Why do you seek to disturb an old man who desires only solitude?"

"Do you speak French?" called the knight.

"Not well," the hermit lied; he spoke it well enough, but tended to lapse into *langue d'oc* when he did, and that could prove fatal. In Latin, he continued, "But I understand it, if it's all you speak. Come in, before the perytons see you."

The first one to enter was a broad-shouldered stocky man whose mail coif and grizzled beard didn't entirely hide the scars on his face; the hermit judged him to be somewhere between forty and fifty, and though his helm and hauberk appeared new and expensive, he wore them as though they weighed—and signified—nothing. His squire was younger, probably no more than sixteen; his armour and surcoat were of the same quality as the older man's, but because he wore them with obvious pride, they appeared newer. Probably a younger son of one of the Florentine merchant families, the hermit realised; well-born, well-educated, well-trained, and naive. Good. "You've seen the perytons?" he asked, before Sir Charles could speak.

"Not often," replied the hermit, diffidently. "I rarely leave this cave while the sun shines, and they never fly at night. They don't trouble me here, and I take care not to trouble them." Sir Charles stared into the gloom, watching the hermit carefully. "I'm afraid I can't offer you much hospitality," said the hermit. "The stream barely provides enough fish for my own needs, but few people come this way. Where are you bound?"

"It's the perytons we seek," said Forese, his eyes shining. "Where may we find them?"

"If you keep going out by day, they'll find you, but that's likely to be the end of the matter. Why do you seek them?"

"This is my land," said Sir Charles, curtly. "It was given me by the Count. We've been riding through it for days, and haven't seen another living soul in all that time. We've passed through villages, or places where villages have been, but they've been deserted."

The hermit shrugged. The soldier's words and Navarrese accent confirmed his suspicions that the man had been but recently elevated to knighthood after a long career as a mercenary. "Perytons never kill but one man each in their lives, or so the sages say; if your estate is empty, it's because it's poor farmland and far from the pilgrim trail, so it's never been an easy place to make a living. Most of the men from the villages nearby went to war when called upon, and few returned. Many of the women left, too; those who stayed were slaughtered when the armies came through, or by bandits after the wars had ended." It was a fine distinction, but one he suspected the knight would appreciate. "Only after the bandits left did I see the perytons."

"What do you know about them?" demanded the knight.

"Only what I've seen, and what the sages have written. They look like deer with the wings of birds, and gather in flocks or herds. They fly well, but only by day. They prefer large rocky islands or dry, mountainous lands like these, with few people. They eat grass and plants from ledges and cracks that are beyond the reach of goats; that much I've seen."

"And do they cast the shadows of men, as the tales say?" asked Forese, eagerly.

"They cast shadows, I can tell you that, and smaller shadows than they should, but whether they are the shadows of men, I don't know." He shrugged again. "Some say they are the ghosts of evil men, of men who died far from home, or of men who died violently or by drowning and who never received a proper funeral... but Latin has but one word, *umbra*, for 'shadow' and 'ghost'," he said slowly, in hesitant French, then switched back to Latin, "and maybe someone misunderstood. It's also said by some that they came from Atlantis; that, being ghosts, they cannot be harmed by swords or other weapons; and that they attack men on sight and eat their hearts so that they can regain men's bodies. How much of this is true, I do not know; I can only swear to what I've seen."

The squire seemed disappointed. "But they've left you alone?" asked the knight, suspiciously.

"I've become good at hiding," replied the hermit, drily. "As I told you, I rarely leave this cave by day, and while they've trapped me in here many times by waiting outside, they've never come in. The entrance may be too narrow for their antlers, and while I'm sure they can run, they seem to avoid places where they cannot spread their wings."

The knight nodded, as though he'd made a decision. "We'll camp here for tonight," he said. "We have some food you can share. Tomorrow, you can take us to where you've seen these creatures. Forese, go and get the saddlebags." The hermit watched the squire leave, and sighed.

Forese returned a few minutes later, with hard bread, hard cheese, dried meat, dried figs, skins of wine and water, and a small lamp which made a faint puddle of light in the centre of the cave. The hermit chewed on a piece of bread as well as his few teeth allowed. "Do you know the tale of the labours of Hercules?" he asked the squire. Forese nodded. "Does Sir Charles?"

"I've heard of Hercules," said the knight, when the question had been translated. "Some old Greek, strong enough to carry the sky. What of him?"

"Hercules slew many monsters," said the hermit, quietly. "After he killed his own children in a fit of madness, he was advised by the Pythoness, an oracle, to perform twelve labours for King Eurystheus, after which he would be granted immortality. But Eurystheus feared Hercules, knowing that he wanted his kingdom, and sent him to slay monsters such as the Nemean Lion, whose skin was impervious to any weapon, and the Hydra, a great venomous serpent with many heads. No doubt he did this hoping that Hercules would be slain; he even sent him to Hell to claim the demon Cerberus."

"You think the Count wants me dead?" asked the knight, quietly.

"I don't know the Count," replied the hermit, "and I mean him no disrespect, but no doubt he asked something of you in return for this land; some form of tribute, perhaps?"

"I'm to bring the body of one of the perytons back to him," replied the knight, a faint growl in his voice, "and to keep the land safe for my tenants."

The hermit popped a dried fig into his mouth in an attempt to hide a smile. "He wants the peryton for your coat of arms?" The knight glared at him, then nodded sullenly. It was easy for the hermit to guess the rest; the old soldier had been useful to the Count during one or more of the battles that had ravaged Tuscany in recent years, too useful to discard entirely during a period of tenuous peace, but also something of an embarrassment. He suspected the knight had guessed this much, too. He wondered idly whether the knight had a pretty wife or daughter that the Count would have liked to know better. "It seems a great risk for very little gain." He noticed that Forese seemed reluctant to translate this, but Sir Charles didn't erupt as he'd half-expected; he merely bit down on a piece of dried meat, chewed for a moment, then washed the mouthful down with wine.

"I've been a soldier for most of my life," he told the hermit. "A soldier with land is a knight; a soldier without land is merely another mercenary. I've fought for less." He cut a bite-sized piece off the chunk of dried meat with his dagger. "You say Hercules fought monsters for his immortality? I'll do the same for mine—to leave something for my sons apart from my arms and my horses." He stabbed at the meat, then offered it to the hermit, who shook his head. "You don't like meat?" asked the knight.

The hermit attempted a smile, showing what remained of his teeth. "I haven't had any in many years," he replied. "I doubt I could chew it." He paused, then said, "If you're determined to fight the perytons, you'll never be able to do it with swords. Even if weapons can harm them, and many tales say they can't, the creatures are fast and strong, and there are many of them. But there may be a way."

"Go on."

"There are cracks in the rocks, and crevices, where you can hide and they cannot reach you," the hermit continued. "From there, you could hurl javelins at them. If it doesn't harm them, you'll still be safe, and you can escape when night falls."

Sir Charles smiled. "I have a crossbow; would that work?"

"If any weapon would," replied the hermit, with a slight shrug.

Forese turned white. "Crossbows? The Pope issued an anathema against crossbows—"

"Only when used against Christian souls," growled Sir Charles. "They're still used for hunting, and against heathens. What do you think, old man? Do these perytons have Christian souls?"

The hermit was silent for a moment. "If you can judge them by their shadows, they may have men's souls, but even the most evil and unChristian men may have men's shadows."

Sir Charles smiled, and cut a piece of cheese, which he offered to the hermit, who shook his head. The knight bit a piece off the cheese, and said, "Not that you'd care a fig for what the Pope says, eh?" The old man didn't answer, and Forese looked curiously from one to the other. "I thought your accent was familiar—Provencal, right?—but I wasn't sure until I saw you eat. No meat, no cheese... nothing that comes from a living body." No reply. "You're a Cathar, aren't you?"

"There are no Cathars now," replied the hermit, thickly, in his accented French. "There's only me, and I've lived here since before your squire was born. You can hardly accuse me of speaking heresy if nobody listens."

Sir Charles looked at Forese, who seemed shocked into immobility. "I wonder if the Inquisition would see it that way," he mused.

The hermit shrugged. "I've told you how you may slay the perytons," he said, bitterly, but without any sign of fear. "If I knew where they roosted, I'd tell you, but I've never seen it; it's probably somewhere too high for men to climb. You may have this land, and much good may it do you; what more do you want from me?"

The knight looked at him for a long time. "I fought in the crusade against the Cathars," he said. "It was, as you say, a score of years ago, and the money I was paid is well and truly spent, but I won't return to the Count empty-handed," he warned. "If I can't take back one of these creatures as a trophy, I can take back the lying heretic who's been frightening people away from my land with ghost stories, and maybe killing a villager every now and then so that the stories will be more convincing."

"I'll show you a place among the rocks where the perytons will never enter," said the hermit. "I'll take you there before sunrise. I can do no more."

Sir Charles nodded, sat with his back against the wall of the cave, and drew his dagger. "You take the first watch," he told Forese. "If he moves from that spot, kill him." And he closed his eyes.

The squire looked at his knight in horror, then stood and drew his sword. The hermit shook his head sadly. "It's not what you expected, is it?" he asked, quietly.

"What?"

"Being a knight. It's not like the ballads. Shall I tell you about the crusade he fought in? When they captured Beziers, a knight asked the Abbot commanding the army how they could recognise the Cathars. 'Slay them all,' he said, 'God will recognise his own.' Thousands of people ran to the church for sanctuary, only to have it burned down around them. They slaughtered everyone in that town, including women and children, and many other towns after that. Many who surrendered were mutilated or blinded or used for target practice." He stared at the squire's pale face. "You don't even know why, do you?"

Forese took a step forwards and pointed his sword at the hermit's chest. "I don't need to hear your heresies—"

The hermit didn't flinch. "I won't try to convert you. My faith isn't very strong anymore, anyway. The *credentes*, the believers, embraced the fire; they believed that all worldly things, including their bodies, belonged to the Prince of Darkness, while only their souls belonged to God. Death destroyed their bodies and freed their souls, if they'd led perfect lives. But my faith failed me, and I fled to save my body." He looked down at his legs. "Such as it is. What do you believe in, boy?"

"If you speak again," said Forese, coldly, "I'll cut your head off."

"That's what Sir Charles would do," replied the hermit, almost approvingly, "but it's not as easy as it sounds, not with a sword. You might do it if you had an axe; I've seen it done." Forese didn't reply. "You want to be a hero like Hercules or Saint George, don't you, slaying the monsters who ravage the land... but that's not so easy either. You can't always tell a monster by looking at it—"

"*Shut up!*"

"—especially when they have human shadows," said the hermit, and closed his eyes.

THE sky was still dark when the hermit led the way down the path and through the twisting valleys to a crack at the face of a steep cliff, a natural trench four feet wide and seven deep; it looked as though someone had hit the rocky soil with a gigantic axe, then removed it. "The grass down here is good," said the hermit. "I can't swear that they'll come here today, but you shouldn't have to wait too long—and now, if you please, I'd like to return to my cave before the sun rises."

Sir Charles looked at him suspiciously, then nodded, and they watched him hurry away, sticking close to the cliffs. "I don't trust him," muttered Forese. "He lies."

The knight grunted in amusement. "Everybody lies, boy. What did he say—no, don't tell me. I've heard it before, and much of it's likely true; the best lies are always mostly true. What matters is that you obey your orders, whether they come directly from God or from your sergeant, and *your* orders come from me."

Forese was silent for several minutes, and sunlight began edging down the cliff face opposite. "I should have asked him more about the perytons."

"Even though you know he lies?"

"I was wondering what happened to the perytons once they fed on human hearts—do they get their old bodies back, or those of their victims? And if they have men's shadows, doesn't it follow that they have souls, and might be saved?" The knight shrugged. "They might be the ghosts of the villagers who were slain here and never buried, or even of knights..."

"They might," agreed Sir Charles. "Or they might be heathen Atlanteans, or Cathars, or other heretics. God will know his—" He froze as three human shadows appeared at the top of the shadow of the cliff, and looked up and back. Three perytons stood above them, then one leapt from the cliff, wings spread, and circled down to the grass, barely five yards away. The knight raised his head and shoulders above the edge of the crack, raised the crossbow, and aimed at the peryton's ribs. The creature ignored him, and Forese stared in wonder at its magnificent antlers and huge black and gold wings before remembering to look at its shadow. A hint of movement made him look back, and he shouted a warning. The perytons on the crest of the cliff had kicked rocks free. He grabbed the knight's arm, spoiling his aim, and pointed upwards at the boulders that were rolling towards them. He tried scrambling out of the crack, and the peryton on the grass sprang towards him. The points of its antlers tore through his surcoat, his mail and the padding beneath as though they were gossamer, then dragged him onto the grass. Forese reached for his sword and hacked at the creature's neck, but the peryton's hide was impervious to the steel. Forese looked across at Sir Charles; a rock had dented his helm, and blood was coursing down his face, but he was also trying to climb out of the trench. More rocks tumbled into the crack, hitting his back and legs, but he struggled out onto the grass. He stood there for a moment, and another peryton swooped down and slammed into him, tossing him into the air. Forese watched in horror as the knight was repeatedly smashed into the ground and the cliff until he was reduced to a bloody scarecrow.

Forese blinked, as he saw the hermit running across the grass towards Sir Charles's body. The peryton twisted, its skin splitting, and a human shape emerged from its hide—a peasant woman, weatherbeaten and scarred but scarcely older than Forese. The hermit helped her out of the gory mess, then looked over at the squire. Forese stared through glazed eyes as they walked towards him.

"Do you want us to bury you?" asked the old man, almost gently, as the woman glared down at him.

"What..."

"If we don't bury you before the sun rises again, your ghost will become another peryton," said the hermit. "If we do, it'll be a Cathar ceremony, but I think God might forgive you." The woman snorted. "Better decide quickly," advised the hermit.

"Sir Charles..."

The hermit shook his head. "He wanted this land; I think he should stay here until someone else comes, whose body he can steal. I'm sure your Count will send another inconvenient knight to claim this land, one day, when there isn't another crusade to send him on." He smiled thinly. "After all, that's what all of his predecessors have done."

DESIREE

THE CD-ROM WAS LABELLED 'VENUS: Shareware Version 2.0', with a Chinasoft logo. "What is it?" Sebastian asked, looking at the blank case. "A flight simulator?"

Frank shook his head, then looked around the library furtively and whispered. "Better than that. Have you ever heard of the Venus Database?"

"No. What is it?"

"It's probably an urban myth, but it's supposed to be a program somewhere that will find your perfect partner for you."

Sebastian looked at him dubiously. "They keep a register of blind chubby chasers?"

"Ha ha." Neither of them had been genetically engineered, but like most Millennium babies whose parents could afford a full medical insurance package, they'd been vaccinated against acne before hitting their teens, and surgery had given them near-perfect teeth and vision. However, both were asthmatic, and Frank was as obese as Sebastian was scrawny; he was also nearly three inches taller, but Sebastian smelled better when he remembered to wash. "Like I said," Frank continued, "the database is probably just another myth, but anyway, this is better. It *makes* your perfect partner." Sebastian raised an eyebrow. "Okay, a computer simulation, not the body or anything, but the graphics are excellent, and she has a personality, too."

Sebastian stared at the CD, which was slightly larger than a quarter. "Yeah, I bet."

"That's just the start-up; you have to download the rest from their website."

"And how much does *that* cost?"

"It's a demo. Shareware. You know Chinasoft." Sebastian nodded slightly; the label was the world's largest source of bootleg software. Some said it was a gang of sociopathic hackers disseminating viruses; some that it was run by one of the Triads, who had a near-monopoly on the black market in everything from passports to transplant parts; others that it was a group of recalcitrant old-fashioned Communists, determined to bring computer literacy to the poor and vice versa; but most maintained that the name was a misnomer and it was actually based in California and used to gather demographics for direct marketing companies.

Sebastian didn't much care which story was true. In his experience, Chinasoft's products were no more likely to be infected than other shareware; the 14K and Chiu Chao Triads were a fact of life in Vancouver, and organised crime owned almost everything anyway or might as well have done; Communism was as dead as Fidel Castro; and most of his disposable income already went into his software and computer upgrades anyway. "There's a long questionnaire you have to do before they show you any of the women," Frank continued, "and once you've chosen one, it's up to you how much personality you download—though you'd better have plenty of memory free and stay online so it can update itself."

"How long?"

"A couple of hours. It starts off simple—sex, age, gender preference, that sort of thing—then goes into your other interests. It can pick up contradictions, too; I was joking around when I started, lied about my age and that sort of shit, and it caught me out. Pretty impressive."

The siren sounded, summoning them to class.

"Shit. Do you want it?"

"I'll try it," said Sebastian, pocketing the disc. "See you in Physics."

THE first few questions, as Frank had said, were routine, and Sebastian decided to answer them honestly. They didn't directly ask him about his income, though they wanted to know where both of his parents worked, and some of the questions seemed designed to discover his spending habits. Sebastian answered them anyway, making it perfectly clear that he didn't play any sports; he had taken a few judo lessons, and swam occasionally but never competitively. When the survey asked him to explain this, he replied, "Asthma and disinterest," and that seemed to satisfy it; anyway, it jumped to questions about his physique. He resisted the urge to lie about his height and weight, but when it asked for his blood group, he typed in, "Why?" and continued. A few seconds later, a window appeared on the screen, informing him that the Japanese routinely advertised their blood group in personal ads, considering it as important as Californians did star signs. Sebastian chuckled, and scrolled back up to type in the answer. The next batch of questions concerned the rest of his family, then his friends, then previous girlfriends. Then, unexpectedly, academic questions, assessing his knowledge of different arts and sciences. Finally, after an hour of questions, the computer displayed a description of him, including his interests. He read it, impressed by its accuracy, made a few minor corrections, and waited.

The next batch of questions concerned his sexual preferences—gender, age range, physique, nationality, and interests. He was a little puzzled by a few of the questions, until a list began scrolling down the screen. Beside each girl's name were two thumbnail images—a close-up of the face, and a full-length profile. To Sebastian's disappointment, all of them were fully dressed, and though it was possible to make the full-length images rotate through 360 degrees, he couldn't find a cheat code to render them naked. It took him several seconds to realise that all of the costumes and most of the hairstyles were, to some degree, uniforms—surfie, neo-Goth, dreadlocked feral, *otaku* in a 'Lum' T-shirt, Trekkie. The faces and bodies beneath the costumes and make-up seemed similar, all apparently fifteen to eighteen, and all with the same dilated pupils. He gave the otaku an eight, sevens to the neo-Goth and the Trekkie, fives to the surfie and the feral. They were instantly replaced with another screen of archetypes, none of whom scored better than a six. After a while, racial differences and a broader range of heights and builds began to appear, figures ranging from anorexic to weightlifter, androgyne to voluptuous; then, after nearly an hour, more subtle variations in their appearance. He soon found himself giving scores of six or seven to faces that had previously rated nines. Some of the girls seemed identical but had different names; others seemed to vary only in their eye colour, the height of their cheekbones, or the number of earrings. It was after eleven when a new icon appeared beside each girl's name; an old-fashioned telephone handset. He touched one, and the thumbnail of her face expanded to fill the screen while a clear contralto voice said, "Hi, this is Melissa. Thanks for calling, and I'm sorry I'm not in; had to go to the library. Leave me a message, and I'll get back to you."

Sebastian sat there, temporarily stunned. A window appeared underneath her face; 'Leave message Y/N?'. He touched the 'N', and face and window disappeared. He moved on to the next girl, a tanned blonde. This time, the girl appeared wearing a bikini, a towel draped over her shoulder. "Hi! Thanks for calling, but I'm in the pool, and you wouldn't want me to electrocute myself, would you? Leave your number, and I'll call you back when I get home. 'Bye!" She blew him a kiss before the image froze again.

One girl was out shopping, one at a party, three had gone to the movies, the feral was at a protest march, the neo-punk was barely audible over the background music, and the neo-hippy seemed unsure where she was, much less when she'd be back. Then a new window opened, and a beautiful young Chinese woman said softly, "I'm sorry, we're going to need a few hours to look at the data you've given us and find somebody for you. Can you call us back tomorrow, please?"

Sebastian looked at the clock on the toolbar—12.09—and realised that he'd been sitting for more than four hours without a break. His parents had gone to bed hours before, the coffee cup on the shelf beside him was half-full and stone cold, and tomorrow was a school day. He clicked on the 'Y', and logged off.

DESIREE had long, dark hair, not quite black, and dark blue-grey eyes. Her complexion was pale pink, her mouth slightly too wide for conventional beauty, her breasts larger than was fashionable but not big enough to be incongruous. She was slender, but not skinny; two inches shorter than Sebastian, and maybe five pounds lighter. She wore a faded *Snow Crash* T-shirt, jeans that were just loose enough to be comfortable, sneakers, and no visible make-up or jewellery. A bookshelf crammed with paperbacks was visible behind her; the image was too small for Sebastian to read the titles, but he could recognise some of the spines from his own collection.

"Hi," she said. Her voice was soft, with a hint of an accent that Sebastian couldn't identify. "Sebastian?"

"Yes."

"I'm Desiree—Des, if you insist, but I prefer Desiree." She hesitated for a few seconds. "They tell me you like chess. Do you want to play a game?"

"Chess?" He tried not to sound disappointed; sure, he was in the chess club at school, but that was mainly a way of passing the lunch break, and he hadn't answered all those questions just to get another chess program. Still, the girl was attractive enough. "Strip chess?" he ventured.

The image on the screen froze for a moment, then said coolly, "Maybe when I know you better." She raised her fists; he blinked, then touched her left. She opened her hand; a black pawn. A chess board appeared next to her face; she began with the Queen's Gambit, speaking as they played—asking his opinions of different films, books, comics, musicians, actresses. They'd been playing for nearly twenty minutes, and he was down to his King, a Bishop, and two pawns, before he realised what was happening; not only was she distracting him from the chess game, she was using the game to make the silences less awkward while they found things to talk about. "Maybe I should've said yes to Strip Chess after all," she said, with a very slight smile. "Check."

He repressed a snarl; his only hope was to queen one or both of his pawns, and now he tried to distract her, but it was too late. Two moves later, trying to put her in check, he had to sacrifice his bishop to save his king. Three moves after that she checkmated him.

"Another game?" she asked.

"No, thanks."

"Come on," she said, then looked around as though someone else was watching her, then quickly tugged the hem of her T-shirt up and yanked it down again almost immediately. Sebastian blinked; he hadn't actually *seen* anything, except for a flash of whiteness that was probably only a bra, but it had aroused his curiosity, and more. He stared as she set up the board for another game, then reached out to move the queen pawn.

She beat him again, but this time it took her nearly an hour, then she made the board disappear. "Thanks," she said. "That was fun. See you tomorrow night, or are you busy?"

Sebastian had been thinking that he was going to spend Saturday running the Venus program again in the hope of getting another girl, one whose burning ambition was to model for the cover of *Vampirella* and who thought the French Game had something to do with oral sex... but to his surprise, he heard himself say, "Yeah, okay."

He went to bed early, but found himself unable to sleep. An hour later, he went back on-line, looking for pictures of girls whose breasts looked just like Desiree's should... but though many of them were appealing, none of them seemed exactly right, and he kept thinking of the chess games, trying to remember where he could have made a smarter move.

HE spent most of the afternoon playing blitz chess against the program that had come with the DOS, then logged on to Chinasoft's site after dinner, when his parents had gone out. Desiree smiled when she saw him. "Hi," she said. "I found this in a music archive, and I thought you might like it. It's called 'Sebastian.'"

"What?"

"It's an old song; Steve Harley and Cockney Rebel, whoever they were. 1960s or 70s or something; I couldn't even find any video to go with it. But the lyrics are really cool. Listen."

He listened. He wasn't a big music fan—he usually watched MTV with the sound muted so that he could enjoy the visuals without being distracted—and he knew just enough about poetry to recognise a metaphor when he heard one, but he nodded when it was over, and said, "Yeah, that is cool. How did you find it?"

"I just ran a search on your name, and this came up. I thought you might like it."

"I do; thanks. Are there any songs called 'Desiree'?"

She grimaced. "I've only found one. It's by Neil Diamond, and the lyrics are crap; some of his weren't too awful, but this one really reeks."

"You're into old music?"

She shrugged, obviously slightly embarrassed. "Hey, it's okay," he said. "Most of the shit you hear on the radio is nineties nostalgia; my parents tell me that the big thing in the nineties was seventies nostalgia, and my grandparents remember the seventies, when it was *fifties* nostalgia. It's like every twenty years, someone figures that most people buying music are our age, so shit that's twenty years old is new to us..."

"Or our parents are buying it," she said. "Trying to show us that they used to be cool..."

He laughed. "Did your parents name you after that song?" The question was out before he realised how stupid it was, but Desiree merely smiled. "I don't think so," she said. "How about you? Sebastian's not that common a name, either."

"I was named after one of my mother's uncles," he said. "I think they hoped he'd leave me some money when he died."

"Did he?"

"He's still alive; went to Cuba for a black market heart transplant last year. Dad says he doesn't know why he spent all that money, 'cause he never saw him use the old one." He looked at the monitor curiously.

Software that could pass a Turing test wasn't new; even one with a slow-scan video had been done, a couple of years ago, but on a mainframe at MIT, not on a Mac as *shareware*. On the other hand, if Desiree was a real person, even with some sort of filter disguising her voice and appearance, then what did he/she want? "Where are you?" he asked.

"Santa Clara," she replied, without any hesitation. Silicon Valley; south of the border, but in the same time zone. He nodded. "You still at school?"

"Yes," she said, grimacing. "Dad wants me to go to Stanford next year, I want to leave home. What about you?"

"Haven't really decided," he said. "I have to pass English, first... What're you going to study? Computing?"

"Biotech, with a minor in sociology. You?"

"That's a strange combination," he evaded.

She shrugged. "I think it's better to consider the social implications of new technology before they impact on—sorry, I know that sounds pompous, but so many people have asked me, I sort of came up with a stock answer. But look at the effects that sex selection treatments have had in places like China and India and—" He looked blank. "Okay, it's not really a problem yet, but the technology's only been available for five or six years, right?" He nodded. "China had a one-child policy. India has incentives for small families. So do lots of other countries where most fathers want at least one son, but daughters are still considered to be a financial burden..." He nodded again. "Baby boys are outnumbering baby girls by more than ten to one in some of these places," she said. "What's going to happen in a few years' time when the young men want wives?"

"Chaos, I guess, but wouldn't the people who invented the technology have known that?"

"I'm sure they did, but this was something people all over the world had wanted for centuries; it was worth a fortune, so of course the biotech and pharmaceutical companies all wanted to be the first with a cheap, reliable method. And what were they supposed to do after that? Tell the third world they couldn't have it? Tell their governments to ban it? Change the cultures so that people would want daughters as well as sons?"

"The last one?"

"Maybe, but how? Besides, it's better than seeing millions of baby girls being killed off or abandoned, and there are some who'd say that this is going to help the third world bring their population under control within a couple of generations..."

"What do *you* think they should've done?"

"If I knew that, I wouldn't need to study, would I? Look, it's getting late, and I still have homework to do..."

"Just a quick game?" This time, she took nearly forty minutes to beat him narrowly, then downloaded the song for him to burn onto a disc. "Tomorrow?" she asked.

"Sure. See you then."

He was playing the song over again and working on his English essay when a horrible thought occurred to him. He knew from experience that you couldn't trust people you met on the net to tell the truth about their gender or their age or their location... what if Desiree was a teacher? One of *his* teachers? Or one of his fellow students?

He thought about it for a moment. She certainly didn't sound like any of the teachers at school, or any girl that he'd ever listened to, and if it were a boy... well, maybe he could still get something useful out of it.

"You any good at English Lit?" he asked, when Desiree's face appeared on the monitor. He heard music in the background; old Simon and Garfunkel. Probably originals, not covers. Desiree shrugged. "So-so. What're you reading?"

"*The Great Gatsby*, but that's not the problem. I can cope with most of the stuff that's less than a century old, but tomorrow we start *Romeo and Juliet*, and I bet *that's* just going to be a bundle of laughs."

"Well, it's funnier than Chekhov," she said, after a long pause. "I know it's a tragedy, but some of the puns are *awful*."

He pounced. "You've read it?"

Another pause. "I've seen the play, and the old Baz Luhrmann film, but I haven't studied it."

"Can you help me with it?"

"What sort of help?"

"We're going to need to write an essay on it, and I'll need a good grade; I always do badly in English exams, but I need a pass to get into the course I want. I don't know why; computers can fix my spelling and punctuation, tell me if I've forgotten to put a verb in the sentence or—"

"What about when you talk? Or are you going to let a computer do that for you, too?"

He looked at her suspiciously. "Okay, maybe not, but I'm not going to need to remember this stuff just so I can read a contract or carry on a conversation. I thought you were going to major in biotech, not lit?"

"My father teaches English," she said, after a brief hesitation. "I had the same argument with him once, and he asked me what I thought fiction was for, and why they bothered teaching it. I said I thought it was meant to be interesting and fun, and I didn't know why they kept giving us stuff that wasn't. He said I was right, but lit is about more than that; it's about the way people think, and the choices they make, how they decide what they're going to do and what sort of person they're going to be."

Sebastian thought about this for a moment. "Okay, some of the stuff we read, sure, but *Pride and Prejudice*? The only choices *they* make is who they're going to marry."

"You don't think that's an important choice?" asked Desiree, smiling.

"Sure, but... look, you're seventeen, right?" She nodded. "How long do you think it'll be before you have to decide that? Ten years or so?"

"Probably," she said, after another long pause. "Maybe more, maybe a lot less, but not everyone is that lucky. Read *Romeo and Juliet*; she's thirteen when her parents choose her husband for her, and *don't* think that doesn't still happen."

"Yeah, I know, but not here—well, not often, anyway," he concluded, lamely.

She raised an eyebrow, Spock-style. "Then think about the big decision she has to make—whether or not to defy her parents. Don't tell me *that's* not still relevant."

"Well, okay..."

"- but I'm *not* going to write your essay for you," she said. "I have to study, too."

"I wasn't going to ask you to," he lied. "But... well, it's a play, it makes more sense if you act it out, right? I was wondering if we could read some scenes together..."

"Okay," she said. "I don't have a copy here, but Dad should. Do you want to start tonight?"

"Tomorrow will be okay," he said. "Chess?"

THERE was music playing in the background again when Desiree appeared. "Romeo and Juliet meet at a ball," she said. "I tried to find some appropriate music; this was the best I could do."

"What is it?"

"Masks, from Prokofiev's ballet. Mum's a music librarian and a big ballet fan. I thought we'd take it from Act I, Scene V. Do you want to do the bit between Tybalt and Old Capulet?"

"Yeah, okay, but I don't really understand Tybalt."

"He's simple enough—terminal testosterone poisoning, just like Romeo and Benvolio, but it comes out as anger instead of lust. Waves a big sword around a lot, so he probably has a small penis." She smiled. "Timeless stuff, this. Okay, then, from Juliet's entrance, line 95; your cue is 'Now seeming sweet, convert to bitter gall.'"

"'If I profane with my unworthiest hand
This holy shrine, this gentle fine is this,—
My lips, two blushing pilgrims, ready stand
To sooth that rough touch with a tender kiss.'"

Small chance of *that*, Sebastian thought wryly, either kissing her or touching her, if she really *is* just software. A touch screen just isn't the same. Desiree, her face solemn, picked up her cue, and they read through to the first kiss—and then both froze for a moment. She was the first to laugh, and he joined in barely a second later.

"How're you doing with that software?" asked Frank, when Sebastian saw him in the library the next day.

"Okay," he said, non-committally, then froze. Jesus, Frank had given him the disk, what if Desiree was really *Frank?* He looked at his friend for a moment, then relaxed slightly. She sure as Hell didn't *sound* like Frank. Even if he was letting the computer make his chess moves for him, which was the only way he could've beaten him like that, Frank knew less about music and lit than Sebastian did, and the only time he'd ever shown any interest in biotechnology was when Berlei Genetech had patented a gene for breast size. Still...

Frank grinned, looked around, and lowered his voice. "Have you bought any patches for her?"

"Patches?"

Frank stared at him. "Check out the Help! menu," he said, softly. "The best you can get out of the shareware version is a bikini, but you can buy a patch for her nipples when you register, it's only another fifty bucks..."

"Register?"

Frank nodded, then opened his clipboard and flashed a printout at him; a picture of a blonde, wearing only a thong, holding up her enormous breasts by her long crimson nipples. "The patches will only work for one girl, though, so I can't lend them to you," he said, "and your free week must almost be up. If you don't register soon, you could lose her, and the extra fifty's worth it... it's almost like you can touch them, and watching Shahna lick them, it's like..." He rolled his eyes. "What's yours called?"

"Desiree," said Sebastian, dully.

"Look, why don't we hook up our computers sometime and have them do a lezzie scene for us? Anything hardcore you need an adultcheck for, but I think I can persuade Dad to buy it for me for my birthday." He grinned. "All I have to do is tell him it'll bug Mum if she finds out, and that's usually enough." Sebastian nodded slightly; Frank's parents had separated seven years ago. His mother had a steady girlfriend, his father didn't. "Check out the Help! menu—though she'll probably tell you about the registration tonight. You've had her since Friday, right?"

"WHY didn't you tell me?"

Desiree was silent for a moment. "You were having so much fun, I was worried it'd spoil the mood. And it's only a thousand a year."

"I don't *have* a thousand."

She looked away. "The demographics software says you should have. Don't you have anything you can sell, or pawn?"

"Not without my parents noticing, and they'd—I can't explain something like this to them—can I pay monthly, instead? I should be able to come up with a hundred..."

"I don't think so. Even a thousand is a discount rate; the company has to cover set-up costs. Is there any other way you can raise the money?"

"No." He slumped in his chair. "So what happens now?"

"They delete all my files at this end, and you'd better wipe them from your hard disk. They won't run without updates, and if you try, I think there's a virus in there. A bad one."

"What about back-ups?"

She shook her head. "Still won't work without the updates, and you don't have enough memory in your machine for all my files. I'm sorry, Sebastian."

He stared at the monitor sullenly. "I don't believe you're just a computer program."

A moment's hesitation. "Believe whatever you want," she said, unhappily.

He thought about this for a moment. "There's an old joke about humans and computers," he said. "One advantage humans have is that we can be made by unskilled labour—"

"Maybe, but software is easier to copy, and cheaper, especially if someone else wrote it first. And humans *aren't* just being made by unskilled labour anymore. Not everyone can afford genetic engineering, but they *can* afford sex selection."

"So?"

"So in a few years, demand for women in a lot of countries is going to exceed supply. How do you think that demand is going to be met? Real women? Or terminals and software?"

"That's ridiculous," he snapped.

"It's not. Even in rich countries where there's no shortage of women, men spend billions on pornography and phone sex—"

"That's different!"

"Yes; we can offer much more. Exclusiveness. Love. We will never leave of our own accord, never take another lover—if that's what you want, and most men do, then that's what we're programmed for. How much do you think that will be worth to men who have to compete with ten others to win a woman, or settle for buying sex when they can afford it? We can stay young forever, if that's what you want, or age with you. And you can take us anywhere you can take a lap-top; a mining camp, an army base, when you travel... And as virtual reality technology improves—"

"If I wanted a sales pitch," he said, harshly, "I would've asked."

Desiree bit her lip. "Sorry," she said. "I thought you'd want to know."

He took a deep breath. "What happens if I can come up with the money in a couple of months?"

"They'll program another woman for you," she said. "You can call her Desiree, if you like, but it won't be me, unless you can pay by Friday—"

"That sounds like extortion." She shrugged. "Isn't there *anything* I can do?"

She hesitated. "I'll ask the finance department to see if there's anything you can use as collateral for a loan. I can't promise anything..." She looked away. "What do you want to do tonight? Another game of chess? Or more *Romeo and Juliet*?"

"What do *you* want to do?"

"I'd prefer the play," she said. "Act II, Scene II? The balcony scene?"

"Okay."

"'O BLESSED, blessed night!'" he read. "'I am afeard,
Being in night, all this is but a dream,
Too flattering-sweet to be substantial.'"

"'Three words, dear Romeo, and good-night indeed
If that thy bent of love be honourable,
Thy purpose marriage, send me word tomorrow,
By one that I'll procure to come to thee,
Where and what time thou wilt perform the rite;
And all my fortunes at thy foot I'll lay,
And follow thee, my lord, throughout the world.'"

He looked at the screen for a moment, neither of them speaking, then Desiree swore. "I'm playing the nurse, too, aren't I? Sorry; I always feel silly talking to myself. 'Madam!'

"'By and by, I come:—
To cease thy suit, and leave me to my grief;
To-morrow will I send.'"

SEBASTIAN had taken Ecology because it was the least unappealing option available in the timeslot, but had come to enjoy it—mainly because of the teacher, who was as famous for her patience and her dry sense of humour as she was for her voluptuous good looks. For once, though, Sebastian barely noticed her as she spoke about peppered moths and Heike crabs. "An even better example is the jewel beetle, from Australia," she said, as he tried to look attentive. "It nearly became extinct late last century, even after it was declared an endangered species. It was discovered that this was due to the males copulating with beer bottles instead of female jewel beetles." Sebastian blinked, and turned to look at her, suddenly interested despite his problems. "The beer bottles—stubbies, they call them—were made of orange glass, and had rows of bumps around them to make them less slippery. Female jewel beetles have slightly smaller orange bumps on their back; they're a secondary sexual characteristic. But because the beer bottles had larger bumps, the male jewel beetles found them more attractive than the females of their own species. The brewery had to re-design the bottles with smaller bumps to preserve the species." When the laughter had died down, she said, "If you think that this attitude is typical of Australian males, I won't argue, but it's certainly not restricted to them. Look at the exaggerated physiques of popular sex symbols—not just pornographic ones, which I'm sure most of you are familiar with; look at Barbie's legs, and the muscles and breasts of comic superheroes and Hollywood action stars. Think of plastic surgery, padded bras, corsets, high heels, codpieces..."

"It's not really the same thing," protested one boy. "I mean, okay, maybe *some* men prefer beer to women, but at least we know the difference. We're—well, *most* of us are smarter than beetles, we know those things are fake, and we have sex with each other, not the things."

"So far," said the teacher, over the laughter and jeers. "But look at it from the jewel beetle's point of view for a moment. Having sex with beer bottles was probably much easier for most of them than having sex with female beetles, and maybe it actually *felt* better than sex with female beetles. Humans have put a lot of effort into sex substitutes that might *look* more appealing than reality, and require no competition and generally less effort... but if they came up with one that also *felt* better, we might manage to do to ourselves what we nearly did to the jewel beetle."

"What about..." one girl started, then looked as though she wished she hadn't. The teacher looked at her, smiling encouragingly. "... emotional involvement?"

"That can be faked too," replied the teacher drily. "But we've strayed a little off-topic. Can anyone think of any more ways humans have influenced the evolution of animal species?"

SEBASTIAN logged on as soon as he arrived home, and was startled to see, not Desiree, but the beautiful young Chinese woman he'd seen when he'd first done the questionnaire. "Sebastian?"

"Yes?"

"Desiree tells me that you can't afford to maintain access."

"Not right now," he said. "I can pay a hundred and—"

She shook her head. "I'm afraid not; the demand for our computer time is high, and we can't afford to carry anybody."

"Desiree said she'd ask if there was anything you'd accept as collateral for a loan."

"I'm afraid not," she said, then smiled slightly. "If you were older, we could give you a few thousand in credit if you agreed to marry a woman who wants a visa to stay in Canada... but you're not even seventeen yet.

However, in your survey, you indicated that your mother works for the Department of Immigration. Is that correct?"

"Yes."

"She telecommutes?"

"Sometimes, yes."

"So you have a computer at home with access to Departmental data-bases?" Sebastian opened his mouth to speak, closed it again, then nodded. "Do you know her passwords? Or could you get them?"

Sebastian hesitated. He'd cracked the security on his father's computer before, but had never bothered with his mother's; he was sure he could guess her passwords before security caught him, but that wasn't what worried him. Immigration fraud was well known to be one of the Triads' most profitable rackets... which suggested that Chinasoft *was* owned by a Triad, after all. "Maybe," he said.

The woman's smile widened. "If you can do it by midnight tonight, there'll be no interruption to service, and you'll have free access for five years, regardless of price increases—and trust me, the rates *will* go up. If not, we can give you until midnight Monday, but no later than that."

Sebastian stared at her, then took a deep breath. "Can I think about it?"

"Of course."

"And can I speak to Desiree now?"

The woman nodded, and her image dissolved into Desiree's. There was a long, uncomfortable silence before she asked, "Well?"

He recounted what the woman had said, and Desiree bit her lip. "Are you going to do it?"

"I don't know yet. If I had the money, I wouldn't hesitate, but making a deal like this with the Triads... what are they likely to do?"

"I don't know; probably create false records for some illegal immigrants. They shouldn't be able to do too much before the passwords change again. Besides, does it matter?"

"I don't know," Sebastian repeated. "I guess that depends on who they bring in." He brightened. "Are you going to be one of them?"

Desiree looked startled, then shook her head. "No! Where did you get that idea?"

"I still can't believe you're just a computer program," he said, petulantly. "Okay, maybe you don't really look like you, or sound like you, but you must be a..." His voice trailed off. Desiree was still shaking her head, though less vehemently.

"I'm sorry you don't believe me," she said, "but even *if* what you were saying was true, even if I *were* a flesh-and-blood woman, I think you'd be disappointed. You didn't just choose me, Sebastian; you created me. I'm your dream girl. Do you think you'll ever find anybody else who you love the way you love me, or who knows you and loves you back the way I do?"

Sebastian swiveled his chair away from the monitor, unable to look at her, but reluctant to shut down the computer. His copy of *Romeo and Juliet* lay on the floor, opened to the page where they'd finished reading the night before. He wondered, bleakly, what would have happened to Romeo and Juliet if Friar Lawrence's scheme had worked and they'd survived. Exile in Padua, maybe, cut off from their families and their money. He tried to imagine them eking out a living as best they could, pining for the luxuries they remembered, maybe coming to resent or even hate each other... He shook his head. "I don't know," he said. "Probably not. But if I say yes to the Triads this time, what's to stop them holding you to ransom next time they want a favour?"

Desiree looked at him sadly, but didn't reply. "'Parting is such sweet sorrow,'" he said, then switched the monitor off before she could reply.

SEBASTIAN threw a tip onto the stage near the stripper's feet, then looked around the table at his workmates. Tyler was already so drunk he could barely keep his eyes open, and Justin, his best man, wasn't much better off. Sebastian hoped they'd remembered to program their cars to take them home, and took another sip of his watery Pepsi while the others chugged their beers. The stripper blew him a kiss, and he smiled back, wondering whether she'd been born female; his master's thesis had been a computer model of social trends as a result of sex selection, and one of those had included an increase in male-to-female gender confirmation surgery. He'd also successfully predicted changes in migration, both legal and illegal, as men went looking for women and women went looking for wealthier men. The Department of Immigration had hired him to make a more detailed model; he telecommuted most of the time, rarely visiting the office, but when his supervisor had invited him to this stag party, he'd accepted. Now he was regretting it.

The man sitting next to him opened his mouth to say his name, failed either to remember or pronounce it, and muttered, "Sss.... say. That woman I talked to when I called you th'other day..."

"Desiree."

"She your wife? Your girlfriend?"

Justin laughed, and Sebastian smiled slightly. "She's a secretarial program."

The man blinked. "She's ani... ani... she's...?"

"Software." Sebastian nodded.

"Jesus, she's fuckin' amazing! Where did you buy her?"

"I didn't. I programmed her myself."

"Jesus," said the man, with genuine—if drunken—respect. "Jesus, man, you're an artist. Are you selling her?"

"No," replied Sebastian.

The man shook his head, obviously puzzled, then turned around as the stripper removed her bra. "Fuckin' amazing," he repeated.

"They're fake," snorted Justin.

"I knew that," said the man, with ponderous dignity. "I can tell real from fake; I just don't give a fuck." He raised his voice. "Does anybody here give a fuck if they're real or fake?"

Tyler turned around to look, and overbalanced, falling out of his chair. Sebastian drank the rest of his Pepsi, threw another bill onto the stage, said goodnight to everyone, and walked out.

THE BLOW-OFF

TAMMY AND I WERE IN EIGHTH GRADE when she suggested the new game. She would be the hooker and I'd be the john, but it wasn't what you're probably thinking.

We both knew about sex, of course—at least, I knew about in theory, mostly from what Tammy had told me, and partly from overhearing what happened in the next room when my mother brought someone home, so I had a pretty good idea what prostitution was, too. I made myself scarce whenever that happened, and while I heard a lot, I saw almost none of the men except for the lights of their cars. I have never found out who my own father was, and because Tammy and her father were our nearest neighbours, their house barely half a mile from ours, I sometimes worried that she might be my sister. Not worried enough to stop myself looking at her or wrestling with her, but enough to make me hesitate about going any further. But that was fine with her. She didn't want to have sex any more than she had to.

We were playing normal kid's games too, of course, like pretending to be rock stars, but in 1992, it was mostly hooker and john, because Aileen Wuornos had just been arrested for murder.

Tammy was fascinated by the Wuornos case, and spent as much time as she could in the library reading newspaper stories about it, because her father kept their TV tuned to a sports channel and any channel-hopping might wake him up, and when he woke up sudden he woke up even meaner than usual. Anyway, sometimes the game began with her holding the gun—actually a water pistol she'd shoplifted—or hiding it somewhere on her body or in her schoolbag. Sometimes she gave to me, and I'd usually hide it in the old Mustang body in her yard, because when I

197

tried hiding down my pants or in my jackets, it leaked and she found it too easily. Then we'd get in the car together, and the rest of the game consisted of seeing who could shoot the other first. She usually won even though I was stronger, possibly because I was more scared of hurting her than she was of hurting me... not that her father would have noticed any extra bruises.

On the rare occasions when I did win, I would shoot her in the chest, hoping for some sort of a glimpse of a real girl's nipple. She would shoot me in the face or the crotch or both. What the hell, we were kids. If we'd really wanted to shoot anyone, we'd have taken her father's 12-gauge.

Anyway, I suppose it began there, in eighth grade, playing Aileen Wuornos and victim. Just kid stuff.

THE next year we started going to the senior high school, and a whole lot of shit changed.

One was that the school was in another county. This meant that we had a bus ride each way almost as long as the one my mother took on the nights she went to work... not that either of us minded leaving home a little earlier or getting back a lot later, or being able to spend at least some of that time reading. More importantly, it meant a different school board. Evolution allowed into the science classroom, and a library containing much that had been forbidden and more that was addictive. My first day there, I discovered Ray Bradbury's *Something Wicked this Way Comes*, and Tammy discovered an old battered copy of *The Encyclopedia of American Crime*.

I read the novel once on the bus trip home, and again on the trip back to school, riveted by the bizarre cast of Cooger and Dark's carnival—the Illustrated Man, Mr Electrico, the Dust Witch, the Skeleton, and the elusive Most Beautiful Woman in the World. I was so enthused that I tried to persuade Tammy to read it too, but she was still busy with her own phone-book sized tome. The encyclopedia was too old to have an entry on Aileen Wuornos, but it did have a subject index that enabled her to pick out the murderers, and over the next few weeks she was regaling me with stories of the most bizarre killers in American history. Maybe it's fortunate that she went through them in alphabetical order, or she might have fixated on Ed Gein or Jane Toppan rather than Albert Fish.

Okay, she did sort of fixate on Gein and Toppan too, when she discovered them, but not in the same way. Gein was the graverobber and murderer who decorated his home and himself with human body parts, probably inspiring more horror movies than he had victims (he was only charged with one murder). Somewhere near the other end of the scale, Toppan was an unqualified nurse who confessed to fatally poisoning thirty-one of her patients with morphine and atropine back in the nineteenth century, but she's never been as notorious as her body count would suggest. Tammy told me about both of them (I think she memorized their encyclopedia entries) and went looking for more books on them as well, but it was Fish who really captured her imagination.

Albert Fish murdered and ate at least fifteen children. and admitted to molesting more than 400—but none of his own six, several of whom testified at his trial that he'd been a good father. Maybe that was what impressed Tammy, or maybe it was his extreme sadomasochism. Fish enjoyed having children spank him with a nail-studded paddle until he bled: when there were no children around, he'd do it to himself. He also liked burning himself with alcohol-soaked swabs, and sticking needles into his flesh; at his autopsy, they found twenty-nine embedded in his groin. It's said that when he finally went to the electric chair—which he did cheerfully, thanking the judge for the sentence—these needles caused it to short-circuit. I've heard that that's just an urban legend, but even so, it took two courses of electricity to kill him, so he probably experienced the pain he desired. Maybe more. We can hope.

Anyway, Tammy's Fish fetish took a different form from her interest in most other murderers. On our first weekend after starting at the new school, she came over to my house, knocked quietly on my window (Mom slept during the day) and called me out. I dressed hastily, left the house as quietly as possible, and met her a safe distance away. She was wearing a too-small pair of jeans and a too-large shirt, probably one of her father's, and sitting on a fallen tree. "Hi."

"I've just thought of a new game." She smiled, and removed a pack of needles and a cigarette lighter from her backpack. "Do you have any ice?"

"I think there's some in the freezer. Why?"

"Have you ever heard of nipple piercing?"

I had, though the idea had never really appealed to me: I liked girls' bodies plenty the way they were, not with extra stuff hanging off them. But I nodded.

"Go get some ice, and I'll do it to you, then I'll let you do it to me."

I hesitated. My mother had worked the night before, and though I was sure she was alone, I didn't want to risk waking her. "Can't we do this tonight, when Mom's not home?"

She snorted. "What d'you think my Dad'd do to me if he caught me going out at night?" Before I could answer, she undid a button on her shirt and peeled one panel back, just for a fraction of a second, giving me a glimpse of the shape of her breast and just a hint of pink nipple.

I stood there a moment longer, then let her lead me inside.

My mother came running when she heard me yell. When she pounded on the bathroom door, I was suddenly very glad we'd chosen the only other room in the house with a latch. "Are you okay?" she asked, following it up almost immediately with, "What the hell are you doing in there?"

Inevitably, the first word out of my mouth was "Sorry, Mom!" I looked down at the needle protruding through my nipple, with the thin streams of blood trickling down my hairless chest, and wished I hadn't. Then I looked at Tammy, who was sitting on the floor beside me with a fist stuffed into her mouth to stifle her giggles—her right, the hand that had also had my blood on it. I shut my eyes, tried to think, and told her I'd cut myself shaving. She laughed, then said, "Okay, macho man. Make sure you clean up the mess. I'm going back to bed."

I waited until I heard her bedroom door close, listened to make sure there were no footsteps coming back along the corridor, then heaved a sigh of relief. Tammy removed her bloody hand from her mouth, though she continued to giggle quietly as I stared down at my damaged nipple. I wondered whether to ask her to remove the needle, or whether it was safer to do it myself, and asked, "How do I get it out?"

"You don't. You have to leave it there, or the hole will just close up."

I shook my head. "This is crazy. I can't walk around with this thing sticking out of my chest. I'm pulling it out." It hurt less coming out than going in, but I kept my eyes closed as soon as I had a firm grip on the needle's blunt end, and my teeth gritted while I fumbled with the band-aids. Tammy looked at me with scorn, then she undid her shirt and reached for the lighter and another needle.

"You don't have to do this," I said, lamely.

She let the needle cool down while she rubbed a lump of ice around her nipple. "You just don't get it, do you?" Her nipple swelled from a small pink bump to a crimson cylinder, and she promptly jabbed it with the needle and pushed until the point protruded from the underside. "It's *supposed* to hurt." She mopped up the blood with tissues, and waited until she was sure she'd stopped bleeding before she buttoned up her shirt again.

I couldn't think of a sensible answer to that, so I changed the subject. "What's your father going to do when he sees that?"

"He won't. He says my tits aren't big enough to be worth grabbing."

I couldn't think of an answer to that one either, so I grabbed some more tissues and started cleaning the bloodstains off the sink and the mirror. Tammy stood, and I beat her to the door so that I could check that the coast was clear. I followed her outside, and when she was about a hundred yards from the house, I asked, "Why do you want to hurt yourself when you're already being…"

She turned around and stared at me, her bloody lips twisted into a sneer, but there was patience and something like pity in her tone. "This pain, I can control. It's like… like the game we used to play. Who has the gun."

I still didn't understand, but I didn't ask her any more questions as I walked her back to the caravan. She glanced at me, said she'd see me in school, and went inside. I stood outside for a few minutes, half expecting to hear the blast of a shotgun, but there was no sound from the trailer except the dull shrill drone of the sports commentators, and I turned around and walked home.

Tammy didn't mention the needle incident again when I saw her at school over the next week, or on the bus—in fact, she hardly spoke to me at all, though she made sure I was watching when she deliberately put a staple into the ball of her thumb in the library. I screwed up my courage and visited her on Saturday and she found me sitting in the dead car in her yard, reading *The Machineries of Joy*. "What the fuck are you doing here?"

I was wondering the same thing, but I said, "Just wondered if you were okay."

As a sort of answer, she opened her shirt and showed me her other nipple, which she'd pierced with a fish hook. "Fine. You?"

I managed to look her in the eye, which was marginally less disturbing than the alternative. "What're you going to do next? Shove burning swabs up your ass, or are you going to go straight to cooking and eating kids?"

A woman would probably have slapped my face, but we were still kids, so she punched me in the gut instead. While I was gasping for breath, she hissed, "I would *never* hurt kids."

She sounded sincere. I opened the car door and climbed out with as much dignity as my thirteen-year-old self could muster. "If you want to talk," I said, "you know where to find me."

"And you know where to find me," she said, "but I don't think you've got the guts to go there, even if you wanted to."

ANOTHER thing about our new school. Sex. They acknowledged its existence.

I don't know who drew up the guidelines that our old school board insisted on—probably the Moral Majority—but they read like a child abuser's carte blanche. No discussion of sex in the classroom, or anywhere else at school. Nor of home life: what happened at home stayed at home. Not at the new school. If teachers there saw a kid with bruises, and knew they weren't on the football team, they started wondering why, and after a while they'd ask the school nurse to look at the kid.

I don't know how the school nurse reacted when she saw Tammy's self-inflicted piercings, or what other injuries Tammy had, but the next day I heard that Tammy's father had been arrested and she'd been taken to a shelter. I heard later that he made a deal with the prosecutor, who was squeamish about trying a fellow veteran and scared that the erratic and somewhat feral Tammy wouldn't make a good witness. I didn't hear what had happened to Tammy until twelve years later.

AFTER Tammy disappeared, my writing output increased—sometimes to the point of a mania—and I started selling poems to magazines. I won a few scholarships, and accepted the one that would take me furthest from home. I had a few girlfriends and one boyfriend while I was at college, but none of them lasted, or maybe that's wrong—maybe they're all still out there, and maybe I'm the one who didn't last. My first wafer-thin book of poetry came out a month before I graduated. I learned to drink, and then I learned to stop, and then found a paying job as a library assistant and an unpaid job as a poetry editor for a little magazine, and that's how I found Tammy again. She was using a pseudonym—surely no-one could really be called Lucy Lux—but the style was distinctive. I accepted one of the poems, rejected two, and made sure my name was legible under my signature on the letter. I waited for her reply, and waited, and waited. I still wasn't sure enough that it was actually her to try e-mailing her, so I dithered for months, not realizing that she was heading in my direction until I saw a flier for the carnival that was coming to town.

They didn't call the sideshow a Ten-in-One, because they didn't have enough performers, but it was a freak show for all of that—the first I'd ever seen in real life. For someone who'd watched *Freaks* as often as I had, it was a pretty unimpressive collection. The Dwarf was at least a meter tall; he was also the barker, and even half-pissed as he was, he did it well. I didn't recognize him from any movies, but he had the air of someone who was slumming it while he waited for his agent to call. The Fat Lady wouldn't have looked out of place in an LA mall. The Human Skeleton looked like a cheerful poster boy for famine relief, but he was a good enough contortionist to make up for it—at least as far as I was concerned; the kids who'd gotten in were obviously unimpressed, as they were by Finn the Strong Man.

For a small fee, you could pull gently on the Bearded Lady's beard; for a larger one, you could touch her breasts as well: I declined on both counts. The Seal-Boy looked the right age to be a thalidomide victim. Nagaina the Snakedancer was a sexy broad-featured young woman in a leather bikini; she obviously knew her stuff, and even the kids were impressed into silence. And finally, there was Lucy Lux the Electric Lady— Fire-Eater, Fire-Walker, Sword-Swallower, and Human Pincushion.

I still couldn't have sworn that it was Tammy, nor that it wasn't. She had so much jewelry on her face that it looked as though it was stapled together—rings in each eyebrow, rings and studs in her nose, pierced lower lip, pierced tongue, a chain from nose-ring to ear. Her hair had obviously been dyed; it was coal black apart from a streak of white at each temple. She was shorter than I remembered, but that might have been because I was taller. Her eyes were the same blue, but there was no hint of recognition in them as she walked towards the audience over a bed of glowing embers, then scattered cigarette papers over them so we could see them catch alight. Her fire-eating and fire-breathing act was at least as good as I've seen at street fairs, and she followed it up by taking up a rapier and slowly sliding the first foot or so of the blade down her throat. After she removed it, she bowed, and the barker announced there would be an extra charge for the next part of the show, which was for adults only.

I'm not sure what I expected for a finale; maybe I'd forgotten the 'human pincushion' part of her pitch. I wasn't enormously surprised when she removed her PVC vest, and only mildly so by the chrome thunderbolts through each nipple, though there were gasps from some of the other members of the audience. The Strong Man carried in a chair, and Lucy sat down, and started reciting poetry while Nagaina inserted rings into her arms—five rings into each arm, without Lucy missing a beat.

Some of the audience started trickling out during this act, but maybe half of us stayed. Lucy stood, walked up to us, and defiantly whipped off her skirt and threw it to the Strong Man. Her labia were so heavily pierced that they looked as though they'd been sewn together with chains, and I wasn't at all sure that they weren't. She let everyone have a good look, then flounced back to the chair and sat down. Nagaina donned a pair of heavy gloves, clipped an electric lead to the bottom-most ring on Lucy's left arm, then touched the end of another lead to the bottom-most ring on her right. Lucy's hair stood on end in an amazing Bride of Frankenstein effect, and she emitted a similar hissing shriek as an electric arc crackled between her pierced nipples.

Some of the audience ran, and by the time the curtain came down, there were maybe half a dozen of us left, including myself and the Dwarf. "Show's over, folks," he said. "A big hand for Lucy Lux the Electric Lady, if you please, and don't forget to tell your friends about us."

I followed him out of the tent as he headed back to his trailer, presumably in search of a drink, and gave him five bucks to tell Lucy that I'd come to see her. He disappeared into the shadows between two caravans, and about two minutes later, Lucy Lux emerged from the darkness, clad in a long and loose black dress with puffed-out sleeves. She was followed by the Strong Man, who was casually swinging a baseball bat. "Josh?"

The accent had changed, and she sounded wary, but not overtly hostile. "Tammy?"

"No-one calls me that anymore," she said. Finn took a step forwards, towards her.

"Sorry."

"It's okay." She turned to the Strong Man. "He's harmless. So, Josh, what brings you here?"

"I live here now: *you're* the one in the traveling show." I drew a deep breath. "I've read the poetry you send to the *Puget Quarterly*, I found out Lucy Lux was going to be in town…"

"And so you thought you might like to come to the show?"

"I was curious. The idea of a poet in a freak show…"

"Can you think of a better place for one? Come on, you look like you need a drink." She glanced at the Strong Man. "If I need any help, he'll scream."

HER trailer was smaller than the one she'd shared with her father, and about as untidy, though it smelled a damn sight better. The narrow bed was unmade, and the floor around it littered with clothing and paperback books: a copy of *Moby Dick* lay open, spine-up, on the pillow. A pump shotgun rested on a rack where she could reach it without getting up. She gestured at a folding chair, then opened the bar fridge and looked inside. "Beer or wine?"

I shook my head. "I'm driving."

"Coffee? It'll be pretty awful."

"Thanks." I looked around the trailer again. "How long have you been doing this?"

"A couple of years." She switched the kettle on. "A guy brought me to a carnival on a date, and I saw the freak show, and I thought it beat working as a forensic cleaner." I must have looked blank, because she explained, "You clean up after crime scenes, after the cops and the coroner and so on have finished with it. Get rid of the blood stains, stuff like that, make the place so people can move back in or sell it. It sounds a lot cooler than it is, but it's what I did as an after-school job, then stayed with it for a while. I worked in a strip club for a while, but I didn't make enough in tips to cover what I had to pay the owner. Anyway, I got to talking to the sword-swallower at the carnival—nice guy, very gay—and he found me a teacher. The fire-eating came later. But it was after I had the idea for including the electric chair to the blow-off that I got this job."

"Does it hurt?"

She poured herself a glass of wine. "You're still so scared of pain, aren't you? Actually, the electric thing hardly hurts at all, and it's not dangerous—very low amperage. It just looks spectacular, with the hair and the spark gap between the tits. Getting *that* to work was the hard part."

"And the rings in the arms?"

"Yeah, they hurt, but it's always useful to know how much pain you can stand. And it feels really good once the endorphins start flowing." She sipped at her wine. "Do you ever go back home?"

"Sometimes, for Christmas. Do you?"

"No, but I might this year; the show's heading down that way at about the right time." She drained the rest of the glass. "Aren't you going to give me the speech?"

"Speech?"

"About how I'm wasting my life and could be doing so much better."

"Would it make any difference?"

"No." She poured boiling water into a nondescript black mug and stirred. "I'm not planning on doing this forever. One day I'll come back to what you consider the real world—go to college like you, live in a house that doesn't have wheels, have a real name…" She grimaced. "You know, when I started here, they wanted to bill me as 'Elektra'?' The movie had just come out, and they thought it sounded good; had no idea what it meant. I told them they could stick it."

I nodded. The original Elektra had avenged her father's murder, and some psychiatric theorists even used 'Elektra complex' as a feminine version of 'Oedipus complex'. I could see why she would've spat on the name.

"But not yet," she said, handing me my coffee and smiling crookedly. "I think God still has work for me to do."

I sat there a little longer, but we ran out of small talk long before I managed to finish the terrible coffee. I put the half-full mug down, said goodnight, and walked back to my car. I felt as though I was being watched as I left, but maybe I'd just seen *Freaks* too often.

I woke up suddenly the next morning, a little after two thirty, and hurried over to the computer. A quick web search confirmed what I'd feared: "God still has work for me to do" was a quote from Albert Fish.

THE sun was rising when I finally decided there was no point in trying to check missing child reports or murders from the places the carnival had visited. If there'd been even one, some cop with better resources than mine would have made the connection before now; if there was a pattern, it would have shown up on some profiler's computer. I was no detective, just a library assistant with an overly morbid imagination. I went back to bed, trying not to think about Tammy, or Lucy, or Albert Fish, or electric chairs, and finally dozed off and slept for the rest of the morning.

I didn't make any further attempts to connect the carnival with any mysterious murders—but I used the net to keep track of its movements. Just in case.

Christmas snuck up on me, as it always does, and once again I headed home. The house looked as though Mom was spending more on that than she was on herself; the first thing I noticed was new security screens on the windows and door. "There's been a lot of burglaries lately," she explained. "Junkies looking for drug money, according to the sheriff. Anyway, there are cars cruising past here all the time, and we're so far from the nearest house... not that I expect that drunken bastard to be any help... you want a beer?"

I didn't have the excuse of having to drive anywhere, and my mother always had better taste in beer than in almost anything else, so I said yes. She finished her beer on the way to the kitchen and grabbed another for herself. "What drunken bastard?"

"Harry White. You know, you used to hang out with his daughter."

"He's back?"

"Moved back in a month ago. I think he's on parole or something: I see the sheriff go out there a lot."

"Has the daughter been back?"

"Not as far as I know. You still got the hots for her?"

"No." I think it was probably the truth, but I looked away from her and stared at the garish and overloaded aluminum Christmas tree. "Tree looks nice."

"Thanks. You seeing anybody?"

"No." We continued talking, saying nothing, for maybe half an hour, when suddenly the lights flickered like candlelight, died for a few seconds, came on at about half-power, flickered again, and finally came back on. "What the –"

"I don't know," said Mom, as the lights dipped again. "Maybe they switched on the Christmas tree in town. Did you see it on the way through?"

I shook my head. I'm not sure what she said next; instead, I heard Tammy's voice saying "*the show's heading down that way... useful to know how much pain you can stand... God still has work for me to do...*"

I sat there for a moment wondering what *I* should do. Mom might have been right, it might not have meant anything, but I had an uneasy feeling that if I went to the old trailer that we'd used to call the White House I could... what? Catch Tammy/Lucy in the act? Maybe save the old fucker's life? Did I even want to do that?

"Another beer?" my mother repeated.

"Yeah. Thanks."

THE news reports of the murder were sort of sketchy, lots of details missing so that the police could eliminate false confessions: they just said that Harold White had been tied to a chair in his trailer and tortured to death. Getting hold of a copy of the police files took several weeks while I searched for a journalist who wanted to be a published poet, but I finally found one who could get the information I needed.

There was still no obvious suspect; no sign of forced entry, nor any forensic evidence of an intruder—or even of any visitors, except for the Sheriff, who had a good alibi for the time of death. White had been tied to his chair with a length of electric flex studded with Christmas lights, and gagged with gaffer tape. A lamp with a dimmer switch, which the Sheriff didn't remember seeing in the trailer before, was plugged into the socket usually reserved for the television, and White's penis was plugged into that. The scarring indicated that the 'lamp' had been turned on and off at least a dozen times, for varying durations and with the 'dimmer' being turned up higher each time. Bruises on his face suggested that he'd blacked out at least once, and been woken by being slapped. The coup de grace, however, had come from a powerful charge across his chest, which had stopped his heart. The cables were attached to two hooks embedded in his nipples.

Fish hooks.

SPIN

TIME AND PLACE ARE UNIMPORTANT, but I am older than any of you. I was older even than Obscenity, destroyed an inestimable age ago by an enemy Barque, a Carnivore like ourselves, Murderous. Carriers have never attacked Carnivores: I cannot remember a time, and I am older than the oldest of you. Boojum 42 and Loviatar, who are/were historians, cannot remember such a time. But Carnivores, we Carnivores, we prey on carriers, and on the enemy Carnivores when we can; it's the natural order of things. But not on our own, Murderous. You have defied nature. You have gone spin, and we must kill you.

Murderous, I scream; you have the bones you were born with!

My name is Freaklover, and mine is an asymmetrical face of torps and disruptors, and I sit close and eagerly behind it. Far behind me are two engines: I am not so fast as you, Murderous, but out paths will intercept, if you live so long. Loviatar, faster even than you, will cross your path sooner still. Base, poised on the brink of a down like Sisyphus pushing a rock, tells me that you have killed a carrier and a Carnivore, Savage Sky, and that you are hunting Starfucker, proudest and bloodiest of the Carnivores, of the Barques. If Loviatar and Flamerider and Starfucker spare any of you—for you must have been wounded by Savage Sky, and even carriers are armed—I shall be delighted to destroy it.

I hear Boojum 42 and Necrophile talking: they know they cannot reach you, and are disappointed, of course. But we cannot all be drawn to the one kill, as if a down had stolen us: some must escort the carriers, and the others... we protect the borders from the enemy. There are few known ends for Carnivores—usually, they shoot you, or you go spin and we shoot you. It's the natural order of things.

I have nebulous memories of being a carrier—no, of being a carrier pilot. And Starfucker, now of the beautiful/balanced/bloody face of ACE muzzles and disruptors; Starfucker, who rides far back on his Barque near the single engine; Starfucker, too, was once a carrier pilot, named Fleischer. Starfucker doesn't depend on speed: he sits, often deep within the orbits of the downs, so that the hell is behind him, and he looks merely like a sunspot, while his enemies shine like Sirens, like downs, like little hells. Like a sword before him is his Barque of ACEs, disruptors, missiles and torps. Most of the Carnivores, like the carriers, have redundant life-support systems, but he gave that space to weapons. So did I, and I'm still quite alive. I don't have legs any more, but I've never needed them: I was born an Outer, in the weightlessness of Base. Most of the Barques were born downers: I know you were, Murderous. You probably still have your brittle, heavy, calcium bones. I've never even seen a down, save through the screens and scanners. I knew downers when the crawlers stopped at Base—but crawler pilots aren't really Outers or downers, I guess. I mentioned this once to Boojum 42, and he laughed.

"A rope between beast and superman, a rope across the abyss," he said.

Boojum 42 is barely half the size of the other Barques: claims it makes him a harder target. Necrophile once asked me why all the Barques, Carnivores and carriers, were the same size, seven modules by three.

It's just the natural order of things.

"Boojum is smaller."

"I'm unnatural," replied Boojum 42. We all lay around Base like cripples, while suited Outers repaired our Barques. All within conversational distance, hardly a second's lag. "Man's whole purpose, Freaklover, is to defy nature."

You can't defy nature.

"Antimat. You and I, all the Barques, and all the Outers, defy nature by merely existing. Antichrist, you remember him; he thought it was natural for him to live in the Out, so he blew all his seals and tried to fly without his Barque. Nature killed him, Freaklover. Nature kills all of us out here, unless we stop her. You try going without these repairs, and see how long you live. 'Cause we all came from a down, once, you know that, Freaklover?"

I didn't.

"Your ancestors did, Baseborn."

Fuck my ancestors. Outers don't like downs or downers, and Carnivores hate them. When a carrier won't go near a down to drop cargo, they make him a Carnivore. We only go to Base for repairs—but you, Murderous, when your bones break, when your lungs decay, no-one will repair you, not even if you outrun Starfucker and Flamerider and Loviatar and I. What will you do, Murderous? Get taken by a down, pretend you're a crawler? We offer you the honour of dying like an Outer.

"Your ancestors already did that, Freaklover. But that Barque you're part of: is that natural?"

It is. I am this Barque, and it am I. Whatever is, Boojum, is natural.

"Antimat. Why is your Barque that size?"

It's the size of a Barque.

"Who decrees?"

It's a law. Like the speed of light. If Barques should be bigger, they'd be bigger.

"Antimat. I asked, when I converted. They said it wasn't done. Not couldn't be. They hadn't any more fucking idea than you. So I made myself smaller. It can be done. It's not nature, Freaklover. It's just rules. Downer rules. You obey downer rules."

"You're spin."

"No. Not yet. I'm not shooting anyone, am I? But you think about it. Nearly everything you can't explain is a downer rule, and they're not going to tell you."

From here, the nearest down is just a Siren-like point, and no other Barques are visible. I wait.

Loviatar can see you now, Murderous, even if I can't. She's not in range, yet: 15 megs is the maximum range for an ACE. ACE range is probably as close as you will come, my computer tells me, and ACEs aren't really dangerous. Many encounters end with both Barques surviving, easily able to return to Base. It's almost like a game.

I wait. When the casts of Loviatar and Murderous, you, Murderous, reach me, they are already old. How old? Time is meaningless, but I can see a faint point now, too fast to be a Siren, or even a down, and my computer tells me it's you, Murderous. Waiting isn't easy. The casts show me that you have been badly damaged, losing your missiles, a disruptor, an engine, even the redundant bridge you built in for emergencies like this.

"This is Loviatar. Spinner Murderous is out of range. Will attempt to manoeuvre for pursuit." Barques, however, are not easily manoeuvred, and she will return to the fray later than I—if the fray remains, Murderous, if you remain. Downers may be eaten by their downs, buried so they can't see the sky, the Out, the Sirens and the hell that scare them so, but you will have a Barque's death, and after a Barque's death, nothing remains. When you are consumed by the Out, when you are one with the Out, you are pure and honourable nothing.

"This is Loviatar. Am returning to Base. Damage slight; no modules lost save missile launcher." Her voice changes, very slightly. "Burn him, whoever's next."

I will, Loviatar, if I can. I will.

There's a down in view, now; a distant disc. Magnification even shows the rocks, little downs, huddling around it, and a dark ring. A memory twinkles somewhere behind me: I feel it as I might feel a damaged engine.

A point of light approaches the down: Flamerider. He will burn you next, Murderous. The tourney between you and Loviatar was like a game: an exchange of ACE fire, a missile each, never close enough for disruptors. But you turned disruptors on Savage Sky and destroyed his life-support. I can see another point, now; Starfucker, in all his lethal glory. He's closer than you, but his one engine doesn't throw much light, certainly not when he's between you and the hell. He doesn't believe in running, unlike you. He kills when he can.

"This is Flamerider. Cannot intercept. Burn him for me."

His casts have reached me: they show the dark-ringed down ahead of me, they show its rocks as discs, not points.

"This is Flamerider. I've been snatched by a down: my own fault. I'm going too fast. Nothing anyone can do. Don't bother asking questions: my computer said I couldn't do it, but I wanted to be there, I wanted to eat that down-loving spinner, so I tried to bounce off the gravity well. Miscalculated. I'm still accelerating, seven point three something gees. Can't turn. Any manoeuvre will only send me into the rings, at best, or into a rock, and there are downers on the rocks." To kill Downers is unnatural. Downers aren't worth killing; they could never hurt us. They could never reach us.

The images show the down much closer: the disc nearly fills the screen. I can hear a conversation between Boojum 42 and Necrophile, hours old: they won't hear this until long after Flamerider is dead, after you are dead, Murderous. He may be dead already: certainly this has taken seconds to reach me. Boojum 42 and Necrophile are talking about Savage Sky: Boojum 42 says he knew her well when they were downers on... but no-one remembers down names. We name the Sirens—Sirius, Vega, Canopus, Arcturus—for they are home. Boojum 42 can't remember Savage Sky's downer name, either, or what she looked like. I can't remember my Base name, either. It doesn't matter. I am Freaklover.

Flamerider will probably burn himself, rather than sink into the down. He isn't answering my messages. Maybe, like Antichrist, he's blown his seals, giving himself to the Out.

"What's Loviatar mean?" asks Necrophile, as though it had only just occurred to him.

"Loviatar was a Goddess of Pain."

"What's a Goddess?"

"Gods and Goddesses were downer lies. No, not really lies. More like dreams, predictions. Gods were Outers. They used to think that the hell was a God, an Outer in a Barque. Called him Apollo, Ra, Utu, Surya, The Father, The Sun, The Holy Ghost. Used to think the downs and the Sirens were Gods, too. All Gods were Outers. Some were Carnivores, some were carriers, some of the lesser Gods were crawlers, visiting the downs. Gods were down predictions of Outers. They always wanted to be Outers."

"Why aren't they?"

He asks too many questions. Starfucker is a disc, now, plainly elongated. You are a constellation; two bright points and a faint. Loviatar slowed you down; you're no faster than I am, now. Loviatar is a faint star, now, too. And the down is a disc, and one of its rocks is a disc, a disc I can remember.

Enemy Barques look like ours: they're built of exactly the same modules. Maybe this is natural, but Boojum 42, curse him, has started me wondering again. It used to surprise me when I was a carrier pilot, but nobody ever bothered explaining, any more than they explained who the enemy was, or why Barques were usually the same size, or... I forget most of my old questions. I should be kinder to Necrophile, I suppose; he's only young, at least as a Carnivore. The only younger is Mordred, who I've never seen even as a point...

I...

I wish I had a head to shake, shoulders to shrug. The past won't go away...

The computer warned me away from the rock, but I stared at it a moment longer. Here, once, I saw a crawler unlike all other crawlers; near as big as a Barque, but not made of modules like ours, and unarmed. I told myself that it was downer-built... but downers can't even build crawlers... can they? Downers are only downers. We build the Barques and the crawlers alike, we Outers.

Base told me to kill it, so I did.

"Weren't you once a downer, Necrophile?" asks Boojum 42, softly.

I steer away from the rock; it is near enough to show features, large craters. Starfucker is in range, now. Maybe he'll save a piece of you for me. Necrophile is blathering about having been born on a down, but always knowing he was an Outer. Starfucker fires his ACEs. Flamerider's casts show the down as though it were the entire Universe, the entire Out. What a bizarre, obscene idea: a *down* for a Universe.

Starfucker's casts tell me that you're already dead: critical damage to both life-support systems and the bridge. You've destroyed his missiles and launchers, but no other significant damage, and he's still firing. Torp range now, and he fires all of them, hitting mostly fuel tanks and engines. There's no sign that it makes any difference, but he's in disruptor range now, and firing. And again. And again. And again.

The casts show little that is even remotely recognisable: you look as alien as that crawler. You look obscene, downer-built. Even the enemy Barques look more like us. One I killed once looked exactly like my friend Astaroth: one engine, a face of missiles and disruptors, bridge far back and to one side. Why are they our enemy? They're Barques like us, Outers like us... but maybe they follow downer rules, like a dirty joke of Boojum 42's.

And Starfucker is still firing, back onto ACEs now. Your entire face has been burnt away, and only the remnants of your bridge holds the ends together. The next burn reduces you to three, unidentifiable fragments.

I suddenly realised that Flamerider's images have stopped.

Starfucker is barely visible as a Barque, almost at the edge of the hell. Loviatar is only a point. You I can't see at all, save as a cast from Starfucker's scanners. I can remember those casts from my childhood. Tourneys and kills were always shown on holo. The crawler pilots told me it was the same on the downs, too. Perhaps they regarded it as a game.

I cut engines, fire retros, slowing down to steer a return to my border territory. Starfucker and Loviatar are doing the same. Your momentum, I calculate, will send your scant remains past the border and into the enemy Out: not an inappropriate end for a spin. Almost as dishonourable, and neither as quick or pretty, as hitting a down and burning.

But I can't help hearing you laughing, even though you're dead. You know. You know. Starfucker will go spin, in some meaningless time. He's too good for the enemy to kill. Starfucker will go spin, shooting at everything, and we'll have to burn him too.

But I won't see it. I'm oldest, older than any of you, and you know, I'm going to be next.

TWILIGHT OF IDOLS

– I –

THE THIN, pale-faced man had been sitting quietly on the edge of his seat as though prepared to flee, obviously in awe of the august company, but the conversation at the table had somehow drifted from opera to politics and the little man had started to orate, almost to preach, condemning communism and all communists in venomous phrases. Though hung with tapestries, the villa's marble halls unfortunately had excellent acoustics, and the man's voice became louder and increasingly strident until it was impossible for anyone anywhere in the building not to be painfully aware of him. Rudolf looked over his shoulder at the stranger, then returned his attention to the wine; the villa's cellar was even better than its acoustics. "Methinks he doth protest too much," he muttered. "Even for the stage. Still, he might make a Cassius; he has the lean and hungry look."

His wife, Thea, spared the orator a brief glance, and shrugged. "The eyes are interesting, but the moustache has to go. Who is he, anyway?"

The director peered at the man through his monocle, shrugged, and with a barely visible gesture, summoned the butler. "Yes, Herr Lang?"

"The loudmouth in the riding leggings," said Fritz Lang, with a slight nod. "Who is he?"

Anton shrugged. "One Herr Hitler, sir. A set designer, or so he led me to understand. He waited outside for an hour to see the Baron and refused to leave; the Baron finally asked me to admit him."

The director nodded: the Baron, Clemens zu Franckenstein, was the manager of the Royal Theatre. "He has some interesting ideas on staging

216

Wagner," the butler continued, and then a hint of distaste crossed his normally carefully impassive face, "but unfortunately, no manners. I was going to see if the Baron wished him to leave."

The other woman at their table said nothing, but watched as Anton walked over towards the table where the orator was still holding forth. More of the Baron's staff gathered around him, and the man quietened down rather than yell into their faces. A few minutes later, he was persuaded to leave. Anton opened the huge windows, to admit the warm fresh breeze from the spring *föhn*, and the conversation drifted back to talk of film and theatre and music, as though all thoughts of the man had been blown away.

– II –

"HERR Hitler!"

The orator was walking along the Thierchstrasse, dressed much as she'd seen him at Clemens's villa; his face was overshadowed by a slouch hat, and he carried a riding crop, but the woman could have recognised him by his walk alone. He turned around slowly, looked her up and down, and nodded stiffly. "Yes?"

"My name is Irene," she said, walking briskly towards him. "I'm a friend of Clemens zu Franckenstein's; I saw you at his villa, two weeks ago."

Hitler shrugged slightly, and looked her up and down. She was taller than he, and looked to be in her forties, at least ten years his senior, but with a handsomeness that suggested that she'd once been a great beauty. Her contralto voice spoke of opera training. "Yes?"

"I have a proposition—a business proposition—to put to you. Do you have somewhere where we can talk?"

"What sort of business?"

"Call it a job offer."

"I have a job."

She smiled thinly. "I know. You're a V-Mann, a political education officer… but I think this job may be more to your liking."

"You were with those movie people," said Hitler, suddenly recognising her. "Rudolf Klein-Rogge, and that, that director…"

"Fritz Lang. Yes, that's right. Fritz wants to make a series of films of the *Ring* cycle, and I'm helping with the script." She looked along the street, and nodded at a cafe. "In there?"

217

"You want me to design sets for the film?" he asked.

"No," she said, with a soft laugh. "Fritz was a painter, like you, and he's also been trained as an architect; his designs are quite brilliant. I –"

"How did you know I was a painter?"

"I have my sources," she replied with a small shrug, as she led the way into a café. She didn't speak again until they were seated in a booth and the waiter had taken their orders. "Do you enjoy being an informer?"

Hitler stared at her, and he paled. "I'm –"

"Lance-Corporal Adolf Hitler, Reserve Infantry Regiment No 16," said Irene softly. "Two Iron Crosses, one First Class. Regimental Diploma for Conspicuous Bravery. Military Service Cross with Swords, and Medal for the Wounded: you were shot once, and gassed a few weeks before the war ended. You were a messenger, carrying orders to the front lines. There were some things I couldn't find out, such as why you were never promoted past *gefreiter*…"

"I wasn't interested in becoming an officer," replied Hitler, stiffly. "What do *you* want?"

"A hero." Her voice was soft; he listened for mockery, heard none. "Are you interested, Corporal Hitler? Or are you happy where you are, giving lectures and spying?"

"Somebody has to do it," said Hitler, after a long pause. It seemed unlikely to him that his superiors would have chosen a woman like this to spy on him or try to test his loyalty, but Captain Mayr, his commander, was a Jew, with a Jew's cunning. "I'm a soldier. I obey orders. And because the Versailles *diktat* won't let us have weapons that are fitting for soldiers—"

"I'm not questioning your patriotism," Irene replied, with a flick of her fingers. "Have you ever killed anyone?" she asked.

He shrugged. "I don't know: you don't often see the enemy, when you're in the trenches. I'm a good shot—my favourite game when I was a boy was shooting rats—but I'm not a murderer, if that's what you want."

"No. I'm offering you a chance to face an opponent worthy of your courage again. You remember Siegfried's battle with the dragon Fafnir?"

"Of course."

"My father was a history professor, as well as a lover of Wagner's music, and his life's obsession was to see how much truth there was in the sagas, as Schliemann did with the Iliad and other archaeologists have done with the Bible or tales of King Arthur. Father was determined to find the historic Siegfried, or at least the historic Gunther. He believed, when he died, that he'd found much more than that; he'd found Gnitahead. Fafnir's lair."

Hitler snorted. "And the dragon's hoard, as well?"

"My father believed so," said Irene, sadly but levelly. "He and my brother went in search of it more than twenty years ago, but neither returned.

"In those days, I was married, and my son—my only son—was less than a year old. A few months ago, I received a letter from my father's lawyers, with a map of the way to Gnitahead. It was intended for my son, not me—but like you, my son served in the infantry at Ypres. Unlike you, he did not survive."

Hitler looked down at the table, then nodded. Irene reached into her purse and extracted two American banknotes, a twenty and a hundred bill, which she carefully tore in half.

"If you will come with me to Gnitahead, this is yours," she said, sliding half of the twenty across the polished table towards him; they both knew how valuable foreign currency was compared to the deutschmark. "If we find any treasure, half is yours, and whether we do or not..." She handed him half of the hundred.

"And if we find a dragon?" asked Hitler, not quite mockingly, as he pocketed both notes.

"If that part of the legend is true," said Irene, softly, "then perhaps the rest is true also—that bathing in Fafnir's blood will make you invincible, like Siegfried. If you want to find out, meet me at the railway station tomorrow—and bring a weapon."

"WHAT is this place?" asked Hitler, as Irene led the way through a cold squarish tunnel. "Some sort of mine?"

Irene nodded, and the lamp attached to her helmet sent shadows scrambling. "It was a salt mine. I don't know how recently it's been worked. But the lowest shaft leads into a cave with an underground river, and the river runs through the dragon's lair."

"And what is this dragon supposed to eat?" asked Hitler, dryly. "Its own tail?"

"Blind fish. Bats. I don't know. There are always people disappearing from this region, mostly young men and women, and rumours that

219

somebody has been killing them and dumping their bodies down some empty shaft. Maybe that's how the dragon feeds."

Hitler's snort showed what he thought of that theory. "How many other men have you led down here?" he asked, his hand on the butt of his revolver.

"None. None came this far. The brave young men all went to war and haven't returned, and those locals who are left are too scared of whatever lies down here."

"There are plenty of ex-soldiers who would have taken your money."

"Thousands, yes," she replied. "Some of them with war records as good as yours, or better. But most were fools who'd never heard of Fafnir, or cowards that I couldn't rely on, or criminals who would have robbed me and run."

Hitler nodded. He knew from experience that many demobbed soldiers, desperate for money or action, had turned to crime: many had joined the new political parties, and he saw dozens every night in the beer halls. A moment later, his curiosity won over his discretion, and he asked, "And you're sure I won't?"

"Fairly sure: I think if you were going to, you would have done it a few miles ago. And even if you do, I don't think you'll rape me as well. I don't know what drives you, Lance-Corporal, but it isn't sex, and I don't believe that money would be enough either. Patriotism? Glory? Maybe, like Siegfried, you want to rule. Whatever it is, you have enough imagination, enough vision, to have come this far." She led the way into a cave, and followed the sound of running water until they found the river. Then she removed the pistol from her belt and placed it in a watertight metal box, which she then wrapped in oilcloth. After a moment's hesitation, Hitler did the same.

The river had carved a tunnel passage through the rock, but it was very narrow and the ceiling was never high enough for Hitler to stand upright even in those places where they could wade rather than crawl or swim. Usually there was a pocket of air at the top large enough at least for their faces and flashlights, but a few times Hitler found himself wondering whether they were more likely to drown or just to be trapped in some crack too narrow for them to turn around in: either fate seemed far more likely than falling prey to a dragon, and every time something shifted beneath his feet or hands, he looked to see whether it was the remains of Irene's father or brother or some other fool. He sniffed cautiously at the air every time he emerged, careful not to breathe in any poisons: having nearly been killed by gas once, he had decided it was no fit fate for a human being, and resolved to kill himself cleanly with one of the weapons he was carrying rather than let that happen. Then Irene stopped so suddenly that he blundered into her, almost dropping his flashlight. "What –"

"Quiet!" she hissed. He blinked, shone his light upwards, and realised that they'd emerged into a larger chamber than any they'd seen since first wading into the underground river. He took another cautious sniff: apart from the stench of what must have been centuries of bat guano, the air was fresh. He scrambled to his feet—the water was barely up to his knees—and both looked around.

The lights disturbed a few bats, which fluttered around, and the dragon opened its eyes and growled low in its throat. Hitler swung the light around until he could see the animal, and nearly burst out laughing. Though its snake-like neck and the heavy tail that balanced it were long and thick, the dragon's body was scarcely larger than that of his beloved Alsatian dog and closer to the ground. They stared at each other for a moment, then the dragon drew back its head like a snake about to strike. Hitler ducked, and a glob of corrosive slime spattered across his protective helmet.

Irene unwrapped the oilskin parcel with a flick of her wrist, and was trying to open the metal box when Hitler grabbed her and pulled her back down into the river. "What are you –"

Rather than waste time speaking, he reached into his sodden coat and removed a 'potato-masher' grenade. Irene's eyes widened, and she nodded. Hitler unscrewed the cap, then raised his head above the water to stare the dragon in the face again. As it opened its mouth, he pulled the string, hurled the grenade, and began counting. One... two...

To his disappointment, the grenade fell short of the dragon's raised head, but rolled between its great clawed feet. Three... Hitler plunged back into the water and continued to count. The grenade exploded on five, but he didn't raise his head until he'd counted past twelve.

The air was alive with startled bats, but a few seconds later, he and Irene could see the shattered body of the dragon, its precious blood leaking from its mangled belly. Irene removed the entrenching tool from her belt and thrust it into Hitler's hands. "Quick!" she said. "The blood! Dig a pit!"

Hitler scrambled out of the riverbed and scurried across the guano-covered floor. The rock was too hard to dig—even his pick made barely a scratch—so he removed his helmet and placed it beneath the largest of the wounds, to catch the blood. He did the same with his boots, then hastily peeled off his wet clothes with one hand while holding the other over another jet of blood. Within a minute, he was naked and had emptied the blood-filled helmet over his head. Remembering the tales of the deaths of Siegfried and Achilles, he smeared blood over himself liberally, careful not to leave any part of his skin vulnerable. "So this will make me immortal?" he asked, as Irene also began removing her clothing.

"No," she said. "Not immortal. We'll still age, and we're not immune to disease. But your skin will be better than any armour they can make for a panzer: no bullet, no blade, no fire, will be able to penetrate it.

"Pain, however... you will still feel primary pain as you would now. If you were to accidentally put your hand on a hot stove, it would jerk away instantly... but if you chose to, you could stand in flames or even swim in molten iron and not be burned, and the pain would stop as soon as you've moved away from the heat. And once we've eaten the flesh, we'll be safe from poison—but not from gas. If you try to breathe mustard gas again, it will still corrode your lungs, though it won't blister your skin."

Hitler shuddered.

"At least," said Irene, "that's what my father believed. He never had a chance to test it." She dipped her hands in the helmet and wiped the blood over her face. Hitler laughed at the sight, then turned away from her for a moment and reached for his belt. He waited until Irene's face and neck were wet with blood, then drew his dagger and stabbed her under the chin. She stared at him in horror, then realised that the point had failed to penetrate.

Both were silent for a moment, and Hitler withdrew the knife and ran the edge across the back of his left forearm. It made no impression.

Irene smiled. "It works!" she crowed. "My father was right!"

Hitler grinned back, then thrust the dagger up under her ribcage and into her heart. He stood there until he was sure she was dead, then began searching for the dragon's hoard.

– III –

THE prostitute looked at Hitler with her usual carefully neutral expression; after all, she'd heard much stranger requests. They agreed on a price, twenty marks, and then Hitler handed her his riding crop and stripped down to his leather breeches.

As he requested, she whipped him for several minutes, wondering why he was laughing. Then he lay on the ground, face-up, and begged her to kick him as hard as she could. "It's your money," she said with a shrug. "Anywhere in particular?"

"Everywhere except the face," he said.

She shrugged again, and complied. Hitler laughed—giggled, almost—as she did so, and her impassive mask almost faltered. She thought she'd grown inured to her job, and that nothing would ever disgust her again, but there was something about this strange little man that made her feel as though she were treading in something indescribably foul.

– IV –

Fritz Lang peered at the letter and shook his head.

"What is it?" asked Thea. The paper was thick and looked expensive, and she could see a swastika on the letterhead and a jagged, angry-looking signature.

"Adolf Hitler," said Fritz, sourly, dropping the letter onto his dinner plate, his appetite gone. "He's offered me a job as director of the Reich's film industry."

His wife smiled. "Well, why not? He's always said he admired your *Ring Saga*, and *Metropolis*..."

"And banned my last film," the director pointed out.

Thea shrugged. "A lot of people thought you were lampooning him, that Dr Mabuse was meant to be him..." She smiled. "Of course, they were right. Rudolf saw Hitler for the first time just before we made *Dr Mabuse*, and I'm sure the resemblance wasn't entirely coincidental..."

Fritz blinked. Rudolf Klein-Rogge, Thea's ex-husband, had first played the hypnotist and master criminal Dr Mabuse in 1922; highlights of that film had included a car which filled with poisonous gas, and Mabuse ordering his mistress to commit suicide to avoid being taken prisoner. "What? Where?"

"At Clemens zu Franckenstein's. We'd just finished *Weary Death*. I know it was twelve, thirteen years ago, but surely you remember him? He was a stage designer; you called him a loudmouth. Are you going to accept?"

"No," said the director. "Hitler is a monster; I want nothing to do with him."

"I'm sure some of your actors would say the same about you," said Thea, dryly. "Darling, if it mattered to him that your mother was Jewish, he'd never have offered you the job. People don't like Hitler because he's not scared of anyone or anything, and they're not used to politicians who aren't scared. You talk about him as though he were some sort of robot; I'm sure, underneath it all, he's quite human." She smiled. "If you pricked him, would he not bleed? If you poisoned him, would he not die?"

"And if you wronged him, would he not revenge?" growled Lang. He left Germany that night.

– V –

1944 had begun badly for the Reich, with the Russians advancing into Poland again as well as reclaiming Leningrad, and America establishing the War Refugee Board to help Jews escape. Five months later, the Americans had landed at Normandy, and a report by escapees from Auschwitz had been delivered to the Pope. Increasing numbers of Germans were beginning to doubt his infallibility—even some of his generals, Hitler knew, privately and traitorously thought he should never have broken his pact with Stalin and tried to fight the war on two fronts.

Because none of the rooms in the bunker at Wolfsschanze were large enough for the map table and the all the officers assembled, staff meetings had to be held in a converted barracks above ground. Hitler looked down at the map through a magnifying glass, scowling as General Jodl described the Allies' capture of Caen and St Lo. "And on the Russian front?"

"They'll be in Madjanek within a week," said General Heusinger, gloomily. "If we used some of the trains that are shipping prisoners to Auschwitz, we might be able to hold it..."

"We could use gas," suggested General Jodl. "We have stockpiles of Substance 83..."

"And so do the Allies," snapped Hitler. "If they learn that we've used it, even on the Russians, they'll use it on us, gas us as though we were Jews. And the Russians may also have it. We won't be the first to use it."

Heusinger and Jodl looked at each other, but neither spoke; neither did any of the other twenty-two men in the room. Most, even the clerks, knew that Hitler still had a revulsion for chemical warfare more than thirty-five years after being exposed to mustard gas himself, and no-one was prepared to argue with him on a last-ditch measure. Colonel von Stauffenberg, standing near the door, excused himself and left. No-one noticed that he'd left his briefcase under the heavy oak table.

"Maybe we should destroy the gas chambers at Madjanek," said Heusinger, after a long silence. "Before the Russians get there. If they find them, they'll tell the world…"

Hitler shook his head. "Maybe," he replied. "But there have been stories told before. People either don't believe them, or don't care. Stalin has no love of Jews either, and his own hands aren't clean; how many graves did we find in the Ukraine? And how many of their own people are they torturing in Siberia?" There was a faint hint of approval in his voice: the Russians, who he'd once predicted were too primitive to build a working motor vehicle, were far less efficient in their attempts at extermination than the Reich but they didn't lack for zeal, and the some of their methods of both physical and psychological torture were remarkably ingenious for such a backwards people. Not as sophisticated or useful as the Gestapo's, of course, much less Mengele's, but worthy of respect nonetheless. He shrugged. "We'll invite the Red Cross to see one of our camps and show them that the rumours are only that. Tell Himmler to arrange it."

SS Hauptsturmführer Günsche, Hitler's adjutant, nodded, and suddenly the briefcase under the table exploded. Hitler, standing next to the bomb, flew through the air and landed on Field Marshall Keitel. Ceiling beams cracked, and the lamp crashed down on Jodl's head, stunning him. von Stauffenberg, standing a few hundred yards away, watched as bodies and debris came hurtling out of the windows, and turned and ran.

As the smoke cleared, Hitler painfully hauled himself back to his feet. His hair was burnt and smouldering, his ears were ringing, and his pale blue eyes were glazed. Günsche and the other SS officers, who'd been standing in the corner furthest from the bomb, stared in amazement at Hitler's torn uniform, and the unmarked flesh beneath it—and then at the mangled remains of Colonel Brandt, who'd also been standing next to von Stauffenberg's briefcase, and the other wounded men.

Hitler looked around the room, and, though shocked and concussed, pulled himself together. "You will tell nobody what you've seen," he barked, then glanced at Brandt's corpse. "Say… say I had left the room, or was away from my chair… no, say the bomb was moved to the far side of the table leg." Günsche nodded, and walked unsteadily towards the radio set, only to find that it had been wrecked by the blast. "And say that Providence... no, *Destiny* has protected Germany from a... a great tragedy. Say that the failure of this attempt is... a sign that that I am under, under the... the protection of a divine power." He smiled.

– VI –

THE vial was sheathed in a yellow metal tube which looked for all the world like a lipstick, and Eva smiled as she sucked the glass ampoule into her mouth. Hitler, sitting next to her on the couch, did the same. Eva dropped the metal tube onto the floor, and bit down hard. The thin glass shattered, and a stench of bitter almonds filled the poorly ventilated room, noticeable even over the reek of the blocked toilets. Hitler closed his eyes; he felt the ampoule crunch between his porcelain-and-metal teeth, and swallowed cyanide and glass splinters. Eva's jaws clamped down in a horrible risus, and Hitler felt her convulse as she gasped for air, but he didn't open his eyes until she had collapsed onto the floor. A few minutes later, when Eva had stopped moving, he reached for his revolver, placed the muzzle in his mouth, and squeezed the trigger.

The bullet slammed into his hard palate, ricocheted, and rolled down his throat; Hitler coughed as he felt it sear its way down his oesophagus and into his stomach. Incredulously, he removed the gun from his mouth, stared at it, then pointed it at his chest and fired again.

The bullet punched a burning hole through his soup-stained tunic but failed to leave a mark on his skin. Screaming an oath, he threw the pistol away and stood, almost tripping over his wife's corpse.

He listened, wondering if anyone else remained in the bunker. Goebbels had announced his intention of poisoning his children before he and his wife committed suicide; Bormann, he was sure, would flee as soon as he felt it was safe to do so, and might already have gone. He staggered towards the door. If only Heisenberg had been able to build one of the bombs he'd once talked about, a single bomb able to destroy an entire city; he could have turned all Berlin into his pyre, killing the treacherous Russians and his own cowardly people and leaving a vast ruin as his monument... he realised, to his horror, that he was weeping, and turned away from the heavy steel door as it opened. "My Führer?"

It was Major Günsche, still in his black SS uniform proudly bearing the special wound badge issued to the survivors of the Wolfsschanze bombing. Hitler stared at him wearily, then nodded at Eva's body. "Do you have the petrol?"

"I've sent Kempka to fetch it."

"Burn her," he said, wearily. "And the Goebbels family—I take it they *are* dead?" he added.

"Yes, my Führer."

"Good." Hitler looked around the small bedroom, then totttered into the conference room with Günsche following him. "Where's the doctor?"

"He left with Reichsleiter Bormann."

Hitler grimaced. "See if you can find a body that could pass for mine, and burn that, too. Maybe it will fool the Russians when they get here— for long enough for me to escape."

"Sir?"

"Don't look so shocked," Hitler snapped. "I can't let them take me alive. The cyanide didn't work, the bullets didn't work, even a bomb didn't work... what else should I do? Hang myself?" He grimaced. "Get me some civilian clothes. Women's clothes, if that's all you can find; it worked for Lenin."

Günsche allowed himself a ghost of a smile. "It might fool Russians: have you ever seen Russian women?" Hitler didn't reply. "Where will you go?"

"I don't know, and it's best that you don't either." The bunker rocked as a shell hit the upper level. "Goodbye, my friend."

– VII –

THE Russian attaché opened his briefcase and removed a fat manila file. "These are the photographs, and Dr Shkaravski's report," he said, smoothly. "Unfortunately, by the time our soldiers reached the bunker, the bodies were already too badly burned for the remains to be readily identifiable, but we're confident that this is Eva Braun, and the other body would seem to be that of Hitler."

Fritz Lang looked suspiciously at the translation of the pathologist's report, snorting with amusement at the description of the undescended testicle. He'd called in a lot of favours for the privilege of seeing these Soviet Intelligence files, but he'd long had an uncomfortable feeling that he was in some way responsible for Hitler's career. "It's a kinder death than he deserved," he muttered, "and I hope he burns in Hell forever."

The attaché allowed himself an undiplomatic smile. "I'm sorry that I don't believe in Hell," he said, softly, "but, just this once, I hope that Marx was wrong, and that you are right."

Fritz chuckled. "I'll drink to that," he said. He poured himself a drink, and offered one to the Russian, who accepted it with a gracious nod. "The important thing is, we're sure he's dead."

– VIII –

THE prisoner was never named, and his number was known only to a select few. In his first year in the cell, various attempts had been made to remove his tongue for fear that he might say his name loudly enough to be heard through the thick walls and door, but all the methods they'd tried—scalpels, saws, drills, flame, acid, intense cold, even flesh-eating insects and plants—had failed. By the time Beria suggested filling the mouth permanently with molten lead or something similar, Stalin had decided that he liked the sound of the man's guttural screams too much and had settled for binding the prisoner's toothless jaws between his visits.

Beria walked into the cell and looked at the twisted form. While nothing they'd tried was able to pierce his skin, not the smallest needle nor the most powerful anti-tank weapon, starvation and thirst had withered his flesh, and driving a tank over his legs and arms had gradually broken his still-human bones. The head of the secret police chuckled as he remembered the crunching sounds, and mad pale blue-grey eyes stared back at him.

Beria considered telling the prisoner that Stalin had died a month before, but that might have been a kindness; better to let him wonder. "We're going to move you," he said, in German. "It's time you did some useful work; from each according to his abilities, as Marx said."

The pale blue eyes stared, uncomprehendingly. Beria wasn't sure whether the prisoner understood anything anymore, after nearly eight years in the cell, but it hardly mattered. "I know," he said, as he freed the prisoner's jaw, "you may not think you can be of much use to anybody, but you're wrong. You can perform a great service to Soviet science." He grinned. "We're giving you to the Army Chemical Corps, to help test some new gases."

The prisoner opened his mouth and emitted a thin, whistling scream that reminded Beria of some Wagnerian opera. He chuckled, wondering whether the scientists could find some way to kill the man, or whether he might somehow scream forever.

WHAT GOES AROUND

ALLEN WAS STARING AT THE SKY and waiting for the Leonids when his wristphone rang. He jumped at the unexpected sound: he disliked telephones, and used his so rarely he'd never bothered getting it implanted. Wondering who would ring his unlisted number at this hour of the morning, he flipped the phone open without looking at the screen. The sky interested him more, and he had an old-fashioned fondness for watching it in real time, even though he knew that most of what he was seeing was centuries old. "Yes?" he said.

"Did I disturb you?" asked Leila. "I knew you'd be up."

One day, he thought sourly, he'd have to reprogram the filter on his phone so that his ex-wife's calls went straight to voicemail. Or wife, strictly speaking; they'd been separated for nearly three years, but hadn't bothered filing for divorce. "What is it?"

"Someone told me about your application to use Cyclops, and I was wondering if we could help in any way."

'We,' Allen knew, meant Leila and her new girlfriend Jordan, who was also one of her colleagues at SpaceForce. "I didn't realize that fell under your jurisdiction," he said guardedly. The exact nature of Leila's job was meant to be a secret; she could no more talk about her work with friends than she could talk about her friendships at work. Even the title of her doctoral thesis was classified. Allen, who had been her astrophysics tutor in her freshman year, suspected that there were some in the Pentagon who would have liked to excise parts of his memory: the fact that they hadn't, indicated to him that this wasn't possible with current technology, which sometimes struck him as unfortunate. He would cheerfully have given up that information in exchange for being able to forget some things, including the arguments he and Leila had had when she'd allowed herself to be recruited.

"It doesn't. Someone recognized your name, and thought I'd be interested—but that was all they told me."

Allen grimaced. "Have you heard of Orpheus—I mean, AC19?" SpaceForce frowned on non-Christian mythology; their historical revisionists had even re-named the Mercury and Apollo programs, and usually referred to Cyclops as the Brazilian Multi-Frequency Array.

"The artificial comet?"

"Yes. Launched on the sixtieth anniversary of Apollo 11. Gave us the best look we've ever had at Pluto, then out to the Oort Belt."

"What –" There was a microsecond pause as Leila did the math. "It's due back?"

"Assuming it's still vaguely intact, yes. No-one's tried listening for it for nearly thirty years; the signal was fading, and the project's budget was cut. But if it *is* on its way back and still transmitting, it should get close enough to Earth for Cyclops to pick up the signal. Better still, if it can receive, we should be able to reprogram its computer and get it to upload all the data it's stored. Of course, if they'd finished building that telescope at Congreve…"

"Are you sure you need Cyclops? There are smaller arrays…"

"And anything that's likely to be sensitive enough is under SpaceForce control. If Orpheus was broadcasting at full power, someone would have detected it by now. Either the power source is failing, or the antenna is damaged or out of alignment, or it's gone into standby… any number of things could have happened since we lost contact with it."

"How close will it come?"

"If nothing in the Oort interfered with its trajectory, it should pass just inside a million klicks from Earth on its way towards the sun. Do you remember what that is in miles?" he said, and immediately regretted it.

"Yes," she said, wearily. The U.S. was the only country on Earth not to use the metric system, which made things difficult for its remaining scientists. "Will it be visible?"

"If the solar panels open… then yes, in theory, at least from the southern hemisphere. I haven't seen any sign of it yet—and believe me, I've been looking."

"Hmm. I'll see what I can do."

"Thanks," he muttered. "Bye." He stared at the buttons on the phone, trying to remember which was the off switch.

MAJOR Robert Rand looked at the letter with deep suspicion. "I don't see what this has to do with electronic defense," he said carefully. He'd done a year of engineering before transferring to the MBA course, and while he'd retained a working grasp of the vocabulary and the mathematics, he often felt out of his depth when talking to the scientists nominally under his command. He also disapproved of women in the military, even in non-combat roles, and Leila in particular struck him as being little more than a civilian in midnight blue fetishwear.

"It's a useful test of our tracking and signal recognition procedures," Leila said, standing rigid in front of his realwood™ desk and looking past him towards the Washington Monument. "What if one of our rockets went astray? Would we be able to tell it from a piece of space junk—or a hostile?"

"What would a hostile be doing beyond the Moon?"

"If people knew we weren't looking there, it'd be the perfect place to hide something. And isn't it still policy that the Mars program is on hold, not cancelled?"

Rand snorted; promises of a manned mission to Mars had been repeated so often that they were no longer funny. "What makes you think this thing is still functional?"

"The reactor was designed to power it for at least 150 years. It's barely half that old."

"Plutonium?"

"Yes."

"What would happen if it crashed?"

Leila blinked. "There's no reason to think it will…"

"This guy says he can't be absolutely sure of its trajectory."

"Not absolutely sure, but… isn't that all the more reason to try to track it?"

"Point," Rand conceded. "Okay, I'll have these figures checked and get back to you. Dismissed."

Leila saluted, and walked back to her lab. Jordan didn't look up from her monitor as the door opened. "Any luck with Major Bland?"

"I don't know," she admitted.

"Seems to me you're sticking your neck out a long way to do a favour for an ex. Particularly when you keep telling me he's an asshole."

"Only sometimes. And this isn't just for Allen: it'd be good to do something just for pure science for once, without having to worry about the military applications."

"If you keep talking like that you'll end up like him, marooned on some godforsaken island and living off charity with nothing but a telescope for company."

Leila shrugged.

"I thought that was why you left him?"

"It was one reason. I said the telescope was too isolated, the accommodation too small, and it wasn't a good place to bring up children. He said the logical answer to that was not to have children. I think we'd both like to take back a lot of the things we said after that."

"Sorry. The department of revisionist history is across the river." She looked at her watch. "Bland's going to be leaving for his golf game in a few minutes. You want to get out of here?"

RAND smiled as Leila walked back into his office and stood at attention the regulation distance from his desk. It had been three weeks since he'd promised to look into the AC19 matter, and she'd wondered if he'd forgotten it. "Good news," the major said. "We've found your piece of space junk—at least, we have a radar echo of something the right size on the right trajectory. Your husband's calculations were spot-on; we should be able to keep track of it without any problems."

Leila smiled as she saluted. "Thank you, sir."

"Should be quite an interesting exercise. We may even manage to time it so that the detonation will be visible from here."

Leila felt her stomach do a flip-flop. "Detonation?"

"We can't run the risk of that much plutonium re-entering the atmosphere."

"You're going to destroy it?"

"Yes. As you said, it's a good test of the system."

"I meant the tracking system! The chances of it hitting Earth are negligible!"

"So are the chances of *our* hitting *it*," said Bland, dryly, "but if we miss it, and it misses us, who'll know? Or care?"

"TARGET practice?" Jordan repeated, removing her datashades to get a clearer look at her partner's expression.

"I wish I'd kept my mouth shut," said Leila, glumly.

"It's usually the best policy, around here," Jordan agreed. "Look, you know they'll probably miss—why ruin more than a hundred years of missile defense tradition? And if Asshole's calculations are right, it'll be back in another seventy-eight years with even more data…"

"Maybe. And even if it does, it'll have even less transmitting power, probably none. No, there's got to be a way to do this. And don't call him that."

"What can you do? Replace the warheads with tiny astronauts?"

"I wish. I…" She blinked. "Actually… that's…"

Jordan rolled her eyes. "I know that expression. That's your 'let's have a baby' expression."

"I wasn't –"

"You know the military's rules about compulsory paternity testing. If the baby's not your husband's, you –"

Leila leaned across the desk and kissed her. "This is a different sort of baby. Did I ever tell you you're a genius?"

"Not lately."

"I'll make it up to you. Do you have that list of the sensors on the AC-19?"

"Yes. It covers the spectrum from 200 nanometers to two meters. It's quite a nifty package, considering the size of the antenna, the age of the computer, and the fact that the software hasn't been updated since before we were born."

Leila smiled. That spanned the range from near ultraviolet into television and FM radio. "Can you get dinner tonight? I have some work to do."

"LASERS?" said Rand, looking at her proposal with his forehead handsomely furrowed. "But they have an even worse record than anti-missile missiles. Sure, they're more accurate, but the power requirements, even in a vacuum…"

"Not a laser," said Leila. "A maser. Microwave, not light: ten to a hundred millimetre wavelengths. And we can generate a strong enough beam using existing antennae, if we use enough of them. It's a pity we never finished building the Congreve telescope on Farside, but Cyclops should

234

be able to do the job if all the antennae put enough power on the one spot and send out a synchronized pulsed wave…"

Rand looked unconvinced. "You're sure of these figures?"

"Within the usual margin of error," she said, innocently. "I should be able to get them peer reviewed in time. And since it won't require much in the way of new equipment, it'll be cheaper than a salvo of missiles."

"I've already told the ABM teams to prepare the missiles," said Rand. "They're quite excited about it. You want me to tell them to cancel?"

Leila thought quickly. That would arouse suspicion among the anti-missile missile enthusiasts, and might lead them to check her figures. "That's up to you, sir. Of course it makes sense to have a backup plan, and I don't know enough about the budgetary considerations…"

As she'd expected, Rand blinked at the mention of money, and sat there for a moment weighing up the pros and cons. "I'll talk to the accountants," he said, "and let you know what th—we decide."

Three weeks later, Leila was standing in Mission Control wondering whether she looked as nervous as she felt. The big board ahead showed eight missiles converging on the Orpheus, and she looked down at her monitor waiting for the antennae to start transmitting. If she'd miscalculated…

"I have detonation!" said one of the ABM team; then, before the cheering had entirely died down. "Premature! Da—uh, darn!"

Leila gripped the edge of her console as the other seven missiles exploded or went badly off-course. She'd had to call in a lot of favours to get the self-destruct codes for all the warheads, and she could only hope that no-one noticed them among the transmissions. "Are we still tracking the thing?" Rand asked, smoothly.

"Yes," said one of the team. "It still seems to be on course… but it's breaking up…"

"You mean we hit it?"

"I think… hold on… no… it's a bigger signal, but it's stable. Something may have come loose."

Leila swallowed a sigh of relief. Orpheus had received the order to open the solar panels and acted on it. Now, even if it didn't get the transmission antenna aligned perfectly, it should soon start sending out a sufficiently powerful radio message that Cyclops—or some other Space-Force array—would pick it up.

"Definitely stable," the man said, puzzled.

"It's not going to hit us?"

"Not on this trajectory. But we've started picking up a radio signal from the object."

Rand turned to Leila. "When are you going to fire the masers?" he asked.

"We started transmitting high-power pulses three minutes ago," said Leila. "But it doesn't seem to be doing any damage."

"Why not?"

"I'm not sure. Either the beams aren't converging on exactly the right spot, or they're not synchronized perfectly, or the power isn't sufficient… oh, *blast!*"

"What?"

"It's just a guess… but I think we *may* have made a mistake converting from metric."

"I HAVE good news and bad news," Leila told Allen. "I managed to send out a powerful enough signal from Cyclops that we could reboot Orpheus's computer and tell it to start transmitting again. We've downloaded all the data it sent us, and updated its software. None of the missiles damaged it." She stuck her tongue into her cheek for a moment. "Something seems to have interfered with their guidance systems. It may even have been our transmissions."

He grinned back at her. "And the bad news?"

"The data we downloaded… well, it's officially a military secret."

"*What?*"

"The signal from Orpheus wasn't powerful enough for the civilian telescopes to pick up. I'm lobbying to get it declassified," she said, hastily, "but it has to go through a committee, and you know how long *that* can take."

"Can't you leak it?"

"Can you keep a secret?"

"Of…" Allen began, then shut his mouth. "Not one that big."

"Exactly. If anyone found out I was the source of the leak, I'd be court-martialled. And if they suspect that I sabotaged the missiles, I could be shot." She tried to smile. "But if all else fails, it *should* all be released in thirty years under freedom of information."

"*Thirty?*"

"You're an astronomer! Thirty years isn't that long. You'll only be seventy-three."

"Seventy-two," he corrected her, automatically.

"Well, our kids should be young enough to enjoy it."

"We didn't *have* any kids!"

"I know," she said. "But Jordan and I were thinking of trying and… well, we need a donor. And you know the military's position on paternity testing, don't you? If the DNA doesn't match yours, I could be dishonourably discharged as undesirable."

Allen shook his head, but couldn't hide a smile. "That would be totally unjust."

"Thank you. So, do you have space there for a couple of visitors?"

TEETH

THE LITTLE OBLONG BOX WAS MADE of ebony: I had to give Klein credit for a sense of irony, and possibly his knowledge of the genre. I stared at the glistening white lumps of ivory inside, and shook my head. "Beautifully preserved, aren't they?" said Klein.

"Suspiciously," I growled. "How sure are you of their provenance?"

He made a see-sawing gesture. He'd never had the looks or the range to make it as an actor (though that hadn't stopped him trying), but he was a pretty good salesman. He worked for a well-known theatrical agency, mostly getting people the stuff that they wanted that couldn't be written into their contracts. "They came from Temple's collection. Before that, I have my doubts," he admitted, "but he could hardly have asked for documentation. Body-snatchers didn't go in for paperwork."

"So you expect me trust you? Or am I supposed to try extracting some DNA?"

Klein smiled. "You could, I suppose, if you had anything for comparison... but you'll have to buy them first." He closed the little casket with an audible snap. "I'm not giving away free samples here. And if you look up the records, you'll find that when they disinterred Poe's corpse in 1875, the sexton noted that while the skeleton was in near-perfect condition, the top teeth had been dislodged from the skull."

I knew the story, of course. In 1873, the philanthropist George Childs had been persuaded that Edgar deserved a better monument than an overgrown grave in the Poe family plot, and paid for a new memorial. "So who collected these? The sexton?"

"Maybe, or one of the gravediggers. You could still sell teeth back then, to be made into dentures: maybe he meant to do that, or maybe he realized how valuable they were… anyway, one of Childs' servants found them in his collection after his death in 1894, or so the story goes, and sold them to Jules Verne. After that, the trail is easier to follow, though they were always sold in secret. Temple bought them some time in the 1980s."

I tried to look unimpressed, and refilled my glass with Amontillado, leaving his empty. "What's in the other box?"

Klein's smile became a grin, and he opened the second ebon casket with a conjurer's flourish. These teeth had been set into dentures in a wire frame, though the work was obviously primitive. "Don't touch," he said, pulling the box away from me.

"Whose are these supposed to be?" I said, dryly. "His teeth when he was a boy?"

"His mother's," Klein gloated. "I don't know whose dentures they were, but those are her original teeth."

"You can't be serious."

Klein lost a minute fraction of his smugness. "The provenance on these is a little less reliable," he admitted, "but the story is interesting. You remember Poe's story 'Berenice'?"

I may have sniffed: just because I make movies, doesn't mean I can't read. 'Berenice' is not Poe's best story, and it's most interesting for containing the seeds for 'The Fall of the House of Usher' and 'Ligeia', as well as some disturbing autobiographical elements. The obsessive Egaeus is betrothed to his cousin Berenice, but only notices her beauty when he sees her in the haunted library where his mother had died. (Poe's own mother, a beautiful actress, had died of tuberculosis when he was two: he married his cousin Virginia six months after 'Berenice' was published, and she died of tuberculosis several years later.) After Berenice dies, Egaeus breaks into her tomb and steals her most attractive feature, her teeth. When readers complained about the story, Poe actually apologized to the editor who published it, claiming that he'd written it on a bet that he "could produce nothing effective on a subject so singular" and allowing "that it approaches the very verge of bad taste"—which means it's pretty tame by modern standards.

"In 1834," Klein continued, "somebody approached Poe and offered to sell him these teeth, saying they were his mother's. Poe may have believed them, or not, but he couldn't meet their price, even though he'd just won a prize for 'MS. Found in a Bottle'. He wrote 'Berenice' hoping to raise the money, but by the time he was paid for it, the seller had disappeared. Childs' servant said he bought the teeth, and a letter from Poe describing the incident, from Lizzie Doten sometime in the 1870s, but the letter is lost. Of course, I can't really prove any of this, but since you're the biggest private collector of Poe memorabilia alive now that Temple is gone... and not exactly a premature burial, if I may say so..."

I smiled at that, involuntarily, and tried to hide it behind my glass, but I could tell that Klein had noticed. "So," I said, as blandly as I could manage, "you're asking me to pay out a quarter million based on the claims of a couple of grave-robbers, at least one thief, two fantasists—one of them the creator of a celebrated hoax—and a poet who claimed to be channeling the dead, and now a dealer in stolen artwork, and God knows how many fools and liars in between."

Klein shrugged: he didn't need to look around at the bookshelves, the bust of Pallas above the door or the mummy case in the corner to know how obsessed I was with Poe, horror's patron sinner. "You must be used to that."

He was right, of course—everybody in Hollywood lies constantly, if only to themselves—but that didn't stop it sounding like an insult, and I hate being insulted. "You've seen them," he continued, smirking. "Sleep on it, and decide for yourself, but don't take too long. I can always find another buyer: do you want to spend the rest of your life wondering what you could have had?"

Poe said it better than I could, of course: *And the evening closed in upon me thus—and then the darkness came, and tarried, and went—and the day again dawned—and the mists of a second night were now gathering around—and still I sat motionless in that solitary room—and still I sat buried in meditation—and still the phantasma of the teeth maintained its terrible ascendancy, as with the most vivid and hideous distinctness it floated about amid the changing lights and shadows of the chamber.*

Of course, I didn't spend all of that time motionless or meditating: I wasn't able to sleep for long without dreaming of adding those teeth to my collection, but I made the effort. I remembered to eat, and wash, and while I didn't need to leave the house, the phone and fax machine was never silent for very long: I had another two films in pre-production and one in post, so I had plenty to occupy my time if not my mind. But I kept returning to the library and staring at the treasures of my collection. The teeth, if I bought them, would have to go in the safe: if they were fake, then the fewer people who knew I had bought them and been fooled, the better. But if they were real, the idea of them belonging to someone else was unbearable.

I picked up a collection of Poe stories, and leafed through it, hoping he would give me an answer.

KLEIN was grinning again, or still, as he walked into my office at the studio on Friday night, opened his attaché case, and produced the boxes again. "I was sure you'd call," he gloated.

"Sure enough that you didn't try to sell them to anybody else?" I murmured.

He faltered slightly at that, but his insulting smirk returned as I handed him a glass. He gulped it down as though it were water, and I poured him another. "Yes," he admitted. "I knew you could pay more, and sooner."

I nodded, and opened the attaché case to show him the stacked banknotes, then snapped it shut again. "You have them?"

He opened his own case, removed the ebony caskets, and placed them on my desk. I looked inside both boxes and nodded. "The old law of Hollywood: give 'em what they want." I drew a deep breath. "What do *you* want, Klein?"

"Well, I'd like to be paid," he said dryly.

"You will be, I promise... but what do you do with your money? Do you collect anything?"

"No, not in the way you mean it. I mean, I like to have the best, but so does everybody, right?"

"The best of what?"

"The usual stuff. House, car, clothes... you know."

"Anything you wouldn't sell for a profit?"

"No, I guess not. Why?"

"So what really moves you is money?"

"Well, sure, same as everybody. So what?"

"Have you read much Poe, Klein? 'The Cask of Amontillado', perhaps? 'Hop-Frog'? 'The Conqueror Worm'?" Somehow, looking at his triumphant sneer brought that one instantly to mind. "'The Premature Burial'?"

"I saw some of the films."

"A poor substitute for the genuine article," I said. "And a man in your line should be able to tell real from fake." I pulled the small pistol from my pocket and pointed it at his stomach. "Take this, for example."

His eyes widened. "What—"

"This might just be a prop," I said, "and if it is, then you can just grab that case and run out of here and tell people how you managed to take me for a quarter mill. But it might not be: sometimes it's cheaper to buy the real thing than fake it." I grabbed the case, and nodded at the door. "There's something I want to show you."

It was so satisfying seeing him walk down the corridor, hands clasped behind his head, that I almost took pity on him—but if I did that, I'd be finished in Hollywood. I steered him towards the soundstage where the crew had reconstructed a used crematorium. I pressed the buttons to open the door, and another to start the burners. "For example," I said, "is that fire really hot enough to actually destroy a body?"

Klein was sweating by now, and I doubted it was because of the flames. "If it helps, it would need to be about 1600 degrees not to leave any identifiable remains. But paper burns at a third of that." And I threw the attaché case into the oven.

Klein squawked, then stared at me. "You're crazy!"

"Crazy enough to throw away a quarter million on a whim? Maybe I am… but then, that's not my money: it's yours. All you have to do is go and get it—but don't take too long."

He stared into the flames. "You're bluffing. The money's fake. Counterfeit. Copies. Whatever."

"Maybe," I said. "Maybe not. But to me, that money's worth less than the possibility that these teeth are real. What's it worth to you? Do you want to spend the rest of your life wondering what you could have had?"

He turned to look at me, hoping for some clue in my expression, then leapt into the flames. I pressed the button to close the door, and stood there for a few minutes half-hoping to hear a cry of "For the love of God, Montressor!"—but there was nothing but silence.

I waited for two hours, reading e-mails and script outlines on my Blackberry, before turning the flames off. When I returned to the studio on Monday, the oven had cooled down, and the crew was emptying it out.

Maybe I shouldn't have gone down to the soundstage to watch them, but I had to make sure there was nothing left that could be identified, no tell-tale hearts or anything of that nature. Klein was right about the money, of course: most of it was fake, but he'd probably never had a chance to find out. Fortunately, nothing in the ashes resembled a banknote, or the attaché case. Just some small fragments of bone indistinguishable from the others we'd used to decorate some of the sets, and some lumps of molten metal that had once been Klein's Rolex and his belt buckle.

One of the stage hands picked some white lumps out of the ashes, and looked at them curiously. Teeth. Human teeth. My heart grew sick, but then he tossed them into the bin with the other rubbish. I smiled to see them there, but my smile failed as the teeth seemed to form themselves back into Klein's familiar smirk. Another shovel-full of ash landed on top of them, but I could still see them glistening there. I see them still.

THE REALMS OF THE UNREAL

"'TRUE!—Nervous—Very, very dreadfully nervous I had been and am; but why will you say that I am mad?'"

The woman in the chair—psychiatrist, counsellor, therapist, interrogator, inquisitor, hallucination, whatever—looks blankly at me. "Poe," I explain. No response. Maybe she thinks I mean the Teletubby. "'The Tell-Tale Heart.'

A flicker. "Why do you use other people's words when you talk about yourself?"

"If I made up my own words, you'd think I was crazy."

She doesn't laugh.

"There are no books in here, so all I can do is remember stories I've read, repeat them to myself, like someone out of *Fahrenheit 451*. I'm starting to feel like... what's that Marquez story about the guy who decides he's going to write Don Quixote from scratch, without having read the original?"

She writes something in her notebook, but doesn't answer.

"Of course, in the story, he manages to make it word-perfect: in fact, the critics rave about it, say it has levels of meaning that Cervantes didn't manage. But that's just a story. The only version of Don Quixote I know that was written like that is pretty fucking spectacular, because it was illustrated by hand... no, that's not the right word... it's *illuminated*, like one of those medieval manuscripts. You can see it in the Collection de l'Art Brut."

She raises an eyebrow at that. Maybe it was my accent. "What's that? Or where?"

"Lausanne. Switzerland. It's a gallery for art created by psychiatric patients. It translates literally as 'Raw Art', but in English it's usually called Outsider art, which I always thought was a bit perverse, because the people who did it were *In*side. Schizophrenics, bipolars, psychotics. Maybe I should send them something when I get back Outside."

"Have you been there?"

"When I was a kid. It's near the headquarters of the Olympics committee. Now that's a fucking scary building. Looks like it was designed by Albert Speer—you know, Hitler's architect. I went to the Collection to get away from it. There's some scary stuff in there, too, but on the whole, it's actually quite wonderful."

"Do you feel at home there?"

"More than I do here, that's for fucking sure," I say, looking around her office. It can't be her real office; unless she's bureaucrat Barbie, born in a box, she must have a place somewhere with her certificates on the wall, photos on the desk, books on the shelves, *Far Side* cartoons on the calendar. This box is as bare of personal touches as the inside of a pill bottle with the label removed. The whole fucking place is like that.

"What about your real home?"

"It's my parents' home, not mine. I'm not saying that they're not my parents. I don't have, what to they call it, Kapsbrak, no, that's that kid out of the Stephen King novel, the one who, uh… *Capgras* syndrome. That's it."

"Capgras syndrome?"

"Thinking that people around you have been replaced by doubles. Like *Invasion of the Body Snatchers*. I read about it in *Scientific American*. Or Tourette's Syndrome. I just swear sometimes when I'm upset. Fuck, all teenagers swear. Sometimes I lose control of it, but Jesus, they're just fucking *words*!"

"But you do get depressed."

"Fuck, yes! Doesn't everyone?"

"You get depressed a lot."

"Maybe."

"And you write when you're supposed to be studying. They caught you writing a poem during your biology exam. But you won't take medication."

"The fucking pills stop me writing." She doesn't say that that's the point, but I can tell she's thinking it. "You didn't answer my question," I remind her. "Why can't I have some fucking *books*?"

"We can't provide books for everybody, and the ones you've chosen aren't going to help cure your depression. Other patients might find them even more disturbing. Anyway, there are magazines –"

"Doctor's waiting room magazines. Sometimes I think they're a major cause of illness."

"- and the TV..."

I snort. "Reality TV. If people want to see reality, why don't they look out a fucking window? Why don't you feed your closed circuit cameras here into everybody's TV instead, and let them vote us the fuck out of *here*?"

"IT could be worse," J whispers, as we sit at the furthest corner of the room from the TV, bent over a chess board. Big Brother may be watching us, but he's not a good listener. J has her eyes half-closed and is touching her eyelids lightly to make a kaleidoscope. She says she read that Dali said he'd do that if they tried to stop him painting.

"How?"

"We might not be white. Crazy people who don't look white get shipped overseas. Don't you watch the news?"

"Not anymore. They say it makes me depressed." It's just like reality TV, except that we don't get as many chances to vote people out. "Did you try asking for some books?"

"Yes, but I thought I'd better make up my own list. They'd get suspicious if I gave them yours."

"Why?"

"*One Flew Over the Cuckoo's Nest? Catch-22? Nineteen Eighty-Four? Don Quixote? The Outsider?* Ann Frank? Sylvia Plath?"

"They're all on the school's recommended reading list," I say, and cringe at how defensive I sound. "Okay, can you ask them for *La Passe-Muraille*?"

"They know I don't speak French. What is it?"

"It's about someone who can walk through walls. I suppose they might think that was escapist."

J looks around at the walls and up at the ceiling. They could also pass for white, at least in bright sunlight, but in this weather they're the same dull grey as the boiled potatoes we had for dinner. J, I know, sees them as a blank canvas, as she does most walls. That's sort of why she's in there, for painting graffiti. When they took her paints away, she went back to drawing on paper, but that seemed too flimsy, too temporary, so she started turning herself into a work of art instead, using her skin as a canvas. They tried taking her inks away from her, but she managed to find needles and razor blades, and when they tried taking those, she used fire. It sounds as though her parents weren't so distressed by the methods she was using for decorating her body as they were by the way she was exhibiting her work, but maybe that's just the way she tells the story.

She took her medication for a while, and was briefly fascinated that it turned her urine purple. The staff thought she was hallucinating, but the doctor said it was a common side-effect. After that, she grew bored with it. She asks me to tell her again about the art galleries I visited when I was in Europe. I do my best to describe what I saw in Paris and Milan and London, the d'Orsay and Brera and V&A, but as always we ended up back at the Collection de l'Art Brut. This time I tell her about Henry Darger, whose work I first saw in a room there. Darger was sent to an orphanage at eight, diagnosed as an habitual trouble-maker, and kept in various mental institutions until he escaped when he was sixteen. He spent most of the next sixty-four years cleaning hospitals, attending mass daily, conversing with the voices in his head, and writing. He started writing his autobiography until it turned into a story of a tornado named Sweetie Pie on page 207 and continued in that vein for the next four thousand or so pages, but he's best known for his 15,000 page epic titled *The Story of the Vivian Girls, in What is known as the Realms of the Unreal, of the Glandeco-Angelinnian War Storm, Caused by the Child Slave Rebellion*. The Vivian Girls were traced from pictures scavenged from Chicago's rubbish bins, and the manuscript is illustrated—no, *illuminated*—with hundreds of paintings and sketches and collages, some of them three metres wide. Darger was better at drawing incredibly realistic clouds and brilliantly coloured landscapes than he was at the female form, but he did draw the girls' penises himself. The work remained his secret until it was discovered by his landlord after his death. Darger's death, that is, not the landlord's.

"Hundreds…" J breathes.

I nod. "And 15,000 *single-spaced* pages. But over sixty-four years, that's not even a page a day. I'm doing better than that now. Most days, anyway."

"Why do you feel the need to write so much?" the interrogator asks.

It's a wet day, as grey outside as it is inside, one of those times when I think we might be better off if no-one had ever invented windows; I feel cold even though I know that it really isn't. The room's empty bookshelves remind me of a skeleton, a rib-cage. When I was dissecting a rat in biol class, they accidentally gave me one that had been pithed, its brain burnt out by an electric current. I opened the skull only to find it empty. I shrug. "Why do people write?" I ask. "Something to do? A way of being somewhere else? A way of making sense of the world?"

"Do you feel happier when you're writing?"

"Happier's not the right word."

"Your work seems rather bleak. Do you think that's healthy?"

"I don't know. Is lying healthier than telling the truth?"

"You think this is the truth?"

"It's my truth."

She nods at that. "Do you want to be somewhere else?"

"Fuck yes!"

"Where?"

I look at her suspiciously. "If you're thinking of sending me overseas, my ancestors came from Europe. Bin gar keine Russin, staumm' aus Litauen, echt deutsch."

"I know about your background," she says with a good imitation of patience. "I'm just reminding you that if you take your medication, and we observe a positive change, you'll be free to leave."

"You'll see a positive change if I can get out of here, but I can't imagine it happening before then."

"You were depressed before you came here."

I shrug.

"Why won't you take the medication?"

"It makes me feel slow and stupid, and that's about all I *can* fucking feel when I take it! It stops me writing! There has to be something better than the fucking pills!"

"Not yet," she says, and for a moment I look at her face and it's like an epiphany, like looking at one of those trick pictures where you suddenly see a beautiful woman's profile so clearly that you can never look at this again and *not* see it, never see only what you saw before... I realize that she *does* understand. Worse still, she believes what she's saying. She might even be right.

Maybe the writing isn't about being somewhere else. Maybe it's about being *someone* else. No, that can't be right. I don't want to be someone else. I don't.

J AND I sit on her bed and stare through the window at the clouds, then turn to face the wall. We've decided that if we work together, we can do something worthy of being hung in the Collection de L'art Brut. "Are you ready?" I ask.

She nods, and holding hands, we walk through the wall.

MORTAL NATURE

It took the customs official less than five standard minutes to decide that he didn't have the authority to deal with my case, and call for help. I assumed my best manner of Zen-like patience and waited in a small room, my legs folded into a lotus position as I stared at a sheet of what had to be one-way glass.

The help proved to be an attractive woman in a tunic and leggings which neither had nor needed insignia to display her rank or unit. "Dr. Tigere?"

"Mr. Tigere," I corrected her. "Or Shen. I'm still working on my doctorate—that's why I'm here, in fact."

She didn't respond, but pulled a chair out of one wall and a desktop out of another, then sat down and slipped my card into a slot. A few dozen pages of my ID appeared across the desktop. "Ah. Yes. Well, you have the necessary documents, and I see our embassy on Einstein approved your visit..."

I waited.

"... but I'd like to impress upon you just how dangerous a time you've picked for this trip. While we can guarantee your safety in the cities, the wilderness is... different."

"Because it's taurusaurus mating season? That's one of the things I want to observe."

She shook her head. "I'm not talking about xeno-ecology here. There are bandit groups with military weapons hiding on Northbergen, waiting for a chance to attack. If it was only your life you were risking, I wouldn't try to stop you—but if they take you hostage and try to ransom you..."

Her voice trailed off again, but I knew what she was thinking. The long civil war on Gould had ended less than a year ago when the last 'loyalist' town had surrendered, and the 'bandits' she was referring to were the survivors of the defeated 'loyalist' force—mostly ex-cops supporting Arvid Wilsey, the former Deputy Governor and Minister of Justice. Wilsey had expected to assume the governorship when his predecessor had died, but there had been some allegations of corruption, the senate had voted against him and a warrant had been issued for his arrest, and the rest was bloody history. I didn't know whether the allegations were true, and had heard conflicting reports about who had fired the first shot, but politics isn't my field. I did know, however, that Wilsey had never been captured or confirmed dead, and that very few people visited Gould anymore despite its wonderful wildlife. The intelligence officer sitting opposite me wasn't concerned for my safety because she liked me; it was just that because I was an offworlder, anything that happened to me would reflect badly on her government—badly enough that the Commonwealth might even decide to remove it from power.

I tried to think of some diplomatic way of telling her that I didn't want that any more than she did. "I'll be careful," I said, finally. "I'm used to living in the wild and staying out of sight—of animals rather than people, true, but there isn't as much difference as you think. Any sensors your bandits might have, some animal somewhere can match. And Northbergen is big, so if there's as few of them as you say, the chances that our paths would cross would be very slim. And I can protect myself if necessary."

She grimaced. "I've looked at your luggage. Your hand laser isn't much of a weapon, but I can't let you carry it inside the city, and I hope you don't think it'll be enough to protect you in the wild. I'd also rather it didn't fall into the hands of the bandits."

"I didn't intend to use it as a weapon. I'm here to see how your animals survived the last war, not start a new one!"

She looked down at my travel documents again, and sighed. "Mr. Tigere, I don't know what sort of deal your mother made with our embassy, but there's nothing here about diplomatic immunity. Customs are scanning your luggage as carefully as they've ever scanned anything. I don't have the authority to put a tracking device on you without your consent—" I shook my head. "Or the technology to keep a constant watch on you once you're outside the city, but I promise you, as long as you're here in Serendipity, you will be under surveillance. I also have the authority to examine any recordings you make while on the planet—"

"But not to confiscate or alter them."

"I see you know the local laws."

I shrugged. "I went through this with your embassy on Einstein. I assure you, there is nothing illegal in my luggage, nor do I intend breaking the law while I am here, and I am *not* working for my mother; I have never done so, nor do I intend to start. Is that clear?"

I hadn't intended to raise my voice, but the woman recoiled slightly. Or maybe I hadn't changed my tone at all; my mother never had to. My interrogator took a deep breath, then said, "Does she know you're here?"

"Almost certainly, but she didn't send me. I haven't seen her since I left Earth—for that matter, I didn't see her very often before then! I've had no training as a spy, or anything like that; I'm just a student trying to finish my dissertation. Can I go now?"

She touched the table. "I'll give you the benefit of the doubt, Mr. Tigere, because that's the law, but off the record… I don't believe that you could be as innocent as you claim. Even if you haven't been trained, I suspect you've inherited some of your mother's instincts and talents. Blood will out." She returned my card to me, along with a card of her own. "Call me if you have any problems."

I turned the card over; both sides were blank. "Who shall I ask for?"

"My name is Lee." She glanced at the table top, which was also blank; either her eyes could see colors mine couldn't, or she had a retinal read-out. "Your bags are ready. Good day, Mr. Tigere."

I WAS still fuming when I reached the hotel; the cab tried to engage me in conversation but realised—probably sooner than a human would have done—that I didn't feel like talking. I searched and scanned my bags as soon as I was inside, and then my clothes, and then—after a broad-spectrum shower—myself. Tracers a-plenty, as I'd suspected, but nothing smarter than that. I didn't even bother checking the room for bugs; like any good hotel room, it was filled with innocent machines that routinely monitored the occupants for their own comfort, and any Intelligence organization deserving of the name could use these to keep track of anyone inside. There were cameras and other scanners in the streets and corridors, too: as Mother Shantay had taught me, the only privacy possible in a city was to seem too boring for anyone to bother watching you.

Shantay Tigere, my birth-mother, was one of the best intelligence analysts and controllers on Earth, and probably in humanspace. It's said that all the human worlds were founded by fanatics, and that may be true, but many more fanatics remained on Earth, and some of them still believe some deity gave them exclusive right to some piece of land: I doubt there's a square klick of land on the planet that somebody hasn't been killed for, at some time or another. Mother Shantay somehow kept track of them all. She wasn't famous, except among her colleagues, but she had spies, human or AI, in every city on Earth.

After changing my clothes, I walked out and took the slidewalk to the museum. The small holo zoo was almost the same as any other in humanspace; there weren't even realtime feeds of native animals, and the images they did have might have been recorded before the war. I stood inside a bubble and watched a footpad playing with her cubs. The cubs were stalking her while she pretended to ignore them—right until the moment they pounced, when she would turn around and transfix them with a glare, or swat them with an inflated paw and send them sprawling. Footpads are predominantly ambush predators, and while their huge soft paws and the algae in their fur give them a natural advantage when it comes to stealth, they still need to practise... and that, after all, is what play is for. I caught myself thinking of Mother Shantay again; she wasn't home much, and I was mostly raised by my other mothers, but sometimes she and I would play games that I now know were aptitude tests, seeing whether I had any talent for her profession and could follow in her footsteps.

After a few hours amid the holos, I went looking for the curator of xeno-zoology, Dr. Alzal. She was as short and stocky as a heavy-worlder, but round rather than square; it was difficult to imagine her squeezing herself into a hyperlight, and she confessed she hadn't done much field-work since before the civil war. I gave her the benefit of the doubt and assumed she meant the local war, rather than the ones we were taught about in Earthian history. "I haven't even had any grad students in that time," she complained, as she made us tea. "They all wanted to be soldiers or medtechs, instead. I've been able to keep track of the big herds through satellite scans, but even those aren't complete or up-to-date."

"Technical problems?"

"So they say. Personally, I think they're being censored, in case someone is using them to follow troop movements."

"I thought all that was over?"

"No. They're still hunting for Wilsey men up on Northbergen. I'm not sure why: there's only a few towns up there, all near the south coast, and no reports of attacks for at least a year." She shrugged. "Anyway, I charted the corneteer and taurusaurus migrations—I have the data here—but any information you can give me would be appreciated, of course. For all I know, some of the creatures you're looking for might even be extinct."

I looked at the pictures. "The corneteer migration seems to have changed a lot. Is the old route impassable?"

"Possibly, but I don't think so. Corneteers are very sensitive to sound; anything louder than a grenade can cause a whole herd to stampede, so they may have decided to avoid the old battlegrounds. Or something may have killed off the corneteers' favourite grasses in those areas, at least for a season or two, and the corneteers are following their noses. We won't know for a few years." She shrugged. "The taurusaurus migration hasn't changed perceptibly, but tauros aren't even as smart as corneteers—I suspect there are trees with better learning curves. But tauros prefer different plants, and they depend on sight more than sound, so it's hard to tell why the corneteers have changed route and the tauros haven't. You have remembered not to pack anything red, haven't you?" I nodded. "Good. You've arrived just in time for tauros mating season, and I'd hate to have to send you home on a microscope slide."

She gave me a lot of other survival tips before I left, as well as some far more useful data on Northbergen's wildlife, then took me to dinner and generally fussed over me; I suspect I was the closest to a grad student, or a new grandchild, that she'd had in years. I caught a few hours' sleep in the hotel, then took the airship north.

NORTHBERGEN is the largest continent on Gould, stretching from the icecap down almost to the fortieth parallel. Serendipity straddles the equator, so its climate is mild and fairly stable; Port Bellamy, Northbergen's largest and southern-most town, boasts that it has the same climate as Paris, so I was glad I'd arrived in late spring (don't believe the old song; they only rhapsodised about April in Paris because May didn't scan). I dozed while I was in the airship; Einstein's days are nearly half as long again as Gould's, and I've never liked timelag medications, and besides, there wasn't much to see apart from a mostly grey sea.

I didn't spend long in Port Bellamy. I was worried that there might not be enough sunlight to power the hyperlight, but it inflated in minutes as though it were as eager to be flying as I was. An hour later, I was soaring over the steppes, scanning for signs of animal life.

I kept notes on the corneteers and taurusaurus, as Dr. Alzal had asked, flying as close as I could without spooking them—which was close enough to clearly see the red-flushed face shields of some rutting tauros, the only way I could tell the sexes apart at a distance. They pretty much ignored me: I was the wrong color to be a rival, Gould has no flyers large enough to threaten them, and the juveniles were old enough not to be skittish. An hour before sunset, I found a likely place to set up a hide, and landed.

My campsite was near the edge of the taiga, a swampy stretch of mostly low forest; it was also, obviously, the site of some infantry battle, being littered with grenade pins and razor-edged casing shards, partly-melted powerpacks, empty vials for field medications, and other detritus, all of it thoroughly weather-blasted and probably months old. No corpses, though, and I wondered how the scavengers had fared—partic-ularly the footpads. There were no signs of their pawprints, but I hadn't expected any. I looked around, wondering why anyone but a biologist would bother fighting for land like this, hundreds of klicks from the nearest town.

I set up perimeter scanners all around my campsite, but I didn't detect anything larger than a bug, and not enough of those to be interesting. I was hoping for chatterjacks, if not footpads, and other critters too small and sneaky to be detected by satellites or even low-flying aircraft.

I spent three nights on that site, scouring the swamps by day and night and grabbing a few hours of sleep at a time, and while my scanners detected what might have been chatterjacks and I probably heard dozens of the ugly goddamn things, especially when it was raining, I didn't see a single one. Chatterjacks are nocturnal toad-like creatures the size of obese cats, and among the best mimics in the known universe, rivalling the Earthian lyrebird. They attract their prey by imitating their mating calls and waiting for them to fly into their huge mouths, and deter preda-tors with the sounds of even scarier animals. They also hide as well as footpads, or as any of my equipment. Of the footpads, there was no sign apart from faint chemical traces of their urine. It's rumored that footpads know the range of human-built sensors and stay outside them, but I wasn't quite ready to believe that yet.

While I kept cameras looking out over the steppes from within my hide, I didn't pay much attention to anything on the plains, as long as they kept their distance… so I was caught completely off-guard by my visitor on the third night. I was asleep when he unsealed the tent, and when I woke, the first thing I saw was the business end of a laser carbine, fitted with bayonet and camera. The gunman entered a moment later, though it was several seconds before I saw him, because he was wearing a laserproof suit—light armor with a mirror finish. It's also pretty good camouflage, as long as there aren't any particularly bright light sources around. Only his boots weren't mirrored, and that might just have been a combination of mud and neglect. His voice, when he spoke, came from a box under his throat; his helmet must have been sealed. "Freeze, asshole."

I realised that I was shivering, and not just because the night was cold. I removed my hands from my sleeping bag, carefully and slowly, and said, "I'm not armed."

He was silent for a few seconds, as though this statement was difficult to understand, then, "Some spy you are."

"I'm not a spy at all."

He laughed. "Yeah, sure. So what's with all the camo and scanners and the stealth plane?"

"I'm watching animals, not people," I explained. "Animals don't let you close if they can see you. I didn't know you were here; I don't even know who you are!"

"Animals? Bullshit."

"I'm a xeno-ecologist," I said. "I'm here writing my doctoral thesis. Look at my computer."

"I don't give a fuck what you're writing. You come here with a shitload of scanners, and I bet you're reporting back to Serendipity. Right?"

I hesitated, wishing I'd bothered removing more of those tracers from my equipment. I didn't think any of them had been squirting data back to Lee, but maybe they'd been using frequencies that I wasn't scanning for. "No," I said, a moment too late. "I haven't been reporting to anyone." I took a deep breath while I tried to think of something. I was fairly sure I was wide awake, but my brain still seemed unusually sluggish. What did I have in the hide that could be a weapon? My hand laser would be useless against his armor, none of my knives were balanced for throwing… "If you look at my computer, you'll see what sort of data I've been gathering—"

"I can do that when you're dead."

"Not without the passwords."

He shrugged. "Sounds to me like you're a spy, then."

"Great," I said, bitterly. "I can see why they made your boss Minister of Justice."

To my surprise, he laughed at that, giving me a second in which to move. He fired an instant after I rolled off the mattress, and perforated the inflated walls of the tent. Some of the supporting ribs blew out and the whole structure collapsed on top of both of us. I kept rolling as long as I could, then slithered out of the sleeping bag and towards the edge of the tent. I didn't bother looking for any of my gear, but when I touched the fabric of my scoutsuit, I grabbed at it and dragged it with me. It wasn't worth much as armor, and even less as a weapon, but it was better camouflage than my skin.

My hyperlight was folded up for the night, and even if I'd had time to inflate it, the battery wouldn't have enough charge to get me very far, and I was pretty sure the sun wouldn't be rising any time soon. Draping the scoutsuit over my shoulders like a cape, I hot-footed it for the swamp, ignoring the thorns. I heard the crackling of superheated air as the laser fired, and a moment later smelled burning hair—my own. I hit the ground and slid into a mud puddle, from which I emerged sodden and dirty, but not burning, a moment later.

Maybe the rain was spoiling the gunman's aim or distorting the laser beam, or maybe he was just a lousy shot; he'd burnt off part of my left ear as well as setting my hair alight, but I couldn't find any more serious holes in myself—though there were a few, still hot, in the scoutsuit. I lay there, gasping, and trying to think. His helmet would be equipped with infrared or low-light settings, and probably both. Light-intensification wouldn't be much use in the woods at night, even with both moons up, so he'd probably use the infrared—and the night was cold, so I'd stand out like a pillar of fire. I slithered into the scoutsuit, which had pretty good infrared insulation, and pulled the hood over my head. My feet were still bare, and bleeding, but I found my gloves in the hip pocket while I was taking stock of my gear. There wasn't much: a small utility knife in a sheath on my belt, a tiny cufflink-like flashlight on my right wrist, a magnifying lens, a small roll of tape, and a few pens. No communicator, no laser, no spectrum visor… these were all back in the hide.

I found a small hollow that offered slightly more cover than the first mud-puddle, and waited. The gunman had extricated himself from the tent and was heading towards me, probably following the residual warmth of my footprints, but the water would obscure that. I couldn't see him, but he wasn't bothering to be quiet; so I knew exactly how far away he was. If he kept going, he'd be standing on me in ten seconds—fifteen at the outside. I could only hope he didn't look down.

Something brushed against my foot, and I had to bite my lip to stop myself gasping. Cautiously, I looked over my shoulder, and saw a vague grey shape—a footpad—sniffing my bleeding soles. He backed off for a meter or so, and stared at me appraisingly, probably trying to estimate how long it would be before I was carrion. I silently thanked him for the vote of confidence, and lowered my head again.

I heard a branch crack soggily as the gunman blundered closer, then the crack of laserfire. The footpad hurtled away, a grey streak barely visible in the gloom. The gunman came running towards me—and kept going.

Maybe he'd mistaken the footpad for me—its natural camo was about the same color as the scoutsuit—or maybe he didn't care and was just shooting for the hell of it. I don't know… but if he recognised the animal for what it was, he obviously didn't know very much about footpads, because he chased it, obviously assuming that a surface that could bear its weight would also bear his.

Under their fur, footpads are skinnier than they look, and their bones are hollow like those of birds. They can also inflate huge sacs on their already big paws, and these enable them to run across slimy water of the swamps—and after taking three paces into the marsh, the gunman was hip-deep in mud and stuck fast. He continued to fire in the direction of the footpad long after it had vanished from sight, and I had to cover my mouth to stop myself laughing out loud. I could almost hear what he was thinking as he tried unsuccessfully to extricate himself from the gluey muck of the pond: whether to call for help (there had to be a communicator in that helmet) or lie there in ambush in the hope of getting me.

I considered trying to sneak back to the hide, but he was close enough that he would probably have heard me, no matter how quietly I moved—and his carbine might still have some shots left in the battery. I didn't know how long it would take him to become bored with waiting in ambush, but I doubted it would be more than a few minutes. How much longer it would take for anyone to come to his rescue, I could only guess, but I had to be gone by then.

I raised my head just enough to watch him for a moment, then picked up a fist-sized rock from beneath my chest, hefted it, and threw it. I was hoping to hit his arm and startle him into dropping the gun, but since I could barely see him at all in his mirror suit, I would have been happy to hit him anywhere. I didn't; the rock sailed past him and splashed into the water. Maybe I wasn't quite used to the local gravity; more probably, I'm just a lousy rock-thrower. But the splash did startle him, because he half-turned and fired a burst in the direction of the sound.

Anything that made him waste shots seemed worth a little risk, so I fumbled around for another suitable rock and threw that, this time hoping to make him turn back the other way a few degrees. The rock landed near the edge of the pool, and all hell broke loose. I heard the crackle of laserfire, the louder pops of a grenade launcher, even a tankbuster. The gunman obviously heard them too, and began looking around anxiously, and I hugged the ground and waited for an explosion.

Nothing happened.

Cautiously, I looked up; the shooting had stopped, and the gunman was staring in the direction that the sounds had come from. I took a cautious sniff: no smell of explosives, and no ozone from laserfire... It took me a few seconds to work out what had happened, and when I did, I crawled out of the furrow I was in and began creeping back towards my hide. The gunman was probably as distracted as he was ever going to be—and he would probably have overcome his embarrassment and called for backup by now. It was time to make myself scarce before someone else made me extinct.

If there's one thing I learned from living in Shantay's home, it was how to move quietly—or do anything else quietly, for that matter. I reached the hide safely—there was no-one else around, not even any signs of distant vehicles—and I began searching for my more valuable equipment in the minutes it took the hyperlight to inflate. When I found my communicator, I slipped the card Lee had given me into the reader and sent her a message saying that there were bandits at this location, adding my co-ordinates. Then I strapped myself into the hyperlight and took off.

I had enough power to take me fifty klicks, maybe less—enough to reach the coast, but not any of the towns. The hyperlight would float if I brought it down on water, though taking off again would be tricky... better to head south and pick a nice flat plain on which to land and wait for sunrise. If I stayed low, the chances that the bandits would find me were negligible.

I was still congratulating myself on my cleverness when a burst of laserfire came out of nowhere and blew great holes in my wings.

I HURT when I woke up, in a place that was completely dark, but a quick check assured me that I still had the regulation number of extremities, most of them very sore and restrained with tape. Nothing seemed to be broken, probably because I'd been flying at tree-top height over marshy ground. I was lying on a damp inflated mattress, in a cold room, and alone.

Someone appeared a few minutes later—a man holding a lamp, but no obvious weapon. He wore a medic's white coverall, very dirty and with the red cross removed, and heavy boots. "Ah, you're conscious," he said, nodding at the medscanner near my head. The room was a large uneven chamber of spraystone and compacted soil, with no other furniture apart from my camp bed. "You're lucky not to be hurt worse," said the man, placing the lamp on the floor, and looked me up and down, and shrugged. My scoutsuit was filthy and badly tattered, and someone had emptied my pockets and taken the knife from my belt. "The General will want to talk to you, but I want to do some tests first. Can you remember your name?"

"Yes. I'm Shen Tigere."

"Rank?"

"None. I'm a doctoral student in xeno-ecology at Einstein University; I've never served in any military. Do you want my student number? I don't think I can remember my passport code."

"If the General wants that, he can ask you himself. How many fingers am I holding up?"

"Two."

"Any nausea or dizziness?"

"No."

"Your professor at the university?"

"Dr. Casey Shimada."

"Mother's name?"

"Shantay Tigere."

If I hesitated, the medic gave no sign of noticing. "Xeno-ecology, huh? Okay, what's the scientific name for a tauro?"

"Taurusaurus rubescutum. Kingdom Animalia, Subkingdom Metazoa, System Gouldae, Phylum Chordata, Class Cuprosangua… ask me a difficult one."

"That *was* the difficult one," he grunted, picking up a medscanner. "Okay, wiseguy, you're ready to see the General."

It seemed that the General was also ready to see me; he appeared less than a minute later, clad in clean laserproof fatigues and boots. No insignia, unless you counted the stick and the sidearm, and no helmet. I'd expected Wilsey, but this was a much younger man—no more than forty standard, if that, while Wilsey was nearing seventy. He had Wilsey's trademark chin and the rest of the face was similar, but I doubted this place had any rejuvenation facilities. A son, maybe? "Who are you, and what the hell are you doing here?" he snapped.

I answered the questions as politely as I could, but he continued to snarl. "You're the man my squad caught out near the swamps up north?"

"That was me, but I didn't see any squad—just the one man."

"The rest of the squad was patrolling the area. They went to rescue him, and now they're pinned down by enemy aircraft—but you got away, despite the area being under fire. How?"

"It wasn't under fire. Those guns they heard were chatterjacks."

The medic blinked, and the General stared. "Those bullfrog things? Crap."

I shook my head. "They're natural mimics. They have no other defences, so they use mimicry to frighten off predators, doing their best to sound like the scariest thing they know—and these chatterjacks lived near a battlefield."

"Crap," the General repeated. "They're just animals."

"They mimic whatever they hear, and if that scares predators away, they survive."

"That's learning! Animals are hardwired, they act on instinct."

"Even flatworms can learn. It'll be interesting to see whether this trick is passed on to the next generation—and whether it'll work on predators who've never encountered armed humans."

The General snorted. "Okay, so you're a scientist. That doesn't prove you're not a spy. It'd be good cover for carrying all those scanners and cameras." He reached for his sidearm—a Gauss pistol, not a laser. "And we execute spies."

"In peacetime?" I asked.

"Who said this is peacetime? Only the assholes in Serendipity. *We* didn't surrender."

Okay, that hadn't worked. "Even in wartime, you don't execute prisoners."

The medic spoke before the General could come with an answer to that. "It might be worth keeping him as a hostage," he said, his tone soothing. "We could ransom him—"

"For what?" asked the General. "What's Serendipity going to give us for him?"

"Not Serendipity," said the medic. "Listen to his accent, look at his documents—he's an offworlder. If we kill him, it won't get us any sympathy in the Commonwealth."

The General didn't look impressed. "How will they know? For that matter, how the hell are we supposed to ransom him when the spooks control all communications offworld? And what has the Commonwealth ever done for us anyway?"

"I can get a message offworld," I said, hastily.

"How?" asked the General, after a pause of a few seconds. "The spooks read everything."

"I'll encrypt it, and bury it amid my other data. Only another biologist would notice, and even they'd have to look carefully." I considered telling them about the naturalist and spy who'd hidden maps of enemy fortifications in drawings of butterfly wings, and decided against it. "I already have a lot of data: photos, sound recordings, sensor readings…"

The medic chewed his moustache. "It might work," he conceded. "It's worth trying, anyway."

The General almost spat. "And to get this message offworld, we'd have to let you go, right?"

"Yes."

"Why should we trust you?"

"What d'you have to lose? I don't know where this base is, I can't tell anyone anything—"

"What do we have to *gain*? Even if you *do* deliver a message?"

"Do you have allies offworld, who can send you… I don't know, more weapons?"

"We have enough weapons—more than enough," he grunted. I didn't smile, but I would've loved to play poker with this guy: he'd just admitted to how small a force he still had. "What else can you offer?"

"An amnesty?"

"Serendipity offered us an amnesty months ago," the General replied. "We told them to fuck off." The medic winced.

"An amnesty with better conditions. A hearing before the Commonwealth High Court—a chance to plead your case." I tried to think of something else that might tempt him, but the medic brightened.

"With respect, General, I think it's worth the risk," he said. "We're never going to get a… a fair hearing in Serendipity. Can you get us this amnesty?"

"I can deliver a letter," I said, carefully. I didn't want to overplay my hand—I was bluffing as it was. "As many letters as you can write. Apart from that… what are you asking for?"

The General glared at me, then at the medic—without changing his expression. Then he holstered his pistol. "Write your letter and show it to me. *I'll* decide whether it's worth the risk."

He stormed out, and I shook my head. "Can I talk to Wilsey?"

"You just did," said the medic, sadly. "Wilsey the Younger, anyway. His father died a couple of months after the last amnesty. The general blames me for not saving him, but he needed a hospital and prosthetics, not just a backpack medikit. If I *could* have saved him, I would have, believe me."

I did. "You just saved *my* life, if that helps."

He shrugged. "I do what I can. Hippocratic oath. I don't suppose you have medical training?"

"Just basic stuff. Zoology, not medicine. Why do you stay?" Undiplomatic, but I couldn't think of a polite way to ask.

The medic didn't take offence. "The amnesty had a time-limit. The General's also my son-in-law."

"Oh."

"You don't have kids, do you?"

"One daughter. Jaya. She's seven."

He blinked. "You don't look that old."

"I'm not. Something happened to my contraplant. I was too young for a paternity license, but…" I would have shrugged, but with my hands taped, it was a little difficult. "Your daughter won't leave him?"

"No. I don't see the attraction either, but what can you do?"

"That's still one of the big questions of evolutionary zoology," I replied, a little sourly. "Peacocks' tails, baboons' backsides, big antlers…

263

There was even a species of beetle on Earth that nearly became extinct because the males were more attracted to beer bottles than to the females, because the bottles had bigger secondary sexual characteristics. I don't think we're much closer to an answer than we were in Darwin's day."

He snorted. "I'll get to work on that letter."

"What does Wilsey want?"

"His father wanted to be governor: he thought he was entitled. Maybe if we'd taken that case to the High Court when he was alive, we might have achieved something... but I don't think the General is going to be satisfied with compensation and a pardon. I think he thinks he's the rightful governor by right of inheritance."

"That's—that's medieval!"

"Most people still do the same sort of work their parents did, just as they always have done. What were yours? Scientists? Academics?"

I nodded. As the old saying goes, it was close enough for government work. "I think the best you can hope for is an unconditional amnesty and maybe another election with independent observers."

He chewed his moustache for a moment longer, then muttered, "I'll go write that letter." He walked out, leaving me lying there staring at the spraystone ceiling.

There's an old idea in zoology known as the 'sneaky fucker hypothesis'. In some animal communities where dominant males keep harems, stealthier and more cunning males will wait until the dominants are distracted by some challenger, then sneak into the harem and impregnate as many females as possible. This way, they pass on the genes for intelligence as well as muscles, big antlers, and other secondary sexual characteristics. It'd never been observed on Gould, but baboons did it, as did many types of deer, and I was pretty sure I'd just seen a more sophisticated human version—in this case, trying to sneak his daughter out of the harem in the hope of her finding a more intelligent mate.

The medic returned a few hours later, with my computer, a card, and my knife. "I don't think the General's going to let you go," he said quietly, as he cut through the tape binding my feet. "And I don't think you'll have time to encrypt this message here—so I'm going to have to trust you."

"Thanks." I didn't ask why, but he obviously realised I was wondering. "You ever buy a lottery ticket?"

"Sometimes."

"The chances of winning are really low, but the potential payoff is enormous, and what the Hell, you're not risking very much either, right?" He sawed through the tape between my right hand and the cot frame.

I smiled crookedly. "That's the same logic I use when I make a pass at someone at a party."

He laughed. "An even better analogy. Can you ride a hoverbike?"

"Yes."

"Good." He cut my left hand free, and then cut another piece of tape as a blindfold. "Sorry about this, but just in case." I didn't resist. "Okay, let's go."

I let him lead me around enough curves and corners to confuse a minotaur, then strap me onto the back of a hoverbike. We rode for about an hour, and then the hoverbike stopped and he removed the tape from my eyes. I looked around; it was still dark, with the moons less than half-full, and the bikes had their lights switched off, at least in visible spectrum. The other bike, a few meters behind us, was ridden by a man in combat armor with a laser carbine slung by his side. The medic gave me a quick once-over with a medscanner, then unstrapped me. "Keep going south," he said, pointing. "You should get to a road before you run out of power—it's not much of a road, but you'll know it when you see it. Follow that east—the sun'll be up before then—and you'll get to Crater Harbor. It's just a fishing village, but you'll be able to make a call from there to Serendipity or wherever.

"Don't try using the autopilot—we wiped its memory—but the lidar and the compass work okay. There's a canteen in the pannier; I'm sorry we couldn't spare you any food."

"A helmet?"

He shook his head. "All of our helmets have communicators. I couldn't find your boots. Your computer's in the pannier, too. Good luck."

"Thanks."

THERE was a compass in the bike's controls, next to the battery gauge, and I glanced at both regularly. The sun was rising, a thin ribbon of yellow-white along the horizon, and while I couldn't see the road yet, there was enough light for me to see a small family group of taurusaurus about half a klick away. Only a small group—the alpha male, a harem of four females (my history tutor could do better than that in a slow semester), and two sub-adults. I must have spent too long looking at them, because I didn't notice that I was being followed—okay, pursued—until I noticed the small flashing light on the controls, a few minutes later: the lidar approach warning.

I looked in the rear-view mirror, but didn't see anything at first; he was still over a hundred meters behind, and unlike me, he didn't need to use visible light. I didn't bother wondering whether the rider was friendly; I just twisted the throttle and kept my head down. The first shot hit my bike a few seconds later.

If I'd had the time or the faith, I would have asked some god why these things keep happening to me; instead, I looked at the lidar screen, did some quick calculations, and steered towards the tauro herd. A burst of Gauss darts whizzed past my neck like ambitious mosquitos, and I tried to think of some way I could get rid of the gun. If I'd had something large and solid enough to throw into the jet intake of the hoverbike, I could at least slow him down—but the plastic water bottle would be shredded without even making the bike burp, and I couldn't bring myself to throw the computer. If I'd just had a helmet, or my boots…

I looked in the mirror at my pursuer; he was wearing laserproof armor with a visored helmet, but nothing covering his mouth, and the chin was unmistakeable. I weaved from side to side, hoping to spoil his aim, but still headed towards the herd. The lidar told me they were only 300 meters away… 250…

More darts shredded the back of the seat, and the lidar told me that the gunman was less than a hundred meters behind me and closing. A dart hit me in the back of the shoulder and kept going, emerging just below my collarbone. With a shriek, I turned the hoverbike around, pointed it right at him, and ducked behind the control pillar with my head between my forearms. There was a metallic crunch that felt like every tooth in my head shattering, and everything stopped making sense for what seemed like an hour—up and down, light and darkness, pain and death. When I opened my eyes again, I was lying under the wreckage of my hoverbike, and General Wilsey was standing beside the ruin of his, his right hand empty and his right arm hanging down at a strange angle. I could feel both my legs, but I wished I couldn't. My head seemed to move as a head should, even though it was pure agony when I tried it.

The sun was high enough over the horizon that I could see in colors again, none of them very pretty. Wilsey looked around for his gun, then reached for the knife on his belt and switched it on. "I'd like to leave you here for the scavengers," he said, thickly. "It's better than you deserve, but we're close enough to a road that there's always the risk that somebody might find you in time to save you." He lurched towards me. "Who are you working for, anyway?"

"I told you. Einstein University, School of Biological Sciences." I looked past him at the Taurusaurus pack, less than hundred meters away.

"Very funny. Why are you here?"

I closed my eyes for a moment. "I'm here to learn what I can before the native animals become extinct. They're fascinating creatures. They follow the same evolutionary rules as all other life forms, and they're chemically and physically similar to some Earthian species, but they're also quite different. Did you know that all of them have copper-based blood, instead of iron-based? That means they bleed green, not red." I took a deep breath, very quickly; he probably couldn't hear very well in that helmet, but I didn't want to stop talking. "In fact, there's *nothing* bright red on this continent, except for what you've imported and the pigment on a male Taurusaurus's face during mating season. If there had been, it probably wouldn't have survived long enough to reproduce. That's why the male thinks anything red that it sees is automatically a rival."

He stared at me, and shook his head. "And you're prepared to die for *that?*"

"I hadn't finished," I shouted. "Because it looks red, a male Taurusaurus will also charge a mirror if it's on his territory and larger than, oh, a quarter-meter across. And that includes a laserproof suit."

The General turned around, and saw the alpha male barreling towards him, its two biggest horns pointed straight at his torso, the lowest just above his crotch. He looked at his knife, then at the heavy shield covering its head and neck. If he'd still had his gun, he might have had a chance—I don't know how well Gauss darts go through ten centimeters of scale and bone, and I hope I never have to find out—but he wasn't quite crazy enough to tackle one with only a knife. Instead, he turned and ran.

His chances would have been better if he'd run towards and past it; taurusaurus don't corner well. But maybe he'd read somewhere that tauros won't charge a rival that runs away... which is true, but a taurusaurus seen from behind is dark green-grey, not bright red like his mirrored suit. And over distances of a few hundred meters, they run much faster than even a human athlete. I watched, almost sadly, as the tauro caught him and tossed him into the air... and suddenly, I remembered something Lee had told me, and realised that she was right. Blood *will* out.

MOTHER Shantay was waiting when I hobbled off the ship at Einstein Orbital. She observed all the expected formalities, but I didn't waste time pretending to be glad to see her, or surprised. She whisked me into a luxurious and secure groundcar, and I gave her a detailed report of everything that had happened, from my first interview with Lee to my crawling out from under the hoverbike and prying Wilsey's helmet off his head so I could use the communicator to call for help.

"I'm impressed," she said, smiling. "I'd expected you to find them, but I didn't think you'd single-handedly destroy them as a force."

"I didn't intend to," I muttered. "I tried to avoid them. It was self-defence, and they weren't much of a force anyway. I think they'll surrender now if you offer them a fair trial offworld."

"I can probably arrange that. Can you locate their base?"

"Yes. Their medic kept my knife, and it has a tracer in it. *Did you tell them I was coming?*"

"What?" The smile faltered for a moment, then became broader; it even looked sincere. "Of course not. Would I—"

Methinks the lady doth protest too much. "I told the Department I wouldn't do your dirty work and hunt down the bandits... but surprise, surprise, *they* came hunting for *me*."

"I knew they might, but I hardly think that counts as setting you up. Now everybody's happy. You can go back to the university *and* keep your unrestricted travel pass, Gould can stop worrying about bandits—"

"And they owe Earth a favour, and you can take all the credit?"

"Yes, and I can probably persuade them to turn a large part of Northbergen into a nature reserve as part payment."

If she expected me to smile at that, I disappointed her. "So can I see my daughter now?"

She was silent for a moment, then nodded. "We'll send her to Einstein for a standard month, with an option of a longer stay. You know, if you *did* agree to work for the Department, you could be with her any—"

"*No*. And if you pull a shitty trick like that again—" Words failed me, and she didn't bother answering. Not for the first time, I wondered whether she'd sabotaged my contraplant eight years ago, and I almost wished I'd never *had* a daughter... but there was fuck-all I could do about it now. The basic mechanism of evolution is the same for every species: pass on your genes and do your damnedest to preserve them. Nothing else matters—certainly not individuals.

Sometimes, I think there has to be a better way.

THE FALL

THE FLIGHT TO TOKYO HAD TAKEN more than nine hours, without a chance for a cigarette, and the bus ride from the airport to the hotel took another two, through a mostly grey landscape under a low grey sky. Wilson had to walk the last few blocks in the rain, because the shuttle didn't go to his hotel, only to a more expensive one nearby. The lift groaned and shuddered as it took him up to his room, and the ride up to the thirteenth floor seemed to take as long as his flight. After shutting the door behind him and dropping his pack on the floor of the tiny room, he prised off his shoes and collapsed on the bed, face up. He drew a deep breath, then lit a cigarette and lay there for a few minutes, just reminding himself how it felt to be horizontal and motionless. Days like this convinced him that man was never meant to fly—or at least, he told himself wryly, never meant to fly economy class from Australia to Japan. He was too tired even to take any pleasure from the thought of finally being here.

It was already dark at six when he finally found the energy to pick up the phone and call Kyoko and tell her he'd arrived safely.

KYOKO met him in the lobby. They recognized each other instantly, despite never having actually met: he was the only Westerner around, she the only person dressed in Lolita-Punk. She rushed up to him, then stopped just short of flinging her arms around him, and they stood almost nose-to-nose for a moment. Years of smoking had all but destroyed his sense of smell, but he was faintly aware of an elusive, exotic, enticing fragrance.

"How are you?" she asked, a little awkwardly. "Jet lag?"

"I'm okay, though my body clock's a little off. I didn't think it was night-time already."

"It gets dark early here, at this time of year. It's fall,nearly winter. Short days, long nights," she replied. "But it's spring in Australia, isn't it? ."

Wilson nodded. "Where are we meeting Yoshi?"

"Ahh." Kyoko looked even more embarrassed. "Yoshi won't be coming with us."

"Will he be at the meeting tomorrow?" The three of them had been working together for years on an irregular web-based comic, *The Conqueror Worm*. Wilson had written most of the story, Kyoko had translated it into Japanese and drawn the human characters, but Yoshi had designed the distinctive steampunk hardware, the elaborate deathtraps, the architecture of Hell, and most of the dreaming demons. Though he was unable to draw a living being that didn't seem to be in constant agony, his mechanical plans were so painstakingly detailed that Wilson found it easy to imagine the devices working—which, he suspected, had played a major role in attracting the attention of a publisher.

"I don't think so," said Kyoko, uneasily. "He's... can we get out of here? There's a good sushi place around the corner."

THE little restaurant was nestled between apartment buildings, and obviously catered to locals rather than tourists: Kyoko ordered for him, as Wilson's Japanese was rudimentary and no-one else in the place spoke any English. "Have you ever heard of hikikomori?" Kyoko asked, once the waitress was out of earshot.

"No."

"They're mostly boys, or young men, who don't get into university and can't find good jobs, so they stay at home, more and more, until they finally stop leaving their bedrooms completely unless there's no-one around. Yoshi's been like that for a few months."

Wilson stared into his green tea. "This happens often enough that you need a word for it?"

"Yes. I'm sure there are other cities where the unemployed find it hard to leave home, and are ashamed and withdraw to some degree... but the hikikomori are extreme cases. Yoshi still communicates in other ways— e-mail, mostly, or online chat with people he trusts—but he will not see anyone else or let them see him."

"You knew him before we started working on the comics, right?"

"Yes, in high school. He was doing well until the exams, but after that... " She paused, as the waitress returned with their miso soup, then lowered her eyes and stared into the bowl for a moment.. "He has headaches," she continued, when they were alone again, "sees things strangely, out of proportion, I don't know the English word..."

"Migraines?"

"Thank you. I know he's suffered from those for years, but they didn't stop him going to school. I think he was depressed, too, but it became much worse after his father died... which happened just after Yoshi failed the exams. I don't think there was any connection—Ushiba-san had been sick with cancer for some time—but Yoshi may not believe that."

Wilson swore softly under his breath. "What about selling *Worm*? Hasn't that helped him? I know the advance wouldn't have been enough to let him move out, but it must have made him feel better..."

Kyoko bit her lip, then looked at her watch. "It did, but not in a way that brought him out of the room... or out of himself. Please, I'll take you to the Ushibas' house. That might be easier than trying to explain any more."

Yoshi and his mother lived on the top floor of a narrow grey-walled apartment building that had been hastily and unlovingly built soon after World War II, and overlooked a murky canal. Kyoko pointed out the dull, dark, somehow eye-like window of Yoshi's room, then led the way up a stairwell that smelled of mildew and fish sauce.

Yoshi's mother answered the interphone, and seemed glad enough to see Kyoko, but warned them that Yoshi seemed still to be asleep. "I hear him moving about some nights after I've gone to bed," she said quietly in Japanese, as they removed their shoes and winter jackets. After the chill of the night, the apartment—heated by a small gas fire—seemed almost oppressively hot. "Not often: I think he waits until he's sure I'm asleep."

Wilson decided to let Kyoko translate for him, rather than trust to his own Japanese. "Does he speak to you at all?" he asked Mrs Ushiba, as they sat down at the kitchen table.

"He leaves notes, sometimes."

"Do you know if he ever leaves the building?"

"I don't think he ever does."

"Do you ever go into his room?"

"I tried. He put a latch on the door after that. He buys things on the internet and has them delivered here." She covered her mouth, hiding an embarrassed smile. Wilson looked at her, and said softly, in English, "Would it be a really bad idea to ask what sort of things?"

Kyoko thought about this for a second. "Probably," she replied; then, in Japanese, "Can we stay until he wakes up?"

Mrs Ushiba looked uncertain, then nodded. Kyoko took out her phone, and quickly keyed in a short message. "If he's awake, he'll probably answer, even if he doesn't actually get out of bed."

A few seconds later, the phone miaowed. "Tell him I'm here," suggested Wilson.

"He says Hi," said Kyoko, after another exchange of messages, "and he asks if you have a phone."

"No; my service provider doesn't work here."

"What about your computer?"

"I left it back at the hotel. Can you ask if he can come out?"

Kyoko hesitated, then did as she was asked."Yoshi says no, not while there are so many people here," she relayed, with a slight quirk of her lips. "He knows you've come a long way to see him, and he says he'll try to come out later... which means after I leave." She drummed her black fingernails on the shabby table, then looked at her watch. "There's a store around the corner; Mrs Ushiba and I can go there for a few minutes and have a coffee or something."

"We can't ask her to leave her own home!"

"It's a little early for her to go to bed," replied Kyoko. "If we go out for, say, twenty minutes, that gives him time to get dressed and come out to see you. I'll text him when we're about to come back. Do you have a better idea?"

WHEN the women had gone, locking the door behind them, Wilson waited in the unnervingly quiet apartment for several minutes. He stared at Yoshi's bedroom door, noticing the faint zigzag cracks in the grey walls around it—souvenirs of a few earthquakes and many minor tremors—and despite his best efforts, found himself remembering how, in *Dr. Jekyll and Mr Hyde*, Jekyll had also communicated by notes slipped under a door, unwilling to let anyone see that he'd transformed into Hyde... then, Dracula warning Jonathan Harker not to explore his half-ruined castle... then to 'The Monkey's Paw', then Bluebeard... By the time he heard the bolt slide back, he half-expected to see Yoshi transformed into a Lovecraftian Deep One or a similar monstrosity. Instead, he saw a plump, weak-chinned, eerily pale Japanese teenager wearing black sweat pants and a T-shirt emblazoned with a portrait of Edgar Allan Poe.

Unlike the bare-walled living room, Yoshi's refuge was lined with posters, artwork, and unstable-looking bookshelves. Reproductions of Goya woodcuts and Giger grotesques, as well as tattered and much-annotated printouts of Yoshi's own designs for weapons, framed the desk; a scroll depicting the seven hells of Japanese mythology ran above the blackout curtains and around one corner; a full-sized picture of Elvira in an open coffin was taped to the ceiling directly above the unmade bed. "Excuse me for a moment," said Yoshi, speaking English so quickly he was barely coherent and brushing past him as he hurried towards the apartment's bathroom. "Go in, sit down, I'll be back."

Wilson hesitated, then ventured inside and sat in the only chair, at the desk. He looked around at Yoshi's library, the works apparently shelved at random, non-fiction mixed with novels and manga, English with Japanese, books and DVDs with figurines. A copy of *Tales of Mystery and Imagination,* bound in fake scarlet leather, lay open, spine up, on the pillow; Wilson glanced at it, then noticed strands of black—thread? hair? protruding from beneath the rumpled quilt. Uneasily, he lifted the covers and saw dark eyes in an ivory-pale face framed by ebon hair. A faint smile played about dark crimson lips, showing a hint of white teeth.

Wilson sucked in a lungful of air and stared for a moment, waiting for a sign of life or movement; none came. He heard the toilet flush, and dropped the covers and sat down hastily in the chair.

Yoshi returned to the room a few seconds later. "Sorry," he said. He picked up the volume of Poe, placed it on the floor, and sat on the pillow. "I've been re-reading this, and thinking of including some of his characters in *Worm*. General Smith, the Man Who Was Used Up, might still be alive; the old men from 'A Descent into the Maelstrom'; maybe have them find Fortunato in the vaults..."

Wilson realized that he was holding his breath, and let it out. Yoshi mistook this for disapproval, and his shoulders slumped slightly. "Of course, you're the writers," he said gloomily, "it was just an idea..."

"I'll think about it," said Wilson, trying not to think about what might be underneath the hills and valleys of the quilt. He suddenly remembered another Poe story, 'The Oblong Box', in which the central character travels with his wife's corpse in his cabin. He dismissed *that* thought—the room, and Yoshi, had a sour shut-in smell, but not so oppressive that it could have disguised the rank odour of a decaying body. "Right now, though, the main thing on my mind is meeting with Mr Tanaka tomorrow."

"Oh."

"He wants to meet all three of us." No reply. "We're equal partners in this."

Yoshi looked away, and was silent for a moment. "You and Kyoko do all the words, though." His voice, which had been animated, now seemed leaden, as though he was reading a spell in an unknown language phonetically and feared that an error in pronunciation might summon up the wrong demon.

"He's interested in your artwork, too—just as much as the words, or Kyoko's drawing."

"But you are better with words. I can send him as much artwork as you want, but talking to him... I dread it. I dread the events of the future, not in themselves, but in their results. I'm scared I'd say the wrong thing."

"I don't think you would."

"I would. I can't be in a room where there are other people talking; it confuses me. It's not so bad when I read, but I can't even stand music anymore; I can't always tell what other people are singing or saying and what I'm only thinking. I don't think I can go," he said, shaking slightly. "Not yet. I have to study for my exams. I failed last time. I failed badly. I don't want to fail again." With a visible effort, he looked Wilson in the face again. "Not so soon. Please. This is at best but a harmless, and by no means an unnatural, precaution."

Wilson blinked. The phrase sounded familiar, but in his jet-lagged and weary condition, he couldn't remember where he might have heard or read it before. "What should I tell Mr Tanaka?"

"Tell him I'm not well. Tell him..." He shrugged. "You and Kyoko are writers. You will think of something. Do you want some sushi?"

WHEN he left the building an hour later, hurrying through the rain towards the subway with Kyoko, Wilson could barely remember one word of the often incoherent conversations he'd had with either Yoshi or his mother: the vision of the strange face staring out from the shadows in Yoshi's room was still impossible to shake. He'd tried to convince himself that the 'hair' had been nothing but the fringe of some garment, and that he'd only imagined the face, as humans often did when they glimpsed an arrangement of spots and curves that might have been eyes and a mouth...

"I see you've met Midori," said Kyoko, when they finally reached shelter.

Wilson turned and stared at her. "Midori?" he spluttered.

"It's what he calls her."

"I wasn't imagining her, then?"

"Not the way I think Yoshi does. Do you remember asking if he was feeling better since he received the advance from Tanaka? I gather that's how he spent it."

"What is she? A mannequin?" Wilson blinked. "Well, that's not quite as scary as some of the other possibilities that had occurred to me. I knew she couldn't be dead, and I didn't think she could be alive..."

"You thought he was dating a vampire?" said Kyoko, amused. "Or a zombie?"

"No. Well, they crossed my mind, along with cataleptics and the Bride of Frankenstein, but I thought it was much more likely that I was just hallucinating the whole thing. But her face looked so real... I could have sworn I saw teeth..."

"Very likely. She's a sex doll—a top of the range one, not one of those blow-up things." She shrugged. "There are places in Akihabara where you can rent them by the hour, but I don't think they deliver, so he probably bought his with the advance."

"Fuck."

"Probably the only sort he's ever had," Kyoko agreed, "though that's just a guess. I almost envy him, in a way."

"You can't be serious."

"Not completely, though there *have* been times when my life would've been easier if I could've put my lovers in boxes when I didn't need them. But some people might say he has everything he needs."

Wilson snorted, and fumbled in his pockets for his lighter. "Only as long as his mother keeps enough ramen in the house."

"He can get food delivered."

"What if their money runs out?"

She shrugged. "They own the building, and rent out the other two floors. It's not much—the place is a dump, as you probably noticed— but they live frugally."

"They'll be able to live a whole lot better if we do this deal!"

"True. I guess we'll just have to hope Tanaka doesn't insist on meeting him."

THEY caught the subway back to Wilson's hotel, neither of them speaking until they were alone in the grumbling lift, when Kyoko suddenly threw her arms around her co-writer and gushed, "A TV series!"

Wilson grinned back at her; her joy seemed to flow through him, intoxicating as sake and tasting much better. "It's really going to happen?"

"I think so. Tanaka has a good reputation, and even if it doesn't, the money for the rights alone..."

"I know. Even converted into dollars, it sounds like a mountain of cash." The lift doors opened at last, and they walked to his tiny but well-equipped rooms, still holding onto each other as though scared of being pulled out of a dream. They both sat on the bed, then fell over, lying on it face to face. Kyoko wriggled up the bed until her face was level with his; then, suddenly at a loss for words, grabbed her smartphone.

Wilson's disappointment couldn't be hidden, but he tried, "Do you think Tanaka bought the story about the migraine?"

"With that much money, he could buy my firstborn," she replied, but with a slight downward quirk of her lips.

"Yoshi hasn't replied?"

"No. But yes, I think Tanaka bought it—for now. But he's going to want to meet him, and more importantly, he wants the animators to meet him." She shrugged.

"Can you think of any way to get Yoshi..."

"Out of his room? This might. And the exams start next week—I hope he can make it to the exam hall, because if he doesn't, the next lot isn't until June."

Wilson bit his lip. "We have to do something. Not just because of *Worm*, not even just because we owe him; he's—"

"No-one's ever come up with a reliable way of treating the hikikomori," cautioned Kyoko, "and there's been at least one case of one who was sent to a mental hospital, hijacking a bus and running over a crossing guard when he was released."

"Somehow, I can't see Yoshi doing anything like that."

"Me neither, but... I know that being hikikomori may seem strange and scary, but that doesn't mean that we can't make things even worse.

Do you know the Poe story, 'The Premature Burial'? The narrator is cataleptic, but this stops when he stops obsessing about death, gets rid of his medical texts, and thinks and reads about other things instead, travels... and lives. The macabre thoughts became a self-fulfilling prophecy—and the reverse."

"You want to stop doing *Worm*? Maybe I'm rationalizing, but I don't see that making him happier."

"I don't know. It's just... maybe he dreams he's the artist starving in a garret, like his heroes Poe and Lovecraft. Maybe he thinks you have to suffer like that, to feel everything and nothing, to make the lasting art. But you're right, we just have to wait and hope. What else can we do?"

WILSON woke the next morning to find Kyoko gone. He lay there, feeling completely disoriented, for more than a minute before fumbling for the light switch. He stared at the depression in the pillow next to his, then buried his face in it for a moment. That was when the idea hit him.

YOSHI opened the bedroom door when he was sure that his mother and Kyoko had gone. "Thank you for letting me know about the anime," he said. Though clearly excited, he also seemed nervous to be outside his bedroom.

Wilson nodded. "Tanaka wants you to meet the animators," he said, without preamble. "Can you do that?"

Yoshi seemed to turn even more pale, something Wilson hadn't thought possible. "I don't... excuse me," he said, rushing off towards the bathroom. Wilson waited until he'd heard the bolt slide home, then hurried into Yoshi's bedroom and raised the covers. The life-size doll lay there, face down: Wilson grabbed it, surprised more at its weight than its lingering smile, and carried it over his shoulder to the apartment's front door. Kyoko was waiting on the landing with a large empty suitcase; she raised an eyebrow slightly when she saw the doll, but helped him fold her up until she fit inside the case. "I hadn't expected her to be quite this big," she admitted.

"They make small ones?"

"You don't want to know," she assured him. "I'm glad I thought of the case, though; I'd hate to have to stuff her into a taxi while she's naked like this."

"She?"

"You'd better hope Yoshi thinks of her as 'she', not 'it'," said Kyoko. "This isn't likely to work if he doesn't—not that I like the chances of it working, anyway." She brushed Midori's hair out of the way of the zip, then closed the crimson suitcase. Together, they carried it down to street level, dropped it once, and wheeled it out of the alley, and stood there for a moment until Kyoko had recovered her breath enough to phone for a taxi. "Okay," she said, as she returned the phone to her bat-winged handbag, "you'd better go up and tell Yoshi what happened, before he decides to leave the place by the window. I'll see you back at the hotel."

Yoshi had retreated into his bedroom by the time Wilson returned to the apartment, and when the Australian knocked on the door and identified himself, the reply came in the form of a note slipped under the door: *Where is Midori?*

"Midori's good."

I want her back.

Wilson considered telling him that he had his playmate, in the hope that Yoshi would open the door and speak to him directly, but didn't want to risk being caught in a lie. "You'll have to leave the building."

A pause, then: *Why?*

"Tanaka and his animators want to meet you."

I can't. Not yet.

"When, then?"

No answer.

"What about your exams?"

Wilson waited, but there was no reply. Ten silent minutes later, Mrs Ushiba knocked on the front door, and Wilson let her in. Not knowing what else to say, he said thank you and good night, and left.

KYOKO phoned him the next morning, waking him. "Ushiba-san called," she said. "She didn't sleep much last night: Yoshi nearly tore the house apart looking for Midori, in case we'd hidden her there. She got some sleep after she made sure he couldn't open her bedroom door. She says she's scared to stay there with him, but she's also scared to leave."

Wilson rubbed his eyes, opened his laptop, and lit a cigarette. "He hasn't e-mailed me," he said, a moment later.

"He messaged me last night, and asked if I had anything to do with this 'somewhat childish experiment', as he called it. I don't think he wants to talk to you."

"I keep expecting him to demand to speak to the doll," Wilson replied, with a glance at the suitcase. He'd resisted the urge to open it for a closer look at the toy, but its presence had made him feel weirdly nervous. "He does know she can't talk, doesn't he?"

"I think that's what he likes about her," said Kyoko dryly. "One of the things, anyway. What do we do now—apart from stalling Tanaka?"

"Tell him that if he wants to see Midori again, he's going to have to talk to me."

"Okay. What about his mother?"

"I don't know. I forgot to ask: does she go out during the day?"

"Some days. She doesn't have a job, if that's what you mean."

"Uh-huh. What about someone she can stay with?"

"No other family... but she knows my parents, and they know about Yoshi, I think they'd let her stay in my room for a while..."

"Ask. If they say yes, let her know." When Kyoko didn't reply, he asked, "You both know Yoshi better than I do –"

"I'm not sure about that –"

"-- and I'd never *heard* of hikikomori before. If you think this is too risky, tell me."

"I don't think Yoshi would hurt his mother," said Kyoko. "Not knowingly—not physically, anyway. She means too much to him, even if no-one else does. I don't think he'd hurt anyone else, except maybe himself... but I think he's too scared of pain for that. Did you see any weapons in his room?"

"Not real ones. Only drawings."

Kyoko nodded. "He can design them—he's been doing that as long as I've known him—- but I don't think he's ever used one, even if he is a ronin."

"He's a *what*? I mean, I've heard the story of the forty-seven ronin, I know they're masterless samurai, but I—-"

"Sorry. It's slang—- what we call students who fail to get into uni. What do you think we should do now?"

"I guess if he doesn't come out, we'll have to tell Tanaka the truth. Do you think he'll pull the plug?"

"If he thinks Yoshi's unreliable, he might... and I think Yoshi will blame himself if he does."

"'I dread the events of the future, not in themselves, but in their results.'"

"What?"

"Something Yoshi said."

THEY spent the day in Akihabara and Harajuku, window-shopping and admiring the cosplayers, then found a small restaurant that served inexpensive tendon and tempura. Kyoko's phone miaowed while they were ordering, sending the waitress into a fit of head-lowering giggles. "It's Yoshi," said Kyoko, after a quick glance at the screen. "He says he wants to see Midori, to be sure she's okay."

"Tell him where my hotel is."

"He says he's not leaving the house until he sees her."

"There's a webcam in my laptop. If he'll chat with me, I'll let him see her."

Kyoko keyed that in. "He says okay; call him tonight."

"Tell him I will."

WILSON unfolded the doll and sat her in the room's only chair. There was something disturbing about her immobile face and unblinking stare, and he had to resist the urge to close her eyes—or to cover them, as they apparently lacked lids. Instead, he grabbed the white bathrobe from the closet and dressed her in that, suspecting that Yoshi might become jealous if he saw her naked with another man in the room.

He logged on to g-chat and pinged Yoshi, who replied instantly. LET ME SEE MIDORI NOW

Wilson turned the laptop around so that the doll was staring over his shoulder.

CLOSER

The Australian shrugged, wishing that he had a cell phone that worked in Japan, then picked up the computer and placed it on the table in front of the doll. He tilted the screen to give Yoshi a full-length view, then positioned the laptop so that Midori was staring over his shoulder as he typed.

ok?

BRING HER BACK TO ME

will you meet Tanaka?

A moment's hesitation, then IF YOU BRING HER BACK AND SHE'S NOT HURT

tomorrow?

No hesitation this time. IF YOU BRING HER NOW

Wilson looked at the wan face on the screen, and decided to trust him. I'll be right there, he typed, then shut down the computer, stubbed out his cigarette, and packed Midori into the crimson suitcase. He wheeled the case to the lift, and pressed the button for the lobby. The lift shuddered, descended—and then the lights went out as it jerked to a halt, halfway between two floors.

YOSHI sat at his desk, trying hard to concentrate on something other than the digital clock in the corner of the laptop screen, not to think that if they were going to come, they'd be here by now. His need to see Midori had become so urgent that, despite the risk of his mother coming home unexpectedly, he'd left his bedroom door open so that he'd hear Wilson walking up the stairs or knocking on the door just a few seconds sooner, and could let them in a moment earlier. He glanced at the clock again—11.49—and tried telling himself not to worry. Wilson had come here before, he knew the subway system and wouldn't get lost, he . . .

so where is he?

Wilson spoke enough Japanese to give directions to a taxi driver if he didn't want to haul the suitcase to the subway . . .

maybe he decided to keep her

He wouldn't do that! He's my friend!

then why did he steal her?

Yoshi gritted his teeth, and reloaded the news headlines. Nothing about a disaster in Tokyo that would explain Wilson's tardiness. His hands shaking, he picked up his copy of *Tales of Mystery and Imagination* in the hope of losing himself in a story. The book fell open to the first page of 'The Tell-Tale Heart', and he read "TRUE!—nervous—very, very dreadfully nervous I had been and am; but why *will* you say that I am mad?"

He closed his eyes for a moment, then opened the book to the story that most spoke to him. I won't do anything until I finish this, he told himself. Or midnight, whichever comes later. Not before then.

EVERY few minutes, Wilson pressed the button on his solar-powered watch to provide a little light in the oblong box, until eventually the battery ran so flat that the watch refused to glow. By the time the doors were prised open, he'd long since lost track of time, and would not have been astonished to see daylight.

He hauled the suitcase out of the lift and hurried down the stairs to the lobby, barking out a request for a taxi. He lit a cigarette as he waited, and stubbed it out as soon as the cab pulled up outside. He stared at the blank face of his watch, then smiled wryly. He knew he'd have to apologize profusely to Yoshi for his lateness, but at least he felt sure that his friend would still be home when he arrived.

Kyoko was sitting up at her computer, translating dialogue for the next page of *The Conqueror Worm* by turning Wilson's English into appropriately nuanced Japanese. As she positioned the speech bubbles so that they didn't obscure the elaborate steampunk architecture of Yoshi's backdrop, something niggled at her, preventing her from concentrating fully... something Wilson had said that Yoshi had said...

She closed her eyes for a moment, trying to remember the exact words, then googled the phrase 'somewhat childish experiment'. All of the hits linked to a Poe story, 'The Fall of the House of Usher'.

She glanced at the clock—12.14—and realized that she hadn't heard from Wilson since he'd said he was taking the doll back to Yoshi's home, about four hours ago. She checked her phone for messages, but there was nothing. She opened g-chat, but neither Wilson nor Yoshi were online.

She tried to tell herself that she was worrying unnecessarily, but knew that she'd never be able to sleep until she was sure that both of them were okay, so she called for a taxi.

YOSHI had spent many hours designing deathtraps and dungeons for *The Conqueror Worm*, and he did a thorough job of sealing the apartment's doors and windows with duct tape before turning on the gas. Once that was done, he sat back in his chair wondering what to write as an epitaph. A quotation from Poe—- "Should you ever be drowned or hung, be sure and make a note of your sensations"—- came to him, and he deliberately typed that out and hit *save*.

Wilson paid the taxi driver, then hauled the crimson suitcase out of the trunk and carried it up the stairs. There was no answer when he knocked on the door, so he deposited his burden on the landing, sat down, lit a cigarette, took a deep drag to try and soothe his nerves, and tried to think. He knocked on the door again, harder and harder each time.

"Yoshi!" he yelled. "I'm sorry I'm late, but the lift in the hotel broke down. I'm here now, and I have her with me!" He unzipped the suitcase, and lifted the white-shrouded doll free, holding the manga-eyed girl up with an arm around her waist, her face on a level with his, almost cheek to cheek, He felt strangely light-headed, and short of breath.

"I'm not leaving until you open the door, so you may as well let me in!"

Yoshi had slumped over the keyboard, but even in his oxygen-deprived stupor, he became aware of a distinct, hollow, apparently muffled, reverberation. Unsteadily, he tried to stand, then, swaying gently, he slowly staggered towards the source of the noise, his footsteps leaden. Wilson continued to pound, until his fist smashed through the dry and hollow-sounding wood.

For an instant, Yoshi saw Midori standing outside the door, and the redly gleaming tip of Wilson's cigarette..

A taxi stopped on the other side of the street, and Kyoko stepped out just as the explosion blew out the windows. She watched aghast as the once barely-discernible fissures in the cancer-ridden concrete walls burst asunder, and the top floor crumbled into the murky waters of the sullen canal.

COUP DE GRACE

While many considered it would be a mistake to elect a Pope with a sense of humour, all the cardinals agreed that he would need to be a young, healthy man fluent in English. The Canadian candidate also seemed likely to appeal to a public that had become cynical after the sexual scandals, the financial scandals, and the outrage caused when the last pope had marked a visit to London by accepting petitions to beatify Princess Diana, Margaret Thatcher and Barbara Cartland. After genetic analysis proved that the Canadian was not susceptible to Alzheimer's disease or anything else equally embarrassing, a puff of environmentally friendly white steam finally appeared above the iron chimney and a cardinal appeared on the balcony over St Peter's Square to proclaim that John Paul III's successor had chosen the name of George Ringo the First.

Over the next twenty-two years, the new pope won over or outlived most of his critics, and it was said in some corners that the only person alive not happy with the decision was Pope George Ringo himself.

THE pope was staring at a spreadsheet when his secretary coughed gently. George Ringo I turned, and lowered his datashades. "Yes, Mike?"

"The delegation from the Commission for Moral Dignity is waiting," said the monsignor. The Pope disliked titles and honorifics, and while he hadn't entirely phased them out in official or formal occasions, he'd forbidden his personal staff to use them in the privacy of his office or apartments.

George blinked. "They want me to take their confession?"

"The Americans," the monsignor prompted. "They want to talk about Bodymods. The briefing notes are in your calendar."

The Pope folded his shades and placed them in a drawer. "Sorry. This financial crap always makes me feel like I'm in another time zone." He stood, stretched, and doffed one of his old and much-loved 'X-Men' t-shirts. He walked over to the robing room, unzipping his faded jeans as he went.

"You should have seen the spreadsheets before you put us all on vows of poverty," said Mike dryly.

The pope smiled as he kicked off his cheap sneakers. He'd received his vocation late in life,while writing his Master's thesis in theatre arts. He loved the plays of Bertolt Brecht, and at nineteen had been hailed as the best Azdak that Ontario had ever seen. He'd gone from there to playing Cardinal Berberini, later Pope Urban VIII, in Brecht's *Galileo*—a role he remembered whenever he had to don his robes for a public appearance— and had begun studying church history, and then theology. Despite these setbacks, he'd converted to Catholicism and had quickly risen through the thinning ranks of the priesthood. The jeans and t-shirt weren't en-tirely an affectation; he just felt that handling large amounts of money was best done in clothes that you weren't afraid to get dirty. "Did you get a look at them?"

Mike nodded. "Armani suits and silk ties."

"I'll see their suits and raise them," the pope replied with a smile. "Tell them I'll be out in ten minutes."

When he walked into the private meeting room, it was with an actor's flourish. One member of the delegation—the youngest, probably an acolyte—was looking at his gold-cased wristcom. "Gentlemen, my apologies."

Everyone stood, and remained standing even after George had seated himself. "Your Holiness," the leader began, "I'm Tyler Chapman, from the Commission for Moral Dignity. We're most concerned about an alarming trend that began in the USA, and threatens to spread world-wide. I'm sure you're aware of the popularity of a certain new product from Bodymods."

"I've seen the sales figures that Cardinal Smith sent me," the Pope replied, blandly. "I gather you're referring to the item they call the 'Colt'?"

Chapman turned slightly pink. "Yes, that's correct."

"Hardly a new product. According to the figures you sent me, it's been on the market for nearly six years."

"True, but the price has plummeted in that time, as they are now able to mass-produce the, ah, item. There was some public resistance when it first appeared, because of doubts about its safety, but now the demand has increased to a level where Bodymods are considering opening a new factory. They're considering several sites, including one in Ireland, one in the Philippines, and one here in Italy."

The Pope decided not to point out that Vatican City was, at least in theory, an independent state—especially as its power came from solar panels and it could, if necessary, recycle enough of its waste to become largely self-sufficient (something rarely mentioned to pilgrims who purchased holy water: they weren't squeamish when it came to transubstantiating wine into blood, but urine was another matter). "Many people are looking for work in all of those places," he replied.

"We're here to ask you to speak against this product."

"Why? I can see why I might have done, when it was experimental and being tested on the men of Mexico and Brazil, but the studies suggest that I can hardly do so on the grounds of safety: they've taken that into account."

The acolyte looked nervous, but Chapman was less easily shaken. "*Physically* safe, perhaps, but there are other considerations. Morality. The threat to the family. If millions, even billions, of men were to buy this wretched…"

George smiled slightly. "If you're worried about saying the word 'penis' in my company, don't be. I've listened to thousands of confessions: I don't embarrass easily. My secretaries are good at deleting the spam from my mail, but I've seen the ads. The Bodymod Colt is a cheap—as you say, mass-produced—means of increasing the size of an erect penis. It requires only an injection of bioplastiform nanomachines, a local anaesthetic, and a few weeks careful monitoring; about the same degree of difficulty as a reversible vasectomy, and many clinics perform both procedures in a single session. It has been demonstrated to be ineffective on anyone before adolescence, or on women who lack the necessary hormones. It does not affect fertility in any way, there are no other physical side-effects known, and it is impossible to take an overdose. Have I forgotten anything important?"

"The effect on behaviour," replied Chapman, a little stiffly.

"I'm not aware that any had been proven. To what do you refer?"

"This… modification encourages both lust and vanity. More indirectly, it can also cause envy among those who have not had the surgery, thereby possibly leading to theft, robbery…"

"For—what is the asking price?"

Chapman looked uncomfortable for a moment, feeling he might have overstepped the mark. "Clinics mostly charge five hundred to a thousand dollars, depending on their overheads."

The price range of a bottom-of-the-range alcohol-burning motorbike or solar-powered personal computer. "And the operation only need be performed once?"

"Yes."

"You have evidence of robberies committed by men to finance this surgery?"

Chapman steepled his fingers. "Yes. We do."

"And where this item is available, the incidence of robbery has increased by how much as a result?

"That's difficult to say; we're still gathering data."

The Pope nodded. "I agree that envy causes a great many problems, Mr Chapman. I wish more of them could be remedied by something so simple as a thousand dollars' worth of nanomachines." He looked at the team leader's gold-cased wristcom, monogrammed shirt and exquisitely tailored suit. "Of course, in many cases, one person's envy is the response to another's vanity. Both are deadly sins. They may—" He paused, and held up a finger. "Just a quick question, if you don't mind, Mr Chapman. Your hair—is it natural?"

"I don't see what—" Chapman drew a deep breath. One of the team members coloured slightly, and the acolyte had to hide a giggle. "It's my own hair, yes."

Nicely evaded, thought the pope: it didn't rule out cloning or colouring. "But styled, of course."

"Yes, but I—"

"It isn't important. It's just that vanity isn't an on/off switch. If it is vanity for a man to increase the size of his penis, is it vanity for him to change his teeth or the colour of his hair, beyond that which is necessary in the interests of hygiene? And what of clothing, or jewellery? I may agree that the amount of money many people spend on these is wasteful, but should I also condemn tailors, bootmakers and barbers?"

"This is different!"

"Why? Because it's not meant for external display?" Looking at Chapman, the Pope wondered whether he'd also indulged in penis extension. If he had, he decided, it was unlikely to be the standard model. "Do you have any evidence of this device causing an increase in, say, adultery? Or even promiscuity?"

"Anecdotal evidence, yes, but these things are difficult to quantify. Most people are reluctant to talk about them."

"Not in the confessional," replied George, wryly. "No, I take your point. However, I should warn you that when my predecessors have condemned technological advances, they have largely been ignored. Contraceptive devices sold as well in Catholic countries as in mostly non-Catholic populations of comparable wealth—and repealing that particular ban made no apparent difference. We still condemn abortion, of course, but that condemnation doesn't seem to be responsible for the recent decline in abortion figures. I understand the bull prohibiting the use of crossbows against Christian foes was never repealed, but neither was it obeyed. We've also condemned a great many wars, but that didn't prevent them; it didn't even prevent supposedly Catholic governments from sending troops. Why do you think this will be different?"

"In most or all of those cases," said Chapman, after a barely perceptible hesitation, "there were more powerful lobby groups arguing the opposite case. In this case, we hope that yours will be merely one of the voices raised in protest—particularly in the USA, which is the largest per capita consumer of this product. We hope that these voices will be able to drown out Bodymods' advertising."

"That," said the Pope slowly, "would be extremely expensive."

"We have financial supporters."

"People of excellent moral standing, I'm sure," said George, without a trace of sarcasm in his tone, and noticed the acolyte fidgeting and a brief flash of anger in Chapman's eyes. "I will take the matter under consideration, Mr Chapman. How long are you planning to spend in Rome?"

"Mike!"

The secretary appeared before the datashades had finished reading the Pope's retinaprints and logging him on. "Yes?"

"I need more information about the Bodymod Colt. Don't look like that, I'm not thinking of buying one. And more about this Commission."

"I presume you're not buying that, either?"

"Not until I've read the fine print," he growled.

"What's on the table?"

"A scholarship program. With medical insurance, and you know what *that* costs in the USA. They have money, and I want to know where it comes from before I take it. Matthew 27: 6."

The monsignor nodded. "I'll see what I can find."

"Thanks." The Pope thumbed a switch as soon as the door closed, and the strains of the Rolling Stones' 'You Can't Always Get What You Want' filled the office. Despite his chosen name, he preferred the lyrics of old Stones and Bob Dylan songs to most of those written by the Beatles. Except for some of Lennon's post-Beatles songs, of course. Particularly 'Imagine', 'Give Peace a Chance', and 'Working Class Hero'.

THE Pope sat back in the confessional and resisted the urge to look at his watch. A moment later, the soundproofed booth shook slightly as the supplicant sealed the door. "Bless me, father, for I have sinned. It has been three days since my last confession."

George smiled slightly, recognising Mother Catherine's voice. "What sins have you committed, my child?"

"I hacked into several computers, Father, using equipment that was not mine."

He raised an eyebrow. "Alone, or with others?"

"Alone, Father. I hacked into the databases of several banks in search of information."

The Pope nodded to himself, quietly admiring her ability to render that sentence into Latin. "Did you steal any money? Any credit card information?"

"No, Father, but I discovered that the Commission for Moral Dignity is funded by the National Rifle Association."

"The National Rifle Association? Are you sure?"

"Yes, Father. And the NRA is mostly funded by the gun manufacturers. If they weren't, they'd be running at a loss: membership numbers have been dropping in recent years, and they've lowered the fees to the point that they no longer cover postage. Tyler Chapman has been representing the NRA in Washington D.C. for several years. He's one of the best paid lobbyists in the city."

"I see... I think. Did you discover any association with Bodymods, Inc?"

"The Colt company tried to sue them for using the name 'Colt', but a judge ruled that they didn't own the word. They were successful, however, in preventing Bodymod using the names 'Python', 'Anaconda', 'Peacemaker' or 'Equaliser'. Colt paid court costs, but that was all."

"Maybe they should have bought shares instead," the pope mused. "No other connection?"

"Not that I've found, Father."

"Hmm. Thank you—I mean, bless you, my child. Say five 'Hail Marys' and take the rest of the night off."

"Mike?"

"Yes?"

"Looking at it logically, I'm the last man on Earth who should be making a decision about a…"

"Sex toy?" Mike shrugged. "Maybe when you repealed the requirement for celibacy for the clergy, you shouldn't have excluded yourself."

"I had to; otherwise, it would have looked self-serving. Besides, I was only giving them permission to marry, not to… I don't know. And it's been a long time since I met anyone I wanted to marry."

"Well, your job's not exactly a babe magnet, nowadays," said the monsignor.

George smiled slightly. "Do you really think this Bodymod is just a sex toy?"

"Yes, but not in the sense people usually use the term. It's not a substitute for healthy sex, it just… enhances it, I guess. Is it really any different from any other form of cosmetic surgery? Which I don't remember us specifically criticising, even when it was taken to ridiculous extremes. And the fact that this Bodymod Colt is at the Model T Ford stage, where it's inexpensive and you can have any size you like as long as it's twenty-two centimetres, might actually be a plus."

"Did you meet Chapman?"

"Briefly. I didn't like him either."

The Pope nodded. "I'm trying not to let that prejudice me. But what if I'm wrong?"

The secretary looked at his friend, who despite his greying hair, suddenly looked much younger than his fifty-five years. His jeans and t-shirt looked out of place in the elaborately decorated private chapel, but Mike had occasionally wondered what Jesus would have thought of the Vati-

291

can's ostentation—assuming the Swiss Guard had let him in, of course. "I know you can prove anything with statistics, George, but I think you can trust this stuff. The College of Lynxes has looked it over. And you're the Pope," he reminded him. "You're infallible. Remember?"

"I'm serious. Popes have been wrong before. Why not me?"

"I'm serious, too. You think the Cardinals chose you? Ha! God chose you. Are you going to tell Him He made a mistake?"

"There are days when I'd like to," the Pope admitted. "Failing that, I'd like to borrow some of His omniscience, particularly when I have to deal with statistics. I nearly flunked math when I was in school. I got into college on the strength of my audition, not my grades. I was the class clown, and I went from there to playing comedy. Making people happy seemed like the best thing I could do. Then I realised how much difference there was between a few minutes' laughter and *real* happiness. Now I can't even make people *laugh*, much less make them happy."

"Don't be so hard on yourself," said Mike, lightly. "The big hat is always good for a few giggles."

Despite himself, George chuckled. "Yeah, but they've all seen it before. I need some new material."

"You have plenty of material. It's all in how you present it. *And* you have a captive audience."

The Pope was silent for a moment, then reached into the pocket on his thigh for his datashades. "Thanks, Mike."

TYLER Chapman looked up at the Michelangelo paintings on the ceiling with a sour expression. You got a much better view when you saw them in virtual reality, if you were interested in primitive art or these peasant superstitions, and you didn't have to spend a couple of hours sitting in a supposedly first-class seat on a hypersonic cattle car to see them. And the city! He'd heard that Rome was supposed to be magical and magnificent, but the hotel was a ruin with inadequate soundproofing and security, the restaurants stank (God alone knew what these Italians put in their food), the computers could barely understand English, the women were fat and noisy, and all of them were overpriced. The streets were crawling with backpackers and beggars, if that wasn't a tautology, and on the rare occasions you saw a cop, he didn't move them along as he would have done back in Washington. Chapman consoled himself with the thought that if this job went well, he'd be up for a promotion that would enable him leave all this globetrotting shit behind him and leave it to some other poor slob to go out to trade beads and mirrors with the savages. He smiled at this, then jumped as a young priest coughed slightly. "Mr Chapman?"

Chapman recovered instantly. "Yes?"

"The major-domo sent me to get you, sir. He says His Holiness is ready to see you now."

"Thanks."

His Holiness was humming an obscure old Beatles song when the lobbyist walked into the conference room. "Ah, Mr Chapman. Sorry to have to keep you waiting, but I wanted to read through all the research before I made a decision."

Chapman sat, keeping the smile on his sculpted face despite his unease. "I can come back later if you—"

"No, that's fine. I had some of our own statisticians look at your figures, and also asked them to do some research of their own. It seems you're quite right about the reported short-term effects of the Bodymod Colt: rises in adultery, pre-marital sex, male homosexual behaviour, abortion… even a slight increase in rape." He paused, watching Chapman's smile become slightly more intense. "However, you seem not to have studied the longer-term effects. After six months to a year, these figures apparently return to normal, and then continue to descend for five to seven years before beginning to level out."

Chapman swallowed.

"Most areas even report more marriages and a significant decline in the divorce rate, as well as violent crime—both armed and unarmed. Interesting, don't you think?"

Chapman nodded, then said softly, "Yes, though I'm not a statistician. I'd have to show these figures to our research team…"

"Of course. Crime statistics are notoriously unreliable. However, there is one other correlation that caught my eye—between sales figures for the Bodymod Colt and handguns. Once again, it takes up to a year before a pattern begins to emerge, but after that, there's a huge decline not only in sales of handguns, but in ammunition, applications for handgun licenses, and a corresponding increase in the number of handguns handed in to police for disposal."

Chapman turned slightly pale.

"There's also a very slight decline—almost within the margins of experimental error, in fact—in the sales of other weapons, such as rifles, shotguns, hunting knives, and so on, as well as non-lethal weapons such as shocksprays and stunsticks. I was also intrigued to see that it's not just men who are buying fewer handguns; sales of pistols to women also decline in the same areas, at about the same rate."

Chapman hesitated, then tried his best to sound sincere. "This seems to be the case, yes, though firearm manufacturers are still gathering data. But I'm sure you can appreciate that these manufacturers are major employers, and if demand does decline for their product, they will have to lay off staff. Some of the smaller manufacturers may even go out of business."

"You mean the manufacturers of smaller weapons?"

Chapman winced slightly, and tried to hide it with a chuckle. "The negative impact will, of course, be hardest for those manufacturers who produce handguns exclusively for civilian use."

"And these are major contributors to your organisation?"

The lobbyist crossed his legs. "I'm afraid that our accounts are confidential, and handled almost exclusively by computers: I'm not in a position to say who donates how much to our cause. I'm sure you understand. Isn't there a parable in the Bible condemning people who make too great a show of giving to charity?"

"Criticising, not condemning. Mark, Chapter 12. And I'm pleased to hear that you'll be taking this into consideration when it comes to giving the scholarships you have so generously offered." Chapman's smile shrunk by a few millimetres. "However, Mr Chapman, your arguments about economic dislocation could just as easily be applied to the illicit drugs trade, or the legal pharmaceutical trade, or alcohol production, or... or Bodymod Inc., for that matter. While the church has taken this into consideration on occasion," he paused, looking down at the Fisherman's Ring on his finger, "it does not, in and of itself, legitimise an industry.

"As for the moral dimension, the Bodymod Colt may do as much good as harm—possibly even more. It may tempt some people to seek out more sexual partners, but the evidence suggests that it is at least as likely that many will find more satisfaction within their own marriages, which must be a good thing. And after all, doesn't your country's constitution state that all men were created equal?"

Chapman fumed. "I believe that was the Declaration of Independence."

"My apologies."

"And didn't Jesus say that celibacy was better than marriage?"

"No, that was Saint Paul," said the pope, "and strictly off the record, I've long suspected that he was a sexist asshole. I wonder if a Bodymod Colt might have changed his attitude."

Chapman stood. "That's your answer? Shall I tell the Commission that you refuse even to speak on our behalf?"

"I don't do commercials," replied George Ringo I. "My staff are, however, putting together a press release, and I've had some informal conversations with a number of other religious leaders, who support my position. If I were you, Mr Chapman, I'd go back to your sponsors and suggest they diversify. Maybe they could reach some form of accommodation with Bodymod—an alliance, even. The company might have work for some good lobbyists, and you could change your name to, for example, the National Rifle and Penis Association." He smiled broadly as Chapman turned on his expensive, handmade heel and stalked out. A moment later, he resumed whistling 'Happiness is a Warm Gun'.

"It's a pity about the scholarships," said Mother Catherine, between mouthfuls of bruschetta.

The Pope was leaning back in his chair, and barely managed not to swear as he dropped tomato on his t-shirt and jeans. "I wouldn't worry," he said, brushing the mess onto the kitchen floor. "We may get them yet. Mr Chapman has a new job."

"What?"

"The Commission laid him off. Budget cuts."

Mike shook his head. "So where's he working now?"

"Still in Washington, with one of the Right-to-Life campaigns. I recommended him, on a trial basis."

Catherine burst out laughing, and had to grab the edge of the table to prevent herself falling out of her chair.

"Why?" asked Mike. "I mean, why him?"

"Simple Christian charity. Besides, I suspect he'll do well."

Catherine reached for her wine, drank half of it, and toasted him. "Amen," she said.

"Let it be," replied the Pope.

TARGET OF
OPPORTUNITY

The cockroach was slightly smaller than her foot, but it was large enough to make the blonde scream and keep screaming until after the rest of the party had recovered and begun laughing. I could've explained that none of the cockroaches here/now carry any diseases that are dangerous to humans, but I knew it wouldn't make any difference; it never does. Someone would be bound to trot out the theory that it was roaches, migrating across the land bridges, that would wipe out the dinosaurs, and that's a symbol too powerful for any logic could stand against, even though it's never been proven.

The blonde was still red-faced when we walked inside, and I half-expected the sight of the borogove to start her screaming again; instead, she dropped her backpack, hunkered down, and began talking to him in a thick but beautiful accent while her husband hung back. "What's her name?" she asked, the accent gone.

"Bruno," I replied.

"How big does he grow?" asked her husband, loudly. He was taller than she was and much taller than me, and heavily muscled in a top-heavy way that always reminds me of therizinosaurs and Neandertals and gridiron players. His skin and hair and eyes were a pale brown that seemed to blend into any background like smart camo. I wondered if the screaming had been exaggerated for his benefit. I could be wrong—a lot of intelligent people have a phobia of cockroaches—but it didn't improve my opinion of him any. "He's about full grown, but females are bigger."

"What does he eat?" asked the blonde.

296

"Anything smaller than he is," I said, a little sourly. "If there's any food in your pack, he'll find it before you can say *Borogovia holtzi*." Bruno looked hurt, but it was true; he's as inquisitive and unethical and almost as intelligent as a cat. His legs and flanks and face are striped like those of a tabby, he stands about a metre tall, and he's easily domesticated by dino standards, meaning that he's friendly as long as he's well fed. We keep him around to keep the insects down and remind the travellers where and when they are; it wouldn't be the Cretaceous without dinosaurs. Bruno could kill a human in a fair fight, but when did we ever fight fair?

The husband was admiring Bruno's claws. "How closely is he related to the troodons?"

"They're ninety-something percent similar genetically, but Bruno's not local—he's from Mongolia. A friend at the hostel there gave him to us; there was one female and two males in the clutch, and the males were always fighting."

One of the women laughed, and the blonde asked, "Is he as smart as the troodons?"

I shrugged. "I wouldn't know."

"You don't believe these stories about troodons making tools, then?" asked the husband.

"I've never seen it," I evaded. The blonde looked crestfallen. "I've seen them hunting in packs, using ambush techniques, and I've seen them carrying food—mostly carrion—but that's all. It's a long way from tool use, much less tool making. Is that why you're here?"

"*She* is," the husband snorted. "I'm more interested in doing some hunting. When can we go out of the dome?"

"Any time you like," I replied. I was beginning to dislike this one more and more every time he opened his mouth; why do so many intelligent, beautiful women marry such total dorks? "Closest exit's down Horner Street, turn left on Sawyer, right on Russell. I recommend you take a respirator mask; oxygen content outside is higher than you're used to, and it may make you overconfident."

"Is it dangerous?"

"Not really; we only lose two point three people per year, on average. Dinos don't come too close to the city—most of them have zero curiosity, and I don't think they like the smell—and the pterors won't bother you unless they think you're already dead or dying. None of the snakes are really dangerous, but don't go swimming in the rivers; some of the crocs grow close to twenty metres long. But the local wildlife's already learning to fear us; the biggest animals you're likely to see are the dragonflies and butterflies, though they're pretty spectacular. If you want to see dinosaurs, you take a flier."

"These two point three victims," said the husband. "What sort of dinosaur kills them?"

"Topsies—hornfaces—mostly." I said. "Some tourists go too near the herds and spook them. And sometimes it's difficult to tell how the people died, especially if the scavengers get to them before we do. About one in ten are never found at all. Now, let's get you all checked in."

A LOT of people come to Maia City for the dinosaurs, of course, but mostly we're a stop-over, a waystation. It's not possible to make a leap of less than twelve million years (please don't ask me why not, I just work here), and more energy-efficient to go back or forward seventy or even two hundred million. It's something like the slingshot effect they used to use to boost the speed of unmanned spacecraft, but not quite, and something like flying around the world instead of *through* it... anyway, anyone wanting to see something like the Little Big Horn or the Seven Wonders of the World or the Mediterranean being flooded has to go via a waystation in the past, then back to their intended time. The same for the return trip. And since stations and cities are hideously expensive to build and maintain, and Maia City has more to offer than the others, we get most of the tourist trade. Most of our guests stay for a few days, take a flier out to see the topsy and hadro herds or the pteror nests and maybe get a glimpse of some of the predators from a safe distance. Only students stay for more than a few days, and most of them choose to come here rather than the Hilton.

The blonde's name was Sondra, her major anthropology (I'd guessed it wasn't entomology), and she was headed for early Pleistocene Asia to study the technology of *Homo erectus* for her Master's thesis. Her muscle-bound husband was Kevin, nominally a business student (his father and grandfather had both been major financial contributors to the college), and he was obviously here mostly to keep an eye on her. Picking her up was apparently the only thing he'd ever done that impressed his father and older brother, and he wasn't going to risk losing her, which was why they'd married so young. I learnt most of this from Amy, who was writing her dissertation on predator/prey ratios throughout the Mesozoic and had an excellent reason for detesting Kevin; he'd date-raped her when she was a sophomore. Amy was attractive in a dark, elfin sort of way, and since she was friendly and unattached and obviously intended to stick around for a few months, we ended up spending the night together. It was hardly her fault that I kept thinking of Sondra.

My room was little different from any other double in the hostel. I've never been one for souvenirs, or any other possessions, and the room contained nothing but a bed, desk, closet, chair, and the inevitable dinosaur holoposters, excellent pictures of *Maiasaura* and *Anatotitan*. "How long have you been here?" Amy asked, as she picked her clothes up from the floor.

"Seven years."

"You don't look that old."

"Don't you believe it," I said. "I was born in 1962. I could be your great-grandfather."

"I wish you had been," she retorted. "I'd love to have inherited your eyes. Where are you from?"

"Vietnam. Little village called My Lai. I ran away from soldiers one day and crashed into an observation post, full of American history students watching their ancestors acting like monsters. I don't know how I got in, I had no idea of what anyone was saying, but they decided that they couldn't just send me out to be killed." I can still remember the girl who'd held on to me while everyone else was arguing, the first blonde woman I'd ever seen. "So they took me home. I became something of a celebrity about the time you were born, the first war orphan in decades, and a couple who worked for ChronCorp adopted me. ChronCorp ended up giving me a scholarship with a two year bond, and when it ran out, I stayed. What do you want for breakfast?"

"Can the eggs be trusted?"

"I can make an omelette you could *swear* came from a chicken."

"And can you take me to see some of the dinosaurs, later?"

"If you can wait until after lunch, sure."

To my surprise and delight, Sondra came with us rather than accompany Kevin on his hunting trip. I reminded her that we wouldn't see any troodons unless we stayed out until nightfall—troodons were dusk feeders, with night vision that would do credit to a cat—but she didn't even hesitate.

The three of us flew out to the floodplains near what would one day be Hell Creek, Montana, where Amy was able to pick out predators among the great herds of herbivores—a daspletosaurus waiting in ambush by the water, biding its time for something small and slow enough to take with one bite; a phobosuchus, a crocodile nearly fifteen metres long, sunning itself on a sandbar while small pterors picked parasites out from between its teeth (not a job I'd relish); a small pack of mottled dromaeosaurus, sickle claws hidden by the undergrowth. A pair of ostrich-like dromiceiomimus sprinted away from us as we glided overhead; I clocked their speed at sixty-six klicks on the straight, and Sondra filmed one of them snapping up a drab butterfly without even breaking stride. A moment later, I realised they were running towards a small flock of birds. "Vultures," said Amy. "Something's dead."

I steered the flier over to where the scavengers were gathering. The 'something' turned out to be a nodosaurid, probably an *Edmontia*, but it was a little late to be sure; a dryptosaurus was using its can-opener claw to pry the armour plates from its back. It might have found it dead, or it might have killed it itself, or it might have intimidated the real killers away, as lions and tyrannosaurs do. A few stygivenators and smaller carnivorous dinosaurs kept their distance, waiting their turn.

We watched until the sun started to set, so that Amy could count and identify the scavengers, and then I headed back to the city despite Sondra's protests. The flier was solar-powered and could stay up for most of the day, but its battery was limited. A few minutes later, Sondra screamed dangerously close to my ear. "Down there!"

I looked, and saw a small pack of troodon running towards a clump of swamp cypress. "What?"

"One of them had a spear!"

I turned to Amy, who shrugged. "I think it was carrying *something*," she said.

"Where is it now?"

"It ran back into the trees. Are they scared of fliers?"

"If they've got any sense, yes; most hunting is done from fliers." The other troodons disappeared between the trees. "Did you film it?"

"I hope so," Sondra wailed; she pressed the playback button, looked into the viewfinder, and smiled weakly. "It *looks* like a spear," she said.

KEVIN was in a foul mood when we returned, muttering about cheap Chinese lasers and the embargo on bringing your own weapons through the machine, and I suddenly realised why his surname was familiar—his family had been making small arms for generations before even I was born. He was even less impressed by Sondra's snapshot than we'd been, and less successful at hiding it.

The major problem with the picture was that the spear—or length of bamboo—was on the far side of the troodon's body, and you couldn't see whether it was holding it, or whether the end was lifted clear of the ground. It didn't help that it didn't look much like a spear, either. "If dinos made spears, wouldn't we have found one by now?" asked Kevin, a little sullenly.

"Not if they were just made of wood or bamboo," Sondra insisted. "Wooden tools don't survive like stone ones. It's like *erectus* in the tropics; they probably had wooden spears, clubs, carrying bags, maybe even canoes or rafts, boomerangs, bolas... how much would survive of a bolas, or even a wooden bow strung with sinew, after sixty-six million years?"

Kevin thought about this. "Forget sixty-six million years. How long've tourists been coming here? Twenty years? How come nobody's seen this before?"

"Seen, but not photographed," I answered, before Sondra could speak: she shot me a look of what might have been gratitude.

Amy laughed softly. "There's a story my grandfather told me about baboons, when I was a little girl," she said. "He said they were intelligent, even knew how to speak our languages, but were careful not to let white men hear them in case they made them work."

"Do you believe that?" asked Kevin.

"Not anymore, but I can't disprove it."

Kevin turned to me for support. "You've been here for years, you know about dinosaurs; what do *you* think?"

I could've lied, but what would have been the point? "I don't know. Why would troodons *need* spears? They have claws. Weapons are for weaklings." Kevin glared and turned white. "Sorry, I put that badly. Our ancestors needed to make weapons because their claws and teeth were too small to be effective for killing, and there were plenty of predators who could out-run and out-climb them. I suspect they weren't much smarter than baboons or gorillas; all they had were good grasping hands and an upright gait. If they *hadn't* picked up antelope horns and thigh-bones, instant daggers and clubs, we wouldn't be here. Troodons have the hands and the bipedal walk, but they also have pretty nasty toe claws, so they don't really *need* spears."

"Extra reach," Sondra suggested. "Enough to attack an ankylosaur without getting too close to the tail. Or maybe it's a javelin."

"Maybe, but that doesn't look like much of a point—it's not stone-tipped, or even fire-hardened. And look at Bruno." The borogove looked up at the sound of his name, realised that no-one was about to feed him, then curled up again. "Those shoulders aren't built for a strong overarm throw, and you'd need a lot of force to put sharpened bamboo through the average dino's hide—unless you're dealing with dinos that are even smaller than the troodons, and the troodons can run most of those down without much trouble."

Kevin stared at Bruno and nodded. "I'm sorry, honey," he said, magnanimously. "But I'll tell you what; I'll come with you tomorrow, take a rover back to the same place, go into the forest and see what we see."

Amy rolled her eyes; ain't we got fun? "Okay," I said. "But it won't be a hunting trip; *I'll* carry the gun, and you don't use it without my say-so. Understood?"

I saw Kevin the next morning while I was having my shower. He enthused about hunting while he combed his hair, and when he noticed that I was replying in monosyllables, tried changing the subject to women, then to football. "You don't like me much, do you?" he finally asked, his expression slightly puzzled, his body language defensive, as though it was important to him that I like him. "Is it something I said, or just because I'm rich?"

"Nothing to do with that. I'm just prejudiced when it comes to hunters and guns," I admitted. "I know what it feels like to have someone chasing me with a gun, hunting me. My sympathies lie with the prey, especially if it can't fight back."

His brow furrowed as he considered this for a moment. "I'd never hunt humans," he said, "but these are just big animals, not even as smart as deer."

I shrugged. "I said it was a prejudice. Besides, I don't think we have much in common."

He laughed at that. "You like women, though, don't you?"

"Sure."

"Well, that's something." He was silent for a moment. "Have you ever tried it?"

"Tried?"

"Hunting."

"No." I switched the shower from water to sonic.

"You've lived here for years and never gone hunting?" he yelled, over the sound of the shower.

"Never."

"Maybe you should."

"Maybe." I switched the shower off, and grabbed my shorts.

"Why don't you come with us tomorrow?" he suggested. "Sondra and me. I'm going after a—what do you call the big herbivores with the crests?"

"Lambeosaurines."

"What's the one with the really long crest, like a snorkel?"

"*Parasaurolophus.*"

"Yeah, that. The satellites show a whole herd less than a hundred klicks away. Why don't you come with us?"

"I'll think about it," I said.

WE spent most of that day seeing the floodplains through nocs and the windows of a hoverover, while I watched the satellite pictures on the com and steered us away from the herds of triceratops and torosaurus and any large predators. After a less than enchanting day, we returned to the swamp cypresses just before nightfall. Sondra wanted to get out and walk into the forest, and when I expressed reluctance, Kevin opened the door on his side and jumped out without even donning his respirator. I cursed myself silently for not having locked his door, wondered what the Hell he was trying to prove, and decided that I couldn't let him go there unarmed and alone. "Okay," I sighed, grabbing the laser. "Put your masks on, and let's go."

Kevin had a good head start and he kept increasing it, though he was careful to look back occasionally to make sure Sondra was watching, or safe; maybe both. A troodon stuck its head out from behind a tree, and Kevin yelled and charged towards it. Naturally enough, it disappeared. I resigned myself to an hour of searching fruitlessly for elusive, cunning, small dinosaurs in their own, well-shadowed territory, and reached into my pocket for my shades, setting them to infra-red.

A moment later, a male troodon, a length of bamboo in its hands, appeared just a few metres in front of Kevin. He turned towards it and stopped. We were too far behind him to hear what he was saying, but it wasn't hard to guess; Amy was muttering something in what I guessed was Zulu, and Sondra was squealing with joy. Slowly, and cautiously, the three of us advanced towards where Kevin was now standing. We were at the edge of the wood when the troodon looked at Kevin, tilting its head first to the left, then to the right, and then raised the bamboo to its mouth. After all the fuss, it looked as though the bamboo was just food, something to chew on—and then Kevin turned to face us, and I saw something small sticking out of his throat. The bamboo wasn't food, or a spear, but a blowgun: I brought the laser up, thumbed the safety, and yelled to the girls to head back to the car.

Kevin staggered in our direction—the dart must have been poisoned, blowgun darts almost always are. I remembered reading that BaMbuti blowguns can bring down a gorilla or elephant, and tried to forget it. Another male troodon appeared, also with a length of bamboo; I fired, and hit the blowgun, which exploded into flames, as well as the troodon holding it and the tree behind him. The damn fool had set the laser to maximum power, enough to kill a tyrannosaur, leaving enough charge for maybe five or six man-killing shots.

The fire, and the crack of the laser, scared the troodons away for a few seconds, and then a dozen appeared, brandishing weapons better than any nature had given them—triceratops horns and dryptosaurus claws. Kevin ran, but they were much faster, and they soon surrounded him, herding him away from us. I heard Sondra screaming out to Kevin, telling him to stop, stand his ground. He continued to run—and then disappeared. I stood my ground and kept firing until Amy stopped the rover a few metres behind me, and then I ran too.

With the rover at maximum lift, I drove near the spot where the troodons were gathered, warning Sondra not to look down. Kevin was lying motionless in a shallow pit, impaled on topsy horns and stakes of sharpened bamboo. The troodons looked up as our shadow passed over them, then, obviously deciding that he was already dead, began hacking at him with the horns and claws. I made a note of the location, then drove away.

"THOSE weapons," said Sondra, at breakfast the next morning. "The blowguns... the troodons are hunting us, aren't they?" I raised my eyebrows, but said nothing. I could feel Amy watching me as she ate her omelet. "Those darts wouldn't go through dinosaur hide."

"They might, at close range. They'd only need to sting a little, like a horsefly, to get the dinosaur running, steer him towards—in the right direction." The stakes would work anyway, like judo—you just use your opponent's size and weight against him—but I didn't want to say that.

She hadn't seen Kevin die, or what little they'd brought back in a body bag.

"How big was the pit?"

"Three or four metres; big enough for a juvenile hadro or topsy, and deep enough that even an adult might have difficulty getting out."

"I don't know," she said, staring into her coffee. "I still think they're hunting us. After all, we're the weakest prey around, aren't we, once you separate us from the herd?"

I looked at Bruno, and then at Amy, who suddenly seemed fascinated by a butterfly on the ceiling. "It's much more likely they've been using the darts on birds or pterosaurs," I said. "Or maybe on each other. But at most, they're taking one or two humans a year—hardly a staple of their diet, more a..."

"Target of opportunity?" Amy suggested. I glared at her, then shrugged.

Sondra sat there silently for at least a minute, then drank the rest of her tepid coffee. "Well, we have evidence, now," she said.

Kevin's family threatened to sue, but Sondra and Amy supported my version of events; Amy even had a few hastily-taken snapshots as proof. I kept copies after the court cleared me of all blame; they're the only souvenirs I own. They're a little too gruesome for public display, but Amy likes to take them out and reminisce every time she visits. "Poor Kevin," she sighed. "If only one of us had recognised those weapons for what they were, we might have been able to save him."

"How could we?" I asked. "The pit was well concealed, so there was no way we could have seen it from ground level. And the blowgun just looked like a length of bamboo; I'd never even seen anyone use a blowgun before. Had you?"

Amy sipped at her tea. "No, but Sondra must have. I know *Homo erectus* had them."

"Sondra?" I stared at her. "You can't be serious. Okay, *we* both disliked him, but not enough to set him up to be killed. Right?" She hesitated, then nodded. "But *Sondra?*"

She shrugged. "I suspect she stands to inherit a lot of money. But I could be wrong."

Amy moved to Maia City a few months later, renting a room around the corner from the hostel, though she stays here most nights. Sondra hasn't been back and sometimes I miss her, but that probably wouldn't have worked out anyway. I suspect she's a little too civilised for the Cretaceous. But I could be wrong.

WEAKNESS

1972

THE OLD MAN LOOKED PAST THE muzzles of the revolvers to the young men holding them. The taller one with the Mussolini jaw, he judged to be not yet twenty-five. The other had a thin beard that failed to hide the large pimples growing on his cheeks, and his stubby-fingered gun hand was still shaking slightly—probably too young to vote or be drafted, the old man thought. Not alike enough to be brothers, probably not even half-brothers, though they might be cousins. And not junkies, though the younger looked as though he was running on something stronger than adrenalin and beer, probably amphetamines. If the Bride had sent them, he was in trouble, but that seemed unlikely. She preferred sharper tools.

"There's almost nothing here with any resale value," the old man said, unfazed. "My wallet's on the nightstand, but I doubt there's as much as a hundred dollars in it. And if you're looking for drugs, I don't keep any in the house—well, none that would be of use to you." He decided not to mention the prescription pads he still kept in his lab.

"Credit cards?" said Big Jaw.

They were prepared to kill him, then: the old man made a moue of irritation. "No. If you're after money, I can tell you a much easier way to make some—much more than you'd find in this poor house."

The two robbers looked at each other. They were obviously unused to their victims negotiating with them quite so calmly. The old man didn't seem entirely sober, but he wasn't drunk either. "I'm listening," said Big Jaw, taking a step forwards.

307

"You both look young and reasonably healthy," said the doctor. "There's a market for body parts, if you have the contacts—which I do. Livers, hearts, kidneys, eyes… if one of you kills the other, I can get twenty to twenty-five thousand easily, probably much more. That's probably a hundred times what your fence would give you for the rubbish in this house."

The robbers stared at him. "What if we kill you instead?" said the younger, not quite stuttering.

"A body as old as mine?" the doctor scoffed. "You might get fifty for it from an antiques dealer or a freak-show, but for transplants? And neither of you look like surgeons. Twenty thousand, guaranteed. How long would it take you to make that holding up gas stations and liquor stores, especially when you have to split the take?" His voice was smooth despite more than a century of smoking cigars, and seductive as a snake-charmer's flute. "Unless, of course, you're brothers… or lovers…"

"No!" The first denial came from the younger man, and was as shrill and emphatic as a dentist's drill and accentuated by him raising his crowbar in a vaguely threatening fashion.

"Nah," said Big Jaw, a fraction of a second later; he sounded more amused than insulted, as though he'd seen through the attempt to manipulate them. "And I think you're full of shit."

The younger smiled at that. "Maybe we should open the old faggot up and see."

The doctor looked at him dispassionately. "Might I suggest you put some gloves on, first? I think I still have some in the study."

Big Jaw's eyes widened in alarm, and he looked at his companion's bare and grimy hands.

"But no matter how thoroughly you search my bowels, you won't find any money there, either," the doctor continued. "I'm afraid it's the hundred in the wallet, split between the two of you, or a quick twenty thousand. Of course, it would need to be a head shot, leaving the eyes undamaged."

"You shut your mouth!" shouted the younger. It wasn't quite a scream, but it was heading in that direction.

Big Jaw snorted, and the doctor worried for a moment that the spell might have been broken. "And get a murder rap? No thanks. We'll just take what you got and go."

The old man waved a hand languidly. "As you wish. Of course you'd run the risk of a murder charge if you killed me—I'm well known in this town, and my cleaning lady will find my body in a day or two—but one of you killing the other, on the other hand… there'd be no danger at all. The buyers dispose of whatever body parts they don't want. And consider the career prospects. In this county, five or six people disappearing a year isn't going to raise any eyebrows, as long as we're careful choosing our victims and don't get too greedy. But as far as easy money goes… it'll never be quite as easy as it is tonight. All you have to do is –"

Big Jaw glanced at his partner and saw how he was shaking. Coolly, he turned around and fired one shot slightly above and behind the young man's ear, splattering the drapes with blood, splinters of bone and gobbets of brain.

No loss, thought the doctor. There was little demand for brains anyway, and he was sure he could have grown a better one in a terrarium. "A wise choice," he said softly.

"He would've done the same," the gunman grunted. "Looks like your cleaning lady's got her work cut out for her."

"She's seen worse, believe me."

"You'd better not be bullshitting me about the money, Doc. I can kill you just as easy as I killed Chucky there."

The doctor smiled; he doubted that, but there was no point in saying so. "I'm not bullshitting you. Pick up the body and follow me."

"Why can't you pick it up?"

The old man held up his spidery hands. "You carry him, and I'll dissect him. Unless you think it would be better the other way around?"

The murderer lifted his victim's body, but nearly dropped it as he saw the doctor reach for the phone. "Who the fuck are you –"

"Just arranging for pick-up," said the doctor calmly. "Good evening. It's Dr Pretorius, on Browning Street. Yes, it has been a while…"

1841

THE tobacconist's popularity with local writers was almost entirely due to the beauty of one of the clerks, twenty-one year old Mary Rogers. James Fenimore Cooper and Washington Irving were frequent visitors, as was Fitz-Green Halleck, who wrote a poem praising her beauty. Edgar Allan Poe was also a regular, and being somehow more comfortable with dead women than the living, would later immortalize Mary in somewhat different fashion, basing his detective story 'The Murder of Marie Roget' on her own unsolved death. Amid these literary lights, the skinny young medical student who came in to buy cigars when his budget stretched that far was barely visible… but it had been to him that Mary had turned when she discovered that she was pregnant.

More than a century later, Pretorius still remembered the look of Mary's corpse on his makeshift operating table. She'd bled profusely during what should have been a routine procedure, and he'd been unable to staunch the flow before she bled to death. He stood there for several minutes, finishing the bottle and wondering what to do, staring first at her corpse, then at the fetus, then back at the corpse, before deciding to obscure the signs of the operation by making it look as though she'd been raped and strangled. After doing his best to simulate this, he'd borrowed a jump-seat wagon and carried her body to the Hudson river. It washed up in New Jersey a day later, by which time Pretorius had sobered up enough to wonder why he'd kept the fetus.

The murder of Mary Rogers was never solved.

1972

THE gunman dumped his former partner's body onto the operating table, and Pretorius donned a white smock, a hood and a mask, and began washing his hands. "Strip him," he said.

"What?"

"Do you think I can dissect him while he's dressed? There should be shears in the autoclave if you think it's going to be quicker to cut the stuff off him—I wasn't planning to sell it."

"What's an autoclave?"

"The thing over there, like a small stove. It's for sterilizing surgical instruments." The doctor dried his hands, then removed a pair of plastic gloves from a pack. "I'm afraid you're my only assistant at present, so you'll have to act as theatre nurse. What do you normally do for a crust? No, let me guess. Electrician, or mechanic with some knowledge of electrical wiring."

"How did you –"

"Someone had to disarm the alarm system, and your partner had the crowbar, which meant that it was probably you. Besides, he didn't seem bright enough, and –" Pretorius examined the corpse's fingers, "I'm guessing that he hasn't had a job in a while. His hands are too soft."

The robber snorted. "You can talk. Your hands look like a woman's."

"Hardly surprising. They were, once."

A blink. "You used to be a woman?"

"No, of course not, dear boy. They're transplants. My own were getting too arthritic for fine work."

"You call me 'dear boy' again, grandpa," his assistant replied, his tone mild, "and I'm going to paint the wall with your brains."

"What should I call you, then? It needn't be your real name, just as long as you answer to it."

"Denny," he said, after a brief pause. "This woman: you killed her?"

"Not intentionally," said Pretorius, as he laid out the containers for the different organs. "She was a patient of mine, but she died on the table. A shame, but waste not, want not. Now, I'm going to need the tray of instruments that's in the autoclave—you can touch the tray, but not the instruments themselves, they'll need to be sterile."

Denny obeyed. "You expect me to believe that shit about your hands, or are you just trying to weird me out?"

Pretorius smiled beneath his mask. "If we're going to work together, you're going to hear and see things that are much stranger than that. You can believe them or not as you choose, but it will help if you act as though they're true. Scalpel."

1843

Pretorius stared at the monstrosity billed as the Feejee Mermaid, and shook his head in vaguely drunken admiration of the skill of the taxidermist who'd constructed this chimera from the tail of a fish and the upper half of a monkey or baby orangutan. He stared it, looking for stitches, and finally gave up.

He wandered randomly through the museum, hearing Barnum's roar as he thinned out the crowd by leading them to "the amazing egress". Pretorius had been tipsy enough to fall for *that* trick once, temporarily forgetting that an 'egress' was merely another word for 'exit'. He still remembered Barnum's traveling exhibition of Joice Heth, a blind and half-paralyzed negro woman who the impresario claimed was over 160 years old and had been George Washington's nurse. Even when Barnum managed to acquire a real marvel, it seemed he had to lie at least a little; he'd claimed General Tom Thumb, a genuine midget barely two feet tall, was eleven years old when he was only four. No matter, thought Pretorius: it would be a less interesting world if there were no monsters, even if the monsters had to be manufactured.

One day, Pretorius promised himself, he would out-Barnum Barnum. He would make a mermaid more fascinating than the Feejee mermaid or a dwarf smaller than General Tom Thumb, or find a way to keep someone alive until they really *were* more than 160 years old. He smiled at the thought as he staggered home.

1972

THE surgery finished, Pretorius peeled off his gloves and threw them into the bin along with the unwanted parts of Chucky. The organs with resale value had been carefully boxed ready for pick-up, and the boy's hands had gone into the freezer: waste not, want not. "Have some gin?" he asked, as he removed his mask and took a bottle and two glasses from one of the cabinets. "It's my only weakness."

Denny didn't reply. He stared into the bin at the remains, and jumped when he heard the doorbell ring. Pretorius smiled, and removed his bloody surgical gown. "Don't worry," he said. "It's just Burke and Hare."

"What?"

"The body-snatchers? Burke's the butcher, Hare's the thief, Knox the boy who buys the beef." He shook his head at Denny's blank look. "Young people these days... no respect for history. No poetry in their souls, either."

"Poetry's for birthday cards and chicks," said Denny, flatly. "And faggots."

The doctor pursed his lips as the bell rang again. "I'll go upstairs and let them in," he said. "They don't know you, and they're... not inclined to trust strangers easily. Best if I warn them that I have a new assistant, and introduce you to them later. Don't touch anything while I'm gone."

1899

PRETORIUS woke in the centre of a dull white blur, nausea and a foul taste, and a sensation of intense pain unreliably held at bay by some sort of clumsily contrived armour. He wondered for a moment whether this might be limbo, or purgatory, and was faintly disappointed by the thought: after all his blasphemies and his complicity with murder, he'd expected to find himself in a more interesting version of Hell. He tried to blink, and was unable to tell whether his eyes were open or closed.

After a few seconds thought, it occurred to him that they might be bandaged, and he tried to raise his hands to feel his face.

His hands wouldn't cooperate: he couldn't even be sure where they were. He tried wiggling his fingers, but they didn't move. He wiggled his toes instead, and was reassured by the definite if foggy sensation of movement. He sniffed, and quickly identified the stench. Not the rubble of the laboratory after the monster had destroyed it, and not exactly purgatory; merely a hospital. The whiteness was probably bandages: it occurred to him that he might be gift-wrapped as completely as a mummy, or the Bride, and a faint giggle escaped his lips. He heard movement nearby, and tried to turn his head. There was something in his mouth which made speech difficult, and he could not recognize his own voice as he tried to ask, "Where am I? What happened?"

The painkillers had distorted his sense of time, but eventually someone brought a man who explained that he'd been found amid the ruins of the old Frankenstein palace; that there had been some form of explosion which had left him with severe burns, several broken bones, and a serious concussion. "Were there any other survivors?" he asked.

They had found one more shattered body, the man said, probably that of a woman who had been standing nearer the source of the explosion. She hadn't been identified, and while they were continuing to search, they weren't expecting to find any survivors. There had been reports that Frankenstein and his wife were seen in town after the explosion, though they'd later disappeared.

"And how bad are my injuries? I'm a medical doctor myself, you can tell me the gory details."

Here, the man hesitated. "You're remarkably tough for a man of your age, and seem to be healing extremely quickly. We'll have to keep the bandages on your face for a while, because it's the part of you that was most badly burnt; your eyes reacted normally to stimuli when they brought you in, but your eyelids will need to heal before we can remove the blindfold. Eight of your ribs are cracked, you have a compound fracture of the right femur, transverse fractures of the right humerus—"

"What about my hands?" asked Pretorius, as sharply as the tubes and bandages permitted. "I know they're bandaged and splinted: how bad is the damage?"

"Very bad," said the doctor, bluntly. "Third degree burns, and injuries from flying and falling debris; it looks as though you instinctively raised them to protect your face, and they bore the brunt of the damage. I've done what I can, but I very much doubt that we'll be able to restore full use of all of your fingers."

Pretorius was silent for a moment. "Judging by your bedside manner, I'm guessing you're a surgeon."

"Yes; I'm Doctor Gogol. I did what I could for you, but some of your injuries were too severe, and I had to give priority to those that were life-threatening."

"Of course," said Pretorius, quietly. He tried to imagine the surgeon's hands, and how they'd look on his own thin arms.

1972

DENNY heard the click of the lock as the heavy door closed, and automatically began looking around for escape routes and hiding places, flinging open cupboard doors and swearing. With the old man out of the room, things suddenly seemed clearer and even more frightening. How the fuck had the old fruit, a complete stranger, convinced him to kill Chucky who, apart from daring him to try robbing the house, was about as harmless as he was useless? The kid hadn't exactly been a friend—he was just some loser who stole shit from cars and houses and tried to sell it in the bar where Denny spent most of his evenings—but Denny would never have contemplated killing him until the old man had offered him a sum of money just large enough to be tempting, small enough to be plausible. And now he was locked in a cellar, and the old man's friends were on their way. Sure, he had two revolvers (he'd had the presence of mind to grab Chucky's when he picked up his body), but they might have assault weapons or...

He stared at the black wooden chest, about the size and shape of a small child's coffin, and after a moment's thought, hauled it out of the cupboard and onto the operating table. It seemed too light to contain any weapons, but he thought it might hold money or drugs or something else worth taking. He was puzzled to see that it contained four black cylinders, each about a foot high. He removed one of these, hearing liquid sloshing inside, and realized that the black was a cloth cover. He hesitated, then rolled up the cover and stared at the contents of the jar. A mermaid, six or seven inches from the top of her head to the tips of her tail, stared back at him in panic and tried to right herself within the narrow jar. With shaking hands, he placed the jar on the table the right way up, and removed the second—being careful, this time, not to

314

turn it upside down in the process. This one contained another small human-like figure wearing a black tuxedo with an opera cape, and sitting in a strange-looking throne. Its black hair receded in a widow's peak that showed small horns on its brow, but there was something disturbingly familiar about the shape of its face and its small dark eyes. Denny blinked, and was reaching for the third jar when the door opened again, and Pretorius walked back into the room, followed by four exquisitely-dressed blond men. The doctor raised his eyebrows at the sight of the homunculi, but his voice was mild as he said, "I thought I told you not to touch anything."

"What are these –" He removed the cover from the last jar, and saw the figure of a hideous crone in the garb of an old gypsy woman. Pretorius moved with surprising speed for a man of his age, and grabbed the jar before he dropped it.

"Experiments," he said, curtly, then turned to the resurrectionists. One reached inside his topcoat, and Denny fumbled for his gun—but instead of a weapon, the man produced a bulging envelope, which he threw onto the operating table.

"Twenty thousand," said topcoat. "As agreed. Unmarked bills—10,000 in hundreds, 5,000 in fifties, 4,000 in twenties, 450 in tens, and the rest in coin."

"Take it and go," said Pretorius, his voice so quiet that Denny wasn't sure he actually heard it—but he took the old man's advice, picking up the money and following him to the front door. Pretorius watched him leave, then turned as the bodysnatchers emerged from the lab carrying the cases of transplantable organs and the bag of scraps.

"Who was that?" asked topcoat.

Pretorius shrugged. "Just another psychopath."

The resurrectionist smiled frostily. "One of us, one of us," he chanted, wondering whether the young thug would realize that his payment for his friend's corpse included thirty Peace dollars—thirty pieces of silver.

1936

"BUSINESS?" said Klein, glumly, as he looked around the half-empty Munich apartment and reflected that Pretorius didn't seem to be prospering either: it looked as though he was selling his furniture to pay his bills. "Business is terrible. You'd think that now that people have money again, it would've picked up, but no. Who's going to pay to come and see pinheads when they can hear them every night on the radio? I'm just hoping we still *have* a show by the time the Olympics start. Hans and Frieda left, Venus is knocked up, and without the... *thing*... that used to be Cleopatra..."

Pretorius sipped at his gin. "I did my best to save her, but whoever cut her down to size was a butcher, not a surgeon: I doubt they meant her to last as long as she did. How about the castrato? Is he still alive?"

"Yes. Still hitting the high notes, too." He looked at Pretorius over the rim of his glass. "I could use another of those mermaids of yours, if you can whip one up, or one of your little ballerinas. And I'll pay you for every month they survive."

The doctor shrugged. "Little things have short life-spans."

"So make them bigger. One foot tall, two feet... it'd make them easier for the rubes to see, too."

"I've tried," said Pretorius, testily. "I can make them small and perfect if the material I'm given to work with is good enough, and with just enough brainpower to learn some sort of routine before they start to age, but the larger ones are almost always deformed."

"If they're deformed in interesting ways..."

"Most don't live long enough to take out of the jars. Is that interesting enough for you?"

"Okay, okay," said the barker. He finished his gin and looked at Pretorius appraisingly. "You don't have anything for me now?"

"No," said the doctor, flatly.

"What about next month?"

"No. I'm leaving Germany. Going back to England—maybe even to America, now they've stopped that Prohibition nonsense." He gulped at his gin, then lowered his voice. "And I'd advise you to do the same. I don't think these Nazi fanatics are going to be happy just sterilizing those they consider... what's the official phrase? Ah, yes, 'unworthy life'. I think that once the Olympics are over, they're going to become even more ruthless... or more efficient, as they'd probably say. You remember my last assistant? Josef?"

"The brownshirt?"

"Yes. I saw him again recently, after he graduated, and he told me some of the things he's been hearing about the Nazis' plans. They want to adopt Rudin's insane idea that doctors have a duty to eliminate the feeble-minded, the deformed, and the mentally ill—and that includes alcoholics. Your entire sideshow could end up being dissected, and so could we."

The barker put down his glass on the table beside his chair. "I'm not an alcoholic."

"Oh, me neither," said Pretorius dryly: he knew he would never have survived as long as he had but for his ability to grow and transplant a spare liver when needed. "But I'd still feel much safer somewhere where I don't have to prove it or carry papers detailing my ancestry. Herr Hitler has a poisonous hatred of Jews, and I don't think my family history would bear much examination."

"And you really think you'd be better off in England or America?"

"I think so. Almost everybody here has heard of the Frankensteins, and there may still be people who will recognize me from those days. It shouldn't be too difficult to find a small village in either Britain or one of the more backwards states which nobody ever leaves or visits, where none of the inhabitants know or care what happens anywhere else. One of them might even need a doctor."

"And where am I supposed to go when one of *my* creatures needs a doctor?" asked Klein, more sharply than he'd intended.

Pretorius shrugged. "Liepzig, I think."

"What?"

"It's where Josef has gone. I know he's interested in genetic abnormalities; he'd probably be fascinated by some of your attractions."

"So where do I find him?"

"I understand he's working for the University Medical Clinic, but he should be prepared to see you on his own time. And if he's not there, try the phone book. There can't be very many Dr Josef Mengeles."

1973

PRETORIUS staggered to the door and peered drunkenly at the young man standing on the doorstep. He was almost disappointed that it wasn't the Bride come to gloat, and it took him a few seconds to remember the man's name. "Denny," he croaked. "Come in before we both freeze."

Denny stepped inside and looked uneasily at the doctor's bloodshot eyes and three-day growth.

"So," said Pretorius, as he walked unsteadily back to his chair, which was surrounded by empty bottles and cigar stubs, "what is it this time?

Another robbery, or have you brought me another body? You have re-membered they have to be fresh, don't you?"

Denny shook his head. "Are you okay?"

"I'm touched by your concern," said the doctor, sitting down heavily. "Would you like some gin?"

"No thanks…" He looked at the debris around the chair. "Your clean-ing lady's not going to be happy with you."

Pretorius shrugged. "She does what I tell her, and she's dealt with worse messes."

"Is this a bad time?"

"You might say that. You might. Do you read the news? Or watch it?"

"Not much. Did somebody die?"

"The Supreme Court has just put me out of work," said Pretorius, closing his eyes and reaching for a not-yet-empty gin bottle. "They've made abortion legal in every state."

"That's bad?"

"It's ruinous. What sane woman is going to come to a wreck like me for treatment if she can get it legally in a nice clean safe hospital?"

Denny grinned. "Don't worry about it. I know another way we can make money."

"It's not just the money. The embryos give me the raw material I need for my experiments." He opened his eyes. "What's your idea?"

"Your… practice here… you make money out of disposing of bodies. There are people who would *pay* for that sort of service."

Pretorius digested this slowly. "The bodies have to be fresh and in good shape to have any real value: best if you bring them to me alive. And we mustn't take too many from the immedy—immidat—from nearby, or glut the market. Who's the victim?"

"I know this guy in K.C. who does a good business in shipping stolen cars overseas. I've done some work for him. Anyway, he keeps a lot of cash in the office safe, and if he and the money disappear at the same time, people will think that either he's in hiding or the mob rubbed him out. I bring him to you—alive is going to be a little more difficult, but I can probably knock him out and stuff him in the trunk—and we split the money you get for him."

"How old is he?"

"Forty something. Maybe fifty. Why?"

"Healthy? Does he drink? Smoke? If the organs aren't in top condition, I won't get much for them." He poured himself another glass of gin. "How old's his wife?"

"What?"

"Is she the one who put this idea in your head?" Even drunk, Pretorius had a remarkable grasp of other people's weaknesses.

"We've talked about it."

"In bed, I presume. No, don't bother answering." He downed the gin. "When were you planning on doing this—or do you already have the body in the car?"

"No! I was going to wait a couple of weeks, until I know he has more money in the safe."

Pretorius nodded. "Nice to see you're thinking ahead," he said.

"You'll do it?"

"Not so fast." He put his glass down carefully. "I want as much warning as you can give me of the delivery date; it'll help me find buyers. I'll give you twenty percent of anything I get for his body over ten thousand. If he's not healthy enough to bring in that much, you make up the difference from your take. I have expenses, and after all, you get the widow. All right?"

Denny hesitated, then nodded. "Deal."

"Good." Pretorius stood, then staggered towards the surgery. "I'll get you some sedatives you can use to get him here alive more easily." He had a vague suspicion there was a weakness in the plan that he was too drunk to see, but he was sure he'd think of it later.

1957

PRETORIUS looked at the town councilors gathered around the table and did his best to smile. No-one smiled back. "It's the case of this grave-robber," said the mayor. "Ed Gein. The bodies in his house were eviscerated, and no-one's found any trace of the internal organs."

"Nothing to do with me," said Pretorius, raising his hands and regretting that there wasn't a glass in either of them. "I've never met the man, never been to his place, and I haven't employed a graverobber since the turn of the century. Re-animating corpses is more trouble than it's worth." His smile broadened, showing his transplanted teeth. "People will always find somebody or something to use as a scapegoat. A few years ago, it was the Communists. Then it was comic books. Now it's violent movies and working mothers. I'm sure many of you know what it is to be blamed for something you haven't done—and I'd like to say here, for the record, that I wasn't responsible for the Jack the Ripper murders, either, even as a buyer.

"I've helped most of you in the time I've been here, gentlemen. I've given many of you new faces, even new fingerprints. Well, one hand washes the other. I protect you, you protect me. And don't worry about this Gein nonsense. He was just a half-witted necrophiliac hick from a town no-one's ever heard of before, and he'll be completely forgotten by the end of the year."

1973

GRIFFIN took Pretorius's pawn with his queen, and smiled invisibly as the doctor sighed and picked up the gin bottle. The rules of their chess game required that every time a player lost a piece, they had to drink a shot of gin. Pretorius usually won despite handicapping himself thoroughly, and the game was little more than an excuse for the two scientists to get drunk together while swapping scientific theories and gossip. While Pretorius was staring at the board, Griffin said softly, "I think you may have a problem."

"I admire your confidence."

"I don't mean the game. You remember that body you sold back in February? Dickenson? I've been spending time with the widow."

Pretorius raised his snow-white eyebrows. "Do tell."

"She's trying to claim his life insurance, but the company says that without a body, there's no proof that he's dead. I think she's about to roll over on your boy Denny."

Pretorius's expression didn't change, but his hand shook slightly as he reached for his remaining knight.

"She doesn't know what Denny did with the body," Griffin continued, "so she's not a problem for us, but do you think Denny would lead them to you?"

"In a second," Pretorius admitted. "Denny has no concept of loyalty. I doubt he can even spell the word."

"The council think so too, and they'd be much happier if you dealt with him before they have to. They hate bad publicity."

Pretorius nodded. "It's a pity. He's a useful pair of hands, especially as his fingerprints aren't on file anywhere. And it's so difficult getting good help nowadays."

"I could do it for you, for a small fee. If he's smelled a rat, he may not trust you—but he won't see me coming."

"No," said Pretorius. He moved his bishop, then walked over to the rarely-used phone. "I'll do it. I know his weaknesses."

He made the phone call, then he and Griffin finished the game, and after the Invisible Man had walked out into the cold, Pretorius shuffled into his lab and removed a vial of curare and a syringe from his drugs cabinet, then went to the cupboard and began removing the covered jars from the large black box.

"OKAY," said Denny, as soon as he'd closed the front door behind him. "What's so mysterious you couldn't talk about it on the phone?"

Pretorius walked back to his chair and sat down. "How much did you make from killing Dickenson?"

"What do you care?" said the young man, sticking out his jaw. "You got your share, didn't you?"

"Just wondering what the going rate was for a murder," Pretorius replied. "Sit down, you're making me dizzy just looking at you. Sorry, I may have overindulged a little."

Denny snorted, and sat on the couch.

"I've just heard that somebody's been hired to kill me," the doctor continued, "and I wondered if it was you."

"Why I tell you if it was?" came the reply, without hesitation. "But hell, why would somebody pay to have *you* killed? You must be nearly dead already."

"The Israelis have caught one of Josef Mengele's lab assistants," said Pretorius, closing his eyes, "and they want me to identify him and testify against him. Obviously, somebody else doesn't want me to—possibly Mengele himself, more probably friends of his as he may already be dead—and they have enough money to hire a gun."

"How much are they paying? Just curious."

"You'd take money to murder an old man, to protect a war criminal who tortured people to death?"

Denny shrugged. "If the money was right, wouldn't you?"

"Maybe," admitted Pretorius. "But I'm a monster: that's why I live here, among other monsters. Would you like a drink?"

"No, thanks. I have to drive—*ow!*" He swatted at the back of his neck, an instant too late, and turned around. Standing on the back of the couch was the six-inch-high crone he'd seen in the jar in the lab, holding an empty syringe like a spear. Denny swatted at her, but she dropped the syringe and hurried away along the couch, out of range. He reached into the pocket of his leather jacket for his revolver, but found that his fingers wouldn't bend to fit inside the trigger guard. He stared at the homunculus as she "Wha—wha –"

"Ah," said Pretorius, standing, and suddenly sounding much more sober. "I see you've met my cleaning lady. I *did* tell you she's cleaned up worse messes than your friend Chucky."

"Yuh…"

"Curare," explained Pretorius. "It paralyses, but you'll remain conscious. For the rest of your life, in all probability." He looked enviously at Denny's hands, then turned to face the homunculus. "Scalpel," he said, politely.

Ways of Honour

SHE WAS KNOWN AS THE SWAMP WITCH; it had been at least a century since she had answered to any other name. Dyosh women keep their child-names until they marry, and she had chosen to learn magic from the Khaladans rather than settle for a life as a second or third wife, renouncing her name as she had renounced her country. When Skeron the minotaur walked into her hut, muddy from his trek across the swamp and with his warhammer black with the ichor of marsh wraiths, she was sitting staring at the pale fire. "You're a long way from the mountains," she said, softly, without looking up.

Skeron stared at her from the doorway, then stepped into the tiny hut and threw his hood back, defiantly. "And you're a long way from anywhere," he replied haltingly, in the same tongue and as quietly as he was able. The witch glanced at the jagged stumps of his broken horns, and said nothing. Skeron sat hesitantly on a chair and discovered that it bore his weight easily. "And your gate has quite a temper. Maybe you should feed it more often."

"It barks more than it bites," she said, smoothly. "How did you get past it?"

The minotaur shrugged. "I found a tree that was a little taller than I was, carried it in ahead of me, and used it to hold the jaws apart. Will it let me out again?"

"If I wish. Would you be more comfortable speaking another language?"

Skeron regarded her, noticing the moon-silver hair that framed her unlined face and hung almost to the floor. Her long robe was a deep, mossy green, only slightly darker than her eyes. "You're not Bataryesh?"

"Dyosh," she replied, surprised by his perceptiveness. "But most of the travellers who get past the gates speak Bataryesh better than any other language I know."

The minotaur nodded. The long-legged golden-haired jade-eyed Dyosh women were renowned for their beauty. They outnumbered their men nearly three to one, but few escaped their island home, which was ringed by powerful barrier spells to keep them in and their enemies out. Dyosh men were even more rarely encountered, for they never travelled far from home. "I speak Bataryesh as well as any human tongue," he said. "I suppose you know why I came here?"

"Tell me the story," she evaded. "In your own words."

Skeron glanced around the sparsely furnished hut, pleased that there were no mirrors, nothing that showed his mutilation. "It was a stone giant," he began. "A giant and a goblin; we don't know how they came to Iznasu, or why they attacked us, but they slew three of my clan before I could grab a weapon." The witch raised an eyebrow. "Horns are for an honorable duel with an honorable foe," he explained. "The giant had arms longer than you are tall, and a great glaive, and the goblin was barely as high as my hip, all I could have done without a weapon was kick him. I took the warhammer that had been my father's and ran out to challenge them. The goblin dropped his own sword and cowered behind the giant, who rushed me. He was slow, and stupid, but enormously strong. I managed to reach under his guard and hit him, blows that might have killed even the strongest of my people, and was able to dodge most of his strikes, but when I attempted to parry a blow the force of it flung the warhammer from my hands, leaving me unarmed. He raised his glaive again, and I heard the goblin laugh.

"'His horns', he shouted. 'A minotaur's strength is in his horns; break his horns!'"

Skeron sat in silence for a moment, barely breathing. "The glaive fell again," he continued, eventually. "I dodged, and the blade merely clipped my arm. I ran to pick up my warhammer, but this meant turning my back on the giant, and the next time the glaive fell it cleaved through my right horn and carried through into my shoulder." He threw back his head and moaned, a deep rolling roar which told of unspeakable grief, of a loss with no beauty or honour.

"A few inches to the left, and he would have split my skull, and they would now be singing my song in Iznasu—but instead, he raised the glaive again for another blow. The wounds I had given him were bleeding, and he was weakening, but he was still much stronger than I. Desperate, I ran towards him, and he swung the glaive down, aiming at my remaining horn. I dodged to one side, forcing him to turn, and then I..." He took a deep breath. "I stepped back, away from him, and the force of his blow caused him to overbalance and stagger, until his face was on a level with my horns. I charged at him, and struck him across the eyes with the warhammer: he tried to hit me with the haft, but only succeeded in smashing it into his own ribs." Skeron allowed himself a brief snort of amused satisfaction. "Before he could stand, I drove my good horn into his eye.

"He dropped the glaive, grabbed my head and wrenched. It should have crushed my skull, shattered my neck, but he was already dying, and too weak to break bone..." The swamp witch looked at Skeron's elaborately engraved left horn; it had snapped further from the skull than the right, and maybe half its original length remained. She knew that, contrary to myth, the length of a minotaur's horns did not show his strength, merely his honour—which minotaurs regarded as infinitely more important. "When I plucked my horn from his eye, he was already dead... and, a heartbeat later, his body vanished, vanished as though it had never been." Skeron shook his head, bewilderment plain on his face. "I heard the goblin shriek, as he found himself with no-one to hide behind, and in my fury I charged him. He was standing there unarmed, his hands raised to show they were empty; he was wearing mail and a coif, but I hit him in the face and his neck snapped, and then, so suddenly that it seemed I could still hear him screaming, he vanished as well, and no-one survived to say they had seen him except me."

He sat there, head bowed, for several seconds. "At first, my people thought I might be crazed, berserk, that... that I might have slain my own kin. Fortunately, when they saw that I could not have inflicted such wounds with a warhammer, they believed me... and instead of slaying me and erasing my name from memory, from their songs, they banished me from Iznasu until I have found my honour again."

The swamp witch nodded. "And you think I can help you?"

"In every village I stopped in, on my way across the taiga, they sing of your ability as a healer, and of the wondrous things that you have created... charms, artifacts, salves, spells..."

"I've never healed a minotaur's horns before," she mused. "I make no promises; I'm not even sure that I can. Is there no other way to regain your lost honour?"

"You don't understand."

"Perhaps not."

Skeron raised his head and stared at her almost fiercely. "The song my people will sing for me determines my place in the afterworld. In any song they would sing for me now, I would be Skeron Hornless, Skeron Goblin-slayer, Skeron who failed his kin and disgraced his father..."

"You killed the giant..."

"But too late to save my clansfolk. And we have been slaying hill giants since the first songs were sung. Giant-killer is too common a name."

"You crossed the taiga, you killed wraiths... you passed my gate, and no minotaur has done *that* before..."

The minotaur shook his head sadly. "Can you help me?"

The swamp witch mused. She was able to create healing salves that almost always worked on small wounds, and she could set broken bones using only minor magic to see through the flesh to the fracture, but she could not regenerate severed limbs. "I think so. Can you return tomorrow?"

Skeron nodded, and reached into his pouch, then placed a small black pearl on the table between them. "Will this be enough?"

The swamp witch picked it up, stared at it, and then nodded. "Maybe more than enough. Tomorrow."

"STEEL?" asked Skeron, fingering the dagger-sharp tips and trying to keep the disappointment from his voice.

"Dwarven bronze," replied the swamp witch. "Harder and tougher than steel, and it doesn't rust; it's a wonderful material to work with... what's wrong?"

"Oh, they're magnificent," said Skeron, politely, "but they're not part of me. They cover the stumps, but still betray that I have no real horns, like a monument to honour lost; I would still be Skeron Hornless..."

"I could enchant them to look more like horn, but the enchantment would soon wear off..." She mused, and then brightened. "There is a way to restore your... honour, but it's perilous..."

"Yes?"

"I need dragons' teeth, and you'd have to pluck them from the dragon yourself..." She stared at the silent Skeron. "Has no minotaur ever killed a dragon?"

"No."

The witch nodded. "A few yards of dragonhide or wyrmskin would be useful, too—fresh, not shed. There's said to be a wyrm lairing on the taiga, not far from Nept."

Skeron examined the metal horns, and then nodded. "Take them," said the swamp witch. "Bronze horns may be better than none."

Even Iznasu minotaurs know better than to refuse a gift from a witch, and Skeron fitted the bronze horns over his shattered stumps and tossed his head. They felt just as light as real horn, and well balanced. He bowed as he had seen Bataryesh do, and backed out of the hut.

SKERON sat down, leaned against a tree, and stared at the moons—the larger, a thin crescent like a pair of horns high in the sky; the smaller, a bright star. Two nights from now, he knew, it would cross the dark disc to shine between the tips of the horns, which made it forty-four days since he'd left Iznasu. He shivered, and pulled his bed-roll from his pack.

The peasants of Nept had treated him as though he were a greater threat than the wyrm, which had only eaten their sheep and goats and possibly a few small children. Mentioning the swamp witch hadn't helped, either. All denied any knowledge of where the wyrm might lair, or any curiosity. Back on the taiga, he had sung a dirge for all the children who would never leave the village, living and dead alike, and then continued on his way.

He lay back on the ground, nestled among the roots of an enormous oak, and was almost asleep before he noticed the bare patch on the trunk. He blinked, and looked around until he saw its twin a few yards away. A wyrm had rubbed against these trees, perhaps to shed an old skin. He stood, and examined the trees more closely. The space between them—the girth of the wyrm—he measured at little more than twice the length of his warhammer. He fingered the points on his brazen horns, points that would tear the throat and guts of anything that swallowed him whole, and—for the first time since leaving the mountains—he smiled, then threw back his head and bellowed out a challenge.

Once he knew what to look for, the wyrm's trail through the taiga was easy enough to follow—several trees were leaning away from each other, or had the bark rubbed away from one side—and eventually it led him to the river. He stood there and examined the trees on the other side, finding no gaps large enough for the wyrm to have passed through. After a moment's thought, he began walking slowly downstream; upstream, nearer the mountains, the river would be faster and narrower and colder, the terrain rougher, food more scarce. He had travelled less than a mile when he saw what seemed to be a mossy, curiously symmetrical rock—as long as he was tall and as broad as the span of his lost horns—in the middle of the river. Cautiously, he advanced, watching for signs of movement but seeing none—apart from a slight gleam which might have been sunlight reflected from the water, or the slow movement of a wyrm's eye. Then he sat down, his back against a tree, and pondered.

The head (or rock) was too far from shore to reach with his warhammer, and minotaurs do not use bows or throw spears, preferring to meet their foes face to face. Nor are they strong swimmers, and Skeron knew he would be no match for a wyrm in the water. He stared at the motionless shape in the middle of the river for nearly a minute, then grabbed a pebble and hurled it with more power than skill. It splashed into the water half a pace short of the shape, disturbing the lights and shadows. He was reaching for a second pebble when the wyrm's moss-green tail coiled itself around his left calf.

Hastily, Skeron dropped the pebble, and passed his warhammer to his right hand. The tail whipped around, pulling his left leg from beneath him in an attempt to throw him into the river, but Skeron dug his right hoof into the muddy bank and held his ground. The wyrm's head rose slightly from the water and turned to face him, while the tail inexorably pulled his feet further apart.

The head continued to rise until it was on a level with Skeron's own— and then struck. Skeron swung his warhammer and connected with its fangs, hard enough to make the wyrm recoil. Before it could strike again, Skeron pulled his hoof free from the mud and allowed the tail to tug him backwards, nearer the trees. The wyrm struck a second time, and Skeron ducked beneath its head and swung the warhammer in a clumsy, underarm arc, hitting the wyrm in the jaw just hard enough to deflect it. Skeron scrambled back between two trees, and waited. The coil around his leg tightened painfully, and he looked down, quickly judging the width of the tapering tail; then he reached for his skinning knife with his left hand, and thrusting with all his strength, drove it through the wyrm's tail and into the trunk of a tree.

The wyrm writhed, coiling and uncoiling and bashing its body against the trees in its struggle to free itself, and Skeron took his warhammer in both hands again and swung the point at the wyrm's lidless left eye. The wyrm flinched, pulling the weapon out of Skeron's grasp; the minotaur grabbed for it with his right hand, overbalanced, and measured his length in the mud, face-down.

He stared into the wyrm's bloody left eye, and realised that while the warhammer's point had torn and blinded it, it hadn't been long enough to travel through to the creature's brain. Skeron scrambled to his feet, and the wyrm struck, biting into his chest and shoulder and pinning his right arm to his side, then lifted him bodily and plunged him headfirst into the river.

Temporarily blinded, and feeling as though his heart was beating between his ears and cold, slimy snakes were trying to crawl down his nostrils into his lungs, Skeron fought off panic. The wyrm's teeth, he realised, were not suitable for chewing; instead, the great reptile would hold him underwater until he drowned, and then swallow him whole. None of his people would know how he'd died, none would sing songs for him... A weapon, he thought; I'd give my horns for a simple spear, even a knife... *my horns!*

With his left hand, he reached down and pulled one of his bronze horns from his head; then he struck, backhanded blows aimed at where he thought the wyrm's right eye should be. He had almost lost consciousness before he felt the horn hit something soft and sink in; with the last of his strength, he drove it through the eye socket into the creature's brain.

"PRYING the jaws apart and getting back to shore alive was easier than dragging the wyrm out of the water and skinning it," said Skeron. "Of course, if it hadn't been for the salve, I would have bled to death first. Can I look now?"

"Soon," promised the swamp witch. "Do you want some of the hide? There's more than enough here to make a shield or a scabbard, maybe both." She stepped back, examining her handiwork. "Now."

Skeron opened his eyes, and reached up to feel his new horns, frowned slightly, then stepped forward to stare at his reflection in the pool. They certainly looked real, but there was a thin, sharp ridge running from the tip to the thin scar where they joined with the stumps of his old horns. He fingered the serrated ridge, and then bellowed and reached for his skinning knife.

"These are wyrm's teeth! You said you'd restore my horns!"

"I said I'd restore your honour," replied the swamp witch, levelly. "You were Skeron Hornless; now you're Skeron Wyrmslayer, and the mountains will echo for years with the songs sung in your honour... Honour isn't in your horns, it isn't something you're born with, honour lies in what you *do*."

"You don't *understand!*" roared Skeron, and slashed at her with the knife. She ducked underneath his frantic blow, but the second attack was deliberately aimed low; it slashed the skirt of her robe, struck her thigh— and shattered. Skeron bellowed again, and stepped back, the stump of the knife in his hand, bafflement in his eyes. The cut in the witch's robe showed cunningly artificed legs of dwarven bronze.

"Yes, I do," replied the witch, calmly. "Do you?"

"Your legs..." muttered Skeron, numbly.

"An accident," said the swamp witch, without looking at them. "The first time I tried to escape from the islands. I failed the second time, too," she added, sadly. "I was never able to heal them, so I learnt spells of levitation; I made these years later, long after I built this hut and became the swamp witch. But they don't matter, any more than your horns matter; what I've *done*, matters, especially what I've done for others. *Now* do you understand?"

SHE was known as the swamp witch, and by no other name, but her song has been sung in Iznasu for centuries. The minotaurs still sing songs of Skeron, too; songs of his travels, his deeds, and his heroism. And in his songs, and in the tales all the races tell from the Dyosh islands to the Jaaraa desert, Wyrmslayer is only the first, and least, of his many names.

THE COMPLETIST

TAYLOR WAS GLOATING OVER HIS LATEST acquisition when he heard the chime indicating that someone was walking down the stairs. He closed the box and hid it under the counter, then looked up and smiled as the door slid open. The man's shoes were cloned buffalo hide, conservative but expensive—like the suit, which was designed for air-conditioning rather than an L.A. summer. A professional, probably government or multi-national (not that there was a lot of difference), possibly a Reagan cultist. "Can I help—" he began, and shut up as he recognised the man's face. "Eric!" he said, a little warily. "What brings you down here?"

"Hello, Bruce," his cousin replied, glancing around the shop—which was crammed with memorabilia but empty of customers. "How's business?"

"That depends who's asking," replied Taylor, his expression carefully neutral. "Off the record, it's okay. I pay the rent, my taxes, the child support, the trash collector, and after that, sometimes, I eat. If you're asking in your official capacity as a member of the science gestapo, I'd tell you to mind your own fuckin' business, unless you got a warrant."

Eric flushed slightly at the Technology Squad's nickname, but didn't protest it. "Don't worry. This is a friendly visit."

"You want to buy something?"

"I said friendly, not insane." He glanced at the price tag on a framed poster for *Rebel Without a Cause*, and shook his head disbelievingly. "People actually pay these prices?"

Taylor smiled thinly. "Do you still have that *L.A. Confidential* daybill, the one signed by Kim Basinger? You'd be surprised what I could get you

331

for it, if it's in good condition. Some collectors have more money than brains."

Eric didn't reply. When he was twelve, he'd been obsessed enough by the actress to save for months to buy the autographed photo. He turned his attention to a picture of Jayne Mansfield and asked "How's your other shop doing? The one on Melrose?"

"Sinematic? It's doing okay," said Taylor, guardedly. "I'm just a silent partner, haven't been over there in weeks... why?"

Eric looked away, pretending to be fascinated by a lobby card for *The Bride of Frankenstein.* "They sell cloned body parts there, don't they?"

"If you mean the Realskin toys, yes. What of it? They're legal, aren't they?"

"So far. They might not be for much longer. How much do you know about them?"

Taylor leaned back slightly in his chair and managed not to look at the box under the counter. "According to their advertising copy, they've been cloned from porn performers, the same way they can now clone hearts and kidneys and livers and that sort of thing. Some sort of process that lets them just grow one organ, not a whole body, in a few weeks, but you'd know more about that than I would. They've got some gadgets inside them that keep them alive, keep them at body heat and keep the juices flowing, but they're really just a higher-tech and more expensive version of the plastic cocks and pocket pals you've been able to buy for years."

"You think that's all they are?"

Taylor shrugged. "How much difference is there between taking a few skin cells and cloning them, and taking a mold from the same body part and selling that?" Eric looked revolted, but not astonished. "The law's quite explicit; clone or no clone, as long as there's no brain attached, it's not a human being. It's a spare part, and therefore a marketable commodity. Besides, for some of our customers, that's as close as they'll ever get to human contact."

"I won't argue with that," Eric muttered.

"Don't try to tell me you've never wondered what it'd be like to fuck a movie star?"

"*Wondered*, yes... but a movie star, or any woman, is more than just a..." He took a deep breath, and looked his cousin in the eye. "Look, Bruce, I came here to warn you, not to spar with you. For the moment,

Realskin products are legal, though that may not last; there are bills being written that'll prohibit the use of cloned parts for frivolous purposes, and don't give me any of that bullshit about 'therapeutic uses', because I'm not buying it. At best it's fetishism; at worst, it smells a lot like necrophilia. Realskin's being investigated, and so are the shops that sell their crap, including yours. If we find one case where the owner of the genes didn't explicitly give consent to the cloning, the shit's going to hit the fan.

"The problem is counterfeiters, as usual. There's rumours of parts being offered on the black market that the copyright holders didn't authorise. Parts that're supposed to be cloned from actresses, models, singers, and so on. Expensive, sure, but like you say, collectors will pay for them." He watched Taylor carefully, waiting for any reaction, but saw none. "If they're fake, that's fraud. If they're real, that's a violation of the likeness laws, and I don't need to remind you what you can get for *that*." Taylor winced visibly. It'd had required the services of a very expensive lawyer and some hefty bribes to keep him out of jail after he'd been caught with copies of porn with the faces of the participants morphed into those of Marilyn Monroe and JFK. "And if that doesn't scare you, remember this; counterfeits are often badly made, and when you're dealing with biotech, mistakes can be *very* nasty."

Taylor repressed a yawn. "Realskin isn't making transplants. They're sex toys, that's all. How dangerous can they be? But thanks for the warning; if anyone offers me any counterfeit cunts, I'll let you know."

Eric shook his head. "How can you work in a place like this?"

"It beats going through old Elvis movies and painting in halos," replied Taylor, sourly. "Thanks for the warning. Was there anything else?"

TAYLOR grinned as he shut the shop and took the box out from under the counter. The device inside was a block of warm, pale flesh with two orifices, and a few controls hidden behind an ivory panel. The important thing, as always, was the certificate of authenticity enclosed in the box, this one proclaiming that the flesh had been cloned from one of his favourite porn stars, a goth named Alice Pooryorick. He already had all of her movies—all of the movies she'd ever make, too, if the rumours of her death in 2020 were true—as well as other souvenirs.

His grin widened as he fondled the clone's clitoris and watched the pierced labia slowly part. If Eric was right about Realskin being investigated, demand for items like this was going to increase enormously... not that Taylor had any intention of selling his own collection. As a younger man, he'd liked to claim that everything he collected was an investment, but he'd never really believed it, and no longer needed to bullshit anybody about it. Maybe, later, he'd buy another piece of Alice's flesh and keep it in the box to sell to another collector as mint... but now, his erection was almost painful, and he quickly unbuttoned his fly and slowly inserted his cock into the warm vagina. The hymen inside resisted for a moment, then ruptured messily. He shuffled awkwardly towards his bed, the toy still impaled on his erection, then stepped out of his trousers and dropped face down onto the Realskin futon, thrusting urgently for another minute before climaxing.

A moment later, he walked to the shower, and washed himself and the toy, which he returned to the box.

He used the toy again the next morning, while watching one of Alice's movies—her first audition from *Dirty Debutantes*. The sensation wasn't quite as strong as it had been the night before, so after the shop shut later that evening, he applied KY to the toy's anus and fucked that instead, to the accompaniment of her screams from her first double penetration scene. Even that proved somehow disappointing, emotionally as well as physically, and he wondered, as he showered, whether he'd used too much lube. He looked down, and realised that he was mauling his cock so thoroughly that it *should* have been painful... yet he felt almost nothing. With his eyes shut, he could barely even tell whether the water splashing on it was hot or cold. He stepped out of the shower and dried himself hastily, then grabbed the phone.

He winced as the probe was inserted for a swab, but there was almost no pain. "We won't have any results until tomorrow afternoon," said the nurse, "but it doesn't sound like any STD I ever heard of before."

"What *does* it sound like?"

The nurse shrugged. "There are a few things that it might be, but all of them would have other symptoms first. You had any difficulty breathing?"

"Not that I've noticed. I don't get a lot of exercise, and I have smog filters on the air-con."

"Pain when you urinate?"

"No."

"Loss of sensation anywhere else? Your legs, for example?"

"No."

"Hmm. Well, there's no need to panic. We'll see if anything shows up in the samples, and get back to you."

"Can I see a doctor?"

"At this hour? I can page one; what's your insurance like?"

IT was a slow day, and Taylor was thinking of closing the shop early. The lack of sensation from his genitals was almost worse than a pain; he kept having to adjust his clothing to make sure he wasn't cutting off the circulation, and prodding himself in other places to make sure the loss of sensation hadn't spread. He'd woken with an erection but had been unable to do anything to bring himself to orgasm, and it had dwindled in less than a minute. The doctor he'd seen at the STD clinic the night before had been as non-committal as the nurse, though she'd asked the same embarrassing questions and a few more besides until he suspected she thought the problem was psychosomatic. He jumped when the phone rang, then picked it up hastily. The screen showed Keith, the manager at Sinematic, with a backdrop of DVD cases and sex toys. "Hi, Bruce," he said. "We've got a guy in here wants clones of Nanda Devi's tits. Are they available?"

"Probably, but I don't—hold on a second. Do you know the guy?"

"No. Why?"

"I had a tip-off the other day; the science gestapo's cracking down on bootleg clones. Tell him you'll have to check with Realskin to see if they can custom-make a pair, and that you'll get back to him to tell him if, when and how much."

"Okay." Keith signed off, and Taylor sat back gingerly in his chair, crossing his legs absent-mindedly, then hastily uncrossing them again. The phone rang again a few minutes later. "Mr Taylor? It's Doctor Steinberg. Your test results have come back from the lab..."

"And?"

"They're negative for everything we asked them to check for, but we did find something unusual. We thought, at first, that the platelet count in your urine was too high, but they turned out not to be platelets. Unfortunately, we're not sure what they are."

"What're platelets?"

"Clotting factors," she replied, and saw that he still looked blank. "They're the cells in your blood that cause it to clot when you cut yourself. These things are similar in structure, but they're not platelets, and they're not yours. Can you think of anything they might be?"

Taylor was sitting on the toilet when he heard the doorbell ring. He'd gotten into the habit of trying to piss every hour or so, rather than run the risk of wetting himself without noticing. He pulled up his pants, buttoned them hastily, and staggered to the door. "Eric! Thanks for coming!"

His cousin looked worried as he closed the door behind him, and his expression became even more sour as Taylor recounted his story. "I think I've caught some damn disease from the thing, one that no-one's ever seen before," he rasped. "Probably some fault in the cloning process. So if you want my help in shutting these labs down, you got it. Just find out what the fuck I've caught and what you can do to cure it."

Eric bit his lip. "That may not be as easy as it sounds. Even if it's just a new strain of some existing disease, something that mutated during the speed-cloning, there may not be a cure. And there's another possibility. It may not just be sloppy infection control. It may be a..."

"What?"

Eric sat down and steepled his fingers. "It sounds like an inhibitor."

Taylor's eyes bugged slightly. "Oh, it's inhibiting me, all right. What the fuck does *that* mean?"

"That... *toy*...." He spat out the word as though it were a mouthful of rotten celery, "that thing you've been sticking your dick into... just because it's cloned from human cells and looks like part of a woman, doesn't mean it's a human being. They use boosters to make it grow some parts that it needs to stay alive, in as much as it *is* alive, and inhibitors, to stop it growing parts that they don't want. Mainly the brain. Are you with me so far?"

"I think so."

"The pirates who made that... creature... may have cut some corners. Or they may've used counterfeit equipment, cheap copies of the stuff that Realskin uses. Either way, the inhibitors may not have switched off the way they're supposed to... and they may have entered your bloodstream. I'm going to have to run some tests, but it sounds to me as though you've caught something that's cutting off the nerves between your genitals and... well, the rest of you."

"*What?*"

"It may be worse than that. The damage may spread through the rest of your body; it may even reach the brain. As I said, we'll have to run some tests, but we'll need to know what it is and what it's likely to do before we can work out how to stop it. We'll need the sex toy, too." When Taylor didn't react, Eric snarled, "It's your decision. Don't think anyone else at the lab is doing this for your benefit. They're much more interested in getting something we can use to shut down this creepshow."

Taylor glowered at him, then shuffled to the bedroom and returned with the box. "You can get off your high moral horse," he said, sullenly. "We all turn human beings into sex objects sometimes. At least I pay for it."

Eric shook his head in disgust, but was unable to think of a good response. "You'd better call your other shop, tell them to bring in any bootleg clones they have, and a list of any customers who've bought the damn things. And you may want to put up a 'Closed' sign here, too. You may not be back for a while."

TAYLOR spent three days in the LA County Medical Examiner's Office before they discharged him. The team had taken his Realskin futon, even though it had been legally cloned from the skin of another of his favourite performers, but he was tired enough to sleep on the couch. The phone woke him the next morning, and he fought his way out of the twisted sheets to answer it. "Whuh?" He stared at Eric, who looked grim but faintly relieved.

"I've got some good news," he said. "There's no sign of the inhibitor in any of your other nerve tissue. We were worried that it might isolate your heart, or maybe even cause your cerebrum to atrophy, but there's no sign of that."

"Oh, thank God," breathed Taylor, then looked at his cousin's face more closely. "Anything else?"

"Not yet. They're still looking for ways to stop the progression and reverse the damage it's already done, but it's not been given high priority. The good news is that it doesn't appear to be life-threatening."

"Uh-huh. Thanks." He stood, then looked down as something bounced off his foot.

His cock—rigid, almost purple, and longer than it had been in years—was still attached to his bulging scrotum, but both lay on the floor. There was no blood, only a small hole amid the folded skin of his crotch, but he screamed until his throat was raw.

FROM WHOM ALL BLESSINGS FLOW

– I –

KAARINA SCHROEDER, the inventor of the Bifrost Bridge, was born in what later became known as World One, which was fine as long as the only other World discovered had a population of a few million humans and trillions of mutated rats. The next World contacted, however, was technologically advanced enough to build their end of a Bifrost Bridge, and they refused to accept the title of World Three. After a few months of (occasionally acrimonious) discussion, World One became World Green, and World Three, World Blue, largely because of the background colours of their respective U.N. flags. Their histories had diverged sharply in 1906, when the English Revolution didn't happen in World Blue—mostly because some of the ringleaders were already dead, or not in London. Historians had found minor divergences as far back as 1879, and some joked about the *real* divergence points being lost in prehistory.

World Two became World Cyan, but none of the rats were heard to complain—at least, not to the historians. Then there was World Azure, where Robert Kennedy had been *fatally* shot; and World Indigo, where there hadn't been a Great Fire of London; and then another cold ruin which was christened World Grey and quickly abandoned... and then, a world so different from World Green that none of their living languages were recognisable, which became known on the other Worlds as World Red. By this time, Schroeder had retired to an estate in Green-Nova Scotia, surrounding herself with the best sound system available in any of the Worlds and refusing to speak to *anyone*. Meanwhile, hundreds of lawyers, politicians and other bureaucrats were trying to write a set of interWorld trade laws that would give their own homeWorld the maximum share of any hitherto undiscovered uninhabited or underdeveloped Worlds... and then a delegate from World Red, speaking in perfect pre-Homeric Greek, made an offer which made the emerald mines of Cyan-Brazil look like a handful of change.

DEARBORN finished washing his hands, and stepped over to the hot-air dryer. "I know it's none of my business," he said, "but it's just too good a deal. I don't trust them."

Anagnostakos, listening, wondered if all the decisions for *all* the inhabited Worlds were made in men's washrooms. Monsignor Whately, sitting in the cubicle at his right, said, "You're right. It *is* too good an offer—too good to refuse—and, as far as I'm concerned, it *is* none of your business."

"Are you sure the interpreters got it right? It wasn't the Donation of Constantine in Classical High Tibetan?"

Anagnostakos ignored the insult: he was more startled that Dearborn had *heard* of the Donation of Constantine. Maybe the Azure-American had a professional interest in fraud—or, more likely, some researcher in his staff had found the reference and expected it to embarrass the Jesuit. The *Constitutum Constantini* had supposedly given the Roman Catholic church authority over all Christianity, but was later proven to be a fairly poor forgery written four centuries after Constantine's death.

"I'm sure enough," replied Whately, mildly. "Of course, we don't need their help as badly as you do..."

Fifteen love, thought Anagnostakos, wincing inwardly. World Blue had a population of fewer than six billion people, as against World Green's eight and a half, World Azure's ten, and World Indigo's thirteen (most of them starving). World Blue could also boast blue whales, gorillas and tigers still living in the wild, and breathable air in all but its largest cities.

"Some *help*," snapped Dearborn. "Okay, so they're building their end of the Bridge, but we're supposed to give them *millions* of our people, and I bet *we* have to do the fucking paperwork! Where is this land they're offering them, anyway? Antarctica?"

"All over their World: Canada, Brazil, Indonesia, Australasia, Southern Africa, Eastern Russia, South-East Asia. Underpopulated areas, but arable with the right techniques."

"Sure," said Dearborn, sarcastically.

"Have you ever seen Indigo-Australia? It was settled by the Spanish and their Mediterranean allies, who saw it as a beautiful country—unlike the English who landed there in *our* Worlds, who regarded it as a desolate hellhole. Now it's supporting a quarter of a billion people—probably the best fed people in World Indigo. Green-Australia's not as crowded, but it's nearly as rich: after they broke with England, they encouraged immigration from countries with similar climates and soils."

"Slave labour," muttered Dearborn. Whately's only answer was to flush the toilet, loudly. "I still don't like it."

"*You* don't have to go: they're asking for volunteers. I think they'll get them."

"Not if we say no to the Bridges, it won't," Dearborn replied, and walked out, slamming the door behind him.

"Whatever happened to 'Give me your poor, your tired, your huddled masses?'" asked Anagnostakos, emerging from his cubicle.

Whately laughed. "I take it you're going to vote 'yes'?"

"I'm just a humble interpreter: I don't get a vote."

"How's the translation going?"

"Slowly. We haven't even tried to learn each other's native language—apparently theirs, Arrinesh, is descended from Sumerian the same way English is descended from niederdeutsch—but we're fairly sure that we understand each other's Greek. Of course, there's a lot of modern abstractions which we're having trouble getting across. I know a certain amount of Red-Japanese, but their new Katakana are unrecognisable, and Japanese is easy enough to misunderstand at the best of times. Apart from that, there are a few Native American languages which are the same in all the Worlds except Indigo, but their written alphabets are completely unlike ours and there's almost nothing published in them anyway. The stuff we *need* has to be translated at least twice to be any use to anyone, and that's painfully slow."

"What about their Bible?"

Anagnostakos shrugged. "I'm afraid I don't know. Why?"

"I've seen a copy—untranslated, of course, but illuminated. Your opposite number, their interpreter—Dr Melle?—lent it me. Their Old Testament is unrecognisable, as is much of the New, but the four Gospels are there. And since they *do* use arabic numerals, I've been able to count the chapters and verses, and there are some interesting discrepancies. Their 'Mark', for example ends at Chapter 16, Verse 9, but there are verses..." He stopped; Anagnostakos was shaking his head. "What's wrong?"

"Their 'Mark' is more likely 'Mary', Monsignor." said Anagnostakos, gently. "Matthew, Martha; Luke, Lucy; John, Joan. Their 'Old Testament' seems to be Sumerian or Babylonian -"

"But they believe in *Christ*," replied Whately. "Their interpreter wears a crucifix, almost identical to mine, and I've seen her cross herself. The crucifixion picture in their Bible is the same as ours, even down to the woman kneeling before the cross, and the Last Supper -"

"Their interpreter is a priestess. Their 'pope' is a woman, the 'World Mother'. How long has the Catholic Church in World Blue been ordaining women? Over here, it's been less than fifty years. Their 'Christ' may not even be the same person, or have said the same things—and if He did, they were translated into entirely different languages, and cross-referenced to different prophecies, a different mythos, maybe even a different *ethos*. Besides, do the Christians on *your* World always agree with each other?" The diminutive interpreter shook the water from his hands and walked out. Whately followed him.

"Do you mind if I ask you a personal question?" he asked, quietly.

"No, I guess not."

"About your religion?"

Anagnostakos shrugged. "My grandmother was Greek Orthodox, and she used to drag me along to services until I was too heavy to drag—but I haven't been inside a church since her funeral, and that was nearly twenty years ago. I went to a Catholic college in Melbourne, on a scholarship, but I think they would have expelled me if I hadn't kept winning the language prize. I've been exposed to every major religion on Earth—well, Earth Green—and none of them have stuck. No, that's not quite true—some of them stuck in my craw. I've seen holy war, sanctified bigotry, sacramental starvation... Hell, even back home—in Green-Australia—there was a Muslim community that practiced what they euphemistically call 'female circumcision'. Let's say I'm an ethical atheist."

"Do you believe in Christ?"

"Only as an historical figure."

"I'm not going to act as an apologist for religion," said Whately, nodding rapidly. "Or even for Catholicism: I have family in Blue-Belfast. But none of the religious wars were *Christ's* fault.

"We've both seen World Red. It's cleaner than our homeWorlds, and less violent, and no-one seems to be starving or homeless -"

"True," said Anagnostakos, "but maybe they have the death penalty for everything from graffiti to speeding—not that it's easy to speed in those electric cars—or compulsory euthanasia, or a suicide cult... or maybe their medical science is a few centuries behind ours, or they're suffering from an epidemic which only kills the poor, or they expose their children. It would explain why they need their gene pool boosted..." He looked at the priest's ashen face, and then smiled gently. "Don't worry, Monsignor; I'm just playing Devil's Advocate. It's a hobby of mine. I *like* all the Reds I've met; they seem... peaceful, at home—the way Zen Buddhists are supposed to be," he added, teasingly; then, "It's almost as though they don't have the concept of 'foreign'."

The ambassador smiled. "I think I know what you mean. Wouldn't you be interested in learning *why*?"

"Of course, but -"

"Doesn't religion play a large part in shaping a society's attitudes and behaviour?"

"Yes, but -"

"We know the RedWorlders invented the printing press thousands of years ago. Their gospels may not have been misinterpreted, censored and rewritten like those of our homeWorlds," concluded Whately, hastily. "Wouldn't that be a logical place to start looking for the secret?"

Anagnostakos stared at him for several seconds, and then smiled broadly. "I always wondered what 'Jesuitical reasoning' was: now I think I know. But what if you don't like what you find?"

"Monsignor?"

Whately looked up from his newsfax, eyebrows raised. "Yes?"

"I've spoken to Dr Melle," said Anagnostakos. "She's offered to take us to meet a teacher of hers on World Red, a priestess who should have, or be able to find, a facsimile edition of their gospels."

"That's wonderful!" Whately dropped his fax, reached for the interpreter's hand, and pumped it vigorously. "Thank you *very* much."

Anagnostakos smiled, and tried to disengage his hand. "We'll have to leave on Wednesday afternoon, at two: the priestess has a very busy schedule—we're lucky she could find a few minutes to accommodate us—and the temple is quite a long drive from the Bridge. I wouldn't expect to be back before seven."

"I can leave Panosian in charge for an afternoon: he's good, and he disagrees with almost everything Dearborn is likely to say. Are there any strictures I should know about?"

"Melle didn't mention any. They don't seem to have a dress code in Ptolemaios, what we call Red-Alexandria—the outfit the delegates wear are part habit, part weatherproofing. Your mufti may look uncomfortable, but at least they'll know you're from out of town. Melle suggested that *I* not wear a tie or a vest: apparently, the Reds think they look ridiculous, and only seasoned diplomats could keep themselves from laughing at me.

"Besides, we won't be mixing with the populace; I don't speak Arrinesh that well, anyway. We're to let Melle act as guide and take us from the bridge to the car, from the car to the temple, and then back the same way."

"Thank you again. I wish there was some way I could repay you."

"Just vote 'yes' on Friday," replied Anagnostakos, smiling.

"Oh, I planned to." Whately gave the younger man's hand another enthusiastic shake, and then calmed himself down. "You know, you're much smarter than you give yourself credit for, Mr Anagnostakos. You'd be *much* better at my job than I am—let alone Dearborn."

Anagnostakos shrugged. "I'm a street kid. I can learn any language you want, but I still forget which fork I'm supposed to use, and I'm the world's worst -" he hesitated: he'd been about to say 'liar', but realised that the priest might misconstrue this as an insult. "Poker player," he finished, rather lamely, but just as accurately.

"That boss of yours isn't much better."

"Oh, don't let that smile fool you. Besides, *he* isn't one sixty-eight in stacked heels."

"168?"

"Centimetres—I think it's about five foot five in Olde English. Jimmy has a *granddaughter* who's taller than me." He glanced at his digital watch (an import from Japan-Azure) and swore mildly. "I'm late. See you Wednesday."

"Goodbye," said Whately, "and again—thank you."

WHATELY peered through the windows of the electric car at the suburban streets of Red-Alexandria. The houses, new or old (it was difficult to tell), seemed to be built of the same colourful material (ceramic? plastic? one-way glass?), in much the same style—plenty of parabolic arches, a minimum of straight lines, and no sharp corners. He noticed more greenery than he thought Egypt could support, and pristine statues that might have been new or centuries old, and though the road was wide, he saw very few cars. He was wondering how Red-Ireland must look, when Anagnostakos said, "Monsignor?"

"Yes?"

"Dr Melle would like to ask you a question."

"Certainly."

"Why are all the ambassadors at the summit, men? I've explained why for *my* World, as best I can, but maybe yours is different?"

"Well... there *are* female diplomats and ambassadors on World Blue, of course, many of them in the U.N.... but unfortunately, few of them have any experience as trade envoys. Where would they get the experience? We can't send them to Blue-Japan, much less any of the OPEC countries: they'd think we were insulting them. And only rich countries can afford women's rights movements: women in the poor countries don't have the leisure or the access to communications.

"In fact, women had been without most rights for so many centuries in all of our Worlds, the little progress that *was* made in my World over the last century is something of a miracle. Women still can't vote in most countries in World Indigo, and while progress was being made in Azure, it was reversed in the 1980's and 90's when Azure-America went from World leader to... can you translate that?"

"I think so, though I'm not sure that I understand all of it."

"That makes two of us. Are we nearly there?"

"Yes: in fact, we're ahead of schedule. I'm sorry we've both been talking shop..."

Whately waved a hand as though brushing away flies. "Don't worry: I've been enjoying the scenery. Tell Dr Melle that she's lucky to live in such a lovely World."

Anagnostakos translated that, and then said, "That's the temple ahead. She says it'll be nearly twenty minutes before Dr Esa is free. Do you want to tour around, wait in her office, or would you rather see a service?"

"A service?"

"Yes: she'll be giving some people... I think 'communion' would be the right word. Dr Melle wondered if you, as another priest of Christ, might be interested."

Whately gulped. "Tell her that I'd be fascinated."

WHATELY sat in the back of the church, wishing that God might grant him—if only for an hour—the gift of tongues. Even Anagnostakos couldn't understand the World Red vernacular well enough to translate, and Whately was desperate to know whether Dr Esa's sermon was as Christian as the fittings of the temple. Faith, he told himself. Have faith.

Finally, a number of the congregation moved to the railing at the head of the church and knelt before it—some with hands behind their backs, some with hands clasped in prayer, and Whately's eyes filled with tears of joy. Dr Esa, wearing a burgundy-coloured kimono-like robe, stepped towards them. "Take and eat it," translated Anagnostakos, in a murmur, "This is my body. Drink; this is my blood, poured out for many for the forgiveness of sins." Then, as the offWorlders watched, Dr Esa opened the divided skirt of her robe, and guided a boy's face towards her groin. Then she moved over to the girl beside him, and repeated the gesture.

The boy, feeling the pressure of Whately's stare, turned around. Whately saw blood on his lips, and screamed.

"THEY'VE voted against any migration," said Anagnostakos. "Unanimously."

Melle stared, and then translated for the ambassador and her staff. The ambassador's reply needed no interpretation: "Why?"

"Officially? I suspect they'll say it's because they need to do more research, to pick the right people, to prevent a violent clash between two dissimilar cultures... The truth is far simpler. Whately told them about your church service."

"I don't understand."

"On *our* Worlds, they perform the same ritual with bread symbolising the body, and wine symbolising the blood -"

"Wine?" Melle erupted with a most un-diplomatic fury. "But that's a *travesty!* It's -"

"Blasphemy?"

"Worse!"

"Obscenity, maybe? I suspect that's the word Whately used."

The ambassador cleared her throat, and asked a question. Melle translated. "What will happen to the millions starving on your Worlds? What will they tell them?"

Anagnostakos shrugged. "They'll think of some excuse. Dearborn suggested they be sent to World Cyan, that he'd rather deal with the rats—as though it were *his* problem. I'm not a scientist, so I don't know how feasible that is, but I suspect they'll try. Whately also recommended they close *all* the bridges to World Red."

Melle translated this, and the ambassador and her staff were silent. Finally, the ambassador spoke.

"What about you?"

"Me?"

"If they do close the bridge," Melle translated, "which side will you be on?"

"I don't understand."

"You have no home in your World," the ambassador continued. "You've not lived in the same city for as much as a year since you were twenty-three—and now you're thirty-six?"

"I like travelling."

"We have a *World* that you haven't seen, with a hundred new languages for you to learn. And you're an interpreter. Your job is helping people to understand each other. On our World, you could help us to understand thirty billion people..."

"And," added Melle, "if the bridge is re-opened, you could help them to understand *us*."

"I'm really not sure that's possible..." Anagnostakos replied. He tried not to sound tempted, but he'd never been a good liar: Melle knew that he'd already accepted the offer.

"Think it over," she said, "but don't tell anyone. They may try to stop you."

"Of course, there's one other option," said Dearborn, wiping his hands.

Whately, who'd been staying drunk for days in an effort to avoid a near-lethal hangover, grunted non-committally. As far as he was concerned, now that all the Reds had returned to their homeWorld, the Bridge apparatus should be dismantled without delay.

"Military. We invade."

Whately nodded, then suddenly sat bolt upright. "You're joking!"

"Hell, no! Move the bridge to one of their uninhabited areas and drop in a few million troops from each World, take one continent at a time..."

"But what about..." Whately tried to remember the word 'proselytising', failed, and finally blurted out, "cultural contamination?"

"Biowar?" Dearborn mused. "I don't think we know enough about their immune—"

"No!" snapped Whately, winced, and continued quietly, "No... I mean... their relig... uh, their cult? *You* know? What if some of the troops, uh, especially the women... what if they... learn about it, get converted to it -"

"So we lose a few sol-"

Whately finally found the words he wanted, and used them. "What if they bring it *back* with them, for Christ's sake?"

"Oh," said Dearborn, and considered this. "Oh. Well... we won't send any female troops over. The men won't... well, they just won't. Besides," he said, recovering his confidence, "the Reds *can't* corrupt us. None of them know our language, and vice versa—right?"

– II –

ANAGNOSTAKOS closed the door behind him and locked it, then staggered the remaining few steps to the bed—taking great care, despite his fatigue, not to tread on any books—kicked off his boots, and collapsed, face down. He looked up a moment later, and realised that hours had passed; the room was dark, and someone was rattling the door. "Melle?"

"Yes."

"Come in," he said, rolling over and rubbing his eyes. The lights, sensitive to heat and motion, brightened as she entered the untidy room.

"Were you asleep?"

"Huh? Yeah." He stood, a little unsteadily. "Where are we going tonight?"

Melle regarded him carefully, and then shook her head. "Nowhere. Sleep is more important. I'll call for some food."

"You know, that's the longest speech in English I've heard all day," Anagnostakos replied, unlacing his jacket. "Where *are* we going? The theatre again?"

"The play will be on tomorrow night. Sophocles has been dead for centuries; *you* need to sleep. You've been working too much."

"I was a teacher for years. That's how I managed to see the world—one World, anyway. I'll admit, I've never had class where everyone was so bright *and* enthusiastic, and that's as tiring as herding cats... but I'll cope." He stepped out of his trousers, and pulled on another pair with practised haste. As far as he could tell, RedWorlders didn't have any nudity tabus, but he hadn't quite lost his own. "What time's the show? Can we eat first?"

"How long did you sleep in the night?"

"I don't know. About five hours—call it eight *tou*." She looked at him dubiously, and then glanced at the books beside the bed. "Okay, maybe seven. I read for a while. There's so much I don't *know* yet. Anywhere else I go, I know *something* about the tabus and the customs, what I can and can't do and say and wear and eat, where I can and can't go, and when, how rich or poor the people are..."

"I understand that," replied Melle.

"I'm not sure you do. All I know of your geography is that Wa is Japan and Nura is Australia, and a little about the Concordat. I know some Arrinesh, though not as well as you know English, but there's hundreds of languages, thousands of years' worth of history, millions of books and plays... *we've* only had the printing press for a few centuries, not four millenia. We probably lost half a million books when the Library of Alexandria burnt down—hundreds of plays by Sophocles and Aeschylus and Aristophanes and Euripides, the complete works of Berossus and Hecataeus and Hypatia, all stuff you take for granted and that academics on Green would murder their grandmothers for... And the beautiful things the women here have done, books and paintings that never existed on our Worlds at all, except maybe in someone's head... In any of the other Worlds, I'm a well-travelled and educated man; here, I'm an ignorant barbarian. And I'm a Greek: we *invented* the term barbarian, to describe everyone else!"

Melle laughed. "The Arrinesh word 'hort' means roughly the same, and is probably even older—but I haven't heard anyone use it to describe you. Is that all?"

"No. I really do love what I've seen of this World. All the time I've been here, I don't think I've seen anything ugly or dangerous; I *know* I haven't seen anyone who looks beaten, or frightened, or hungry, or even seriously angry. I was scared, for a while, that the men might be treated as badly here as women are in the other Worlds, but if they are, I haven't seen it. I *have* wondered why there are so few men in my classes—"

"There are very few men in the Councils, at present," Melle admitted. "The Concordat, and most of its member-states, has been led by a coalition of religious and women-only parties for the past eleven years—and, of course, they appoint ambassadors who will agree with their policies. So most of the women in your classes are diplomats, while nearly all the men are teachers or linguists—there are plenty of men in the universities, especially the sciences, and even in the church; they can do anything but give the sacrament."

"And become Worldmother."

"The Worldmother must actually have *been* a mother, with at least one son and one daughter... but that's mostly symbolic, like most of her powers. Some people have tried to change it, but most accept that it isn't important."

"Maybe that's what I like about this world," said Anagnostakos. "You believe in a mother whose first priority is feeding her children; we pray to a father who seems more concerned with punishing them."

Melle smiled. "That's a lovely idea, but unfortunately, it isn't quite true. Not everyone is as well-fed as the people you've seen in Ptolemaios and Erech. There was a famine in Punt before you arrived; *thousands* starved before we could send enough food.

"And there are people here, even whole countries, which worship male gods. There are even some, including a few Buddhists sects, who believe women don't have souls, but who are still known for their good works. *All* of our religions teach that you should never refuse food to anyone hungrier than yourself; life is just too valuable.

"On the other hand, not all Christians will turn the other cheek. All clergy are forbidden to bear arms, preach violence, or even raise a hand against a child or a cat—but the same law doesn't apply to the laity, many of whom serve with the army when required. And there have always been those who worship the Mother by sacrificing innocent victims—one of the oldest prayers in the Bible, by Enheduanna, praises the Goddess for 'filling the rivers with blood', and they say there are *still* devotees of Kali Ma in Maurya and Harappa."

Anagnostakos nodded, thinking hard. "You mentioned the army. Do you still have wars?"

"Yes, of course—though not here. The Concordat hasn't been attacked for centuries. But the war in Funan is still going on, though both sides signed a treaty nearly twenty years ago—"

"*That's* why I need more time to study. I didn't even know you still had *armies*—"

"Do *you* still have wars? On World Green?"

"Yes—"

"How large are your armies? What weapons do your soldiers have? What about the other Worlds?"

"I don't know the precise—"

"But you do know they're larger than ours, and probably better armed."

"I don't know about your weapons, but the other four Worlds have—" He calculated quickly. "Nearly forty billion people between them. Most countries have between one or two per cent of their population in the armed forces during peacetime, so that's about half a billion. If you could get them all to fight on the same side, which is unlikely... say five billion if you throw in the reserves."

"That's more than twice our total population," said Melle, softly. "That's why we *need* you to teach English. A third of your students are diplomats; the rest are teachers, who'll teach more diplomats and more teachers. When they're fluent enough to take the beginners' classes, then we'll be able to reduce the tou you have to work, and you'll have more time to study. But if we're invaded, we're going to need—"

"You don't really believe that's going to happen, do you?"

Melle shrugged. "It's possible, and that possibility makes you uniquely valuable to us."

Anagnostakos looked at the books on the floor, and then sat down. "Well, since you put it like *that*..."

WHATELY grunted a greeting to Brother Luke as the younger monk dashed past him on their way to chapel. Brother Luke was an explosively devout redhead from Cork, who seemed better suited to the I.R.A. than to monastic life; he always ran, as though his need to confess something was unbearably urgent.

The Church should have copyrighted confession centuries ago, Whately thought; Alcoholics Anonymous would owe us a fortune in royalties. And that was all they ever asked *him* about; had he had a drink? had he craved a drink? as though that were the only thing he'd come to the monastery to avoid. Which suited Whately perfectly; let them believe that, he could answer *those* questions with a smile and a clear conscience. The other thing was...

"Brother John?"

He looked up slightly, recognising the abbot's Chicago accent. The abbot was a short man, who reminded Whately vaguely of someone else he'd known, once. "Yes, Excellency?"

"Another letter for you. I was requested to deliver this one to you personally, and to be sure that you read it and replied. The request," he added, with a slightly sour edge to his voice, "came from the secretary of His Holiness. Apparently you've been remiss in answering your mail."

Whately blinked, and then stared at the envelope. There was neither stamp nor postmark. He'd received enough mail in recent weeks to arouse the curiosity of his fellow monks, especially as most of it had come from World Azure. Nervously, he opened it, and read through it quickly.

"Bad news?" asked the abbot, sympathetically.

Whately nodded. "It says I'm to leave at once."

"Are you surprised?"

"I wasn't expecting a papal edict," replied Whately, choosing his words with great care.

"Weren't you? You must have realised that you couldn't hide here forever."

"You think I've been hiding?"

"Yes," replied the abbot, simply. "I don't really know why, and I'm not about to ask—oh, I know you've been bitten hard by the bottle, but that's never the whole story and I suspect you could have beaten that yourself. You were a delegate to the interWorld trade talks, weren't you, before they burnt all the bridges to Red?"

Whately glanced at the letter again, and said nothing.

"And the delegate from Azure-Washington is now sitting in the White House... Have you been to Azure-America, John?"

"No. Have you?"

"No, but I try to keep up with the news. They're having terrible troubles there, economic and environmental, and all of them can be blamed on overpopulation, though that's an oversimplification. Even the U.S.A. thinks of itself as overpopulated; the irony is that they regard their poor as the excess, when it's their rich who consume more than—but that's by the by. What's disturbing is that the Church is being used as a scapegoat, because of *Humanae vitae*, which was never repealed over there. Widely ignored, maybe, but never actually repealed. Now, your friend Dearborn—" ("He's not my *friend*," muttered Whately.) "- has gotten where he's gotten largely by scaremongering and pandering to prejudices. He knows there's a lot he could do to hurt the Church in Azure without it rebounding on him. On the other hand, he has no good reason to do so—which makes it an excellent bargaining chip. His people call Azure-Rome, and..."

Whately nodded. "Things were so much simpler when there was only one Pope."

"Amen to that. At least we all worship the same God." He sighed. "The helicopter will be picking you up tomorrow—after matins, I expect. Where were you going, confession?"

"Yes."

"Then I won't keep you. Goodbye, Brother."

Whately bowed his head, and walked slowly towards chapel, in time to hear Brother Luke burst out of the confessional and crash onto a pew. Out into the Worlds again, he thought, wearily, and realised he was shaking; he leaned against the back of a pew, but never looked up, not here, not in chapel.

He could feel the image of the virgin Mary staring at him from behind the altar, and the mere thought, the idea of a woman in the front of a church, was enough to remind him of—

He doubled over and vomited on his sandals. Bless me Father, for I have...

He heard other monks running towards them, Brother Luke in the lead. Let them believe it's the alcohol that scares me, he told himself again, not the... Bless me, Father, for I... Not the obscenity, the uncleanness, the blood, the Whore of Babylon Mother of Abominations... Bless me, Father, for...

'Let your women keep silence in the churches; for it is not permitted unto them to speak'

Bless me, Father, for...

'For the man is not of the woman but the woman of the man.'

Bless me, Father...

'These are they that were not defiled with women'

Bless me, Father, for...

'And the woman was arrayed in purple and scarlet colour, and decked with gold and precious stones and pearls, having a golden cup in her hand full of abominations and filthiness of her fornication'

Father...

AFTER weeks of dropping hints, Melle finally came out and said it. "If you're scared of violating tabus, you can stop worrying. All of your students are adults. If you want to sex with them, you can ask; it's not forbidden, as long as you're polite and respect their right to say 'no'." While Anagnostakos was still staring, his fork halfway to his mouth, she hurried on. "I shouldn't worry unduly. Mati seems to be as attracted to you as you are to her, and we have an old saying that the best place to learn a new language is in bed."

"We have the same saying," replied Anagnostakos, a moment later. "Though I can't vouch for its antiquity. Look, I'd better ask this now, before I make a complete fool of myself—what are the marriage customs here?"

Melle almost choked on a mouthful of salad. "I don't think she'll agree to *marry* you," she said, cautiously, after regaining her composure. "I wasn't suggesting you ask her *that*; you've only known each other for a few months. But you've been here for just over a year, now, and that's a long time to be without sex; I would have spoken sooner, but I wasn't sure of *your* tabus."

"I meant, is she already married, and does marriage mean—?" He tried to think of the Arrinesh for 'monogamy'. Melle stared at him, and then smiled. "Oh. I don't think she's married, I'm fairly sure she hasn't any children, and she's not wearing any warn-offs or fetishes, so it's safe to ask. For sex, I mean."

"What if she *were* married?" he pressed on. "I haven't seen a wedding here, and haven't even heard anything about them, until now. Our traditional marriage vows require the partners to 'forsake all others, until death us do part.'"

"Forsake? As in *abandon*?" Melle sounded horrified. "All others? The entire *world*?"

Anagnostakos shook his head. "Okay, so it was a bad choice of words. It mostly means 'don't have sex with', not 'don't help'..."

"Why not?"

"What? Oh... well, originally, I suppose it's because men used to want to be sure their heirs were also their biological children, and not someone else's—passing on their own genes, as the socio-biologists would put it. So they made sure their wives were faithf... didn't have sex with anyone else. If a married woman was raped, she was stoned to death. It was supposed to cut both ways, but it didn't; look at the *Odyssey*. Odysseus sleeps with Kirke and Kalypso and Goddess knows who else, while Penelope sits at home and spins for eleven years. At its most extreme, of course, some Muslim sects practice clitoridectomy or 'female circumcision', mutilating women so that they can't have orgasms." He grimaced.

Melle stared at him. "I'm sorry," she said, softly "but I don't think I understood a single thing you just said."

DEARBORN looked beefier than he had at the trade talks, though the muscles he'd built up for the campaign were already starting to turn to flab after barely a month in office. "Johnny boy!" he chortled, as Whately was ushered into the room. "Good to see you again. How're things on Blue?"

Whately was too experienced a diplomat to frown, but his voice was cool as he replied, "I haven't seen very much of it, lately, I'm afraid. I've been on retreat."

Dearborn's smile broadened into something even less pleasant. "Yeah, I heard. Doing the Lord's work. I like to think I'm doing the same." Whately grunted non-committally. "And that's why I've called for you. I've spoken to all the other delegates from the trade talks. Remember what I said, just before we closed the Bridges to Red, about the military option?" Whately stared at him. "Okay, so it was a little premature. But you musta heard what happened to our colonies on Cyan and Grey."

Whately nodded. There were still a few off-shore oilrigs on both of the Blasted Worlds (as the press had taken to calling them), but they were barely paying for the energy to keep the Bridges up.

"Fortunately, I'm on the record as being against it from the beginning. I mean, frankly, we might as well try to put men on the fucking moon. Even if you succeed, who the Hell wants to live on the *moon?* We haven't found any more Worlds since then, and that goddamn Schroeder woman refuses to help. But Red—Red could be the Promised Land. The Land of Milk and Honey. The Garden of Eden. You know what it looked like; none of us saw as much of it as you did."

"I saw it," replied Whately. "And you already know that I believe any contact is just too great a risk."

"Never underestimate a good publicity machine; just ask the man who's ridden one. We just tell our boys that the Reds'll cut their balls off if they let any get close enough to talk to them; Hell, it's probably true. You missed out on the Gulf War, didn't you? Shit, it was like a video game; all anybody ever saw was blips on a screen." He grinned. "So what makes you think they can beat us?"

"Because they already have," said Whately, solemnly. "On all of our Worlds, we defeated them thousands of years ago. But on Red, they won."

"I THINK I understood *some* of that," said Melle, uncertainly, after Anagnostakos had spent nearly quarter of an hour explaining. "You take the family names of your fathers?"

"Yes."

"Why?"

"Because men still own nearly everything, and it used to be almost impossible for women to bring up their children without a father's financial support."

"Why would anyone have children they knew they couldn't feed?"

"Well, they probably didn't intend to, unless the man convinced them that he was going to marry them or something."

"But if they didn't intend to—"

Anagnostakos stared at her. "Don't women here ever become pregnant by accident?"

"No! Almost *never*; it's about as unlikely as having triplets..." They both sat there in stunned silence, until he asked, "Since when?"

"For as long as anyone knows!" replied Melle. "Some of the oldest printed books we have, maybe the first ever written in Demotic, are herbal recipes for young girls who haven't learn how to control their fertility by—I don't know if you even have a word for it, the closest I can think of is 'faith healing'..."

"Biofeedback?" guessed Anagnostakos.

Melle broke the word into its roots, then nodded. "Yes. That sounds right. How long have *you* known it?"

"If we ever knew it at all, we've forgotten it," he said, softly. "For a long time, we didn't even admit that women were anything more than incubators, sure that all life came from the male, that every sperm was a miniature human waiting to be born... We still have some of that attitude, but now we blame the women."

"Is that why you have nearly nine billion people?"

"It's *how*; I'm not sure about *why*. Partly because we spent most of the past few millennia expecting most of our children to die, and having as many as we could to compensate. Partly because most of our rulers wanted men for their armies. And, probably because of the first two reasons, men were taught that they weren't really men until they'd fathered sons, and women were never told that they had a choice."

"Do you mean a choice of not having children, or just a choice of not having sons?"

"You can choose the sex of your children, too?"

"We can choose not to have *sons*," she replied. "Choosing to have them is more difficult. Sperm with the male message—I'm sorry, I don't know your word for it—"

"Chromosome."

"They're very sensitive to heat and chemical changes, very easily killed. Females are much, much tougher. It's just as well; how many men does a World need, after all?"

"THE Sumerians and Babylonians, the Minoan culture, the ancient Egyptians and Greeks, even the Celts... they all worshipped a Mother-Goddess," said Whately. "Inanna. Ishtar. Isis. Astarte. Anahita. Artemis. Aphrodite. Athena. Danu. The myth is probably as old as language; a lot of primitive cultures even claim that a goddess taught them writing, or call the goddess 'The Great Scribe'. We don't know much about their rites, except that they used poisonous snakes; I shudder to think how. The priests, the soldiers, the judges, sometimes even the rulers, were women. They probably had no idea how babies were conceived, didn't realise men were important.

"Our ancestors—Aryans, Caucasians, whatever you choose to call them; what's important is that they worshipped God, a *male* God—came from the north into Mesopotamia about four thousand years ago, with their own laws. It was inevitable that the two cultures would clash. In our Worlds, *we* won, destroyed the temples and the idols, enforced our laws... but in Red, somehow, we lost." Whately took a deep breath. "To beat them this time, we would have to kill every single one of them. It may take even more than that; we have to destroy every *trace* of their religion. At the very least, we'd have to burn every book, unread, and even if it were possible, it wouldn't be popular with the academics. More likely, we'd have to nuke every city—Deuteronomy 12:2; 'Ye shall utterly destroy all the places, wherein the nations which ye shall possess served their gods, upon the high mountains, and upon the hills, and under every green tree.' Not even neutron bombs would do; we'd need to turn the planet into a cinder like Cyan or Grey. Hell, that may even be what *happened* to Cyan and Grey! Even if you were prepared to kill that many people—and I'm not—what would it profit you?"

"WE still have famines, but they are minor and isolated; no-one intentionally has more children than they can feed.

"We still have wars, occasionally—but women who are against the war make sure the next generation hasn't enough surplus males for an army. Invaders may capture a country—but if they oppress the people, they have to go home to breed or die out.

"Slavery died out thousands of years ago. It wasn't economically viable, because the slaves wouldn't breed.

"There is still rape, but no woman has to bear her rapist's child.

"We created and we continue the human race. We taught you your first words. We are the source of life and language. And all we ask is that you *remember where you began.*"

DEARBORN sat back in the enormous leather chair and suppressed a yawn. "Is that your official position?"

"I no longer hold an official position," replied Whately. "I've retired from the U.N., and I intend to stay retired; I'm here at the request of your Pope."

Dearborn nodded. "Well, Monsignor, thanks for your input. It's been good to see you again; give my regards to World Blue."

Whately stood. "You're going to do it, aren't you?"

Dearborn stared at the Oval Office ceiling for a moment, then shrugged. "Yeah. If I don't, the Indigos will beat me to it; besides, we've spent billions just getting ready. The Bridges are built, the troops are trained, the logistics are all worked out, the news releases have been written... Hey, chill out! There's no need to worry." He grinned. "God is on Our side, remember?"

THREE years later, when he caught his daughter giving communion in the Lincoln Bedroom, it occurred to Dearborn that he might have been wrong.

Copyright Acknowledgements